So Screwed

ALSO BY MELISSA MARINO

So Twisted

So Screwed

A Bad Behavior novel

MELISSA MARINO

FOREVER
YOURS

New York Boston

Forever Yours
Hachette Book Group
1290 Avenue of the Americas, New York, NY 10104
forever-romance.com
twitter.com/foreverromance

First published as an ebook and as a print on demand: March 2017

Forever Yours is an imprint of Grand Central Publishing. The Forever Yours name and logo are trademarks of Hachette Book Group, Inc.

The publisher is not responsible for websites (or their content) that are not owned by the publisher.

The Hachette Speakers Bureau provides a wide range of authors for speaking events. To find out more, go to www.hachettespeakersbureau.com or call (866) 376-6591.

ISBNs: 978-1-4555-6954-0 (ebook), 978-1-4555-6963-2 (trade paperback, print on demand)

To the Twilight fandom, the place and the people that gave me friendship, laughter, hope and paved the way to making my dreams come true.

CHAPTER ONE

EVELYN—

It was a proven fact that if you had to be somewhere and looking presentable, Mother Nature would laugh at you while dumping torrential rain upon you...with no umbrella in sight.

Mother Nature was a feisty bitch.

I glanced out my car window, watching the streams of rain try to outrun each other against the glass, as I formulated a plan. My best friend's house, the one she shared with her boyfriend and his daughter, was over a block away. Parking was tight along the Lincoln Park street in front of Callie and Aaron's home, which wasn't surprising considering they were hosting a post-funeral luncheon for Aaron's grandmother who had recently passed away.

"Shit," I whispered to myself.

The rain wasn't letting up, and sitting in my car was only wasting time I didn't have. Stopping by to give my condolences was only a gesture to Aaron, who had become a great friend to me. But gesture or not, I was going to look like a drowned rat, a drowned blond rat with red lipstick and smeared mascara, but a rat nonetheless.

There was no point in prolonging it. I flung my car door open, and as soon as my black patent leather Mary Jane pumps hit the pavement, I was off. Dodging puddles and passing cars, I hurried my way down the street the best I could in heels while attempting to cover my head with my large handbag. When my eyes landed on the path to Aaron and Callie's brownstone, I quickened my steps to get to safety.

I paused in front of the glass storm door of their home, hoping to get a glimpse of the type of damage the rain had caused me. All I could make out was a tangled nest of once perfectly styled hair. While I wasn't vain enough to think that anyone would be concerned with how I looked, I still wanted to appear presentable in front of a group.

I reached into my bag to retrieve a comb or something from my wedding planner emergency kit that I *always* had on me, but the front door opening stopped me.

"Evelyn?" Aaron said. "You're soaked. Get in here."

He held the door for me as I stepped in, droplets of water falling from my hair, trench coat, and everywhere else.

I shook out my hair and attempted to run my fingers through it, but it was no use. "How bad is it?" I asked Aaron.

He gave me a calming smile. "You're never not anything but beautiful, Evelyn."

I patted his chest as I unbuttoned my coat, thankful for the fact I had a water-resistant one. "Always with the smooth talk," I said. "I can see why my best friend fell for you."

He took my coat and hung it up in the closet behind him. "So sweet of you to stop by," he said.

"Of course," I said, rubbing my fingers under my eyes to try and rid them of raccoon-ness.

"You need me to go find Callie?" he asked. "So you can, you know, fix or, you know, borrow a hairdryer or maybe—"

I smiled at his attempt at tact before interrupting him. "Yes, please. I need to be presentable before I can go…present myself."

"I'll be right back," he said.

I watched as he rushed down the marble-floored hallway and disappeared into the sea of the bereaved conversing. Wasting no time to begin cleanup efforts, I began to dig through my bag to retrieve a compact to survey the damage. Once found, I flipped it open and looked at my reflection.

It was worse than I thought it would be.

"Hurry up, Callie," I muttered. "Hideous isn't appropriate in this setting."

"I certainly hope you aren't referring to yourself as hideous. All I see is beautiful," said a low voice behind me.

I didn't turn around immediately with my compact mirror giving me the ability to see behind me; I knew exactly who it was.

Aaron's younger and insanely hot brother Abel.

He also was, according to Callie and her multitude of warnings, a playboy that went through women faster than the swipe right on Tinder he probably found them on.

I turned around to get a full view of the award-winning

eye candy. Abel was dressed in a slim blue suit tailored to perfection. His dark pompadour and closely trimmed beard made his blue eyes stand out in contrast. He had always been extremely handsome, but seeing him dressed as he was kicked his allure up another notch. The entire package was quite startling.

My head lifted because he was *that* tall. The few times we'd met before I'd taken notice of his stature, but standing next to him served as a reminder.

"Abel," I said. "So sorry about your grandma."

"Thanks for coming," he said. The corner of his mouth lifted into a tiny grin while his eyes found mine. Dimples. They were just visible from beneath his beard, extending onto the smoothed skin of his cheeks.

"You're welcome," I said with a shrug. "Aaron and Callie are two of my favorite people."

His eyes scanned up and down my body with deliberate intent. "What do I have to do to become your third favorite person?" he asked. "You know, every time we run into each other, you decline any invitation I've offered to get to know each other better."

Abel and I had ended up at the same functions on several occasions. At every one, he asked me out.

And I said no every time.

"Come on," he said, touching my arm. "I think you and me together would be what Grandma Dorothy would've wanted."

He was a handsome, handsome guy. I'd give him that. No doubt a line of panty droppers wherever he went. Hell. I would've maybe been one of them if I didn't think it would cause drama. My best friend's boyfriend's brother? Not ideal. Plus, knowing his history of getting around? Also not ideal. However, there was still something about him that caught my interest at every interaction.

"Plus," he continued. "Even with you looking like you fell into a very deep puddle, you're still the prettiest thing I've seen today."

"I don't know if that's a compliment or—"

He smiled again, his dimples running deeper, as he stepped in closer. "It's absolutely nothing but a compliment, Evelyn."

He was trying to pick me up again. If I wasn't so attracted him, I would've almost been offended.

"Ev," Callie said, coming up next to me. She took me in a hug as Aaron came up next to her. They were one of those couples others hated. Strikingly good-looking, her with her long auburn hair and perfect skin, and him tall and built just like his younger brother, with a smile that warmed up everything around him.

"You poor thing," Callie said, attempting to smooth my hair down as she pulled away from our hug. "My perfectly put-together Blondie isn't so perfect at the moment."

"She looks pretty perfect to me," Abel said.

"Abel," Callie sighed. "The list of phone numbers you have of willing ladies is the size of the first draft of the Bible. I've told you several times before. Quit creeping on my best friend."

And then there was Callie, who wasn't going to give Abel

any wingwoman support while simultaneously reminding me not to fall under his spell.

That was going to be difficult. While being entranced by a cute boy was certainly out of character for me, there was something about Abel that stuck with me.

"Are you trying to cockblock me?" Abel snapped.

Yup. The handsome boy with the witty comebacks was the sticking point.

Callie yanked on my arm, and tugged me away. "Really, Abel?" she said over her shoulder. "Let's get you all put back together, Blondie."

As we walked away, Abel shouted, "Can I come watch?"

Handsome and ballsy as shit.

She guided me down the hallway with quick steps and hurried me up the stairs to the second floor. Once in the privacy of her bedroom, she closed the door behind us.

"All right," she said, heading into the bathroom with me following. "What do you need? Hair dryer?"

Once I got a solid look at myself in her side-by-side mirrors and realized what terrible shape I was in, there was only one thing I needed.

"A blowtorch?" I asked.

Callie waved her hand at me. "Oh, stop. It's not that bad," she said. She pulled a drawer open and pulled out a hair dryer. "Here."

She handed the dryer to me, which I took with eagerness. I could sit and complain, or I could do something about it.

I *always* did something about it.

"You have a wide tooth comb?" I asked.

She stepped back, leaning against the bathroom doorway. "Yeah. In that same drawer. You know, you didn't have to make an appearance."

I glanced at her in the mirror. "I know. I wanted to," I said, digging through her drawer until I found the comb. "How is it all going?"

"Not bad," she said with a shrug. "I mean, the best a funeral can be, right?"

I began taking sections of my hair, working the comb through the tangles. "How did you get roped into having the luncheon here?" I asked.

She rolled her eyes. "Don't ask. All I'll say is I blame Abel."

"Do I want to know?"

"He knew someone who owned a restaurant near the funeral home, and he said we should have lunch there. And like they do, Aaron's parents indulged Abel in his decision-making."

I plugged in the hair dryer and clicked it onto high and hot. Blowing my hair around, I considered what Callie said. There was never a shortage of her opinions on Abel. I knew she had love for him, and he was a huge help when Callie and Aaron had some troubles in the past, but there was always an undercurrent when she spoke of him. She thought he was immature and ran around with his zipper open. From what I could tell, she wasn't off base.

But what stuck with me was why did he get under my skin every time our paths crossed?

When my hair resembled something decent, I unplugged and returned the dryer to its place. A cleanup of eye makeup and quick reapply and I was almost ready to reemerge.

"Have any hair spray?" I asked.

She raised her eyebrows. "Don't you think you have enough product in that hair already? Plus, only you can get stuck in a thunderstorm and make yourself look stunning in under ten minutes, Blondie."

I turned around and smiled. "Oh, sweetie. What a doll you are, but the hair spray isn't for me. It's for you. Let me help you touch up so you can go back to playing hostess."

She ran her fingers through her hair, bringing out a long strand to look at. "What's wrong with it? I thought it looked okay even though I got a little windblown earlier."

"It doesn't look windblown. It looks...well...it just looks bad," I said.

"I love that we have the kind of friendship where there is no bullshit and can tell each other when she looks like shit."

She opened a closet and took out a bottle of hair spray before handing it to me. I finger twisted some of her natural, auburn waves while giving her a spritz of spray. "Speaking of Abel," I said.

Her head moved back from my primping hands as her eyes narrowed at me. "Were we speaking of Abel?"

"Before, yes, we were," I said, reaching back out for her hair. "If you weren't dating Aaron, don't you think you'd find several things charming about Abel?"

She snorted. "I am dating Aaron, so I don't look at his brother like that, but to answer your question, no. He isn't my type. And furthermore, he shouldn't be your type, either. Haven't we been over this?"

I gave her one final fluff and spray before setting the can down, folding my arms across my chest. "Yes. We've been through it, which is why I'm wondering why you're against Abel and me having a little fun?"

"You can have fun with lots of guys. He certainly has fun with a lot of women. Also, I think—" She paused, narrowing her eyes at me. "Unless you're considering *more* than fun. Are you considering more than fun?"

"Just when I thought you knew me, you throw something like that at me," I said.

"You didn't answer my question."

"Because it's stupid. You know I don't do more than fun with anyone. Plus, based on everything you ever told me about Abel, he's usually one step away from uncivilized. I can deal with that, though, because those dimples, Cal," I said.

Mmm. Yes. Those dimples.

"Let's take Abel out of this for a minute, okay?" she said. "Are you ever going to settle down with one guy?"

Here we go.

"I'm twenty-four years old, Callie. I don't need to settle on anything except my lunch order and how fast I can get to the top of my game in my career."

"Everyone isn't Patrick," she said in a quiet tone. "And that was a long time ago."

I recoiled instinctively at the sound of his name.

Patrick.

Man...that boy took me for a run. Everything from love to hate and everything in between. I did settle. I settled on the other side of victory and I had no intentions of revisiting a time in which a man clouded my goals and my true self.

Callie waved her hand around. "Let's not get into it, okay?" she said. "There's been enough drama today. You know with burying Nana and Mr. Matthews choking on a hard candy at the gravesite."

"Are you serious?" I asked.

"Oh yeah. As serious as the Heimlich maneuver Aaron had to give him."

I laughed and didn't even know if I should, but when Callie joined in, I knew it was all okay.

"All right," she said. "Let's get back down there and see if we can find those yummy croissant sandwiches."

I liked her plan, but it didn't work out that way. Callie was pulled away from me as soon as we reached downstairs, leaving me to fend for myself and fend I did. Meandering between random conversations with strangers, and a rather uncomfortable exchange with Mr. Matthews in which he told me in great detail how he saw a "vision" of his just passed-on mother when he was choking on the hard candy. I snuck away from him as soon as I could while considering making a run for it. I didn't want to leave without saying good-bye to Aaron and Callie, but desperate times called for desperate measures.

Making my way back down the hallway to the foyer, I reached the closet where Aaron had hung my coat. After I retrieved it, I slipped the damp sleeves on and wrapped it around me just as I heard my name called out.

"Evelyn!" Callie said.

Callie and Aaron had found me with Abel following close behind.

"Were you trying to sneak away without saying good-bye?" she asked.

"I didn't want to but didn't want to bug you, either," I said.

Aaron and Callie came to stand next to me on one side, Abel on the other. I once again was made aware of his height, and as he leaned in closer, I caught the scent of his cologne. My head, and eyes turned upward to find him looking down at me as well.

His signature smile appeared. "I would've been disappointed if I didn't get the chance to see you before you left."

"Is that so?" I asked.

"It is so," he said.

Aaron cleared his throat, pulling my attention away from Abel. His eyes shifted between Abel and me for a brief moment. "Thank you again for coming, Evelyn. You're a sweetheart to do so."

"It's what friends do," I said. "I have to run and get back to work, but I'm glad I could stop by."

"I'll walk you out," Callie said, linking her arm through mine.

"Thanks again, Evelyn," Aaron said.

"In my thoughts," I replied. I turned to Abel. "Sorry again."

Callie and I started to walk away, but Abel's hand on my arm stopped me. He stepped close, hovering over me. "How about a drink later?"

"I…don't think so," I said.

Callie remained quiet, but the tug on my opposite arm began to pull harder.

"Please," he begged, batting his dark eyelashes at me. "I'm in mourning. You wouldn't want me to be all alone, would you?"

Callie tugged on my arm. "Abel," she said. "I love you, but sometimes you're as civilized as a toddler on a sugar rush."

"I do have to go," I said, allowing Callie to lead me away. "I'll see you guys soon."

Callie's arm was still linked through mine as we approached the door.

"He's oddly charming," I whispered in Callie's ear.

She stopped in her tracks and spun around, placing her hands on her hips. Her eyes narrowed like she was looking for some hidden message behind my words.

"Oh, shit," she said. "Please don't."

"Don't what?"

"Bang my boyfriend's brother."

And like any best friend could, she read me like a book. It wasn't entirely true, though.

"I'm not," I said. "I won't."

"Good because I love you both. You're like a sister to me and Abel is like a brother. You two hooking up would be weird. Anyway, the more pressing issue is do you want to meet *me* for a drink later?"

I dug my phone out of the bottom of my purse and scrolled through my missed calls. Two from my boss, Bridget, which meant there would definitely be no drinks for me.

There would be a drink for her, though. A green smoothie from the place across the street from the office, and she nicely requested for me to pick it up for her on the way back.

"I can't, sweetie. I have to get back to work, but how about brunch or something on Sunday?"

"Absolutely. I miss you," she pouted. "Your hair looks fantastic, by the way."

"I miss you, too. Now go be the supportive girlfriend, and then mend his broken heart in any way you can."

"And you...go get...to work," she said with an eyebrow raise.

She got me.

* * *

We were full-service wedding planners at By Invitation Only. Bridget and I did everything from venue choices to invitations. Our job was to make a wedding as stress-free for the bride and groom as possible. Also, depending on price point, there could be as little and as much interaction as the couple wanted.

I was lucky to be getting my start in the business with Bridget Harrison. She was *the* wedding planner of Chicago. Celebrities, athletes, political officials...they all wanted her and they paid very good money for her services. With her meticulous organizational skills, calm exterior, and stellar connections, no one could pull off a wedding like she could. In less than a decade, she not only rose to the top of the wedding field, but also opened two other locations, staffed with planners she trained to provide the same grand care she did. I had approached her when I was in my final year of college and asked if she would consider me for an internship. She had told me she usually didn't take on interns, but she had been impressed enough with the small children's party-planning business I had started, along with the social media campaign for our university's chapter of the American Marketing Association, which I was president of, that led to a 25 percent increase in membership. Once I graduated, she offered me a full-time job in the career of my dreams.

Not only was she my top pick to work with, but we also hit it off from the moment we met. We joked and talked like girlfriends. But when it was time to get down to work, we were all business. We both knew our places: her the boss and me the employee. The dynamic worked out perfectly.

She was about refined perfection. Dressed always in designer labels, she was the epitome of professional. She began her career much like I had: interning while still in college, which led to an offered position. Then after a few years, she opened up By Invitation Only. Now, ten years later, she was at the top. My goal was to be her friendly competition someday. I was sure she knew this. How could she not? If I was where she was at thirty-six, I'd be thrilled.

I balanced her smoothie, a large coffee for myself, my phone, and a box of programs as I hip checked the door to By Invitation Only open.

"Anything new?" I shouted. "Green junk is here, by the way."

I unloaded everything onto my desk as she breezed out of

her office. With her hair piled tightly on top of her head and her white silk blouse, she looked every bit as polished as the crystal chandelier that hung above us.

"What the hell happened to you?" she asked. "You look chewed up and spit out by a garbage truck and then dragged for seven miles."

Yes. I wanted to be just like her except for her approach, which at times was about as soft as a scouring pad.

"It's raining and I was sans umbrella," I said.

She dropped a folder onto my desk in front of me. "Here are the proofs from the Hamilton-Norris engagement shoot."

"Why proofs?"

She tapped the plastic top of her smoothie with her red manicured fingertip. "Is this kale or spinach?"

"Half kale. Half spinach. You're always changing your mind on which you want, so I've been getting you half and half for a while," I said. "The proofs?"

"Oh yeah. Courtney Norris wanted to see actual photos because she wasn't sure the proofs online were"—she paused before making air quotes with her fingers—"Save the Date quality."

I sipped my coffee as I rolled my eyes. "They were gorgeous, but of course she would've found something wrong with them."

"Bridezilla?"

"Kind of, but also seems more worried about planning a wedding than knowing her fiancé. She had to call to ask him what his middle name was."

"Aw," she said, carefully inserting a straw into her smoothie. "Is your jaded heart bleeding all over my white carpet again?"

"Hi Pot. I'm Kettle."

"Oh, you know that's what I adore most about you. The one thing I've never had to teach you. You came to me perfectly bitter."

"*Bitter* is a strong word."

"What would you call it?"

My phone buzzed with a text message.

"Honest," I replied to Bridget.

CHAPTER TWO

ABEL—

So, I saw you giving Callie's friend some serious eye fucking earlier," Marshall said.

I was enjoying a quiet moment in the living room, my head leaning back against the sofa, as the remaining guests filtered out, but peace was short-lived when Marshall found me.

"I wasn't eye fucking her," I said, turning my head to see him enter the room. "She was just..."

He plopped himself down next to me. "Hot?" he asked.

Yeah. Hot. Really, really hot. No matter how many times I saw her it still surprised me just how much.

"Obviously," I said. "But she's...I don't know."

"Did you sleep with her yet?" he asked.

I shot him a look. While we routinely dished the dirt at the bar we worked at together, we were still at Nana's funeral. I might have been checking out Evelyn, but I was not crude.

"Wow," he said, extending his hands behind his head, lacing his fingers together. "Either you have and she gave you the brush-off after. Or that look means you're feeling the feels of a different kind."

"I realize this is the pot calling the kettle black, but can you try and not be a shithead while still at my grandmother's funeral?" I asked. "Jesus, Ponyboy."

He earned that nickname years ago and it still fit.

This guy, who was at least seven years older than me, looked like he belonged on the cover of some badass men's magazine. Strategically coiffed hair, blue eyes, and teeth so white they'd blind you, Marshall had the mouth of a sailor with the looks of a bearded pretty boy except for one thing. Any area of his body that wasn't hidden behind clothes was covered in tattoos. He was Aaron's best friend, and now, one of mine, too. He didn't take any bullshit. Ever. It was a good thing, too, because whenever I found myself in a pickle, Marshall was always there to lend a hand or remind me how bad I fucked up. Usually it was both. It was no wonder he and Aaron were tight. They were so much alike.

"I was trying to lighten the mood," he said. "Plus, Aaron agreed with me."

Aaron walked in. "Aaron agreed with what?"

"That Abel was ogling Callie's friend," Marshall said.

Aaron stood in front of us, shaking his head. "I didn't say ogle. All I said was it looked like something was going on between Abel and Evelyn."

"Christ," I said, pushing myself up from the couch. "You two fuckers gossip more than chicks. You sure got the whole bestie thing down."

The two of them looked at each other and started laughing at me, full-on fist pumping occurring. This was what they did, ever since I was a middle schooler and they became the dynamic duo in college. I was the little brother. Always.

Marshall let out one last sharp chuckle. "Oh, relax. You two want to go get a drink?"

"We have a sitter on the way for Delilah, so Callie and I are going to go grab some dinner. Why don't you guys come with us?"

"I don't have time for dinner, buddy," Marshall said. "In fact, I should be checking in at WET."

WET was the bar that both Marshall and I worked at—Marshall as the manager and me as a bartender. WET, a speakeasy lounge, was the brainchild of Aaron and considered one of Chicago's most exclusive bars.

He stood and gave us both a hug before taking off. I wasn't going to wait long to follow his lead. It had been a long day, and with the night off work, I was anxious for some time away from it all.

Hoping for a quick getaway, I waited until I was already at the front door before shouting to Aaron, "Heading out. Love you all."

My hand was on the doorknob but Callie's voice stopped me from moving forward.

"Don't you dare leave without saying good-bye," she shouted back before emerging at the end of the hallway.

"I was saying good-bye," I mumbled.

She rushed down the hallway, calling out to Aaron over her shoulder, "Aaron! Abel's leaving. Isn't he coming with us?"

"Aren't you coming with us?" Aaron yelled.

I sighed as I watched him turn the corner, following Callie's path toward me.

"And watch you two make goo-goo eyes at each other for an hour? I'll pass," I said.

He rolled his eyes. "I'm sure we can contain ourselves. Besides, it's been a long day. We'll share some Chianti and have some bucatini at RPM."

"Nah. A stuffy restaurant isn't what I had in mind. Besides, I got some stuff I need to do."

"Like what?" Callie said, coming up next to me with Aaron joining her.

Her hand slipped into his just as his body immediately relaxed into hers. Everything about them was familiar. They knew each other's looks, their bodies, their touch…it was kind of intense. It was also kind of amazing.

"Just…stuff," I said.

I was intentionally vague because like with playing cards, I knew when to bluff.

Aaron rolled his eyes again while rubbing Callie's back. "He thinks we'll be making goo-goo eyes at each other all night."

Callie gasped. "We do not make goo-goo eyes at each other. I, for one, just enjoy looking at my hot man."

"I mean," Aaron said, stepping back and looking at Callie up and down. "How can I not keep my eyes on this one? If you knew what she was wearing, or lack thereof this morning—"

She playfully slapped his chest. "Some things are private."

He bent down, kissing the side of her cheek. "Like when—"

"Okay. I had enough," I said, walking away. "You two make me sick."

"You both make me sick," Callie huffed. "Both of you can't keep your wieners in check for one night."

I snorted as I stepped aside, Callie and Aaron following behind me, bickering in their lovey-dovey, bullshit way as I headed toward the door. And they wondered why I didn't want to go to dinner with them.

"I can keep my wiener in check," Aaron mumbled. "I was trying to add some humor into a depressing situation. I'm not completely uncivilized, sweetie."

"Oh, please. You grabbed my ass at least three times tonight and—"

Aaron faked shock; it was the same look he gave his daughter, Delilah, when he had to give her a parental talking-to. "You had something on your skirt. Your very tight skirt, Calliope."

"And," she continued and pointed to me. "This one was salivating all over Evelyn. I did all I could to not have him start humping her in front of the buffet table."

"I wasn't humping! Or trying," I said. "I just asked her to go get a drink."

"So, this has happened before?" Callie asked.

"Abel asked me once if he could ask her out, and I told him no," Aaron said. "That and the fact that at Delilah's birthday party last year there was some serious looks going on between the two of them, which I noticed was happening again today."

"I'm free to date whoever I want," I said.

"But you don't date anyone Abel. You screw around with whoever gives you the most attention. I don't want my best friend to be one of them," Callie said.

"Well, unless," Aaron said.

"What?" Callie said at the same time as I said, "Yes?"

"It's not like Evelyn dates, either, really," Aaron said. "She's very career focused, and she just...you know."

"No, I don't know," I said.

"Aaron," Callie warned, pulling her hand away from him and folding her arms across her chest. "I'm going to have to ask you to stop wherever this is going before both you and your brother are single."

He matched her stance, his breath increasing. "What?" he snapped. "There's nothing wrong with two people having casual sex. In fact, I think that was our intention at first, right?"

"No. We were boss-employee with benefits, and it almost wrecked us. Why would you tell him to do that?"

"I didn't tell him to do anything. It was only an idea."

"One second you tell him hands off. The next, to go have a fling. It's not like he needs any help making bad decisions."

"He's not an imbecile. I'm going into business with him, aren't I?"

Yes, he was. My super-successful brother was giving me another handout.

Kind of.

My dream was always to be a teacher, an English teacher. My love for reading and writing was always intense. Books were read as soon as I could get my hands on them, and notebooks were filled with stories of various genres. Graduating from college, I thought Chicago would be in such need for a teacher like me. This wasn't the case.

Now, two years later, I was still bartending at one of Aaron's bars, just like I did when I was still in college. Several months ago he offered me an opportunity for something new: open a new bar with him on the central coast of California. I was going to be part owner with Aaron obviously fronting the initial investment. At the risk of sounding like an ungrateful prick, I was very "meh" about the whole thing. Not only would it be a huge commitment, but more so, it wasn't what I wanted to be doing. At the top tier of concerns? It was Aaron once again helping his little brother out. While the agreement was I would buy my way in a little at a time, at the going rate I was making as a bartender, I'd be caught up in a decade or so.

The bickering continued, but I'd had enough. So much of my life was other people and things making decisions for me.

"Can I go now?" I sighed.

Their standoff posture softened, and with one little grin, they were back to holding hands. Is that what love was? True love? I had touches of it over the course of my twenty-four years, but nothing like that.

"Do you have work to do?" Aaron asked.

He wasn't asking about me pouring drinks, but about the online teaching gig he thought I was doing. It was where he believed the money was coming from for my share of the California bar.

"Something like that," I said.

Poker I wasn't always good at. Bluffing I was.

* * *

Clouds of smoke rose above the green felt-covered table as I and the eight other men and women sharing it with me stared intently at one another looking for tells. After things wrapped up at Aaron and Callie's, I was anxious and didn't want to go home to an empty apartment. It had been an emotionally draining day, not just with losing Nana, but with my screwup over the location of the post-funeral luncheon. How was I supposed to know that my buddy's restaurant would be closed by the health department the day before? And then my dad's near-death experience. Per usual, Aaron was there to save the day and I was just around to watch it all.

Then there was the girl.

Evelyn.

Even her name sounded as beautiful as she was. The fact that thought even crossed my mind, in those exact words, was proof enough there was something different about her.

I thought her *name* sounded as beautiful as her. I didn't do that.

But there was more.

A lot more.

It was her sexy-as-hell, curves-for-days body. It was an adorable smile, and even soaked from the rain, her blond hair was beautiful. It was her voice, sweet with a slight raspy undertone. It was her confidence; the pointed way she spoke during every conversation. It was her eyes and her lips and just the whole entire package.

And she seemed to not want a damn thing to do with me.

At least, that's what she gave me to work with. During our numerous other meetings, there were times I thought I was feeling the vibe that she was interested. But then I'd ask her out, and she'd decline. I wasn't sure if she was playing hard to get or if Callie was swaying her decision, but I didn't give a shit. There was such an insane chemistry between us, judging just by the look in her eyes, and I wasn't going to go down without a fight. I wanted that girl.

My focus returned to the game in front of me. These underground poker games were always in different locations—restaurant basements, empty warehouses, and tonight, a closed-down nail salon that still smelled faintly of whatever the fuck chemicals they used.

I was losing. Badly. My mind was everywhere else except the game, and it was showing. In an effort to try and dig myself out, I was confident when I was dealt a pair of queens and went all in. Everyone began to fold after me, and it appeared that things were going how I wanted.

The girl across from me with very long dark hair and olive skin, who I'd seen at other games, called. Her heavily made-up eyes, covered in purples and blues, were enough of a distraction without her fondling a thin gold necklace that landed right in her cleavage whenever she dropped it. The rest of the table folded.

We were heads up, she and I, and we turned over our

cards. The blood rushed from my head when my eyes landed on her ace and king. The flop came down, and I hit with three of a kind. The next two cards were two kings, giving the lady her three of a kind that trumped me.

I tossed my cards on the table and stretched my arms behind my head. "Shit," I said under my breath.

I drained what was left of my Scotch, and before I could even ask, a cocktail waitress set another one down next to me. It was how these high-end places worked. Paid to get in. Free drinks. Liquor up and spend all your money. I had to take it with a grain of salt, looking at the entire picture as whole. In the several months that I'd been frequenting these games, I had done well.

Very well.

A bad night here and there wasn't going to make or break me, especially since Benji, the ringleader of this gambling circus, had taken me under his wing. The guy wasn't much older than me, but had created an empire in the hidden poker game ring. We met during my run of gambling in college, and when we ran into each other a few months ago, he invited me to one of the games. So, I went, and getting the extra cash was working to my advantage. It was harmless.

He knew I was strong player, and the last couple of losses resulted in a strong pat on the back from him and reassurance there was nothing to worry about.

There was only one very big problem with me being at this table at all.

The thing was, I wasn't supposed to be gambling.

Four years ago, I'd gotten in over my head when a friendly

poker game led to high-stakes ones multiple nights a week. When my debt exceeded far into the six figures, I had no choice but to turn to my parents for the money.

It was one of the most humiliating moments of my life.

I'd given my parents my word that I would never revisit the poker table for money again. The debt I owed cleaned out my trust fund and solidified my forever status as "fuck-up son" of the century. The older son, Aaron, was and still held on to the title of "golden son."

* * *

I pushed off from the table, taking my drink with me and throwing my suit jacket over my shoulder. The alcohol buzz was definitely flowing. Hell, I deserved it. I spent my nights bartending and serving the drunks. It was okay for the tables to switch every once in a while. I made my way to the makeshift bar, which was nothing more than a few large pieces of plywood haphazardly screwed together with a flimsy, booze-soaked top. After settling into an empty chair in front of it, I placed my drink down and my head in my hands.

My mind was spinning; thoughts and decisions hung all over me like spiderwebs. I couldn't shake it and it clouded everything around me

It was more than the funeral and Aaron and losing. It was still the girl. Evelyn. Every time I ran into that girl, I reacted, and it wasn't anything I was used to. She didn't buy into my suave bullshit like so many other girls. I didn't mind the chase, but she acted like she didn't want to be caught. I couldn't put my finger on it, but she stirred something in me in other ways besides what's in my pants.

The stories she must've heard about me, Aaron's playboy, freeloading brother.

I was sure it was all exaggerated even if at the core there was an element of truth.

The cleavage chick from the table was now focused on me and not the game in front of her. She gave me a wink, but I wasn't sure I was feeling it. As she rose from the table, the clingy black dress she was wearing fell to her ankles. With a slit almost up to her thigh, her long, bare legs swayed as she strutted toward me with her red fuck-me heels clicking against the linoleum floor.

I sipped my Scotch just as she slid into the seat next to me. The scent of her perfume overwhelmed me.

"Tough loss," she said with a smooth European accent.

I turned in my seat toward her. "I was…distracted."

Her hand settled on the middle of my thigh, and she looked up at me from beneath her fake eyelashes. "Any reason why?"

Her voice rolled the *r* of *reason* just so, and I knew she had to be Italian. I wanted to ask, but I had a hunch there would be time for questions later.

Okay. Maybe I was feeling it. Or maybe it was her fingers inching higher and higher up my thigh. I wasn't sure. The only thing I was sure of was I didn't care.

Right or wrong. I didn't care.

She was here. The woman I wanted wasn't.

Sometimes you just needed to feel *needed*.

"What's your name?" I asked, placing my hand on top of hers.

"Dafne. With an *f*."

She bit down on her lower lip, and I knew this girl was going to pull out all the stops. Sometimes they worked too hard. I was sure there were classes they took on the art of seduction, but we didn't need all that shit. Men were simple creatures. If we wanted you, we were there. Even if we didn't want you, we'd probably still do it.

I stood and grabbed my jacket. "I'm Abel. Well, Dafne with an *f*, why don't we go somewhere a little quieter and I'll tell you all about my day?"

I extended my hand to hers, and without skipping a beat, she slid her own into it. It was a shitty day all around. I'd be lying if I said that a beautiful woman like this wasn't going to softly massage my ego back into top form.

We headed outside and to my car. As I opened her side, she paused before sitting. Her long hair blew in the wind and across her face.

"No wife? No girlfriend?" she asked.

"Nope. Just you. Just for tonight."

I was nothing if not one thing.

Honest.

CHAPTER THREE

EVELYN—

There were times I ran on caffeine and adrenaline. I glanced at my phone to check the time: 9:48 p.m. Bridget told me before I even started a year ago that the spring and summer months were going to be the busiest. I was unprepared the first time around. This year I knew what to expect. Sometimes it really was all about work. My twice-canceled plans with Callie since the funeral last month was proof of that. Luckily, she was always understanding. Good fortune was also on my side that I didn't have to balance a boyfriend along with everything else. My life, with career first, was designed around my dreams. I created it that way ever since I learned how much of a distraction men were anywhere outside of the bedroom.

I was finishing up addressing invitations for an NHL player's upcoming wedding when it all became very ironic. My ideal job and formulated social life was all thanks to the incredibly hot but very intense hockey player I dated in high school through my freshman year of college. Patrick wasn't a bad guy. We were bad together. It wasn't love, but rather an obsession that led to us shutting out the rest of the world. Learning young that when life revolves around a man you don't have room for much else was a retrospective gift.

Bridget poked her head out of her office. "How many do you have left to do?" she asked.

I checked my spreadsheet and color coded the ones I had marked as *done*. "Seven more."

"Okay. When you're done, we'll go over the itinerary for the Miller wedding on Saturday."

"All right."

It was nearing the end of April, and things were already in full swing.

"Hey. I have an idea," she said, leaning on my desk. "How about when we're done tonight I take you out for drink?"

"Yeah?"

"Do you have other plans?"

I considered telling her I had plans with my *Friends* DVD box set, but I wasn't ready for that kind of truth, especially to my boss.

"Nope. No plans."

"Great," she said, walking back to her office. The door was almost closed before she stuck her head out again. "Oh, and Evelyn? This place where I'm taking you is very—what is the word for it?—intimate."

"Intimate?"

What did that mean?

"It's very exclusive," she explained. "You'll see when we get there."

It was close to eleven p.m. by the time we were headed out to get our much-needed cocktail. The stress of the day weighed heavily on my shoulders, and I hoped that after one drink, I could get home to unwind. Most importantly it'd include me taking off my bra and heels.

"Should I get a cab or I can drive if you want?" I asked as we exited the building.

Bridget adjusted her white raincoat, tying it tight across her small waist. "No need. We're just going around the block. Actually, on the opposite side of the building."

I followed her as we walked toward the corner. "I didn't even know there was a bar on that side. I thought it was offices and the deli."

She stopped, turning to look at me. "That's what most people think," she said with a wink.

We continued along the side of the building and turned when we reached the next corner. Bridget stopped on a neon-orange spray-painted star on the ground. It was odd, but then again, so was Chicago.

"Come stand next to me," Bridget said, waving me over.

I stepped next to her, as she pointed her finger to the ground. "Twenty-eight from the star," she said.

"Huh?"

"The orange star. Count twenty-eight steps forward from standing on the middle of the star."

I stepped alongside her, stopping when we reached twenty-eight. Bridget pivoted and approached the side of the building. As she ran her hand along the brick exterior, I wondered if she was just overworked and in need of a good sleep. None of this made any sense at all.

Her hand stopped on a wooden panel that blended in with the bricks. She knocked three times and stepped back, fluffing her hair as she did. A door, seamlessly hidden, opened and a handsome man, who appeared to be in his early thirties with short, curly brown hair dressed in a dark suit, appeared.

"Well, hello there, Bridget," he said. He held the door open and stepped aside to let us pass.

She walked in, with me close behind, and gave the doorman a playful tap. "Long time no see, Tyler."

I looked around, trying to gauge my surroundings, because this was, in fact, not a bar. All I saw was darkness. A hum of music buzzed around us, and my feet vibrated against the concrete floor. Bridget was standing close and talking softly to Tyler before she looked my way.

"This is Evelyn, and she is wonderful at keeping secrets."

I raised my eyebrows at her. *Secrets? What kind of secrets? Where has she taken me?*

"Fantastic," Tyler said. He reached his hand out to shake mine. "Very nice to meet you. Let me take your coats."

We handed them to Tyler who opened an expansive cherrywood armoire that was hidden behind eggplant-colored velvet drapes and hung them up.

"Now, if you want to follow me," Tyler said.

He stepped ahead of us, and Bridget followed with myself close behind as we traveled a narrow, darkened hallway.

We stopped when we reached a velvet rope, which Tyler unhooked and allowed us to pass before taking the lead again. I tugged on the back of Bridget's shirt and yanked her toward me.

"What is going on?" I asked.

"I told you. I'm taking you for a drink."

This was seriously weird. It was like one of those underground clubs, places I had read about that were sex clubs or something. Could that be it? Was Bridget trying to introduce me to something…new?

Dimly lit lights lined the now-carpeted floor, the hue getting brighter and brighter as we walked toward the sound of the music. I heard voices, laughter, and conversation. Not loud like a dance club or something of the sort, but of a restaurant.

Tyler stopped in front of a leather tufted door and smiled. "Welcome, Evelyn, to WET."

The door opened, and I was relieved it wasn't an underground sex club. No, it was something much different. Golden hues and sparkling chandeliers lit the small room while the mahogany floors matched the small bar. Six high-back stools lined the front of the bar and low marble tables, surrounded by plush burgundy couches and armchairs, were scattered around the room. It was exquisite. And so were the people.

I raised my eyebrows at Bridget, wondering what this wonderland we walked into was.

"Speakeasy," she whispered.

"What?"

"You know, like in the days of Prohibition, they had hidden places to drink booze.

"I know what it is. I just didn't know they still had them."

"I only know of this one. And for the record," she said, leaning over, "that was no joke about keeping this a secret. This place is strictly members only, and you have to be invited to become one. Very private."

"Holy shit!" I pointed to a small U-shaped sofa along the far side of the wall. "Is that what's-his-name from that movie and no! That is *so* not his wife. Do you think—"

She yanked on the edge of my hair. "Private, Evelyn," she hissed.

I tore my eyes away from the movie guy and scanned the rest of the room. There were several other familiar faces, a politician or two. A hockey and baseball player. Yes, this was elite. There was beauty and power, and most of all, money.

"How did you find out about this place?" I asked.

"Seriously?"

It was dumb of me because Bridget knew almost everyone in Chicago. If she didn't know them, she knew someone who did and made whatever connections she wanted with one phone call.

"The owner is Aaron Matthews, super heavy hitter in the hotel and restaurant game in Chicago. He is—"

Bridget kept talking, but I stopped listening. This was one of Aaron's bars? It was strange, but also not. Like Bridget said, I knew he owned several bars, but this place? My eyes scanned around the room again, and then something came to memory. Callie and I had a conversation once regarding a secret club that Aaron owned and took her to.

"My best friend's boyfriend," I muttered, my mind still reeling.

"Huh?" she asked.

My head snapped to her. "My best friend is dating the owner."

Her eyebrows raised. "Your best friend is dating 'the' Aaron Matthews? Wow. That's quite a catch."

He was a catch and I couldn't be happier for her. However, I knew how nosy Bridget could get, and I wasn't going to dish the dirt to her about Callie and Aaron.

"Yes. They are both quite the catch. Come on. Let's go get a drink," I said, tugging on her sleeve.

She shrugged, knowing I was finished with the discussion. As I followed her across the room, a mixture of expensive fragrances and pricey cocktails surrounded me. Once I sat on the seat next to Bridget at the bar, I opened my purse to casually look to see if I had any cash on me.

"Well, if it isn't my favorite bartender," Bridget said.

"Well, if it isn't my favorite wedding planner," a deep voice said, approaching us. "How are you, Bridget?"

"Wrecked."

"I'll ease that out of you. Want the usual?" he asked.

"I don't know. Maybe we'll get a bottle. Evelyn... Evelyn...what are you doing?"

"I was just looking in my purse for—"

"Hey," the deep voice said. "Evelyn."

Shittttttttt...

Because of course, why wouldn't Abel work at a bar his brother owned?

It took me several moments to recognize him. Maybe it was because he was behind the bar and wearing such a slim-fit, white button-down shirt. Maybe it was the lighting or the sheer surprise of seeing him.

Or maybe it was because he seemed even more handsome than the last time I saw him.

"Hi. Wow…small world," I said.

Bridget looked between us, confused. "You two know each other?"

"Yes," he said at the same time as I said, "Kind of."

He bit his lower lip and laughed. "A little of both?"

"He's Aaron Matthew's brother," I said with an eyebrow raise.

"Well," she said, inching forward on her stool. "How come you never told me this before, Abel?"

He smoothed his hands down the front of his crisp white shirt as he shrugged. "You didn't ask," he said, turning his attention to me. "You look as beautiful as ever, Evelyn."

I could see Bridget, out of the corner of my eye, staring at me, her lips upturned in a smirk. "Well, well, well…"

"What?" I asked.

She shook her head. "Nothing. Nothing at all."

I stared at Abel as he added some ice to a martini shaker and fastened the lid to the top. He shook it rapidly, the strong muscles of his arms pulling against the tight white fabric of his shirt. He caught me gawking, but before I could even be embarrassed, he winked.

A wink.

It was such an underutilized gesture. It was subtle in nature, and the recipient could interpret it any way they wanted to. With him, I was conflicted because all I could think about was how hot it was. How hot *he* was. It wasn't that I'd never noticed before. It was hard not to, but there was something different about him I couldn't quite place.

Regardless, he was under a new light now; a new light that made his blue eyes sparkle, made his shoulders and height seem even more impressive. It was the same light that made me aware of those dimples just below the surface of his beard, the beard that I wanted to reach out and touch to see how it felt under my fingertips. The light that made his smile so warm and his eyes turn down coyly.

"Will you answer him for Christ's sake?" Bridget said, poking me in the side. "You look like you were contemplating if Cheerios were doughnut seeds."

And it was the same light that made me appear like a complete jackass.

Abel was now leaned over, laughing. "I'm sorry," he said. He waited until he caught his breath before he spoke again. "I've never seen someone so confused about what to drink."

I cleared my throat. "I wasn't confused. I was—"

"Daydreaming?" he asked.

"Ogling," Bridget said, bringing her martini with three olives to her mouth. She took a sip and set it back down, the clank of her gold bangle bracelet the only sound I heard, even though there were conversations and low music occurring around me. "She was ogling you, Abel. Can't say I blame her. If I was a free woman and ten years younger, I'd do the same."

He started laughing again and turned his attention to a gentleman who came up next to him and whispered in his ear.

"Bridget," I hissed. "You are mortifying me."

"Oh, lighten up. I'm trying to get you laid."

My jaw dropped. Not that I should've been surprised. This was Bridget. I worked for her for close to a year, and in that time I'd never known anyone else to have two completely different sides to their personality. She was the epitome of professionalism in the office. Every aspect of her business from the furnishings to the labels on the clothes she dressed in was perfection. Then, when work was over, and she was in a place where she could unravel, the real Bridget came out. A foul-mouthed, no-bullshit woman who took no prisoners.

I whispered in her ear, "I don't need your help."

"What are you girls whispering about?" he asked. "Cocktail selections?"

"I'll have a Manhattan, please," I said.

He nodded as the dimples reappeared. "A whiskey girl. My favorite."

I heard Bridget snort as she stood up and excused herself to the ladies' room, leaving me alone.

"So, what's new?" he asked, placing a short glass on the bar.

"I wasn't ogling you," I responded briskly.

He shrugged, adding ice to the glass. "I wouldn't have minded if you were."

"You're smooth with the words. You play the bartender role right."

"No role."

He made my drink with a certain artistic flow. He added whiskey, bitters, and vermouth to the glass before stirring it well. After running a thin orange peel around the rim, he threaded two cherries through a toothpick. Just before he slid it over to me, he took a fresh hand towel and wiped the outside of the glass down, ensuring there was no spillage. I was relieved that the liquor wasn't up to the very top because undoubtedly, I'd spill the first time I picked it up. There is little recovery when you have booze running down your chin and a wet shirt that made you smell like a distillery.

I brought it to my mouth and took a small sip. It was sweet and strong, with the right amount of kick back from the slow burn of the whiskey.

"Perfect," I said. "I'm always impressed when someone stirs instead of shakes."

"Not even if someone asks. Always stirred."

"I usually ask for two cherries, but you seemed to have known."

He placed his hand on his chest and gave a little bow.

"How do you know Bridget?" he asked.

"I've been her assistant for the last year. I have to say, I'm a little disappointed she never brought me here before."

"I'm sure she had to be certain you could be trusted. Members can bring in guests, but it's their membership if word gets out. It's why most people don't."

"Ah. I see. Well, I'll consider myself lucky. My lips are sealed."

"And what a set of lips they are," he said as he licked at his own, the tip of his tongue running across his lower lip. It was deliberate and sexy, but I couldn't help but wonder if this was his game.

"Are you allowed to do that?" I asked.

"Do what?"

"That," I said, waving a hand between us. "Flirt. With me. At work."

He took in a deep breath that expanded his already large chest. "Well, if you want to get technical…"

"Yes," Bridget said, sliding back into her seat. "Let's get technical."

"Just the person I need," Abel said. "Do me a little favor, Bridget."

"What's that?"

He grinned, leaning over the bar. "Fire this insanely beautiful girl so I can ask her out for the fourth time."

"What?" Bridget said.

"No," I shouted.

"I can't ask her out if she's a member or with one. You know that. So, fire her."

"Um. Do you honestly think I would risk my job to go on a date with you?" I said, pointing at him. "Arrogant bastard."

"Arrogant maybe," he said, winking again. "But I'm not above playing dirty."

I took a large sip from my cocktail. "Good for you. I'd never give up my dream job for a guy, let alone a date."

I sat back against the chair and folded my arms. Who the hell did he think he was? Figuring this guy out was like dodging bullets, left and right. I never knew where he was coming from or where he was going.

"Oh, please," Bridget said. "You have an in with the owner, Abel. Just tell Aaron to let this one slide."

"My brother might've heard that before," he said.

I ran my finger up and down the side of my glass. "I'll ask him the next time I see him."

His eyes fixated on my finger movements, the gliding across the wet glass. "Maybe," he said, without looking up. "I might have said it before."

"That's what I thought," I said.

He shook his head to clear his thoughts and noticed another customer was ready for her next drink at the other end of the short bar. I watched as his hand brushed the bar's surface, the heat from his palms leaving small smudges across it.

"Leave him your card," Bridget said. When I didn't answer her right away, she nudged me with such force she almost forced me off the stool.

I shook my head. "No. Callie and Aaron don't think it'd be a good idea. Plus, you heard him. I don't want to get you or him in trouble."

She rolled her eyes. "His brother owns the place. He isn't going anywhere."

I looked at him, opening a champagne bottle that cost more than my rent. He was completely engaged with the woman in front of him, the same way he was with me just moments before. Maybe it was just him. Being a flirty bartender was part of the job description, wasn't it? But what about all the other times we ran into each other? Was that him being his regular, flirty self, with the ability to insert a heavy dose of inappropriate?

As if he sensed my stare, his head turned as he poured the champagne, and he smiled. I twirled a strand of hair around my finger and wondered what I was so afraid of. I wanted to know more. I want to know more of him. I knew Callie and Aaron wouldn't be happy about it, but they'd get over it. There was something moving between us, and every time I was near him that became more and more apparent.

"If you don't leave your number, I will," Bridget said. "He's a doll."

"How would you know that?" I asked.

"Because I've been coming here for long enough to know," she said. "He graduated from Northwestern a couple years ago and wants to be a teacher. It's hard right now in Chicago to find something, so he's been biding his time."

"A teacher?"

I had no idea, and frankly, it didn't seem to fit him. I didn't know what I expected, but it wasn't that.

"Yeah. High school, I think." A familiar flutter swirled around my stomach, one that I hadn't sensed in a long time, one that let me know that I was, in fact, swooning. Hot guy, teacher, and a brazen attitude was enough to check off a number of boxes in my imaginary dream boy checklist.

"I can't stay much longer," Bridget said, looking at the time on her phone. "We have a lot of shit to get done before the Miller wedding on Saturday."

I took another sip of my Manhattan and started digging through my purse again. Bridget set her hand on top of mine and laughed. "No. Not now. Just not a lot longer. At least let's finish our drinks."

"Oh, I know. I was looking for this," I said, pulling out one of my business cards.

It seemed silly, considering he knew where he could find me, but it was a gesture. An invitation. One that I hoped he'd accept.

CHAPTER FOUR

ABEL—

Tonight was the best kind of surprise. Not only was her coming into WET one, but that combined with the way her cheeks flushed from the whiskey and her tight sweater dress clung to every one of her curves, I was completely enchanted. On top of all, she always wore the most intense red lip color. She was like Marilyn Monroe, and something unique to her mixed together and created this incredibly sexy, adorable woman.

"I guess I can assume, yes, hot by the way you have that dreamy look in your eyes," he said.

"Fuck off, Ponyboy," I said.

"Did you hear any more about that teaching gig?" he asked.

"No. Well, not since the last I heard. I guess they decided to hire a sub who'd been working there. They said they'd contact me in the summer about any fall openings, but it doesn't look promising."

"That sucks, dude. But the online teaching thing is going good, and you have the California thing in your corner."

I shrugged, immediately feeling guilty not only for lying to Marshall about the online thing, but also because I was coming across as ungrateful for a huge opportunity Aaron had offered me. The truth was I knew it wasn't right for me, but I needed to start stepping up. By the time Aaron was my age, he was already well on his way to being an ultimate success. I wasn't even close, and my family never missed a chance to remind about that even if it came from a place of love.

"It's true," I said. "I'm not complaining."

Marshall was quiet, and I knew why. He knew it wasn't what I wanted to do. I was grateful I had a brother in a position to give me this job and the opportunity tons of guys would jump on, but I was nothing like Aaron. My older brother was everything I wasn't: business smart, serious, and well, more serious. He was a single dad and a hell of an entrepreneur. At thirty-two, he'd achieved more than most people did in a lifetime.

My parents were successful, retired professionals as well. The apartment I lived in was in the same building as my parents' and was paid for by them. I hoped not for long, but at the rate I was going I wasn't so sure.

"I think we're done here," he said, tossing his rag into the dirty pile. "Want to head out?"

"I'm going to stay for a few. Do you mind?"

"No, but are you okay? You've seemed off all night, and it seems like it's something more than just a smoking girl."

"I'm fine. Just a lot on my mind."

I didn't mean to be so blasé, but it was all I had in me.

He shrugged. "All right. See ya tomorrow."

Our small kitchen staff left soon after, and I was alone in the quiet. I sat down at the bar, a bottle of Patrón and a shot glass. It was something I liked to do sometimes, sit in the silence of the room that was once filled with noise and distractions. All of that energy, everything people wanted from me, drinks and my words, left me drained most nights. While tonight wasn't much different, I had a different reason to reflect.

It was almost two a.m., and while most of the city was tucked in their beds, a warm body next to them, I was knocking back tequila and thinking about a girl.

Evelyn.

Shit. The fact that she held her own when I flirted relentlessly, then left her business card, made her that much more desirable. She was making the calls on her terms, and there was something very sexy about a woman doing that. I knew she was going to stand her ground, and because she worked for such a spitfire powerhouse like Bridget, it fanned the flames of want something fierce.

She was *different*. She might be my unicorn.

I needed to see her again. In fact, for a reason I hadn't felt in a long time, I wanted more than to just see her again.

I was going to get that girl.

I took out my phone and looked up the name of a nearby florist. Their website had online ordering, and after some decision-making, I decided on a modest bouquet with mixed flowers. Choosing the right flowers and how big of an arrangement was important. If it was too big, they thought you were overly eager and totally into them. Even if I was eager, and I was, I couldn't let her know that. If I sent something too small or cheap looking, then I looked like a broke asshole, and no lady liked that. I think I chose well.

I knocked back the rest of my Patrón and slid the glass across the bar, stopping it before it toppled over the edge. After walking around, blowing out the rest of the barely still-lit candles and shutting off lights, I locked up. I walked outside, the streets deserted except for a few cars. The night was chilly, but not cold, a sign that the warmth the city waited for was coming.

There was something brewing. I didn't know if it was the girl or the changing weather. Summer was coming, and things were beginning to smell clean and new. It always reminded me of when school was out for spring break. It felt like after the long Chicago winter, it was the first time I could breathe.

I wasn't ready to head home yet. Some nights I was just too keyed up and needed something to help me unwind. Luckily, a last-minute poker game I'd gotten an alert for a couple hours ago was happening only a few blocks away. Good vibes were in the air, and with any luck, they'd fall down on the cards.

CHAPTER FIVE

EVELYN—

I assure you, Mrs. McGovern, the bows on the chairs will be the exact same color as the bridesmaids' dresses. I will check the swatches personally," I said, rolling my eyes at the phone. Not even ten a.m. and I already had to talk down Mrs. McGovern. Her daughter, Maddie, was marrying the mayor's son and having their wedding at the Peninsula. Maddie was one of the most laid-back brides I'd ever worked with. She knew what she wanted, didn't waiver, and let us do our jobs. Her mother, on the other hand, called at least three times a week to micromanage.

Bridget passed by and gave me a thumbs-up before walking back into her office. Lucky bitch. She only had to deal with the super-urgent stuff and vendor meetings. And of course, the wedding day, but I was with her for that. All the cranky phone calls from mothers of the bride or overly involved grooms was handled by me. It was the first thing Bridget taught me: Remain calm no matter what. Tell them it's handled, even if it wasn't. We were getting paid to take care of everything for them.

I was saved just in time as she started asking about how long the chef had been there, and if he had ever done anything as important as her daughter's wedding, when a delivery person walked through the glass doors.

"I'll definitely look into his credentials, Mrs. McGovern, and get back to you, okay? I have an urgent delivery here I need to address."

I sighed loudly as I placed the phone back in the receiver. "Thank you," I said, standing to sign for the delivery.

He looked down at his clipboard. "I'm looking for Evelyn?"

"Yeah, that's me."

"I have a delivery for you," he said, handing me the clipboard to sign.

"For me?" It was unusual for something to come specifically for me because everything was under Bridget's name. I looked down to see where to sign and saw the name of the business at the top. Windy City Florist.

"Hold on. I'll bring it in," he said.

I shrugged it off and signed. It was probably a sample bouquet or centerpiece that I accidentally put in my name.

Then I saw it. Or part of it as the delivery guy was trying to wedge it through the door.

I rushed over to help him. "Here, I'll hold the door." He paused, and I unlocked the side door to give him more room to get through.

"Thanks," he said, lifting an enormous floral arrangement into the office.

No, it wasn't enormous, it was…massive. The white flowers, composed mostly of carnations, were flanked by overflowing greenery while a white satin sash that read BELOVED was draped across the middle.

It was clearly a funeral arrangement.

"Um," I said, handing the clipboard back to the delivery guy. "I think this is a mistake. This obviously belongs at a memorial service or something. This is a wedding planning office."

"You are Evelyn, and this is By Invitation Only, correct?"

"Yes."

"They're for you. Card's at the top."

"Huh?" I looked at the small envelope, and sure enough, my name was on the front.

The guy said something as he left, but I wasn't even paying attention. I was too busy ripping the seal off the back of the envelope.

I slid the small card out and read the printed message:

Dinner tomorrow? Call me: 312-555-0199.

Abel

Oh. Hell. No.

Was he kidding me with this? What kind of idiot sends a girl he was interested in flowers that were more fitting for bereavement than interest? What a—

"What the hell is that?" Bridget shouted, slamming her door and pointing her finger at the atrocity.

"Abel sent it!"

She stepped toward the arrangement, circling it with her lip curled. "And he thought sending you this was the way to go?"

I poked one of the petals. "It's all so weird and…creepy. This is all your fault!"

"*My* fault?" she shouted, slapping her hand to her chest.

"Because you told me to! You encouraged it."

She waved her hand above it. "Well, you have to get it out of here before a client comes in and thinks we're exchanging weddings for funerals."

* * *

I had to say something to Abel. I mean, that was just good manners. Plus, it was going to be a double-whammy type of call. Thanks for the flowers, and never contact me again, weirdo. My judgment was seriously lacking for even considering going out with this guy. Callie was right. I should've stayed clear.

"Anything else?" Bridget asked.

"No. Just Mrs. McGovern. But I have it taken care of."

She smiled. "Just how I like it. Okay, I'm running out to meet the Lake people at Red Loft. I swear to hell if that incompetent coordinator didn't get those extra tables in there for the wedding Saturday, I'm going to level her with one look."

She was so badass. I hoped one day to be just like her.

Once she left, I sat down at my desk and called the number Abel put on the card. I took a sip of my coffee and tried to tell myself the butterflies I was feeling as the phone rang were just my stomach complaining it hadn't had breakfast and not that I was going to be hearing Abel's sexy voice. If anything would be my downfall at that point, it would've been that.

On the fifth ring, he picked up, but I didn't hear anything right away. A rough throat clearing, followed by a couple rounds of coughs were the first sounds before I heard a very raspy, very sexy "Hello?"

"Abel?"

"Mm-hmm."

I cleared my own throat loudly, hoping to rouse him out of his sleepiness. Christ. *Just don't answer the phone if you're still sleeping at ten a.m., especially if you're going to sound so hot doing it.*

"This is Evelyn. Owens. Evelyn Owens. I got your flowers and was calling to say thank you, but that I'd have to decline the dinner invitation."

There was a pause, and I could almost hear the wheels turning in his head. "Wait. The flowers? You didn't slike them?"

"They were...fine."

"Fine? Wow. You must really think I'm a dick to call flowers I sent fine. Don't hold back."

"Look, I said thank you, but you don't have to get snotty because I don't want to go out with you."

"I don't care if you don't want to go out with me. You could at least be cool when you're calling someone to wake them up and then act all ungrateful."

Oh hell *no.*

"First off, I didn't know you'd still be sleeping at ten."

"I'm a bartender. I don't get home until three, and by the time I unwind and shit…well, you get the point."

"Sorry," I mumbled. "In any case, I was being tactful in regards to the so-called flowers. I have no idea what you were trying to prove by sending such an arrangement, but I wasn't impressed. I was secondhand embarrassed on your behalf."

"I very thoughtfully picked out that seasonal mixed bouquet!"

"A bouquet? For what? The cemetery?"

"That vase was extra."

"There was no vase. Where the hell could they even put one?"

He paused. "They didn't deliver the flowers in a vase?"

"No, I think it was a tad too large for one, don't you think?"

"Ah. No. Just how big is it?"

I glanced at it and couldn't even begin to explain. "Let me take a picture and send it to you," I said.

After considering if I should stand on my desk to get the full effect, I decided that if I stood far enough back I could get the entire thing in the picture. I snapped the picture and sent it to him.

"Okay. Just sent it," I said.

He was quiet for several moments before I heard him take in a sharp breath. "What the *fuck* is that? I didn't send that!"

"Your card was sitting all pretty on top of it," I said. "I had to get a ladder to get to it."

"Ha-ha. Let me call you back."

He hung up before I could say another word.

I set my phone on my desk and leaned back in my chair as I considered what my next move should be. Everything about Abel's delivery, both with flowers and in most other actions, was always riddled with ridiculousness. There was an innocence in his ability to be oblivious and a sexiness to his will to behave without fear. He spoke his mind, and while that sometimes included a level of inappropriateness, the boldness was growing on me.

Five minutes later, he called me back.

"So, apparently the flowers I ordered for you were delivered to Vana's Mortuary, and the arrangement you received belonged at a funeral there."

I started laughing, not only because it was the perfect explanation, but also that the guy probably couldn't have been any more embarrassed.

"Thank you," he said with a sigh. "Rejected by the girl who received the Treasured Moments standing spray of flowers."

"No, no," I said, catching my breath. "I feel bad. I do. If it had happened to me, I would've died."

"Would it be presumptuous of me to assume that the flowers were the reason you didn't want to have dinner with me?"

I picked up a pen and started twirling it around my finger. How could I answer that? I wasn't going to let him know I was hoping he'd call or text to ask me out. That I haven't been able to get him out of my head since the night before.

I bit down on the edge of my pen and had an idea. "*Presumption* is a good word for it. For now, I have to do something with the flowers. Bridget was freaking out. If a client comes in and sees it, well, it just doesn't fit in with the rest of the bridal decor. I'm not quite sure what to do with them. I don't just want to throw them in the Dumpster."

"The florist said he would come pick them up, but it would be a few hours."

"Hmm. I guess I could move it down the long hallway or something until they come, but I don't know if I could by myself."

Come on, Abel. Follow me here.

"Of course you shouldn't. In fact, I'm going to call that asshole florist and tell them to come pick it up immediately."

"No," I said quickly. "Don't do that. They already messed up once today."

There was a long pause, one in which I was hoping he was connecting the dots. I casted out, dangling the bait.

"Any maintenance people to help you in the building?" he asked.

Maybe I was losing my touch.

"That's not their job, you know, helping us move stuff. I'll figure something out," I said. "Thanks again—"

"Wait," he said.

Wait.

"You aren't going to try to move it yourself? I mean, I saw yesterday how nicely you dressed for work, and you shouldn't be getting all dirty and stuff," he said.

So close. Bring it around, buddy.

"Do you want me to stop by and move it for you?"

Bingo.

"Would you do that? I'd really appreciate it."

"How about we make a deal?" he said. I could hear the smile in his voice, the smile that drew his dimples in and made me remember what it was like to feel flutters.

"Yes?" I said, smiling, hoping he could hear it, too.

"How about I come by in about an hour, get rid of the memorial of my humiliation, and take you to lunch as an apology."

Fist pump.

"I can't agree to that," I said.

I heard him whisper "shit" under his breath. "You confuse the hell out of me."

"What I will agree to is taking you to lunch for helping me out. Deal?"

He laughed, deep and strong. "Absolutely."

"See you soon."

"Yes, you will."

CHAPTER SIX

ABEL—

Jesus Christ. That girl. Feisty. Sexy. The mix of both was so captivating. She was going to eat me alive, and I already knew I'd let her and enjoy it.

There was no other explanation for me getting up after a few hours' sleep to go move some flowers and have lunch. After a quick shower, where I drank extra-strong coffee from my Captain America shower mug, and deciding that glasses would have to do because contacts weren't happening this morning, I was off.

I thought about driving to her work, but it was a quick "L" trip there. The energy of the Chicago train and streets was just the extra wake-up call I needed. Her office building was situated almost on the direct opposite side of WET. I always loved knowing the white-collar workers probably wished for a hidden bar in the building. They had no idea what was happening right underneath their noses as they left work for the day.

I walked to the elevator, and after scanning the directory

to see where By Invitation Only was, I headed up to the fifth floor. Once I exited, my hands began to shake. I turned the corner, and the glass door was immediately to my right. The first thing I noticed was her.

She was staring at her computer, her eyebrows creased in concentration. She was wearing a white shirt, or blouse, or whatever the hell they called it. It was cut low, but not too low. Her blond hair was tucked behind her ears, and her lips, *Jesus*. They were that same red, like the perfect red, painted with a lipstick that made the color look like her own. My mind wondered what it would be like to kiss her lips, that mouth, and wipe it all away. I didn't even give a shit that most of it would end up on me.

God. Her. Those lips. Around me. I strained against the zipper of my jeans.

"Hi," she said, opening the door. She smiled but looked confused. Well, maybe it was confusion, or maybe it was something more like weirded out. "Why are you just standing there? Come in."

I stepped in, and she was right there in front of me. She smelled and looked like something out of a wet dream, while I sported a Hummer-sized hard-on.

"Glasses, huh?" she asked, grinning. "They suit you."

"Yeah," I said, touching my black rims. "And I wasn't just standing there on purpose. I, ah, was making sure this was it. I wasn't sure, you know. Well, I mean the name was on the door, but you looked busy. I didn't want to barge in and disturb you. Are these the flowers? Duh. Of course they are. Okay, well, I'll take them and be right back."

"Oh, well, there's no rush," she said.

Yes, there is. I need this…covered.

The damn thing was in fact an atrocity and definitely was heavier than I expected. It made the He-Man *let me carry this thing out like the strong man that I am* act look weak. I didn't need any more help looking like a jackass.

"Okay, well, if you want to do it now, I was going to have you put it outside at the end of the hallway. There's only empty offices down there so, until the florist comes to get them, they'll be safe."

"Cool. Yeah. I'll be right back."

I dragged the thing down the hall, which seemed to expand more and more, like the scene from *Poltergeist*. Carnations and huge leaves left a trail behind me, and there was no room to even give a fuck. I was pretty sure I'd blown it, and if she did believe the flowers were a mix-up, I came across as such a huge tool and lost all credibility.

When I got back to the office, Bridget was standing next to Evelyn's desk. As soon as I opened the door, they stopped talking and stared at me. They'd obviously been talking about me. It showed.

"Hey Bridget," I said, shoving my hands in my pockets.

"Hey there, Abel. I saw you picked quite the declaration in terms of flowers for Evelyn."

"It was an accident," I explained. "The flowers I got—"

She walked over and punched me in the arm. "I know. I just wanted to see you squirm. Thanks for getting it out of here because, well, I can't have that shit in my office." She continued past me and into her own office. "I'll need her back in an hour. So, if you want to eat and have a little post-lunch make out, you'll need to make it quick."

"Whatever," Evelyn said. I watched as she stood and was finally able to get the full view of her, without the distraction of flower removal. Her shirt was tucked into a tight, slim skirt and every inch of her curves—*Jesus, that ass*—was perfectly in place.

"You want anything?" Evelyn shouted to Bridget.

"Where are you going?" she asked.

Evelyn looked at me, her eyebrows raised in question. Going out was her idea, her offer, so I wanted it to be all in her hands. Plus, I wanted to see what she would come up with.

"It's up to you. It's your date, right?" I winked, and instead of her looking like she was put off, she smiled.

"Lou Mitchell's," Evelyn shouted.

"Ugh," Bridget said. "Do I eat delicious greasiness or snack on my cucumber slices?"

Evelyn swung her purse over her shoulder. "Let's go."

"Shouldn't we wait and find out if she wants something?"

"It was more of a rhetorical question than anything. She'll sit there and talk herself in and out of getting something while we waited."

I followed her to the elevator, noticing that her shoes were black heels with a small strap that wrapped around her ankle. It was both professional and sexy. It was a fine line, and most women couldn't pull it off, but she did. As I trailed behind, I noticed her strong, toned legs. She had to work out. Or run.

"Thanks for coming," she said, as the elevator doors closed. Her eyes drifted downward, her long lashes following, and I thought maybe she was just as nervous as I was. "You know, for helping with the flowers," she added quickly.

"No problem," I said.

She smelled amazing—sweetness, and vanilla, and something. Without thinking, I moved closer, inhaling deeply.

"Are you…smelling me?" she asked, pushing herself to the back of the elevator and as far away from me as possible.

"No. I mean…it's just, you smell really nice and—"

The elevator opened, and she stepped out as quickly as she could. Meanwhile, I tucked what was left of my dignity back into my pants.

* * *

Lou Mitchell's was a Chicago institution. It had been around for over eighty years and was visited by presidents, celebrities, and average people on any given day. They have the most delicious breakfast that's served all day. There were many early mornings while in college spent there with friends after pulling an all-nighter or partying and needing to refuel my body with enough fat and carbs to send someone into cardiac arrest. It was that good.

I held the door open for her, a gust of wind blowing her hair back into me. It was something she used on her hair that added to whatever else she used to make her smell so good. She had no idea I was sending those flowers or that I'd be seeing her today, so why did it seem like when she woke up in the morning, she made an effort to do everything in her power to assure she drove me absolutely crazy.

"Welcome to Lou Mitchell's," a smiling older woman said. She held out a basket to us. "Would you like a doughnut hole?"

"Yes!" she squealed. "They have the doughnut holes."

She reached into the basket and pulled out two doughnut holes. "Here," she said, holding one out to me.

I didn't know of any other place that gave you warm doughnut holes as you entered, but it was one of the things that made Lou's special. I popped one into my mouth and resisted the urge to groan, they were that good. Good or not, moaning after I was caught sniffing her was just going to up the chances of getting slapped.

We slid into opposite sides of a booth that was tucked away in back near the kitchen.

"Mmm," she said, licking the tip of one of her fingers. "Yummy, right?"

She was fucking kidding me with this, right?

A small dusting of powdered sugar was left on her lower lip. "Definitely yummy. You have a little on—"

I leaned across the table, brushing my finger against her lip. "You have a tiny bit here."

My finger skimmed across her lower lip, pausing movement as I reached the corner of her mouth. The palm of my hand instinctively rested against her cheek, and the moment I realized what I was doing, was when I was going to pull away for fear it was too much.

But the look she was giving me, the way her blue eyes held tight on mine and how still she was as my palm settled against her face, told me I had nothing to fear.

A small smile appeared from her, and while it was fleeting, it was totally fucking there.

I pulled away from her, returning her grin as I did.

"Thanks," she said, picking up her napkin and going over the area again.

The waitress came over to take our order.

Evelyn was ready. "Can I get the Denver omelet, please? And can you add cheddar cheese to that? Thanks. Oh, and a side of pancakes. I'll just drink water, too."

My jaw dropped. A girl who wasn't afraid to eat and eat well. "Nicely done," I said, impressed.

She shrugged. "What's life if you can't…indulge every once in a while, right?"

"I'll have the same."

"So…," she said.

"So…"

"Have you been working at WET long?" She snorted after she said it, covering her mouth. "It sounds so much dirtier out loud than it did in my head."

"Imagine working there." I took a sip of my water as she watched me, her eyes scanning across my face.

"I've been there over two years. Worked there a night a week when I was finishing up school, graduated college and I couldn't find a teaching job. Now, I'm working there full-time. Not my dream job, but I'm lucky to have it."

"Sucks about the teaching thing. I have some friends going through the same thing."

"I had no idea it would be so hard. You figure, we live in Chicago, there should always be a need for teachers."

"What made you decide on education? I mean, no offense, you don't strike me as the teacher sort."

"I get that often, but really I just love kids. I went for secondary education because I don't want to be wiping noses and dealing with vomit, but if I got offered something in elementary, I'd take it in a second."

"You probably get some good practice with your niece. That Delilah is precious."

"She's the best thing in my life. What about you? Any nieces or nephews?"

"I'm the oldest of four, so no nieces or nephews."

"Wow. How's that?"

She thought for a moment, taking a sip from her water. "It's loud and fun. My family is crazy, and my parents are awesome. It's…all those things. My mom was a professional ballet dancer that gave it all up to be a mom. Dad is a contractor."

"How did you end up working for Bridget?"

"Luck. And a lot of BSing on my part. I was looking for an internship. She was my first choice since I wanted to do event planning, but she said she didn't do interns. I pressed and asked for a meeting anyway. That was it. I worked my ass off during the internship, and she offered me a job as her assistant. I'd like to say it was all about my skills, but I think she realized how much she was doing on her own, and she couldn't anymore. With me, she's able to take on more weddings and leave me with details, while her attention can be on the clients. I work hard so I can do it all myself someday."

She continued to impress me. There were so few people,

who were in their twenties like us, that knew what they wanted and went after it. She grabbed her career by the horns and owned it.

"What?" she said.

"What what?"

"You were staring."

"No. Just processing. You're very ambitious. I could probably learn a thing or two," I said, winking.

She smiled and shifted in her seat before reaching back to tuck her hair behind her ears. "I don't know. I saw how you worked last night, and you seemed to do it very well."

I shrugged. "I'm not bad at it, and I don't think I'd hate it if I did it forever. But it's not what I feel in my heart, you know? Plus, it's a killer on my social life."

"Really? I thought it'd be the opposite. I'm sure you meet lots of…interested people."

"Nice choice of words. I work a lot of nights and weekends."

"Huh," she said. "Lucky for you, so do I."

It was then time for me to squirm in my seat. Everything about her made my blood run hot in the most intense way. I could feel it in the way my heart raced and how with simple words or gestures she turned me on. I was sure I was staring again; in fact, I know I was, but this time she was staring back. There was this energy between us, and I was hoping she was trying to make sense out of it all, too.

Our food coming broke the spell, and we ate while we continued to talk. She was so easy and engaging to talk to that when she checked her phone for the time, we'd realized the hour she was supposed to be away had come and gone.

"I better get back," she said, motioning for the check.

"Will she give you shit for being late?"

"Probably, but then she'll forget about it five minutes later."

"I'm glad she finally brought you into WET," I said, my voice lingering on the word *wet*. I focused a hard gaze in her direction in the hopes she would catch the vibe of just how into her I was.

She grabbed hold of what I was sending out, her eyes staring back at mine. My confidence began to rise, along with other things, and I thought she was understanding exactly what I wanted her to.

She rolled her eyes. "Smooth motherfucker, aren't you?"

Or maybe she wasn't.

Shake it off, Abel. She'll get there. She's almost there already.

"I do my best," I said. "Is it working?"

The check was placed on the table, and we reached for it at the same time. She reached it first, placing her hand on top of it, just as my hand landed on hers. I knew she said she wanted to pay, but I wasn't going to let her without a little protest.

"Nope. I said it was my treat," she said, wiggling her hand out from under mine. "You can take care of it next time."

And there was going to be a next time. I knew I better strike while the iron was hot.

"Do you like to run?" I asked.

"After a breakfast like this? Not usually. At the gym later, though."

"No," I said, laughing. "I meant, are you a runner?"

She shook her head and made an adorable *duh* face for not following me. "No races or anything, but yes. I like to run."

"I like to go on Sundays. You can stop by my place, and we can run along the lake if you aren't busy."

"I'm not much of a morning person, plus I have a wedding to work with Bridget Saturday night. How's ten o'clock?"

"Perfect," I said. "I'll make brunch when we get back."

She smiled as she looked through her purse and pulled out her wallet. "A Sunday run sounds good to me, but I think we both should agree on one thing before."

I dreaded what she was going to suggest but asked anyway. "What?"

"No expectations," she said. "Just a run between friends, okay?"

It was nothing to dread, well, except for her using the kiss-of-death word *friends*, but I was willing to overlook that because it made perfect sense.

"Lucky for you, I'm a great friend," I said.

"Oh, I'm sure you have a list a mile long of them, Abel."

Perhaps.

But that was nothing to worry about now. Evelyn in tight running clothes? I was making a mental folder of images as she paid the bill.

* * *

"Ma! I need help!" I shouted, pounding on their door before opening it with my key. "Ma!"

"We're in the kitchen, honey," she called back.

There were certain benefits to having my parents living in the same building as me. For example, when I was supposed to have an extremely hot girl over for brunch in an hour and having no idea what to make or how to make it.

I walked into the kitchen; my father was sitting at the table, reading the newspaper, and my mom was adding more grounds to the coffeemaker.

"Coffee?" she asked.

"Yes. But I also need help with something."

"Everything okay?" she asked.

"Not really," I said, reaching into the cupboard for a coffee mug. I searched, pushing the other cups to the side, to find my Chicago Blackhawks mug. "I need to make brunch for a girl today, and I don't know what to make."

"Today? Why did you wait until the last minute to plan?"

I poured my coffee, filling it up to just below the rim. "I didn't. I'm asking you now."

Mom pushed the sugar and cream over to me, even though I told her every time I've had coffee for the past five years that I took it black.

"Is she waiting now?" Dad asked without looking up from the paper.

"No. Of course not," I said.

"Daniel, really?" Mom said. She sat down next to him and playfully hit him in the arm.

Dad lowered the paper, looking at me over his reading glasses pushed down his nose. Mom didn't need to know about the couple of times Dad ran into me escorting one of my walks of shame out of the building. Not only was it awkward for me, but I knew the girl had to be embarrassed to meet her one-night stand's dad in the lobby of the building that also housed his parents. There isn't a girl alive that would love meeting fuck buddy's dad with sex hair and last night's dress a wrinkled mess.

I raised my eyebrows back at Dad and took a sip of my coffee. "We're going running and back to my place for brunch."

"Well, if you're running," Mom said, "you should have something light and healthy for brunch. Maybe fruit and an egg-white frittata with veggies?"

"A frittata? Really, Mom? Like I know how to make that."

"Oh!" she said, standing up and rushing to the counter. She grabbed a plastic-wrapped loaf and started unwrapping it. "I made babka yesterday. You can have this as a little sweet side with your brunch."

I crossed the kitchen in two steps, yanking the babka from her hands. "Yes, please!"

"Don't bend it!" she scolded. She sighed before turning to the refrigerator. "Do you want some cinnamon butter to go with it?"

"Yes. Cinnamon butter is good."

She handed it to me, and I took it gently. "This is great, Mom. Thanks. Now. Can you tell me how exactly to make a frittata? I mean, I know it's eggs, but what is it *really*?"

She raised her eyebrows at me at the same time Dad snorted.

"What?" I asked.

A crack of a smile appeared on my mom's face. "Sweetie. You know what a frittata is, but more importantly, if you're trying to impress a lady friend I wouldn't leave it up to you to make yourself."

"How hard could it be?"

"Not very, but you don't want to try a new recipe when you're under pressure," she said. "Why don't you go on your run, and I'll have it all ready for you at your place by the time you get back."

She wasn't entirely wrong. I hated her doing things for me because it made me feel as though she thought I wasn't capable. On the other hand, maybe she knew me best and maybe that meant I wasn't.

"Hello!" my brother Aaron said, entering the front door.

"In here, sweetie," Mom said.

"Mom," I said. "Are you sure you want to do that for me?"

My niece, Delilah, ran into the kitchen ahead of Aaron. She was holding her little Minnie Mouse close to her chest, her light blond hair curly and wild.

"What are you whining about now?" he asked.

"I'm not whining. Hey, squirt," I said. I set the babka and butter on the table before turning to Delilah. I tickled her all across her tummy, watching her giggle and pretend not to.

I scooped her up and began to spin her as she laughed.

"More, Uncle Abel," she shouted. "Faster!"

At five, she was so amazing and took completely after my brother, instead of the deadbeat mom of hers. While I was sad Delilah would probably never know her mother, it was for the best. She was strong-willed, wicked smart, and completely lit up a room with her smile. Plus, with the way things were going, Callie was going to be her mom someday.

"What do you want in the frittata, Abel?" Mom asked.

"I don't care," I said, throwing Delilah over my shoulder.

"Well, what does *she* like," she asked, opening the refrigerator again.

"I don't know. We've only been out once."

I remembered the deal I made with Evelyn. It was going to be our secret for now.

"Dude," Aaron said, taking Delilah from me and setting her down. "Do you have a girl waiting at your place right now? Hell. Make your own breakfast for her."

Dad snorted again, his paper held over his face, but I could tell by the way his hands and paper shook he was laughing. "Why would he do that when Mom can do it for him?" he asked.

Aaron matched Dad's laugh. "Some things never change, huh?"

"Shut up," I said. "There's no one at my place. We are meeting in—" I looked at the clock, seeing that I had a half hour before she was supposed to arrive. "Shit, I have to go."

Aaron punched my arm. "Language," he said, pointing to Delilah.

"I have some goat cheese and herbs. I can sauté some veggies to put in there," Mom said.

"Perfect," I said, grabbing the babka and butter. I rushed to Mom, giving her a kiss on the cheek. "Best mom ever."

I patted Delilah on the head, shouting good-byes as I ran

toward the door. I heard my dad ask my mom why she always babied me.

"Because it's what we all do," Aaron said.

I shook it off as I left the apartment, rushing to my own place. After a quick shower and change for the run, I got a text from Evelyn letting me know she was downstairs waiting.

My eyes scanned the lobby of our building as soon as I stepped off the elevator, but I didn't see her anywhere.

I walked toward the revolving door, wondering if she was possibly waiting outside, but I heard her laugh, not just a laugh from her, but a laugh that I already knew was hers, high and full of enthusiasm. She was talking to Rob, the doorman, on the other side of the door.

Even though there'd been ample material collected in my mind, I don't think I adequately prepared myself for how she would look in tight running pants and the fitted zipped jacket that covered up entirely too much of her. She wasn't as done up as I'd seen her in the past, but she looked every bit as beautiful. Her cheeks were flushed pink from the chilly lake breeze, and her hair was pulled up into a tight ponytail on top of her head.

"Hey," I said, emerging from the revolving door. "There you are."

I leaned in and kissed her on the cheek, her skin cool against my warm lips. I instantly noticed her scent, that perfume she'd worn every time we'd been together. I was going to have to ask her what it was.

"Hey you," she said. "I didn't know whether to come in or not, so I started chatting with Rob here."

Rob had been working at our building for the last four years and, suffice it to say, had seen me around with a lady or two.

"I heard your laugh, there is no mistaking it," I said.

I rubbed my hand against her back, as she leaned in against my chest.

"There is for sure no way to mistake my hyena-type laugh. You could hear me clear across a crowded room."

"I think it's adorable," I said.

She snorted softly before playfully punching my chest. "Smooth, but there's no bullshit on my grocery list today."

She pulled her hoodie over her head, tucking loose strands of her hair into it. "Let's go, Abel. Let's see if you can keep up."

Rob cleared his throat as I started to jog off after her. I turned, and he gave me the thumbs-up. "I like this one already. She's different," he said.

"I agree."

She wasn't kidding. I did have trouble keeping up with her. I tried not to be chauvinistic and think that there was no way a girl half my size could give me a run for my money. She totally did.

We started off at a slow jog together, but after about a mile, her stride became stronger and faster. I trailed behind, fighting to catch my breath and stay more in time with her. Not only was she faster, but she was also the worst kind of distraction, especially from the back.

Her jacket hem stopped at her hips, hugging around her waist, while her spandex pants gave me a full and pleasant view of her ass. It wasn't like I hadn't checked it out before, but now, with just a thin layer of fabric covering it, I had to fight off the urge to grab her behind and make out with her until she couldn't remember her own name.

I was imagining what she was wearing, if anything, under those pants when the distraction became too much. I tripped and stumbled, trying to regain my balance before she noticed.

"You okay back there?" she shouted, turning around and continuing to jog backward.

"Fine. I'm great. And you don't need to shout. I'm not that far away."

She adjusted her hoodie, pulling the frayed strings tighter around her face. "Want me to slow down?"

And miss this view. No way.

"Or are you enjoying the view?" She grinned, a wicked, sexy grin that I was sure was going to get her whatever she wanted out of me, whenever she wanted. No doubt this girl could get any man to do whatever she wanted.

But I wasn't going to let her know that. *Yet.*

"Yeah, I am. The lake looks beautiful today."

"Uh-huh," she said, turning back around. "Come on, slowpoke. You're going to have to work harder than that if you want to catch me."

I was beginning to figure that out all on my own.

CHAPTER SEVEN

Evelyn—

Men are so predictable and easy. They see a pretty girl in tight pants, and they think we have no idea that running behind us isn't because they are slow, but because they are checking out our ass.

Or maybe they are slow, too. I was leaning more toward ass patrol.

I would've never admitted it, but I was enjoying it immensely. While I had prefaced this outing with a "no expectations" stipulation, I secretly had many of them.

I expected him to continue to let his eyes roam around my face while his dimples subtly appeared.

I expected him to continue to let me know who he was, what his goals were, and how he was appearing to be nothing like what I perceived him to be while these things were gradually unraveling.

I expected his touch to be somewhere on my body again.

I expected him to kiss me.

Expectations often led to disappointment, but on the rare occasion that they came to fruition, it was so very delicious. It was why I was here. *He* was the delicious.

We rounded the corner by his building, and I slowed, allowing him to catch up. After a few moments, he jogged up next to me, breathless and sweaty.

Walking off the run in circles, regulating my own breathing, Abel was bent over with his hands on his knees, inhaling sharply.

"Maybe you shouldn't do two things at once?" I said, leaning against the concrete building and stretching my legs.

"Two things…such as…huh?" he asked, panting.

He stood, extending his arms above his head, which caused his jacket and T-shirt to ride up. I saw a snippet of his tight abs and smooth skin with the slightest hint of treasure trail. It was maybe the fifth time I had seen him, and I still couldn't get over the size of him. Without knowing for sure, I estimated he was six two and made of iron. He obviously lifted weights, but he wasn't bulky. He was just solid. Solid man.

"What was that about two things at once?" he asked, winking.

I was standing with my leg pulled up behind me by my ankle, stretching, when his abs hypnotized me. Maybe women were as predictable as men.

"Nothing. I'm just really good at multitasking," I said.

"Is that so?"

He smiled slowly, deepening his dimples as he moved toward me, crossing the space between us. The closer he moved, the more his eyes focused on me. His hands lifted above me, pressing into the building, and trapping me in tight to him.

"It is so," I said, trying to keep my cool.

"So you can stretch and check me out at the same time. Anywhere else you can display this multitasking?"

"Many places."

"Mmm," he whispered, his mouth lowering toward my neck. His lips grazed against me, just below my ear. "Interesting. Let's see how well you do up against the side of a high-rise."

"What did you have in mind?"

"Well, I've been wanting to kiss you senseless since the second I saw you today. In fact, I've thought of nothing else for the last couple of days. So, why don't I help you stretch while I kiss you," he said, running his hand down my side. He skimmed across my hip, bringing his touch around, grazing just underneath my ass before sliding his hand down my leg to behind my knee. He lifted it up against his hip, pressing himself into me.

His mouth moved from my neck to my jaw where his nose brushed against it as he inhaled deeply. "You always smell so amazing," he said before pressing his lips to mine.

He held me closer, tighter, moving his free hand up and into the back of my hair. Our kiss deepened, our lips moving together, carefully testing each other out. His hand wrapped around my hair and gripped it roughly, causing my knees to go weak.

But just for a moment.

He pulled away slightly, taking his hand from my hair while running his fingertips down and across my neck. His thumb brushed across my lower lip as his eyes shifted wildly across my face.

I followed my tongue along where his thumb was, licking my bottom lip, as I tried to compose myself. The boy could *kiss*. Shit. He must've had a lot of practice, and in that moment, I couldn't even bring myself to care because there was only one thing on my mind: more. I wanted more of him.

I pushed up on my free foot and gripped his jacket with my hands, pulling him to me and slamming us back against the building. A stifled groan reverberated against our lips as our tongues touched. Then…it was hands, lips, touching…all at once. I felt him *everywhere*. The hair of his beard tickled and was soft and rough at the same time. It was kind of like him. His mouth moved from my lips to my neck, kissing and brushing the tip of his tongue just below my ear. My sweet spot. He'd found it faster than most men.

My hands reached up around his neck, gripping the back of his hair. Without the product he usually used on it, his hair was soft and was curling slightly at the ends from the wind blowing against it. His tongue slid against mine as one of his hands held my knee against him, and the other held my chin in just the place he wanted it.

He shifted his legs open wider, stepping closer and slipping his leg between mine. There was no way he could continue kissing me like that, with his leg pressed tight, and not have me squirm on it. I was only moderately aware that we were still in public, so even though this side of the building was deserted and the desire to hump him there out in the open was fierce, I had to consider families with small children walking by.

My heart raced, pounding against my chest, not only from the hotness of it all, but also that a couple of my expectations were already exceeded.

His eyes.

His hands.

His touch.

Kiss.

It was frightening and exhilarating all at the same time, the push and pull of overwhelming want tempered by fear of letting him in too close.

Only focus on the want, Ev.

I pushed against his chest, separating us. "See? I told you. Multitasker."

He lowered my leg to the ground before wrapping his arms around my waist. "I was just seeing how much you can handle."

"I can handle a lot."

"I bet you could," he said, giving me a quick peck. "For right now, though, let me get you inside so we can eat."

The expansive building Abel lived in was within walking distance of Navy Pier; it stood high above the city, the rotating top floor reserved for the most special of occasions. We crossed the lobby, giving a nod to Rob on the way to the elevator and up to the fifty-fourth floor.

His hand intertwined with mine as we exited the elevator. "You're awfully quiet, Evelyn."

"So are you."

He paused in front of a door, reaching into his pocket with his free hand. "I'm wondering how much more you can handle."

He grinned at me, dimples deep, and like his kiss, it made my whole body react. Heat and butterflies. I wasn't handling things, but a girl never shows her cards.

"Quit giving me that smile. I'm sure it gets you whatever you want, but I'm the one that wants right now."

"Is that so?" he asked, raising his brows.

"Mm-hmm," I said, squeezing his hand. "I'm starving. Feed me or I'm out of here."

"You got it."

I could smell something amazing before he even opened the door. As he stepped inside, I followed, instantly taken over by the scent of cinnamon and eggs, along with the modern, vast space. The open floor plan allowed me to see most of the apartment from where I was standing.

"Are you kidding me with this?" I said.

"What?" He unzipped his jacket, tossing it on a stool before stepping into the kitchen.

It was all stainless steel and fresh white furniture. Everything was perfectly in place, right down to the smooth steel wall sconces and chenille throw pillows.

I moved farther into his home, taking off my own coat and placing it on the arm of the couch. "Your place is…amazing. Beautiful."

"I wish I could take credit for it, but I just told my mom what I wanted, and she decorated the entire thing," he said.

I watched as he placed pot holders on his hands and re-trieved a pie dish from the oven. He set it on the tabletop, which was already set with dishes, silverware, and cloth nap-kins.

I laughed. "Should your mom take credit for all of this, too?"

His head snapped up. "Why? Why do you think that?"

"Well, it seems that Leslie does a lot of things for you. I mean, the apartment, decorating, I wouldn't be surprised if she washed your clothes for you. A frittata is impressive for a guy such as yourself."

He held up a bread basket. "I have babka, too. And cinna-mon butter."

"Did you bake it yourself?"

"No. My mom definitely did that. Coffee?"

"Yes, please. Can I have some water, too? Rehydrating, you know?"

"Of course."

He slid the frosted glass refrigerator open, retrieving two bottles of water.

"What's this?" I asked, pointing to a closed Mason jar on the far end of the granite tabletop. "It looks like dandelions."

He walked over, extending the bottle of water to me. "Yes. That's exactly what it is."

I approached the jar and picked it up, turning it over in my hands. No stems, just the white, fluffy tops. There had to be at least thirty of them in there.

I set it back down and unscrewed the top from my water. Taking a sip, I raised my eyebrows at him, waiting for an ex-planation.

"What do you think of when you see dandelions?" he asked.

It was just as strange of a question as it was to see a Mason jar full of them. I didn't know if it was some spiritual thing, and he was going to spring to his views on life based on the symbolism of the dandelion. Or maybe they really weren't dandelions at all. Maybe they were poisonous bulbs, masquerading as dandelions, an elaborate plan to get women under his spell, like the poppies from *Wizard of Oz*, but instead of sleepiness, we became weary of clothing.

He reached above the stove, the fabric of his white T-shirt stretching across his back and arms. After retrieving two small pods for the coffeemaker, he grabbed two glass coffee mugs.

"I didn't realize it was such a tough question," he said. "How do you take your coffee?"

I placed the water down, fumbling with the lid. "Maybe you should just tell me why you have a jar of weeds on your counter, especially since everything else in the place is so pristine. And black, please."

"Whiskey and black coffee," he said, nodding. He grinned, his blue eyes moving up and down me. "You really can do no wrong, can you?"

"Don't make me take out my bullshit meter. Now, tell me about the dandelions."

He pulled the coffee cup from under the coffeemaker and placed it on the tabletop, sliding it across to me. I lifted it to my mouth, smelling hints of vanilla and cinnamon. "Look at you pulling out this gourmet shit. I would've been happy with some freeze-dried Taster's Choice."

He banged his hand on the table so hard the Mason jar shook. "Bring it here, beautiful," he said, raising his hand. "A *Pulp Fiction* reference has elevated you to an entirely new status."

We high-fived each other, but before I could let go, he laced his fingers through mine and pulled me forward. Leaning over the breakfast bar, he was tall enough to bend down to kiss me.

"They're for wishes," he said, our faces close.

"Kisses for wishes?"

"No." He bent over for one more kiss before pushing back. "The dandelions. They're for wishes."

"Ah. I see. So, you just save them up, and when you need one, you…blow?"

"Exactly."

It was sweet, a side of him separate from the bold, smooth-talking man I'd known. He wasn't afraid to leave a jar of dandelions out and to tell anyone who asked they were for wishes. In fact, he really didn't give a shit what people thought of him.

I took a sip of my coffee while I was aware he was staring at me, wondering what I was going to say.

"What?" he said. "No 'Aw! That's so cute!' or 'That is so sweet!'"

"Is that what you're used to?"

He shrugged. "It seems to be the general reaction of most women."

It occurred to me his jar of wishes was a way to get women, but instead of my initial thought of poisoning them, it was all about appearing endearing. I had almost bought it.

I saw the sincerity in his face, the ribbon of truth in his words, and I was compelled to believe him. I *wanted* to believe him, that whatever was happening between us was for me alone.

I just wasn't there yet.

"I'm not like most women," I said, drinking from my coffee mug.

His gaze fixated on me, his movements still except for the rising and falling of his chest. Silence was all around, even the coffeemaker had quieted. I worried I'd offended him but was reassured when he smiled, dimples displayed, while he ran his hand across his beard. "I'm beginning to figure that out. Ready to eat?"

"Absolutely."

* * *

I didn't care, not one bit, who made the brunch or whom I was eating it with, I ate all of the deliciousness with barely a breath. Abel put the babka in the toaster and smeared it with cinnamon butter. The heated, fluffy bread soaked the butter into the cinnamon swirls, making it impossible for me to eat just one. So I ate another and would've eaten a third if I didn't think I'd come across as a total piggy.

"Mind if I go change real quick?" he asked when we had

finished. He stretched his arms above his head and brought them down, running his fingers through his hair.

"Why?" I asked.

"I'm sure that I don't smell the greatest after the run, and while I'm sure I need a shower, a new T-shirt will be better."

"Oh, sure. Just leave me in my funk."

"Girls don't have funk," he said.

"Yes, we do."

It wasn't a debate that I wanted to have. Body odors weren't conducive to coming across as waking up perfect and smelling like roses at all times.

"Well, you don't. In fact," he said, approaching. His arms wrapped around my waist, and he forced me to him in one commanding pull. "I have to know the perfume you wear. It smells incredible on you."

He dipped his head down, dragging his nose against the skin of my neck, running it down to my collarbone. His touch, every single time, made my body respond, heat and shivers, like a shot of whiskey. When the initial jolt had settled, I had the need for more. He moved from my neck to look at me, waiting for an answer. Everything was so playfully intense with this guy. He demanded attention without being cocky, expecting responses with mischievous direction. There was no doubt he knew how attractive he was and how to use it.

He began moving my hips, casually back and forth, with his hands, almost like we were dancing. "Why do you want to know?" I said. "I mean, it's pretty unique, and I wouldn't want you to share it with anyone."

"What if I promised not to share?"

I held out my pinkie to ensure a promise. He wrapped his own around mine, grinning as he did.

"That smile," I said, shaking my head. "Gets you everything you want, doesn't it?"

He shrugged. "Sometimes. But there are times I really want something and I need to work harder for it."

"Such as?"

"You ask a lot of questions, Evelyn," he said. He closed the space between us again, knowingly taunting me by bringing his lips to mine, barely touching.

It was push and pull between us. He was trying to dominate, but I wasn't going to crumble. It wasn't my style, nor was it where I wanted to be with him. I could feel myself falling under his spell. It was a dangerous place to be. It wasn't about being in charge. It was about showing him that even if we both wanted the same, I was going to be the one to decide.

I shoved his arms off me, startling his confidence as evidenced by his frown.

"Frowns don't suit you as well as your smile does," I said, taking his hand and leading us to the couch.

He followed, and with a gentle push, he sat down. I straddled his lap, wiggling myself into a comfortable position in which I was the one looking down on him for once. A gradual smile returned to his face.

"There we go," I said, gliding the tips of my fingers down his beard, ending where his dimples emerged.

Our lips met, and all of my intent disintegrated. The kisses were all tongue and want, the sugary-sweetness taste we shared making us hunger for more. The once quiet apartment was now filled with our soft moans and shifting bodies moving against each other.

Without a break from lips, he lifted me by my hips just enough so he could change positions and lay down, bringing me down on top of him. My hands slid under his shirt, wanting to feel his smooth skin beneath my touch. The hard muscles of his chest were only matched by the heat radiating off it.

I rolled my hips over him and that one movement showed me how hard he was against my thigh. While I knew he was worried about his post-run scent, there was nothing offensive about him. He smelled of aftershave and man, strong and inviting at the same time. Our movements together became more and more rapid as his hold on me became tighter until all at once, he stopped.

I flipped up, mounting his waist. "Everything okay? Am I hurting you?" I asked, panting.

"No," he said, blowing his hair off his damp forehead. "You're amazing, a little too amazing."

"Then why did you stop?"

"Because we were about to cross over into the point of no return."

This boy was the best thing my body had known in a long time, and if making out was this good, the sex had to be even better.

"You," he said. "You I want to wait for."

My response was to snort and call an off-the-chart register

on the bullshit meter. Instead, I stifled a chuckle and attempted to move off his lap.

"Hey. I'm serious," he said, grabbing my waist to keep me put. "I don't want you to think I'm in this for one thing."

"I'm sure you're serious."

But I wasn't. I didn't know how any female was.

He let out a deep sigh. "I really like you and I must say," he said, brushing his hand through my hair. "You look really good up there on me."

There was no hint of embarrassment, no pause. There was only a wide smile and eyes unafraid, looking straight into mine. His grip on my waist remained, as his fingers dug into my hip farther. He was giving a little of himself, and in return, I knew I should've done the same, but didn't know if I could. As his eyes scanned mine, looking for something for me to give back, I realized I had a choice: Either appease him or not, knowing that I might blow the whole thing.

I decided to meet him halfway.

"I go to a place in Lincoln Park where you can make your own perfume. It's made with vanilla and peony essential oils, plus lighter notes of a few others. You won't find any other girl with it. I'm the one and only."

He leaned up and gave me a peck on the cheek before wrapping me up in a hug. "One and only is right," he whispered.

My bullshit meter went off.

I quickly told it to shut the fuck up.

* * *

I didn't do dreamy. I wasn't one of those girls who laid awake in bed and went over every single detail of a date. I didn't recall his lips on my skin or hands moving across my body. There was never a time I lost sleep reminiscing over the unmistakable desire in his eyes and the way my own body and mind couldn't get enough. No. I didn't do that. But I did. It felt wrong but in all the right ways. I was on a dangerous, slippery slope. It was taking everything in me to keep from falling.

"Ah, Evelyn. Hello?" Bridget shouted.

I jumped in my seat, shaking my thoughts out of my head. "Oh, hi. I got your green garbage drink. It's on your desk."

"What's wrong? You were staring at your computer screen and didn't even hear me come in. What if I was here to murder you?"

"Nothing is wrong and the door was locked to keep serial killers out."

She plopped her Birkin on my desk and unbuttoned her coat. After taking off her coat, she sat down in the chair opposite me while sporting a Bridget-sized stare.

"What?" I asked. "Did you not want your freshly squeezed compost? Should I have gotten you coffee?"

She crossed her legs, swinging her black Jimmy Choos at me. "Are you kissing ass about something?"

"No. I was out early this morning and was being considerate."

I almost asked her if she was cranky, but she hated it when I asked her if she was cranky when she was cranky.

"Thank you. Although it does make me think you're kissing ass about something which also makes me think you have an idea what I'm going to tell you."

"What?"

"Now, I don't want you to panic…"

"Are you firing me?"

She held up her hand to stop me. "Just let me talk," she said, pausing for a moment. "I didn't want to say anything until I was sure it was a done deal, but now that it is, I can tell you. By Invitation Only is expanding into a second location."

"*What?* What does that mean?"

"It means there's going to be a Charleston, South Carolina, office," she said, moving to the edge of her chair. A smile, one that was both warm and excited, took over her face. It was about as rare as snowless Chicago winter.

I was having a hard time processing what she was saying. Another location? Charleston? Was she leaving? Was I? What did it all mean? I lifted my coffee to my mouth, sipping as I chose the most important question to ask so she didn't freak out on me for asking too many questions again.

"I can see by your reaction you have concerns. Sweetie, these are all good things. For the both of us," she said.

"How did this…happen? Why Charleston? Who's going to run it? When is it up and running?"

She rolled her eyes and sat back in her seat. "Charleston has hit a huge boom on the destination wedding front within the last several years. Now, there is going to be some travel for me. In fact, I've snuck away a few times already when I told you I was at conference or something. I've hired a very well-established planner who's already there. Her name is Trinity and is the cutest little Southern belle, but a total tiger when it comes to business."

Dread weighed down my body, and I couldn't even form a question to ask. I'd always thought if anyone would be made a partner, it would be me, not someone who lived one thousand miles away. My expression gave me away and Bridget picked right up on it.

She sighed loudly. "You seriously need to stop freaking out before you know all the details."

"How can I not? This is huge. It's bigger than huge. Plus—"

"And if you'd let me finish," she said, interrupting me. "This is a huge opportunity for you, and one I haven't taken lightly. I want you to go out there for three months in the fall. It's only from September to December, so you'll be home in time for the holidays. Trinity knows what she's doing, but you know how I like things done. I want you to help with the transition, get the office organized, get marketing squared away and all that stuff. You'll be with her on the weddings already booked, but it's to make sure things are being handled with the utmost care. When you come back, I want to start putting you on your own weddings."

This was all too much information at once. My brain couldn't catch up with everything Bridget was throwing at me. The only logical question, which I was sure wasn't very logical to her, was "Huh?"

She smiled. "I'm moving you up, dollface."

"You're making me your partner?"

"I wouldn't go that far. I still pay your salary, but you are ready for this. You could pull off any event, and now is the chance to show me you can pull off another By Invitation Only."

It all began to sink in. It wasn't exactly what I'd dreamed of. I had always imagined going out on my own, but at this stage of my life, what Bridget was offering was the next logical step. I'd worked so hard, and this was a huge move forward.

"What do you think?" she asked.

Pride and gratitude overcame me.

Then something else followed.

All the what-ifs.

What if I really wasn't ready for this?

What if I got homesick for Chicago, a place I'd never been away from for more than a couple weeks at a time, and missed Callie being so close?

What if what was happening with Abel turned into something more?

No. It wouldn't. It couldn't.

It brought back so many painful emotions from when I was with Patrick. How he'd make me feel poorly if I chose work or something to help me further my career over something as simple as having dinner with him. There would be passive-aggression for days after, where I'd have to do all I could to make it up to him. The day I did my first independent event for Bridget, and it went over seamlessly, all I got from him was bitching about how late I was coming home. It occurred to me soon after I had no idea who I was anymore—no idea who I was with *him*. I never wanted to experience that again. I refused to.

I wasn't going to express any of those thoughts to her. I only wanted to tell her what she wanted to hear most and what superseded any other emotion.

"I'm ready," I said. "I'm ready to be all in."

CHAPTER EIGHT

ABEL—

If you don't put that thing away, I'm calling Aaron and telling him I'm firing you."

Marshall shoved my shoulder, but I knew he was all talk. I slipped my phone back in my pocket and mumbled, "No one is even here yet."

It was a Wednesday night, and we were setting up for a private party. Extra champagne glasses, which Marshall insisted be wiped down to make sure they were crystal clear, covered the top of the bar while the kitchen crew began setting out mini desserts for a sweets bar.

"If Aaron walked in and saw you on your phone, my head would be on the chopping block."

"Quit being so dramatic. Since when does Aaron pop in? Never. I was only checking my texts, and besides, no one is getting in trouble or fired, so stop acting like a seven-year-old girl tattling to her teacher."

It had been three days since I'd seen Evelyn, but we had

been texting and talking back and forth during that entire time. With every ding of my message alert, my heart beat a little faster knowing it was her. At the same time, my masculinity deflated, knowing that this girl had me so completely wrapped up in her. It was an ego thing for sure, but I was sure I could handle it as long as no one else saw it.

"Man. That girl has got you whipped already," he said, chuckling.

Wishful thinking.

"Shut up," I said. "I seem to remember finding you crying in the office when Brit broke up with you."

"My hamster had died, you dick. It had nothing to do with Brit."

I picked up another glass, rubbing the crystal with a soft cotton towel. "She died like two years ago."

"Sometimes grief comes over you at unexpected times."

"Yeah, like when your girlfriend finds out that you were planning a three-way with her and her best friend, without either of them knowing?"

"You promised you'd never bring that up again," he said with obvious anger. He started to walk away but stopped after a few steps. "Aaron's brother or not, I could make your life hell."

Watching him stomp off was like watching a four-year-old have a tantrum. He tried to be all boss, but in the end, he was like a big kid.

My phone vibrated in my pocket and I decided one more look before the night got going was okay. I slid it out of my pocket, seeing as I hoped, a message from Evelyn.

Evelyn: I'm so exhausted and nowhere near close to finishing for the day. Is taking a nap at work frowned upon? Listen to me…your night is only beginning. Have a good one!

I started to type a response, but then had an even better idea. After putting my phone back in my pocket, I ran from behind the bar to the room directly behind it. Marshall was sitting at his desk, a small wooden rolltop with an oversized leather-bound chair.

"I need to run out for a few," I said. "Be back in like ten minutes."

He pushed away from the desk, the wheels of his chair squeaking against the tile floor. "The hell you are. People are getting here any minute, and I need you."

"The party isn't due to start for another twenty minutes. I'll be back in time. There's something I have to get real quick around the corner."

"What's around the corner? The drugstore? Let me guess. You need some Midol and tampons, right?"

"Ha-ha," I said, flipping him the bird. "Give me a break here."

He sighed and pulled his chair back to his desk. "If you aren't back before the first guest gets here, your ass is grass."

"Thanks," I shouted as I rushed from the room.

It was a little after seven o'clock, the sky beginning to fade dark in hues of purple and blue. Without a jacket on, the lake breeze washed across my skin, warmer now in early May to prepare us for the heat that would be coming soon. I ran down the sidewalk, jumping between the suits who were rushing from work to get to the train back to the suburbs.

"Slow the fuck down," a guy with a messenger bag and a gold tweed sports coat hissed at me when I accidentally bumped his shoulder.

There was no time to apologize.

I crossed the street, not waiting for the light to change, and came dangerously close to being hit by a cab, which didn't even attempt to brake. If you're in the way of a Chicago cabbie, you move. They don't stop.

I yanked open the door to Starbucks abruptly, swinging it hard into the side of the building. The entire shop went silent and glared at me from behind their laptops and Frappuccinos. If a little bubble would've appeared above their heads with their thoughts, I was sure it would've said, *You…are a dick.*

"Sorry," I mumbled, stepping up to the counter.

I wasn't sure what to get her, but something sweet, hot, and caffeinated seemed like a safe bet. Who didn't like caramel? I glanced at the clock behind the counter and saw this was going to have to be quick.

Luckily for me, there was only one person ahead of me, a middle-aged woman, wearing a fur coat and a plastic rain-cover hat thing over her heavily hair-sprayed hair.

"Oh, I don't know," she whined, tapping her long, fake nails on the counter. "If I drink espresso this late in the afternoon, I might be up all night."

"Well, you can get almost anything in decaf," the teen barista said. He looked past her, and I could see him roll his eyes at me just behind the blond bangs.

"Of course," she said. "But I do need a little pick-me-up, you know?"

"Half cafe?" the barista offered.

I looked down at my phone and realized if I didn't order immediately, I'd be late getting back to WET, and Marshall would need an ambulance for the stroke he was going to have.

"All right. I'll have a half-cafe Venti latte with skim milk, sugar-free vanilla, a touch of whipped cream, and make it extra hot," she said. She slid to the display of pastries and bent down close to the glass. "Hmm. Maybe I'll get a little treat, too. Those muffins look good. What are they, blueberry?"

"Yes, they—"

She continued talking, interrupting the barista. "Oh! No. I'll have that chocolate thingy there."

She stood up, leaving a smudge of her makeup on the glass from her nose.

"Do you know how many calories are in those?" she said, squatting back down. "I'm sure they're too much. Maybe I should—"

I snapped. "Maybe you should stop being inconsiderate of the people waiting behind you and not stand there all day, making up your mind. Have you never been to Starbucks before?" I asked loudly. Probably too loudly.

Again. The room went quiet.

She put her hand to her chest and gasped. "And who do you think you're talking to like that?"

Just before I told her where she could stick her pastry, another employee came up to the register. I moved up next to Ms. Fur Lady, shooting her a dirty look as I did.

"What can I get you?"

"Venti Caramel Macchiato and chocolate croissant, please."

"And that, young lady," I said to the woman, "is how it's done."

The first barista snorted under his breath, but the lady was oblivious. She was mumbling about why there weren't more gluten-free items because why wouldn't she start complaining about something different. She was the exact type of customer the service industry hated.

Then, because I had been so distracted by the lady, I remembered Evelyn was a black coffee girl.

"Wait!" I said to the barista making the drink. "Can I change that? I messed up."

Fur lady snorted, which to be fair, I deserved.

"Um," the barista said over the loud churning of the espresso machine. "You want to change?"

"Just…ugh. Never mind."

By the time I paid and got the warmed croissant and drink, I knew I'd have to hustle. I jogged back across the street and down to the large office building. While I tried to keep the coffee from bubbling up at me, it splashed my white shirt just as I was rushing through the revolving door.

"Shit. Shit. Shit," I whispered as I waited for the elevator.

Checking my phone, I saw I had about two minutes to make the drop-off and get back to work. I also had a text message from an unknown number. I clicked it open.

Matthews: Dropping something off at WET tonight. If I don't hear back from you, I'll assume you'll be there. Benji.

Dropping something off? What the hell did that mean? When did Benji and I ever "friend" outside of the poker table?

I shoved my phone back in my pocket. I'd think about it later.

Once the elevator doors opened, I jumped in and tapped my foot, waiting for it to slowly ascend.

I was off and running the moment the elevator doors opened again, stopping to slow down just before I reached the glass doors of By Invitation Only. She was sitting at her desk, hand under her chin, her hair covering the side of her face. God, she was beautiful. With no one around, she still looked as perfect as she did anytime I saw her. Hell, I could've caught her picking her nose and would still want to lift her up on her desk to have my way with her.

I pushed the door open as her eyes lifted to see who was entering. An electric smile brightened her entire face as she stood from her desk, pushing a slim, very tight black skirt down.

"Hey you!" she said, walking toward me. "What are you doing here?"

"I can't stay. I have to get back to work, but I wanted to bring you something to help you get through the night."

I handed her the coffee and croissant, which she took with a surprised reaction.

"Are you serious?" she asked. "This is the sweetest thing ever."

"I fucked up and forgot that you liked it black. By the time I remembered, they'd already started. So, I got you a foo-foo one. Then I realized as I walked over here that I didn't get it sugar-free, if that is how you would've wanted it. I mean, I guess I thought about it when I ordered it, but not really. I didn't want to assume you wanted the lower calorie one because I know girls don't like that. You get them something lower fat or something, thinking you're being considerate, but then you get frozen yogurt thrown at you for calling her fat. I only wanted to—"

She stood on her tiptoes and kissed me to shut me up. I hadn't expected to remember her touch with such clarity. Or the way she immediately made me want her, how my every sense responded to her, but that was exactly what happened. Her taste, the softness of her lips, the now-familiar scent of her perfume, everything made me realize one thing: I'd missed her.

She pulled away. "Thank you so much."

I brushed my hand against her cheek, pushing her fallen hair behind her ear. "You're welcome, beautiful. Free tomorrow night?"

"Don't you have to work?" she said, wiping some of her lipstick from my lips.

"No. I'm off."

"Well, I am free, but not until closer to eight probably."

"Dinner?"

I was going to play it safe and not ask her out until the weekend, maybe for a lunch or something. That was the plan before I saw her tonight. I knew I wouldn't be able to wait that long. She was getting under my skin, in the best possible way, and it was giving me such a high. I wanted to ride it as long as I could and as soon as I could.

"Absolutely," she said, patting my chest. She pulled her hand away and looked at my shirt. "Shit. You got coffee on your shirt."

I almost didn't hear her because I was too busy staring, but then it registered. *Coffee. Shirt.*

"Fuck," I said, kissing her one last time. "I have to run. Call you later or tomorrow or you know."

I raced for the door and swung it open, stopping to give her one more look. She took a sip from her coffee, bringing it away from her mouth, leaving a hint of foam on her upper lip. She knew I was still watching her because she licked the foam off her lip and winked at me.

* * *

Getting back to work ten minutes later than I'd promised, plus with a messed-up shirt, did not make Marshall happy. I never wanted the fact that Aaron owned the bar to be my Get Out of Jail Free card for me to do whatever I wanted. I tried to be conscious of that, but when Marshall told me he'd fire my ass if I ever did something like that again, I didn't say a word. I needed to be on my best behavior.

Guests for the party, who were in from New York and celebrating some major deal they did in Chicago, were already arriving when I returned. By the time I changed into an extra shirt, a crowd had gathered at the bar.

"Hey there," I said to a woman waiting. I placed a cocktail napkin down in front of her. "What can I get you tonight?"

She pulled her long, dark hair over her shoulders and motioned for me to come close. "Something very strong so I can get very drunk so I can forget about all the bores I'm with tonight," she whispered.

I nodded, understanding exactly what she meant. "Gin drinker?" I asked.

"Vodka would be better. If that's okay, that is. I know everyone else is drinking champagne, but I'd rather not. I could pay if it isn't on the party plan."

She reached for her purse, but I shook my head. "You can get anything you want. Vodka is what you want, so vodka it is. I'll add a little something extra to help you…achieve your desired goal," I said.

"Well, you just might be my new favorite person," she said, smiling and sliding into the chair in front of me.

I was used to sizing guests up and coming up with the right drink to make them happy. Of course, my job wasn't just about making them happy, but about making them want more. I made a vodka martini for her, with a bit of triple sec and a splash of orange juice. It would go down sweet and smooth but pack the right amount of punch that she wanted.

She took a sip, and I saw her shoulders instantly relax. When she took a larger sip, she gave me a thumbs-up, nodding her head. "Ahh," she said. "Perfect."

"That's what I like to hear."

I moved on to helping other guests, stopping to check in

with the only person who was sitting at the bar instead of mingling at the tables and couches, the vodka-drinking lady.

"You're going to make the job you assigned me much easier if you keep drinking like that. Another?" I asked, retrieving the empty martini glass from her.

She rolled her eyes. "Please. Maybe I can fake a headache and head to my hotel room across the street instead. Flying back to New York tomorrow with a hangover sounds awful."

"I think you're right about that," I said, starting her second drink. "What's your name?"

"Abby," she said, holding out her hand.

I shook her hand. "Abel."

"Abby and Abel. That sounds nice together, doesn't it?" she said, running her fingers across her necklace.

I started shaking her cocktail. "For twins, for sure."

She leaned her body in, her breasts touching the top of the bar. "Twins weren't exactly what I had in mind," she said.

And here we go. She was starting to flirt. I knew the routine, and while I'd be lying if I said it wasn't nice that an attractive woman was coming on to me, there were rules. The rules of WET were very strict. No dating guests. It was a rule I followed almost always. *Almost.*

"Do you have a girlfriend, Abel?" she asked.

"Nope," I said, pouring a drink into a clean glass and running a thinly sliced orange slice along the rim.

Technically, I didn't have a girlfriend. I wasn't sure what Evelyn and I were yet. It was too early to even establish that, and even if I was thinking about it, there was no way I'd bring it up first.

Plus, I didn't like people knowing my business so there was never any mention of a girlfriend. My job was to make drinks and hear their stories. The more they knew about me, the less they talked about themselves.

She lifted her glass and winked at me. "Thank you."

I nodded and slipped away to help another guest. I busied myself, making drinks and conversation, to keep my mind off the one thing I wanted to think about: Evelyn. It was quickly becoming my favorite pastime, imagining what she was doing or if she was thinking of me, too. There were moments of feeling completely emasculated, letting a girl I barely knew occupy so much of thoughts, but those moments were mine alone. No one knew I was falling hard for this girl. No one could know because anyone would think it was insane for it all happening so fast. I know *I* would. In a way, I thought it was. It wasn't enough, though, to tell my heart that it was all unworthy.

I motioned to Marshall, pointing my finger toward the bathroom, that I needed to take a quick leak. Abby grabbed my arm as I tried to walk by.

"What time do you get out of here?" Abby asked.

Her long, red fingernails spun a plastic hotel card on top of the bar. I took in a deep breath because I knew how I'd usually respond. I would usually say, "It'll only be this one time." But something was different now. Something had changed.

"Late," I said. "Not until after two."

She stopped twirling the hotel card and pushed it toward me. "It's lucky for you, or really, the both of us, I'm a night owl."

A few weeks ago and this would've been a no-brainer. I was trying to choose my words carefully, walking the line between offending her and encouraging her. Regardless, she was going to be pissed in the end when I turned her down.

"What do you say?" she asked.

I glanced across the room and saw Bridget, holding a Starbucks cup and bag, talking to Tyler. It was a little strange since the private event was still going on, but considering she was one of our most important VIPs, I didn't think too much about it. I gave her a wave before she nodded and started walking over.

"Give me one second, okay?" I said to Abby before shifting over to meet Bridget.

"Hey there," Bridget said, setting the Starbucks down on the bar. "I'm here on official business."

"Yeah? I hope that business is having a drink. The usual?"

"No cocktail for me tonight."

Confused, I asked, "A little something for your coffee? Wait. Coffee at this hour?" I looked at my watch, and it was almost nine. "Burning the midnight oil like Evelyn?"

"The coffee is for you," she said, pushing it across the bar.

"What? Why?"

"Turn the cup around," she said.

I picked it up and spun it to see the writing on the side. In black marker, it read: "Back at you, handsome." Followed by a red-stained lipstick kiss next to it.

"Why didn't she stop by? Tyler's seen her with you, so it wouldn't have been an issue," I said.

"She's still working, and I was on my way out anyway. She

took a little break and came back to the office with this for me to bring you." Her head turned, sensing the stares from Abby who was clearly eavesdropping.

"There's a brownie, too," she continued. "She also told me to tell you that it's no babka, but it was the best she could do. Whatever the hell that means."

I smiled, thinking of her thinking of me, and it made my chest ache. It was fear and exhilaration wrapped up in one bold decision.

I took a sip of the coffee, a caramel latte, which she had no way of knowing was my favorite from there when I wasn't drinking it black. The heat from the coffee warmed my chest every bit as much as the gesture. Without another thought, I jumped off the bridge, without a thought of offending anyone.

"Be right back," I said to Bridget.

I stepped back over to Abby, who was downing the rest of her drink and looking annoyed. Her eyebrows raised at me, looking for an answer to her question.

"Sorry," I said, pushing her hotel card back toward her. "I have a girl, and I kind of like her a lot."

CHAPTER NINE

EVELYN—

W hat the hell is wrong with you?" Bridget snapped at me.

I was dancing in my chair and daydreaming to Beyoncé when Bridget walked into the office. Thinking no one was watching, I was in full-on dance party mode.

"Nothing," I said.

I turned the music off my phone and pulled my chair back under my desk. The smile I was sporting couldn't be contained, though.

She dropped her white Birkin bag on my desk and put her hands on her hips. "If this is how you're going to be every morning from now on, then I might need to fire you."

"Why do you have to do that to the Pretty?" I asked, gently lifting her Birkin and petting it. "You just throw her around like she's a knockoff you found in the bargain bin."

"Can you not fondle my bag, please? It's creepy and weird."

She knew I lusted after this bag, a bag that at over $10,000

I'd never be able to afford, but I couldn't help it. It was gorgeous.

"So, are you going to answer your boss and tell me why you're in such a good mood?" she asked.

"For real, nothing. Fridays are late morning starts and I was able to get a run in. The sun is out, so I just felt...peppy."

"Peppy?" She twisted her upper lip. "I call bullshit. I think this has 'hunky bartender' written all over it."

My stomach tingled and I smiled again. "Perhaps. What did he say when you dropped off his drink last night?"

"I think he liked it."

"You think?"

"The place was packed so I'm sure he appreciated it."

She was skirting around the topic, which just wasn't her. There was something she wasn't telling me.

I set her bag back down on my desk. "What?" I asked. "Did something happen?"

"No, but—" she said, avoiding contact with my eyes. "Can I give you some friendly advice, sweetie?"

"Yeah."

"Don't put all your eggs in one basket, okay?"

So, something *did* happen. It didn't take me long to figure out what she was getting at.

"Someone else there bringing him coffee?" I asked.

"No. But just someone he seemed overly friendly with."

"We aren't exclusive and he's free to do whatever he wants," I said. I mustered up as much confidence as I could when I said this, but the excitement I'd had only minutes before had deflated. It really was no one's fault, especially

Abel's, except for mine. It was too much, too soon. A dangerous combination. I should've known better.

"Don't look like that," Bridget said. "It was probably nothing. You know what a flirt he is, but just in case, I want you to be careful."

Per usual, Bridget was a wise woman.

* * *

Abel: Be there in five. Can't wait to see you.

I closed out my messages and tossed my phone in my purse. Anxiety swirled around my body as I looked in the mirror, checking out my tight black dress with a low back, from all sides. I wasn't sure if it was nerves or…I didn't know what it was.

Yes, I did. It was mix of anger and annoyance. It was strange emotions to have because I usually wasn't insecure about men. I didn't have to be. It wasn't a self-confidence thing. It was a self-preservation thing.

I considered canceling our date, but that would've been petty. I was being petty, and that only fueled my annoyance. Two dates and I thought we had something going. I wasn't out with other guys or flirting at a bar. I was so into him, and now I wasn't sure I wanted to be. As I smoothed red lipstick over my lips, it occurred to me exactly what was bothering me.

I wanted him to act, to do, what I was doing. I expected him to know how I felt and to feel the same way. It wasn't him I was angry at. It was myself.

All these years of being focused on me and I was letting someone else in. It was then that an entirely new emotion surfaced—fear. I was heading into new territory, allowing my heart to be open to Abel. It scared me because I'd known what giving so much of myself to a man did to me. When I allowed Patrick to take over my heart, I lost myself. Once realized, I knew never to make that mistake again. So far, I hadn't. All was good as long as I didn't lose my head.

The door buzzed, and I knew it was time. After slipping my shoes on, I raced from my room, the clicking of my black high heels echoing against the hardwood floors, as my neighbors blasted their Frank Sinatra dinner music.

"Don't lose your head, Evelyn," I said to myself before opening the door.

"Hi there, beautiful," he said, all smiles and dimples.

He came in for a hug, bending his head into my neck where he sighed against my skin. My body went into sensory overload. Everything about him was familiar already. Everything from the woodsy smell of his cologne to the way his beard tickled against my cheek. My fingers swept over the fabric of the back of his sports coat, noticing the strength of him even through layers.

Taking a step back, he bent to kiss me chastely on the lips before taking my hands in his. "You look…" He trailed off, eyes running up and down my body.

"Thanks. We ready? Or do you want to have a drink here first?"

"Hot. You look…superhot," he said.

Smooth as a motherfucker this guy was. No wonder he

probably made every girl he met eat out of the palm of his hand. Teaching may be his calling, but he should quit the bartending job and take up what he'd be really good at. Panty dropping.

"No. I made reservations at RM Champagne. We should probably get going."

"Wow," I said, reaching for my purse off the bench next to the door. "Bringing out the big guns."

He smiled, deep dimpled, and smoothed his hand over his beard. "You have no idea just how big of the guns I'm bringing."

Butterflies, or maybe something that resembled a rhino, spun its way across my chest and stomach. I felt dreamy, almost calm, so that it took a lot of strength to remind myself of the one promise I'd made. *Just don't lose your head, Evelyn.*

"Come on, beautiful."

He was going to make this as hard on me as possible.

* * *

"Have you been here?" He opened the car door for me.

"No way."

When a place was praised as one of the most romantic spots in Chicago, and you've dated guys that lacked in the romance department in general, RM Champagne wasn't a likely place.

His hand slipped into mine as we stepped onto the sidewalk. "Why did you say it like that?" He looked down at me. "You know what? I don't care. I'm glad you're here now."

With the height of my heels, I was taller than usual, making me that much closer to him. His face, his mouth…those lips weren't all that far away when he leaned down. He stopped and smiled, dimples deep and adorable.

"You keep looking at me like that, and we won't make it inside," he said.

A cool breeze blew my hair into my face, which he brushed away before I could. His hand lingered, brushing the tips of his fingers across my cheek.

"I wasn't looking like anything," I said, pulling his hand from me.

I was doing my best to be present, but looking at him, his touch, were constant reminders of what Bridget had told me.

He appeared confused, looking around to see if someone or something had distracted me. When he saw nothing, he shrugged and we returned to walking.

We were about to cross into the next block when he pulled me by the hand down a dark alley. "Wait. Are you taking a shortcut?" I asked.

"Nope," he laughed.

The darkness of the alley gave way to twinkling lights and hanging lanterns draped across the buildings. Our pathway lined with cobblestones narrowed as we approached an outdoor seating area that hadn't been opened yet for the warm months.

"You know all the hidden spots, don't you?" I asked.

"Aside from the speakeasy and this, I don't have much more up my sleeve. However, I would like to take you back here in the summer to sit outside."

"Pretty confident we'll still be seeing each other in the summer, huh?"

As soon as I said it, I regretted it. It wasn't so much what I said, but how I said it with my usual sarcasm taking a backseat to abrasiveness.

"I was hoping so."

His grip on my hand became weak, and he physically distanced himself from me. Whatever I was putting off, which I was sure was every form of bitchy, he was getting it. All of this was going wrong. *I* was being all wrong.

"I'm glad you took me here now," I said. I stopped him before stepping through the door of the restaurant. "Thank you."

His head tilted while a grin reappeared. "Everything cool?"

"Yeah," I said. "Just…yeah."

"You kinda don't seem into this tonight, so if you'd rather not, it's—"

"No. No, I'm fine. I'm sorry. It's just…can I be honest with you?"

"I like honest."

I took in a deep breath. "Look, I like you. I like spending time with you, and you owe me absolutely nothing. So, if you're seeing other people, I'd like you to be up-front about it."

He shook his head. "Wait. What?"

"You're not my boyfriend, and I'm not your girlfriend. So, I don't want any expectations between us. I mean, we like hanging out and I'd like that to continue."

"Wellllll," he said. "I don't have any expectations, either, and I like you, too."

"Good. Same page. Now let's go in."

I wasn't sure if he knew where I was going, but at least I'd said it.

The moment we walked into RM Champagne, I was speechless. It was stunning, let alone romantic. Intimate tables of couples and small groups of friends sat surrounded by candelabras lit by candles and a large fireplace. Crystal chandeliers hung from the ceiling, giving the rustic decor a soft glow.

He waited until I was seated to take his seat, a gesture of a real gentleman that is so seldom seen. I leaned across the table. "This is beautiful."

"I'm glad I'm the first one to show you it."

We decided on wine instead of cocktails, and he ordered oysters, which he assured me were spectacular and not innuendo. As we talked, I tried not to imagine him with another girl or many other girls. My legs bounced under the table as I tried to control my thoughts.

He scooted his chair back and leaned over to the floor. I assumed he had dropped something, but when his head popped back up, I knew it was the thumping of my heel on the floor he was looking at.

"I was wondering what that noise was," he said, pulling his chair back in. "Although I don't mind getting a closer view of your legs in the process, too."

"Sorry," I said.

"You nervous about something?"

"Bridget saw some girl give you her hotel card last night," I blurted out.

He chuckled, throwing his head back with a flair. "I knew you were being weird about something. Bridget has a big mouth."

"She's looking out for me. That's why I said what I did about expectations and shit. If you are sleeping with other women, I'm totally fine with that, but I'm not going to be one of them."

"Totally fine with that, huh?" He smirked, boldly displaying those deep dimples, which I was certain he knew was my Kryptonite at this point.

The server came back with our wine. She babbled about vineyards and specials, but I didn't hear a word. I was mortified because now my neurotic jealous side, which I'd worked so hard to keep in check, had vomited across the white linen tablecloth.

As soon as my glass was filled, I brought it to my mouth and took a large sip. Abel was still grinning, calm and composed, and probably trying to think of an excuse to ditch the crazy girl.

"For the record," he said once the server left. "Bridget saw the key, but I guess she wasn't around long enough to see me slide it back across the bar to the woman who gave it to me. I didn't sleep with anyone last night. In fact, I can't stop thinking about you long enough to even consider it."

"I'm sorry. You don't owe me—"

"Will you shut up for a second?" He reached across the table and took my hand. "Also, I hope you wouldn't be totally fine with it because I know I wouldn't be if the tables were turned."

He squeezed my fingers as my face grew warm from the wine. Or maybe it was me blushing. Regardless, it didn't go unnoticed.

"Blushing is sexy as hell on you," he said, winking.

I let out a long sigh. "I know a lot of girls say they aren't those psycho, controlling girls, but they really are. But I'm really not. I'm me. I'll be me with or without someone. I…" I motioned between us. "I like spending time with you."

He raised his glass to me, and I followed. "As do I. There's no one else I want to be here with. Cheers."

We lifted our wineglasses and clinked them together. I wasn't sure if I believed him completely or not, but I wasn't convinced if you could ever truly know. He said what I needed to hear, and with the slow burn of the candles surrounding us, I let all that was holding me back go up in smoke.

* * *

He couldn't take his eyes off me. Not when he ordered his food or when he sipped from his wineglass. Not when we shared a plate of oysters. Not when he played with my fingers, and stroked my hand, or when I stood to excuse myself to go to the ladies' room. His eyes watched me from the across the room as I walked back to our table. It was intense, the way he looked at me without noticing anyone else in the room. There was a building of desire, a rising of energy between us that was reaching new levels. As I sat back down, I knew we had to get to the hard questions, or we would've just sat there and made goo-goo eyes at each other all night.

"What's your favorite book?" I asked.

The question was general and common, but it was important. There were so many dudes who didn't read at all, but with him wanting to be a teacher I had higher hopes. He lifted his wineglass to his lips and took a slow sip. It was obvious he was carefully choosing, which was a good sign.

"Harry Potter," he said, setting his glass down.

It didn't get more elementary than that or more perfect. No way was I going to let him know that, though.

"Interesting," I said, nodding. "Why?"

"I'm not stupid. I know saying *War and Peace*, or some shit like that would be more impressive, but why lie?"

"I'm all for not lying."

"I'm assuming you've read it."

Since we'd agreed not to lie, I nodded.

He scooted forward in his seat, excitement visible across his face. "I mean, what other books teach so many life lessons? There's the ultimate friendships, being brave and standing up for yourself," he said, counting on his fingers. "The struggle between wondering where you came from and who you think you are. Plus, I think the most important thing of all is what Dumbledore said: 'The truth is a beautiful and terrible thing, and should therefore be treated with great caution.'"

He leaned back, seemingly proud of himself. I could feel

myself trying to contain a smile because he'd hit it out of the park. My swoon meter was going crazy.

"Do you know that quote?" he asked.

"Of course. Do you know what book it's from?"

"Ah. Yeah, *Sorcerer's Stone*."

Impressive.

Our dinner arrived, trout with lemon, capers, and brown butter for me and hanger steak with herbed butter for him. We shared a macaroni gratin, with caramelized onions and Gruyère cheese, which put my beer macaroni and cheese to serious shame. We emptied the bottle of wine as we ate, giggling at the couple next to us who were sitting in silence and appearing angry.

"What do you think he did?" I whispered. "She looks super pissed."

He set his fork down and wiped his mouth. "Why do you assume it's him?"

"I don't know. I just—"

I was cut off by the girl splashing her drink in his face, telling him to go to hell. She stomped away, as her date was left with a wet shirt and a deflated expression.

"Whoa," I mouthed to Abel. "Sucks to be him."

"Okay. So maybe he *did* do something, but that's no excuse for public humiliation."

I could tell by his expression he had some firsthand experience. "Unless he told her that he slept with her best friend, then I agree."

"Or if he had a friend tell her he moved to Paraguay to join the Peace Corps only to have her see you a week later with another girl on the jumbotron at a Blackhawks game."

"Jesus."

"I didn't say it was me. It was…a hypothetical."

I narrowed my eyes at him. "Why don't I believe you?"

He shrugged. "Want to taste this?" he asked, pointing to his steak.

"Yes, please," I said, relieved for a change in topic.

I didn't want to imagine I'd be the girl on the jumbotron or the one being broken up with by his friend. There was always that fear, no matter how much trust was given, that your heart might be broken. I was going to try to not let that fear ruin me, but knowing he probably had a sordid past left me uneasy. It was a dangerous path, so close to jumping off and free-falling through terrifying, bottomless unknown.

He lifted his fork to me and brought the steak to my mouth. I took the bite and nodded, giving him a thumbs-up for how good it was. Before returning his fork to his plate, he put it in his own mouth, licking it off slowly.

"What do you think you're doing?" I asked.

"Getting whatever is left of you," he said.

I laughed, shaking my head and scooping up a petite pea from my plate. "Bonus points," I said.

"I'll take all I can get. So, what's happening at work? I know what you do, but not sure how you do it or whatever."

I picked up a napkin and wiped my mouth, smearing whatever was left of my lipstick on the white fabric. "Funny you should ask. Bridget lined up something big for me. It's going to have me relocating for a few months, but it's very exciting."

He stopped mid-bite, his fork hanging in the air in front

of his face. After he swallowed roughly, he asked, "Relocating? That sounds...cool."

"I think so," I said. "I mean, it's only for a few months, like I said."

"Where?"

"Charleston, South Carolina. Bridget is expanding, and with that area being one of the top destinations for weddings, it makes sense."

He set his utensils down and shifted around in his seat. A tension lowered around us, and it made me pause as well. It wasn't like I didn't know what he was thinking, or what I'd *hoped* he was thinking. If whatever this was between us was going to continue, what would it mean?

"Did I tell you how handsome you looked tonight?" I asked.

His hand slid across the table, and he placed it on top of mine. "No, but that hardly matters. What does matter is, did I tell you how beautiful you looked tonight?"

"No. You told me I looked hot, which in my book is an even better compliment," I said, scooping up a piece of my trout. "Want to try some of mine?"

He winked and then grinned, dimples deep. "Yes, I would, Evelyn."

We finished our dinner while debating our love for opposite Chicago baseball teams. The true deal breaker wouldn't have been over books, but the fact that he was a Cubs fan while I was a White Sox one.

"Star-crossed lovers. We might as well just call it quits now," he said.

"I agree. We were doomed from the start."

Our server came by, leaving a dessert menu on the table, which I only gave a glance to. The food, along with the wine, had left me feeling tipsy and relaxed. Everything about the night had gone so differently than I anticipated, and so much better. There was only one thing that could make it even better.

"Dessert?" the server asked when she returned.

"Dessert?" Abel repeated to me.

I looked at the menu and had to make a quick decision. "Can we get the huckleberry and cacao macaroons and chartreuse cream puff?"

"Sure. I'll be right out with it," she said.

"Actually. If you don't mind, can we get it to go?"

He raised his eyebrows at me, clearly wondering what I was up to. The purpose was served, and I had him right where I wanted.

After the bill was paid, we walked back down the dark alley where all I could imagine was being lifted up against the wall while he kissed me so hard we were delirious. We held hands, quiet until we reached the car.

He started it, but turned to me instead of pulling away. He took my face in his hands and brought me in close. His lips were faintly stained red from the wine we shared, and I wondered if mine were the same.

"Dinner was too long without me having my hands on you," he said, rubbing his nose against mine. "You have no idea how much you drive me crazy."

Good.

I closed the space between us, pressing my lips against his and brushing my fingers against his beard. He kept it short enough for me to trace his skin underneath, feeling exactly where his dimples hollowed as he smiled against my kiss.

"There is something you need to tell me. You never told me your favorite book," he said, twirling his finger around a piece of my hair.

"*Pride and Prejudice*. I'm a classics girl."

"Hmm. I dig Austen."

"Oh, really? You've read *Pride and Prejudice*," I asked in disbelief.

"Don't believe me again, huh?" He moved too close to my ear. "I have been a selfish being all my life, in practice, though not in principle."

I gasped, pushing him back. "Did you just quote Mr. Darcy to me?"

"Believe me now?"

"Perhaps."

He moved closer again, gradually saying, "I was given good principles, but left to follow them in pride and conceit."

"I'm almost convinced."

His lips pressed against my neck, his words tickling my skin. "My feelings will not be repressed."

"I believe you."

I kissed him again, pushing my chest into his and rising up in my seat. His hands wrapped around my waist, but moved down to my ass. No doubt passersby could see my arms raised, pressing my hands into the ceiling of the car, as his tongue sucked at my collarbone. I felt him everywhere, but not close enough at the same time. I wanted to taste his skin, feel the muscles of his chest while he moved above me. I knew what I wanted now. There was no doubt in the way he kissed me, the way he muttered my name against my skin.

"Come home with me," he whispered in my ear. "Please."

Even though I'd promised myself at the beginning of the evening, I went against my word.

I completely, and totally, lost my head.

"Take me," I said.

The car ride was quiet, palpable sexual tension rising between us so thick it was hard to breathe. His hand rested on my bare knee, his thumb rubbing small circles across the skin.

I followed him into his apartment, dropping my purse and the small bag of our desserts on the end table, as he guided me by the hand to his bedroom. The quiet confidence turned me on even more, the way he knew I wanted him, and the way I knew he wanted me just as much. He sat on the edge of the bed and pulled me toward him. I stepped between his open legs and stood waiting. I wanted him to tell me how he wanted me.

He brought his mouth to my chest, placing light kisses where my dress dipped to a V. His tongue swept upward, and his hands shifted down. Cupping my ass, he pushed me closer into him. The heat of his kisses increased, the warm breath of a touch and the tickle of his beard on my skin made me shiver.

He pulled away. "Cold?"

Moonlight came through the sheer overlay of his curtains, creating shadows across his face. He looked worried, his eyebrows pulled together tightly. It made him look vulnerable…unsure.

And this made my emotions, the fear and the uncertainty mixed with the knowledge that this kind of chemistry didn't happen every day, become clearer to me. It was more than the physical. It was a lot more, but I wasn't ready to admit to myself what I knew it was. It was too scary to think about, and in that moment, I only wanted to enjoy it for what it was.

"No," I said, bending down. I pressed my lips to his, sliding my tongue in to join his. I pushed against his chest as I kissed him deeper, hearing him emit a soft groan.

His hands rubbed my back up and down until he stopped at the zipper of my dress. With a slow, deliberate pull, he eased the zipper down. I slid the dress off one shoulder and then the other, as our kiss never broke.

I stepped back, both of us panting, and with my eyes on his, I pushed the rest of my dress down. It fell to the floor along with any inhibitions as I stood in front of him in my matching black bra and panties. He leaned back against his elbows, spreading his legs, showing his visible erection beneath his pants. My heart raced, matching the rise and fall of his chest, as I stepped out of my heels and dress.

"Come here, Evelyn."

CHAPTER TEN

ABEL—

She walked slowly toward me before kneeling in front of me, reaching for my belt. As much as I wanted what she was ready to give, there was something else I desired more. I gripped her wrist and pulled her up to me.

"You," I demanded. "You are what I want right now."

I pulled her onto my lap, which she straddled grinding into my hard dick that was about to bust through my zipper. My hand slipped up her back, her skin smooth and erupting goose bumps. She trembled as I gripped the back of her hair, and brought her mouth to mine. The deeper we kissed, the harder she ground herself into me until I couldn't take it anymore.

I picked her up and stood as she wrapped her legs around my waist. As I carried her to the side of the bed, she buried her head in my neck.

Her grasp on me tightened, and it was then my attention briefly shifted from dick to my heart. She was going to be leaving in a few months. I tried to mask my disappointment over it because at this stage of the game I had no right to feel any other way but happy for what she had accomplished. But the disappointment was there. I didn't want her leaving just as soon as I'd found her.

I didn't want to dwell on it, though. The whole evening was a dance, a movement of words and glances. Conversation and smiles, rising desire and truths all rose around us. It was amazing.

And now I was going to be able to see just how much more amazing it was going to get.

"You better be just as good at fucking me as you are at the art of seduction, handsome," she whispered.

"Jesus Christ," I hissed, laying her down in the middle of the bed.

Instead of staying put, she got up on her knees and crawled to me, bringing her fingers to unbutton my shirt. "Allow me." She looked up at me.

With careful precision, she undid each button with the push of her dark purple fingernails. When she was done, she yanked the sides up roughly to pull the rest out from my pants. She began to crawl back, wiggling her finger at me to follow her.

"You are going to fucking wreck me," I said, pulling my T-shirt off over my head.

I climbed onto the bed next to her, and she pushed me down by my shoulders so she could climb on top. Her take-charge sense was so hot and so different than the girls that made me do all the work. It made me want her more.

Slow and controlled, she moved up and down my waist, grinding herself into my erection. My hands grasped her ass, and my fingers pushed against the delicate lace of her underwear, guiding her. Her moans grew louder as she leaned back and pushed her breasts farther to the top of her bra. I'd wanted to see under that bra for entirely too long, so I pushed the straps and front down.

"You," I said, bringing my mouth to her tits. "Are the"— I licked around her nipple, teasing the skin with the tip of tongue—"the sexiest"—running my teeth gently across the hardened tip—"thing I've ever seen."

She pulled at the back of my hair and rubbed herself into my dick even more. The more I sucked, moving between her perfect, full breasts, the more she responded.

Mental note: This girl loves the breast play. When given the chance after this first night of fucking the sense out of both of us, titty fucking should be on the menu at some point.

I reached around to her back and unhooked her bra, pulling it off altogether.

She flipped her head back, her hair falling all over. "What do you want?" she asked breathlessly.

I brought my thumb to her lips, freed of lipstick and pink and full from kissing. "I want inside you," I said, rolling her under me. "That's what I want."

She smiled and lifted her fist to me for a pump. Man. This was what drove me so completely crazy with this girl. She was off the chart sexy, so fucking hot I was afraid I was going to blow my load in three pumps. But then she was fun, too.

The moment when you first sleep with someone you have feelings for is high pressure. With one gesture, she put us at ease.

I stood up, unbuttoned my pants and eased my zipper down. She sat up on her elbows, watching me with an eagerness that made me move faster. My heart raced as I pushed my pants and underwear down, kicking them to the floor. I reached over to the nightstand and flung open the top drawer to get a condom. I tore it open and rolled it up my dick.

She bit her lower lip as I crawled toward her, kissing my way up her leg, thigh, and stopping to lick across the lace edge of her panties. My thumb dipped down, running across the center of her and feeling her wet with want for me through the silk fabric.

Her head lowered to the pillows, arching her back off the bed the more I teased her. I couldn't tease anymore. My dick was pounding, pleading before I lost all control. I slid my fingers across her hips and under the thin strips of her panties, pulling them down forcefully.

"Come here, beautiful," I said, moving up toward her.

I positioned myself above her and bent my head down to kiss her. She reached between us and began stroking my cock, a firm and steady rhythm, which alone almost completely undid me. My hand joined hers, moving together until I couldn't take it anymore and gradually eased myself into her.

We both let out simultaneous moans as I continued bringing myself deeper and deeper, her fitting around me in the most perfect way. I pulled back and pushed in as she began rocking her hips back and forth to match my movements. Beat for beat, we danced to our own music, something so unique it made my chest ache.

Her legs wrapped around me as I pushed myself harder, deeper, watching her face for any indication it was too much.

"You feel so good," she whispered.

This wasn't just fucking. I'd had good sex before, blind fucking with someone beautiful. No, this was different. The smell of her skin, the remnants of perfume lingering around us, her soft skin, and the way she knew how to move with me—it all came together. Even if I never had her again, I knew I'd always remember this girl for the way she lit me up and how she was no match for anyone else that had been in my bed before her.

I wanted to feel more, get even deeper. "Roll over," I said, my voice strained. "I want you from behind."

I pulled out of her, as she turned and raised her ass off the bed. She flipped her head around to look at me, her face flushed and her hair wild. Sex hair.

Her ass was fucking flawless, a perfect view as I guided myself back into her. I was right. Deeper and a more vocal reaction from her. I gripped her hips and thrusted faster, feeling my orgasm only a few beats away.

"Fuck, beautiful," I said. "Are you close because I can't—"

I stopped mid-sentence as I saw her bring her hand between her legs and start rubbing her clit. "So close," she said.

The sounds of skin on skin and our rough, breathless voices took over the entire room until there was nothing but her loud cries of coming. She was still rocking into me as she tightened around my cock, and I became utterly undone. A guttural sound from an unlocked place in my body cried out as I came, driving into her until I peaked and started to come down.

Our rhythm slowed, both of us struggling to catch our breath, while I stayed in her for as long as I could.

"Shit," I said, panting. "Do they make custom-built vaginas? Because I think we got that on lock."

She wiggled away from me but pushed up on her knees. Her head turned and she kissed my neck, her damp skin meeting mine.

"Who knew?" she said. "Well done, sir."

"I would very much like to do that again once I recover."

"Me, too," she giggled.

Her eyes looked up to me, and I bent my head to kiss her. "And again."

"Agreed."

Kiss.

"Again."

Kiss.

"Often and longer and again."

Kiss.

Before I said it again, she bit on my lower lip gently, teasing before releasing. "Game on, handsome," she said, kissing me quickly on the cheek.

I watched as she moved from me and off the bed. She bent down to the floor, I assumed looking for her clothes, but she picked up my shirt instead.

"Back in a second," she said, walking out of the room, tossing my shirt on as she did.

Before I could tell her that there was a bathroom connected to the bedroom she was out, so I made a quick trip while she was gone. My dick was still in recovery mode when I entered the bathroom, wondering what kind of glorious event I'd just put it through. After a splash of water to the face, condom disposal, and a new pair of boxers, because I didn't care what anyone said, no chick wanted to see a dude they just banged walking around with a semi-flaccid penis, I went back in.

She was already back, laying on top of the wrinkled sheets with my shirt hanging out, exposing the sides of her breasts, breasts that I missed seeing for the 2.4 minutes I'd been apart from them.

"Want a little sugar?" she asked.

She had our desserts from RM on a plate next to her, but was holding the cream puff in her hand, licking the filling from her fingers. Just when I thought she couldn't get sexier, she did.

"I do," I said, sliding into the bed next to her.

She held the cream puff out to me, but just as I went to take a bite, she yanked it away from me. "Hey," I pouted.

"Sorry," she laughed. "Here," she said, holding it out to me again. But for the second time, she pulled it away.

"Two can play at that."

I slid my hand across her tight, soft stomach, dragging my fingers across the skin. Goose bumps erupted all over her, and I knew I found a sensitive spot on her. The sides of my shirt that were covering her fell open, making it easy for me to lean down and kiss around her breast. Using my tongue, I worked my way downward, tracing my tongue around the edge of her nipple while she began to squirm next to me.

"Okay," she said, her breathing quickening. "I'll share."

"Nope. You had your chance."

I picked up the plate of the macaroons and put them next to me on the nightstand. She still held the cream puff as I moved myself above her body. I bent my head to taste her skin between her breasts, working my way back down, feeling the heat of her body radiate onto mine.

Her hips started moving again, up and down as I went down…down. Her pussy was clean-shaven, not completely bald, but perfect for what I wanted to do. I slid farther until my tongue was right by her clit.

I looked up at her, making sure it was okay, and her eyes were already dreamy, sexed. The moment my tongue hit the right spot, her hips raised up to meet me. A soft giggle came from her, no doubt from my beard that I was sure took some getting used to.

She was so fucking wet for me, and I wanted nothing more than to thank her for that. Her hand gripped the top of my hair as I worked my magic, sucking and tasting every bit of her. I followed the rhythm of her hips and wanting her to show me how she liked it. It was a quick crescendo, the rise of her moans, and the rapid movements of her body, to let me know how close she was.

I adjusted ever so slightly, and it was all she needed. She

gave a shout-out to God, me, and an unnamed person called Motherfucker as she came against my mouth. She rode it out like a champ, and I didn't stop until she started to come down.

"Damn," she said, her voice hoarse.

I slid up, bringing myself next to her. Her face was flushed, pink cheeks that made her look beautiful all fucking naked against my white sheets. And she was still holding that fucking cream puff.

With her dazed, I leaned over and took a bite without her even having time to realize what I was doing. I could still taste her, and now it really was all sugar.

"You want the rest?" she asked.

"Nope. I'm good now."

She set the rest of it down on her side table and laughed, shaking her head.

My grin must've come across as arrogance because she punched my chest. "Cocky asshole," she said. "Let me ask you a question."

"Shoot."

"So, the beard."

"Yes. I'm aware I have one."

"Shut up. I hope this isn't inappropriate, but considering you had your dick in me only a few minutes ago, I think I should get a pass."

"By all means."

"So, the beard when you go down on a girl. How does that work?"

I rubbed my hand down the side of it, wondering how to

answer. "Well…you were just a recipient of it, so maybe you should tell me."

"Don't go fishing, handsome. I already told you it was a job well done. But I've never been with a guy who's had one. It wasn't as uncomfortable as I thought it might be. A little tickle, a little brush…you know. But do you get…me…all over it?"

She cast her eyes downward, but after a moment, she peeked at me through her lashes. No matter how confident she was, she was definitely embarrassed.

"Sometimes," I answered, offering no more unless she asked.

"Sometimes? You mean, depends on how into it you are?"

"Yeah. Or if I do it at all."

"It isn't part of your normal repertoire?"

I winked. "Only for the special ones."

She rolled her eyes. I loved that she didn't buy into any bullshit, even if in this case, it was true. It occurred to me that it seemed she might have had some practice at it, not just at detecting a line, but at sex. She was too good at both.

"I'm honored," she said.

My hand slid around her waist, and I pulled her close. "Why don't you just ask me what you really want to ask?"

Her eyebrows raised. "I did."

"You want to know if I'll be able to still taste you even when I'm done."

Her breath hitched, and her lips formed an O.

"Flavor-saver, beautiful."

"Oh," she said. Her eyes scanned the ceiling, mulling over

what it all meant. She shrugged before kissing the side of my head and wiggling out from next to me. "This was fun," she said.

She slipped my shirt off and tossed it on top of the sheets before slipping out of the bed. I watched her bend down, her tight ass putting on a show for me.

"Where the hell did you throw my undies?" she asked.

"I have no idea," I said. "Why?"

She found her bra and turned to me while she put it on. "Home."

"And why would you want to do that?"

It was usually me making excuses to sneak out, or it was me laying in the bed, trying to think of ways to get her to leave. But with this girl, I didn't want her anywhere else but in my bed.

"Ah! Found them." Her panties were at the foot of the bed. She pulled them on and stood with her hands on her hips. "You don't need to be all sweet and make it seem like you don't want me to go."

She was much too smart at the game for my own good. It freaked me the fuck out.

"I don't want you to go. Stay," I said hesitantly.

Maybe she really didn't want to. Maybe she was one of those rare breeds of women that thought like a guy. I wondered if *Wild Kingdom* was aware of this phenomena.

I moved to the side and got up, walking to her. "I'm serious," I said, grabbing her by the hips and bringing her close. "Stay with me."

Her eyes fluttered across my face, looking for something

to hint at bullshit. "Make sure I'm up in time to get home and ready to make it to the wedding I'm working tomorrow at noon?"

"Promise," I said, holding out my pinkie, waiting for her to intertwine hers. Once she did, I gave her ass a tap. "Now get that perfect ass back in my bed."

* * *

I was dreaming of a scantily clad Evelyn, on her knees, in the middle of an empty Wrigley Field, blowing me. The sun warming my face and the feel of her mouth around my dick made me rock my hips as I barely began to wake up.

The vision of her began to darken, but the sensation of her lips working me up and down stayed front and center. It was as if it was…

My eyes opened, and there she was, like I just imagined, with my cock in her mouth. So, it wasn't Wrigley Field, but it was so much better with her in real time and still naked from our all-night fuckfest.

She was looking up at me, the slightest hint of a smile lifting the sides of her lips. I brushed her hair away from the side of her face, running my finger down her cheek, as I felt her bring me deeper and deeper into her mouth.

"Fuck, Evelyn," I growled.

She took as much of me in as she could and used her hand to pump the rest. When she needed to pause, her hand didn't. Firm and fast movements, as her tongue swirled around the tip, and her eyes remained on mine. I wanted it to go on and on, keeping us in this moment for as long as I could, but she felt too good. She was too good. My head, still fuzzy from sleep, couldn't keep up with my dick.

I rubbed my hand across her face again, struggling to get the words out. "Oh God. I...I'm ready to go."

Her rhythm never faltered but instead went hard-core, sucking, pumping faster...harder until I came in her mouth. My closed eyes opened in time to see her swallow what she'd done to me, satisfied and chill.

"Best wake-up call I've ever got," I said.

She sat back on her knees, wiping her mouth like a fucking champ. "Consider it a parting gift."

I looked at the time on my phone next to the bed. It was a little after eight, and I knew she'd have to go soon. "Come here, beautiful."

She crawled up my side while I sat up, lifting her into my lap. I buried my head in her shoulder, her skin smelling like sex and her. All it took was one night, and I knew I was hooked. I had a strong suspicion before last night, but I was sure now. I was totally falling for this girl.

I pulled back to look at her. "There's only one more thing we need to do," I said.

"Already?" she asked, biting down on her lower lip. It was so damn cute because she was seriously considering if I was ready again. I was good, but not that good.

"I'm not superhuman. What I meant was we need to do one thing to lock this thing down."

"What thing?" she asked, making quote marks when she said *thing*.

"Us."

"Us?"

"Yes."

"Yes?"

"Are you going to just repeat everything I say but in question form?"

She wiggled in my lap, her palms deep into the mattress so she could try and move back. I didn't know her well. At all. I didn't even know her middle name, but I already knew that when she was uncomfortable, when she needed to process, she needed space, physical space.

"What I meant by 'thing' is you and me," I said. "Last night, we both said we weren't going to sleep with other people. That means, this thing is you and me. Just us."

Her silent squirming continued, and I had to consider if it was what she wanted, too. It wasn't a label thing I was after. We could call it whatever—hell, I was calling it a "thing." The only thing I wanted was to be with her, preferably alone.

"Look—" I said, but she cut me off with her hand on my mouth.

"I'm sorry. This is all…unexpected. You are so unexpected," she said. "You, the panty-dropping woman getter. You are telling me you want us to be a thing."

"Okay. Let's get this straight, beautiful. Yes, I've been around the block. So the hell what? But I wouldn't be here, I wouldn't have *taken* you here if I didn't want you here. I wouldn't have said what I did. I do what I want, and whether you think that's bullshit or not is your problem. I like you. I have a stupid amount of fun when we're together. And what we did last night? I want that, I want you, to be *mine* and mine alone."

Her shoulders squared off tightly. "I just," she said. "Think this is a big step."

"You just had my dick in your mouth. We fucked four times last night, and you think this is a big step?"

"Aren't you supposed to be all *guy* and be afraid of commitment?"

"I'm not afraid of shit, beautiful," I said, lifting my hand to her face to brush the hair that had fallen into her face away. "Just because I haven't wanted to isn't the same as being afraid."

"No offense, but look at you. You're walking, talking sex and don't even tell me you don't do it often because anyone who can do those moves has been around the block many, many times." She scooted back closer to me, wrapping her hands around my neck. "Can I be honest with you?"

"Of course."

"I've been anti-thing for a long time. I'm not even sure I'd be good at it. You and I haven't been living very different lives. You see a woman you want and you get her. Home, bed, and good-bye. I see a man, and my actions are similar."

"That's what I mean about this feeling different. I don't want it to be that way with you."

Her fingers brushed against my neck and then up through my beard. "Neither do I. I've been anti-thing for a long time and have been able to keep a casual sexual thing separate from emotions. Hell, I've had a regular booty call on retainer for a long time. No drama. No relationship bullshit. But when I found out about hotel room card chick, I reacted. It was strange and scary because it was so foreign for me."

She was a little more cautious about laying it out than I was. That was okay with me, so in an attempt to lighten things up, I knew I needed to show how little all that shit mattered to me.

"So, what you're saying is while I'm the panty dropper, you're the boxer dropper?" I asked.

She laughed and nodded. "Yes. I'm not embarrassed or ashamed. If we are going to have a thing, you need to know who I am. Or was. Or…whatever."

"You think that makes a difference to me?" I questioned.

She shrugged. "It would to a lot of guys."

Women were judged for this kind of bullshit all the time. It was okay for a man to have no-strings attached, but when a woman did it, people got judgy. It drove me insane.

"I can't say this in any kind of delicate way," I said. "But I couldn't give a fuck."

"Good. I don't give a fuck who you fucked *before* me."

She leaned back down, her chest and mine connecting as a soft sigh left her lips. I kissed her shoulder while I crossed my arms around her back.

"The only thing I do wonder is how you learned to do that thing when you're on top of me and roll your hips while tightening—"

She giggled and flipped her head to the side. "It's a gift."

"I should say so. What does this all mean?"

"I think it means that there's a thing. We're a thing."

I winked. "Glad we got that cleared up."

"Good. Okay, I have to get going," she said, giving me a quick kiss before starting to move from my lap.

"Hold up," I said, gripping her hips to keep her put. "This whole thing started when I said there was one more thing to take care of to lock this thing down."

"Right. Okay. What's that?"

"We need to tell Callie and Aaron."

CHAPTER ELEVEN

Evelyn—

I could decide in a matter of minutes to commit to not seeing other guys, which in and of itself was a petrifying prospect, but something even scarier was facing Callie. I wasn't going to worry about that now, though. Even though Abel offered to take me home, I knew he was just as exhausted as I was, so I left him sleepy and completely sexed in his bed after he called a cab for me. As I took my walk of shame from his apartment to the elevator, there was no doubt in my mind I was about to embark on an adventure I'd never known. Whether it was going to be one with a thrilling outcome or a disastrous one would remain to be seen, but it was going to be an adventure, nonetheless.

I stepped inside the elevator and leaned against the back of it as it closed, dreamily remembering every detail of the night before. He was…everywhere. His hands, his mouth, his words encircled me, and no matter which way I turned there was him. The way he moved inside of me and losing my mind in how good he was. I'd push my eyes closed to move with it. Every time I'd open them, his blue eyes, his almost translucent blue eyes, would be watching me. I'd bring his mouth to mine and kiss him, all the time moving our bodies together. When I'd get close to coming, he'd lean his head against mine, whispering, "Look at me when you come." His eyes were on me, followed me, and took me. From the restaurant to his bed, it was all on me. I'd never felt more *wanted* in my life.

The elevator door opened, and as I stepped out still in a daze, a sight made me stop, become instantly alert, and run behind the large potted plant in the lobby. Abel's father was talking to Rob the doorman, holding a coffee cup and I was hoping…leaving. Wait. Maybe coming would be better. I'd wait it out, squatting behind a fake palm tree, let him get in the elevator and then I could be off.

"Did I tell you what little Lauren did?" Rob said. "I know you love these kids' stories, so I always try to remember the best to share with you. So…"

I lost my balance and gripped the end of a palm leaf to stop me from falling. Enough noise was made that both men turned to look to see what was going on, but I'd moved just in time before I was caught. At least I thought I was safe.

"Hold up, Mr. Matthews," Rob said. "Let me check this out."

"Fuck," I whispered.

I was going to be dragged out from behind a lobby plant, wearing last night's clothes, in front of my new boyfriend's father. Rob's shoes moved swiftly across the marble floor until my eyes were looking directly down at them.

"I need out before he," I whispered, pointing a finger at Mr. Matthews, "sees me."

Rob said nothing, just a wink, and I knew I was safe. He stepped away, carrying with him a loud, not very convincing monologue. "Oh, look at that, will you? Water is leaking all over from the pot. I need to get this taken care of before someone slips and gets hurt. I'll catch you later, Mr. Matthews. You go on home to Mrs. Matthews, okay?"

"Need me to call maintenance?" Mr. Matthews asked.

"Nope!" Rob answered. "Got this covered! You go enjoy your cappuccino."

"Have a good day, then," Mr. Matthews said.

Rob's body blocked my view, but based on the distance of his voice, he was close, which meant he was almost to the elevator…which also meant I was almost in the clear. A couple dings of the elevator door later, and Rob stepped away.

He reached his hand down to help me up. "Well, well, well, Miss Evelyn."

"Hi Rob," I said, standing. "Thank you. It's a bit too early for me to have to deal with, well, you know."

"Not the first time I've had to help out a lady of—"

His expression crumpled into embarrassment. Poor guy. He'd just done me a favor. Now I was going to give him one right back.

"I'm sure Abel's love life has revolved more than your door, Rob. You're a gentleman for lending us a hand."

He sighed heavily. "I do my best."

* * *

It was going to be a long day.

Not only was the lack of sleep going to ruin me, but there wasn't a part of my body that wasn't aching from the night before. It was okay, though, because so much fun was had getting that way.

I approached my apartment door and fished my keys out of my purse. What I really wanted to do was take a hot shower and a long nap, but that wasn't going to happen. I had to be at the Drake in two hours to work what was going to be a very long day of wedding activities.

I unlocked the door, and I was almost inside when—

"Evelyn!"

"Shit!" I screamed.

Callie was standing in the middle of my living room, arms folded, and by the way she looked, wearing clothes from the night before as well. I clutched my chest, trying to find my breath again. She ran toward me, throwing her arms around my neck tight before letting go and pushing me.

"What the hell?" I said, almost losing my balance and dropping my purse on the floor. "You scared the shit out of me standing there like that."

"Um, Evelyn. Where is your phone?" she asked. She was staring me down, and the only time she did that was when she was pissed at me.

"In my purse. Why?"

"Is it operational?"

I giggled. "Operational? I'm sure it is—operational, that is."

"Oh, well fine. Go ahead and laugh. I'm glad your phone is working. I'm also glad that you probably know how to use it. But what I can't figure out is why you didn't answer it last night the hundred times I called you. Or why when you saw all those missed calls you didn't call me back. What if *I* had an emergency? What if I needed you?"

"Sorry," I said with a sigh. I walked past her, heading toward my room. "I got caught up and my phone is dead."

"I've stayed up all night. I thought you were dead in the gutter. I was going to start calling hospitals."

"Dramatic much?"

She gasped. "Don't you dare take that tone with me. I was worried sick!"

I stopped and turned, trying my best not to laugh at her. "Cal. I haven't had to tell you where I was going in a long time, let alone if I was or wasn't coming home. I spent the night at…a friend's. And before you ask, yes, a man."

She stood staring, tapping her ratty pink Toms, which she kept at my house to use as slippers on the wood floor. I hadn't seen her this mad in a long time. It rated up there with the time I created a dating profile for her on an online site without telling her. I was sure the "chance meeting" between her and the guy I'd picked out for her would go over perfectly. How was I supposed to know he was a liar and really a sixty-seven-year-old man?

"I'm sorry if you were worried, but I'm going to have to ask for my key back. I'm a grown woman and—"

"No. I'm not giving it back. This is the exact reason I have one. I was so worried I came here at four in the morning. Aaron is so concerned he tried calling Abel so they could split up and see if they could find you, but like you, he doesn't answer his phone, either. I'm sure he was busy with a friend, too."

I snorted. Then I laughed. Snorted again. Laughed. Once. Twice. On the third time, I couldn't stop. This wasn't the way I wanted to tell her about Abel and me, but it looked like there was no time like the present. First running into his dad and now Callie? I hadn't had to do so much sneaking around since I was in high school.

"Okay, fine," she said, throwing her hands in the air. "I'm glad you think this is so funny."

She stormed past me, mumbling about being surrounded by immature sex fiends. "Callie, come on," I said. "Come back and I'll explain."

Her hand fumbled with the knob on the door, but I knew she was being dramatic. There was no way she could stay mad at me. Plus, when I told her what I did and with who, she was going to want to know all the details.

I plopped down on the couch, with Callie following, and kicked my shoes off onto the floor. "Now," I said, turning to face her. "Before I start, you have to promise not to get mad at me."

"Oh no! Nope. You always do this," she said, shaking her head.

"Do what?"

"Make me promise not to get mad and then tell me something that makes me mad, and then I can't get mad because I promised I wouldn't."

"Okay. Fine. I won't make you promise, but please don't freak out."

She twirled a lock of her auburn hair around her finger, as her eyes narrowed. "I don't freak out."

I resisted the urge to snort again. "So, I've been seeing someone. Kind of. It's very new, and we've only been out a few times, but I spent the night with him last night."

"Ev! This is fantastic news! Why would I get mad about that?"

"Because I haven't told you who it is yet."

The strand of hair she was twisting was getting tighter and tighter around her index finger as she considered who it might be. There was part of me that thought it was obvious, but then it occurred to me, several undesirable men have come and gone in my life over the years.

"Wait," she shouted. "It's not that dude who runs the hot dog stand is it? I mean, I guess I could get over it if you were into him, but you have to talk to him about the socks with sandals situation. It's wrong and you know it."

"Will you stop it with your hair? Your finger is turning purple," I said, yanking her hand from her hair. "No. It isn't hot dog Bob."

"Then who is it?"

"It's…well, it's…Abel," I whispered.

My body recoiled on instinct, and I closed my eyes, knowing the rage I was about to endure would be painful. Instead, there was nothing but silence. When I peeked at her out of one eye, I knew she wasn't angry. No. She was beyond that.

"Abel?" she muttered. "You slept with Abel?"

"Yes, but we didn't just sleep together. We're together-together. We're having a thing. We're a thing."

"A thing? You're having a…thing…with Abel," she said, her voice raising an octave with each word. "This is the same Abel I told you to keep your panties on for, right? My boyfriend's very immature, irresponsible, tail-chasing brother? And for the record, the same Abel I love like a brother. A brother who I wouldn't want to date my best friend who is like a sister to me. I don't want my brother and sister to have a thing and do…stuff…together!"

Yup. Pretty much how I thought it would go.

I reached for her hand and held it in a tight grip. "Yes. That's the same Abel. I know you told us not to hook up, and we didn't until last night."

"How did this happen?"

I gave her the rundown on how we started up.

"I can't believe this. Wait," she said, pausing. "He took you to RM Champagne? Wow. How was it?"

"It was fantastic. The restaurant, that is. Now, as far as he goes, well—"

She held up her free hand to stop me. "Please. Let me wrap my mind around the first part of this before we start dishing the dirt on the dirty."

"Fair enough. Look, I didn't mean to lie to you or make you think that I was keeping things from you. I just wasn't sure where things were going."

"Aaron is going to flip his shit. He adores you, and he's Abel's big brother. It'll be so awkward if things don't work out."

I had thought about this, but hadn't really considered it until that moment. This was only starting, and the chances of it making it for a long haul were slim. Would we be able to still be in each other's lives if, or rather when, things went south? I wanted to reassure myself it wasn't worth thinking about now, that I wanted to enjoy the here and now. Unfortunately, actions have reactions.

Callie stood up and brought me up with her, our hands still held together. "You look worried, sweetie," she said. "And I don't want you to be. All I want is for you to be happy. If it's Abel doing that, then I'm fine with it."

This was my Callie. The Monica to my Rachel. She worried endlessly about everything, was neurotic and overall the more responsible one. It was why she was practically married, ready to settle down, and I was the one who freaked out over a "thing" that morning.

"Really?" I asked. "What about Aaron?"

"I will handle him. All I need to do is remind him how you and Abel had both of our backs when we were making a shitshow of things. It's our turn to watch the shitshow."

"A shitshow? We were calling it a thing, but whatever," I said.

"I gotta go," she said, walking us to the door. "First, I'm stopping at the store to get you a portable phone charger, and then I'm going home to sleep."

"I have a wedding to get ready for. I'm sorry you were worried. Really." I hugged her, her scented shampoo lingering in the air. I could never smell lavender without thinking of my best friend. "I love you."

"I love you, too. And hey, now that you've been to WET and you're porking the bartender, maybe we can all go there sometimes," she said.

I watched her walk down the hallway, knowing how lucky I was. We'd been through so much, and no matter what she thought, I knew she'd always be my constant.

"Ev?" she called, holding the elevator door open with her hand. "One question."

"Yeah?"

"How was he?"

I smiled to myself, a flutter of energy running across my chest. "He was…delicious."

Completely yummy.

* * *

Abel: You left something here. I think you should come back and get it.

Me: What?

Abel: Macaroons. They are taunting me.

Me: Ha-ha. Don't be tempted. You go ahead and indulge.

Abel: How is everything you say so sexy?

Me: How's this for sexy? Callie knows about us, and I'm sure by now Aaron does, too. Oh, and I had to hide behind a plant in the lobby of your building to avoid your father seeing me lead the Got Laid Parade.

Abel: Anything to do with my brother or my dad = not sexy. You saying "Got Laid Parade"? Still sexy.

Me: Seriously. You worried? About Aaron?

Abel: Aaron gets his boxers in a wad over everything. Always. He'll get over it.

Me: Callie recovered quickly from the news. She did call you a womanizer.

Me: And a fuckup.

Me: And immature.

Abel: All terms of endearment from her.

Me: She called you a nincompoop, too.

Abel: Okay. That one hurt. Work going okay?

Me: I'm exhausted and we haven't even started. I wish I could just take a nap.

Abel: I love naps and my bed is lonely without you.

Me: In that case, I wish I could take a nap with you.

Abel: I wish we can take off all our clothes and make out.

"What the hell are you grinning at?" Bridget said, coming up behind me while scrolling through her iPad.

I shoved my phone in my pocket, returning my attention back to my own iPad to view the timeline. "Ah. Nothing."

"Well, you look like hell," she said, running her eyes over me. "What gives?"

"Nothing," I said, trying to hide my smile.

Her eyes narrowed as she moved closer to me. Then a

spark of realization, and I knew she had me. "You had *sex* last night."

"Is this appropriate work talk between a boss and employee?"

"Abel?" she asked enthusiastically. "And fuck if it was, I need to know how the boy gets down in bed."

I nodded, embarrassed I was admitting the reason for my bloodshot eyes and excessive yawning.

She yanked my arm. "Come on. Let's go out back and sneak a smoke while you tell me all the slutty details."

This was *major*. Bridget only smoked when she was either super stressed or super excited. I had only moments to wonder which one it was before she was dragging me through the lobby of the Drake. It didn't take me long to realize it was a mix of both, along with the extra thrill of living vicariously through me.

* * *

My eyes were always on the prize. This trip to Charleston was going to change my career, regardless of any guy. No one needed to tell me that.

My phone vibrated in my pocket, alerting me of a new text message. I pulled it out to read.

> **Abel:** Now you did it. All I can think about is you, naked, in my bed, while my sheets still smell like you. You get me hard without even being close, beautiful.

"Okay," Bridget said, swiping her lips with some gloss.

"Are you ready for this?"

I knew she was referring to the wedding, but all I could think about was Abel.

"I'm as ready as I'll ever be," I said.

CHAPTER TWELVE

ABEL—

And that's why I had to leave the gold-digging, cheating bitch."

The customer picked up his glass and swung it around, mumbling about alimony. I wiped away the spilled gin that was spreading out in front of him.

"Sounds like you made the right choice, buddy," I said.

"Women," he slurred. "Nothing but a fucking headache."

I glanced at my watch and saw it was getting close to midnight. WET was still packed, and according to Tyler, the line to get in was still thirty people deep. One right after the other, I made drinks for strangers, but my thoughts never left Evelyn. If she occupied my thoughts before we slept with each other, things were twice as worse, or maybe better, now. I thought knowing her body, feeling and touching places that I'd be fantasizing about would curb the constant obsessing. It didn't. It did the exact opposite. I got a taste, and now, I couldn't stop wanting another bite.

I ran to the back to grab a few bites of a sandwich, and when I came back out, I saw what I wanted. Evelyn was leaning up against the end of the service bar, smiling and talking with Marshall without noticing I was coming up next to her.

"Well, this is a surprise," I said, placing my hand on her back and kissing the side of her neck.

She leaned into me, her perfume giving me the perfect reminder of what I was missing. My hand moved down from her back to her ass where I copped a feel of my girlfriend like the horndog fuck I was.

Girlfriend.

"Watch it," she said, playfully slapping my arm. "I was over at the Drake, and I wanted to tell you something real quick."

Marshall gave a nod and stepped over to the cocktail server who was waiting for him to help her. "See ya later, Evelyn."

"What do you have to tell me?" I asked while giving her the once-over. A black pleated skirt with a lacy red top that covered just enough to be modest, but left glimpses of skin.

"I felt bad for leaving you in such a dire condition."

I bit down on my lower lip when I noticed her heels. Black patent leather heels with a strap around the ankle. Patent fucking leather. It was my Kryptonite, a direct line from eyes to my dick.

I bent down, nuzzling against her ear. "My condition is even more dire now that I see how hot you look tonight."

"The right thing to do is make it up to you."

"Is that so?"

"Mm-hmm."

"Come back in a couple hours?"

She looked tired, dark circles under her blue eyes that were laced red. I didn't want her waiting around for me while I finished up.

"I have a better idea," I said, grabbing her hand. "Marshall. I need a break. Give me fifteen."

"The fuck? We're getting slammed here."

"And it's against the law to not allow me to take a break."

He flipped me off, but gave me a knowing smirk.

I took her by the hand down the back hall and past the kitchen to the employee bathroom. I pulled her inside, slammed the door behind us, and locked it.

"What are you doing?" she asked.

I pushed her up against the door before my hands reached up and gripped her face firmly. "I solemnly swear I'm up to no good."

I turned her head and my tongue reached out to taste her skin. She moaned softly, as her body started to melt into mine.

"I love it when you talk Harry Potter to me," she said. "But we shouldn't do this in here."

"I work here. I can do whatever I want, beautiful. Plus, if I don't get inside you immediately, I'm going to go out there and quit so I can fuck you someplace else."

Before I could move further, I realized we weren't going to get anywhere. "Shit. Can you hang on a minute?"

Her body stilled as she gave me a strong glare. "No."

"I need to go get a condom. I'm sure someone or some-where—"

She let out a sigh. "Were you serious this morning about this being just you and me?"

"I wouldn't have said it if I didn't."

She reached up and kissed my bottom lip before biting down gently. "I'm on the pill, so I'm good to go," she said, kissing me again. "If you are."

I was so hoping we'd be able to work something out on the protection but not condom front. My girl was prepared, and it made me *more* than good to go.

My hand slid down her skirt until I reached the hem, curling my fingers underneath it. As I lifted it, her head leaned against my chest, the warmth of her ragged breath heating me more.

"Do you want to know why we call this place WET?" I said, reaching between her legs.

"Mmm," she moaned. "Mm-hmm."

"I'm not sure that's an answer. But I love the response nonetheless."

My hands dipped down farther, my palm running over the front of her lace panties. "You see," I said, increasing my pressure. "In days of Prohibition, places were dry, with no booze. But then some speakeasies started popping up, and they weren't dry. They were wet."

Her hips rocked into me, finding a rhythm in perfect tune with my touch. "I…see," she said, breathless. Her head lifted from my chest, and she was all eyes on me.

"Those eyes are locked in pretty hard there," I said. "And it's making *me* so fucking hard."

She bit down on her lower lip as her chest heaved from

anticipation. It made my cock throb with excitement, and my breathing began to match with hers. Sensing this, she dragged her hand down the front of my shirt and along the seam of my pants, stopping to feel the hardness.

"Thank you," she said, looking down at where she gripped me. "For that development."

I still couldn't believe how fucking sexy this girl was. Everything about her turned me on, and so much stronger than I'd ever known. Her scent, her skin, her touch…it all drove me to the point of almost insanity. It was why I barely thought about it before I lifted her up against the door and started kissing her madly. Matching our want, with tongue and playful bites, I knew I needed her, wanted her, had to have her.

I spun her around while in my arms and placed her back down facing the mirrors lying above the long counter and sinks.

"You hold on to that, beautiful. Stay exactly like that."

She turned her head to look at me, but I firmly pushed her head back to look toward the mirror. "The mirror. You look right there. I want you to see how sexy you look when I fuck you."

I was able to watch her smile in the mirror as I hiked her skirt up over hips and yanked her underwear down. My hand brushed against her smooth, bare ass, so perfectly round that I had to hold myself back from biting it. Instead, I gave her a playful slap and watched her gasp while I hurried to undo my belt and pants.

"Right ahead in that mirror," I whispered into her ear as I

pulled my dick from my boxers. "And open your legs."

She obeyed, giving herself over to me. I wanted to push into her slow, feel the warmth and wetness of her surround me, but a noise outside the door, followed by a knock, reminded me of where we were.

Slow and leisurely would have to wait. It was all about hard and fast at that moment. I slid myself into her, bringing myself as deep as I could before pulling back and repeating. She met my immediate rhythm as she obeyed what I told her. Even though I'd had her this way the night before, being able to watch her reflection in the mirror and to see her face was fascinating. I leaned into her farther, wanting to get deeper and deeper, which was so much more intense sans condom. It had been a long time since I had a woman this way, skin on skin, no barriers. This woman was the one I'd been waiting for.

Her fingers gripped at the top of the counter, wanting to hold on to something.

I wanted something to hold on to, too.

I gripped the back of her hair and yanked it toward me. Bringing my mouth to her neck, I sucked the skin beneath her ear, grazing my teeth over the tender flesh. "You still looking?" I asked in a hushed tone. "Watching what I'm doing to you?"

She panted and pushed herself into me at a matching tempo. "Yes."

The knocking continued louder and louder as I fucked her harder and harder. The mix of timing and her hot-as-fuck moans was enough to drive me over the edge.

"You there, beautiful?"

The words weren't even gone from mouth before she came, tightening and pulling me to do the same. My head buried in the crook of her neck, and I instinctually bit down, wanting to taste her. It was all animal on my part. Uncontrollable.

Her hand reached around and palmed the side of my face as we both fought to catch our breath. After a moment of us silent, and a few expletives shouted from the other side of the door, we pulled away from each other.

"That better not leave a mark, you asshole," she said, touching over the area where I bit her.

She gave me a hard glare as she walked into one of the stalls, but there was enough of a hint of a grin to let me know she wasn't truly mad. It was a kind of dickhead thing to do. We weren't in high school where you'd leave a hickey to prove you were the shit. It wasn't even about marking my territory, either. It was all about wanting her. Getting her. All at once.

"By the way," she said, exiting the stall, pulling her skirt down over her panties. "I like you like that."

"Like what?" I asked.

"Bossy."

I zipped my pants as I took a quiet look in the mirror. Yeah. We both looked like we'd just had a quickie in the bathroom. "You ready?"

"Yup," she said, turning toward the mirror.

I finished tucking my shirt in as I unlocked the door. A quick button of my pants was happening as the door flew open.

"About time," the gin-drinking customer who'd been sitting at the bar said. He pushed past me before stopping his steps and words. "I almost—"

I turned, and there was Evelyn, applying lipstick in the mirror. She snapped the top back on and smoothed her lips together, slipping the lipstick back into the pocket of her skirt. After she ran her hands down the front of her shirt, she headed toward the door, stopping to giving me a kiss on the cheek.

"Perfect, handsome," she said, exiting the bathroom. "But next time, I'm the boss."

Both of us watched her leave as our jaws slackened.

"Jesus," I said, running my hand through my hair.

* * *

It never let up for the rest of the night. It was a relief because it was going to end up being a killer money night for me, which would help me out. Evelyn didn't stay after we left our bathroom love hut, but she continued to linger all over me. My shirt smelled of her perfume, and the images of her watching her reflection in the mirror as I fucked her from behind was at the forefront of my mind.

Marshall rushed past me, bumping my shoulder as he did, causing me to spill from the bottle of Malbec I was pouring. "Dude," I shouted.

"That's for the shit-eating grin you've been sporting all night since Evelyn left," he said, pounding his index finger into the screen at the register.

"Jealous?"

He cackled, shaking his head. "Yeah, right. I don't get jealous of something I can have anytime I want."

"Uh-huh."

I put the cork back on the bottle and returned it to its proper place before handing the wineglass off to one of the servers.

"I can," Marshall said, rearranging the fruit from which we made fresh garnishes. His blond hair was never out of place. He'd be out all night, drinking, partying, whatever, and the guy never had a hair out of place. His tattoo-covered arms were covered up at WET, but outside of it? It was out for the world to see, and the chicks dug them. They dug him a lot.

"Uh-huh," I repeated.

"Don't make it a regular occurrence," he said. "I'm not running a brothel."

"Jesus. You're testy tonight. No, it won't be a regular thing, but she will be, so please don't refer to my girl as a slut ever again or I'll go from friend to murderer in two seconds."

There it was again. The animal. The protective aggressiveness I was getting over her. Marshall and I always joked about our conquests, but Evelyn was different.

He laughed again while shaking his head at me. "Now who's testy? Isn't it a little soon to be so whipped?"

"It's not whipped if I'm enjoying it."

"And I didn't call her a slut and I never would. No lady deserves that. I'd probably have a few choice words about her if she ever cheated or fucked around on you, but she seems almost as into you as you are to her. Plus, she dresses classy as hell. Those shoes, man," he said, shaking his head.

"Don't talk about her shoes," I warned. "And I know. She's…something else."

"By the way," he said, pushing away from the bar. "There's a girl over on the far back sofa that said she wanted to say hello to you. I was going to tell her you might be occupied in the bathroom, but figured less was more, right?"

"Dick," I whispered under my breath as I emerged from the bar to see who he was talking about.

"I heard that! And same back at you," Marshall shouted.

I weaved my way through the tables and conservations, noticing the familiar scene at two a.m. Boozy expressions and close bodies were the norm, but there were always the sad ones. The investment banker drowning his divorce woes in glass after glass of expensive brandy with a buddy. Or the local weather girl who was in at least twice a week and sat alone reading until she was too drunk to see the words anymore. That was what people liked about this place. They could be themselves, and there was no judgment. Aaron's life was a lot like that. First when he went through his divorce, and then when he started seeing Callie, the nanny, it was all over the city papers. It was why I liked working here for the time being. Outside I had to prove myself as Aaron's little brother, and I didn't think I could ever measure up to him. Here? I was just a bartender.

The room grew darker the farther back I went, but the candles on the table lit her face enough for me to recognize her immediately. It hadn't been that long since our night together, and I hadn't recalled telling her where I worked. We were both so drunk before we stumbled onto my couch, and at that time I could've told her anything.

Shit. What was her name? And how the hell did she get in here?

"Abel," she said, uncrossing her long legs and standing. And her legs were all I saw with her skirt so short, covering only the holy areas of her body.

She pressed her hand to my chest before giving me a kiss on the cheek, lingering a little too long for my comfort.

"How have you been…?" I said, trailing off while still trying to remember her name.

Her eyebrows raised knowingly. "Do you remember me?" she asked.

"Of course. Yes."

"My name?" she questioned.

The accent should've helped me, but it didn't. Where was she from again? Greece? No. That wasn't it.

"Huh?" I said, leaning into her and cupping my hand over my ear to pretend like I didn't hear her.

Her hand on my chest ran down my shirt, her fingertips gliding over each covered button. I backed away while taking her roaming hand in mine.

"Italy!" I blurted out. She was definitely from Italy, but it was not her name.

She winked. "I'll let it slide even though it breaks my heart to think I'm forgettable."

"No. It's been a long night working and—"

"Dafne. And no trouble," she said, her accent wrapping

around each word, each syllable like honey. It was stunning, as was she, but it wasn't where I wanted to go anymore.

This was always so awkward. One-night stands were supposed to stick to the one-night rule. Whenever someone didn't abide by that, I was left standing in front of the "standee" trying to figure out how to make a getaway.

"I wish I could stay and talk, but I have to get back to work. I'll send over another cocktail on me. What are you having?" I said.

She sat down, backing herself into the plush cabernet-colored sofa. With an exaggerated lift of her leg, she crossed it over the other, hoping to give me a glimpse of what was or wasn't under that skirt.

"*Hai preso il mio fiato,* Abel," she purred.

I shook my head. "I…don't know what that means."

"You pretended you knew when I whispered it in your ear."

"I really do have to get back. It was—"

"You took my breath away," she said. She looked around the room, tables slowly beginning to empty. "Almost done?"

Shit. I didn't want to have to use my number two excuse, but she left me no choice.

"You're very beautiful, Dafne. Oh! Now I remember. Dafne with an *f*, not a *ph*. Anyway, I had fun, but I'm seeing someone now. I can't," I said. "Now how about that drink?"

She tapped her long fingernail on the rim of her wineglass. "Merlot," she said. "And you flatter yourself."

"I do?"

"Yes, you do. I'm not here only for you. I was going to meet Benji here, but he had to cancel."

"Benji Wright?" I asked.

She nodded, her eyebrows lifted in question. "That's right. I'm sure you know him as well."

A chill ran through my body at the sound of his name. My debt was increasing and I was grateful he was giving me the time I needed, but even I knew he'd have his limit. My anxiety eased when I reminded myself she'd said he wouldn't be coming, which led me to my next question.

"Why would you be meeting him here?"

She shrugged her shoulders as she lifted her palms up, being coy about answering my question.

I didn't give a shit that Dafne was cozying up to someone new. It was the fact that it wasn't wise with Benji. He was dangerous, and everyone knew it. You had to know that if you were going to be part of anything he was running. Of course, there were some women at games, but it was like *Fight Club*. You didn't talk about it.

"You're…friends with him?" I asked.

She raised her eyebrows as a devilish grin emerged. "You're jealous."

"I'm really not. Like I said, I'm seeing someone now, but that doesn't mean I can't be concerned."

"No concern, Abel. Benji has something I want, and I was here to try and persuade him."

"Look, Dafne, you shouldn't get into anything with him. He—"

"I better say no to another drink," she said, interrupting me. "Even though you're nice to ask."

She gathered her things and stood to leave, only to stop to kiss me, a little too long, on the cheek.

"*Addio, bello*," she whispered in my ear.

CHAPTER THIRTEEN

EVELYN—

"Sex in a bar bathroom?" Callie said.

I was sitting next to her in my bed, nibbling on pastries from Floriole Bakery and sipping coffee. With both of our crazy schedules—she's a teacher—our Sunday morning tradition of pain au chocolat, fruit scones, and coffee was one of my favorite moments of the week. It was also good to get a reading on her after finding out about Abel and me.

She took a bite of her scone. "When I worked at the bar Venom, we had a name for girls like you."

"Slut, tramp, dirty—"

"You know what?" She waved her hand around, crumbs from her scone falling like snow all over my comforter. "It's probably better off I don't say."

"You know what else is better off? If you don't get food all over my bed."

She stood up and began brushing crumbs into her palm.

"I'd think you wouldn't be so grumpy considering how much you've gotten laid in the last two days."

"I happen to get a one-nighter here and there on more occasions. Although having a boyfriend now will have its perks."

She stopped the crumb removal and shook her head. "Wait. What?"

"What? What?"

"A boyfriend? Abel's your boyfriend?"

I shrugged, picking up the bag of pastries. "Ah. Yeah. Didn't we go over this yesterday, and did you get only one apple scone?"

"Shut up about the scone. You, the perpetual bache-lorette? I mean, yesterday you said you were having a thing or something."

"Look, I like him. I'm not opposed to being exclusive be-cause if I'm going to sleep with him on the regular I prefer to be the only one doing that with him."

"Then why call it anything?"

"Because he wanted to…and…I don't know."

She dumped the crumbs into the wastebasket. "I know why," she mumbled.

"What was that?"

"I said I know."

"Oh, really? I get that you know me better than anyone, but I find it almost impossible you know what is happening when I don't."

"Don't be so dramatic. He's your boyfriend because you want to hang out with him, having fun when you do, and not wanting him or yourself to sleep with other people means...he's your boyfriend."

"I didn't say he wasn't."

"Yeah. Whatever. But haven't you considered how this whole thing happened with him?"

"What are you talking about?"

"I mean, I'm with Aaron. You met Abel through us."

"And?"

"And you don't think that's a bit serendipitous?"

"Callie. You don't believe in that bullshit and neither do I."

"I don't know. I didn't think I did, but sometimes things come together in ways that are unexplainable, like how Aaron and I met. We didn't meet at some random bar or the library. We met after you suggested me for the nanny job."

I curled my lip and shook my head. "At a library? You are so twisted."

"It was a hypothetical. I was just sayin'. The fact of the matter is, you met in a very fated way. Plus, the both of you aren't the type for exclusivity. It makes me happy because you're finally opening yourself up again," she said.

"Well, regardless, I'm going to need you to keep an eye on Abel when I'm gone. There's no telling what kind of trouble he'll get himself into," I said, rolling off the bed. "I need a shower. You staying for a while?"

"When you're gone? Where are you going?" she asked.

"Oh my God. With all the boy business, I forgot to tell you! Bridget is sending me to Charleston for three months!"

"What?" she shouted. "Three months? I can't be without you for three months!"

My phone on my nightstand buzzed with a text, and while I wondered if it was Abel, I needed to take care of Callie first—sisters before misters.

"Way to be selfish, you twit," I said. "It's huge. Bridget is opening a By Invitation Only in South Carolina. I'm going there to help get stuff together while she stays here."

"But why can't she go to Charleston?" she pouted.

"Because she has weddings booked through the summer and fall she needs to be here for."

She looked disappointed, turning her attention to those ratty, pink Toms I hated, but did her best to hide it. "This is fantastic. It really is, Ev. You've worked so hard."

I glared at her, continuing to ignore my phone buzzing again, because she wasn't getting off that easy. "You're being a brat. I'm going to miss you, too, but it's only a few months."

"Three is more than a few," she mumbled. She shook off her funk with a shake of her head. "This is great. It really is."

She took me in a hug, and it was the first time I realized I was being selfish as well. Our friendship bordered on codependency. If the situation was the other way around, I'd react the same way. In fact, I was sure I did at first when she told me she was moving out to nanny for Aaron, even though I recommended her for the job, and then the second time when she moved back in after not being the nanny anymore.

"And for the record," she said, pulling out of our hug. "Abel isn't going to need any watching over. It's going to be made very clear to him if he screws this thing up with you that he'll be walking funny for the rest of his life because I'll be ripping him a new one."

"I'd expect nothing less. I think Aaron is still in recovery from when I busted his balls so hard-core when he messed up."

"Also," she said, "you're going to have to trust him. The good, the uncomfortable…whatever. Learn from my mistakes. If you don't trust each other, there isn't any point in having…a thing."

My phone vibrated for the third time. I leaned over and retrieved it from my nightstand. It was Abel.

> **Abel:** Lunch? Dinner? Both?

I smiled at my phone, recognizing the familiar butterflies.

Callie snorted. "Abel? Never mind. You don't have to answer that. It's written all over your face. You two are definitely in the gooey stage. It's so weird."

"It is *so* weird. You going to hang out for a while?"

"I can't," she said, slipping out of her Toms. "Aaron and I have to go grocery shopping and to Home Depot before we pick up Delilah. She spent the night at his parents."

"Boy. You two live the wild, crazy life, don't you?"

"It can't all be sexcapades and sugar," she said.

I followed her out of the room as my phone buzzed in my hand again. I glanced down at it.

> **Abel:** Or you can just get your sexy ass over here, get in my bed, and let me fuck your brains out for the entire day.

Callie was wrong. For right now, it was all sexcapades and sugar.

I waited until she was gone to respond to Abel. I wanted to tell him yes, I wanted it all. In fact, I wanted it all and then some. I wanted to spend every waking moment with him because I couldn't get enough of him. The bar bathroom romp was one of the sexiest moments of my life—the way he wanted me, commanded me, and took me. I'd never felt so desired nor had I ever had such desire for someone else.

I returned to my text messages, grinning again like a high school girl whose crush just asked her to prom.

> **Me:** This is quite an offer. Can you be more specific with the terms?

> **Abel:** Hang out, fuck, cheeseburgers, drinks, fuck.

No need to be coy.

> **Me:** Offer accepted. Meet at your place in a couple hours?

> **Abel:** Cool. Need to check in at my parents' for a few, so if I'm not at my place, I'll be there. 4946.

Wait. His parents? Does this mean they knew? I mean, it wasn't like it was a secret anymore or that I hadn't even already met his parents, but this was different. It was like meeting his parents for the first time as someone completely different.

> **Me:** Are you sure you want me to?

> **Abel:** What's the big deal?

Me: It seems so...official. Meeting your parents. Again.

Abel: It's cool. I was going to hang out with Delilah for a bit, but I don't want to make it weird if you aren't ready for any of that. See you at noon AT MY PLACE, beautiful.

I headed into the bathroom to take a shower, along with the nagging sense I was doing exactly what Abel said I was. The parent thing? Making a big deal out of nothing really? I looked to my reflection in the mirror, staring at the remnants of mascara under my eyes that didn't quite wash off when I removed my makeup from the night before.

I considered what Callie said—if I was going to be with Abel then I was going to have to trust not just him but myself. I'd have to trust that letting go meant going into scary things, like seeing his parents as his girlfriend. There was more unexpectedness than I was prepared for, but the feelings I had for Abel were overriding that.

I leaned over and turned the shower on, knowing anything worth doing was worth doing right.

Message received. Loud and clear.

My excitement got the better of me, and I was ready to go in record time. By the time I arrived at Abel's building, I was over a half an hour earlier than expected.

Rob was outside when I arrived and nodded his head at me. "Nice to see you again, Evelyn."

"Thanks, Rob," I said. "Thanks again for your help the other morning."

He shrugged. His navy raincoat didn't have a wrinkle in it,

and it made me wonder if he steamed it every day. "It's what I do," he said.

"Well, you won't have to anymore," I said.

"That's too bad. So, things are ending?" he asked.

I stepped into the revolving door, shouting behind me, "Nope. Just beginning."

I crossed the two-story lobby, the dark marble floors and matching decor shined to perfection. The shiny, gold buttons next to the list of apartment numbers lined the wall, and I scanned with my finger until I pressed firmly on the one marked 4946.

"Hello?" said a soft voice.

"Ah, hi. It's...Evelyn. I was wondering if Abel was there. I was supposed to meet him but was early. He told me he was going to spend time with you this morning, or well, I guess it's afternoon now, so I thought I'd check in."

Pause.

"I hope I'm not disturbing you. I can come back if he's busy, or if...I don't know."

Pause.

I looked at the buzzer and then my phone to make sure I had the right number. Yup. It was right.

"Um. Okay. Thanks. I'll go get a coffee and check in with him. At his place. If—"

A laugh, one that I recognized, cut me off. "Hey, beautiful."

"Have you been listening to me this whole time making a fool of myself?"

"Yes. You sounded so adorable being all nervous and awkward," he said, chuckling again. "I'll just go get a coffee."

The door buzzed me in, and I briefly thought about ditching him to teach him a lesson. I pulled the door open before I lost the chance as I fished out a lip gloss from my purse. As I stepped in front of the elevator, I used the reflection to apply the gloss, smiling as I did.

"Yeah, right," I said to my reflection. Like I'd ditch that guy now. He was so close, and it was like my body knew it.

Or maybe it was nerves. Or annoyance. It was something because as I took the elevator up to the forty-ninth floor the realization I was going to the exact place I said I didn't want to go was happening.

What was I so nervous about? The parent thing? They thought I was delightful. His mom was always so kind to me as well. Then it hit me. All of the anxiety I had wasn't about Abel's parents *knowing* about us, but how they'd *feel* about us. Mr. Matthews did not have a good reaction when he found out about Callie and Aaron. In fact, the whole thing got ugly before it got better. The good news was Mr. Matthews knew he acted like a jackass and admitted it soon after. Both he and Mrs. Matthews adored her now. Under those circumstances, I had reason to be concerned.

The elevator stopped, and the doors opened to the same burnt-red carpeting that lined the halls of Abel's floor. My footsteps slowed as I approached the numbers on the doors raising to 4946.

"Cut it out," I whispered to myself. "You don't do this. You don't do nervous. You're being ridiculous."

Deep breath. Knock.

The door opened to Leslie Matthews, Abel and Aaron's mom, and her warm smile was enough to take the edge off my nerves.

"Come in, Evelyn," she said, stepping aside. "Abel is saying good-bye to Delilah. It's so nice to see you, dear."

She was so lovely with her ivory cashmere cardigan and the eyes so blue she had enough to pass some on to her boys.

"Oh, thank you. You, too," I said, walking into the home and taking it all in. It wasn't only the gorgeous home I was taking in, it was the fact she wasn't exactly surprised to see me. It meant he'd told his parents. About us. Mrs. Matthews looked at me kindly, her hands held close to her chest.

She placed her hand on my arm and guided me farther inside. "Can I get you anything to drink? I heard you saying you were going to get coffee, but I have a pot all ready here."

"No, no. That's okay. I was only making excuses because your son was giving me a hard time."

She shook her head. "Well, that's Abel for you."

"Is that Evelyn?" Mr. Matthews shouted from another room.

"Yes!" Mrs. Matthews said. "Come say hello!"

"That's okay. I don't want to disturb him if—"

"Well, Evelyn!" he said, entering the room, his loud voice only preceded by his personality. "I knew I saw a love connection with you two!"

"Dad!" Abel yelled.

Mr. Matthews waved his hand in the direction of Abel's voice. "Don't mind him. He hates to admit when he's wrong."

Here I was, worried sick with nerves about how they'd receive the news about Abel and me when I should've been concerned about the reverse of the situation.

"He's down the hall. The first room on the right," Mrs. Matthews said. "There's a tea party in progress."

"This I have to see," I said, stepping away.

Mr. Matthews stepped in front of me, placing an arm around my shoulders and guiding me into the nearby kitchen. "You'll be good for him."

It wasn't a question, but it should've been. I knew he meant well and that his heart was in the right place, but based on his response when Callie and Aaron started dating, I was leery. While Callie hated confrontation, I wasn't afraid of it when I thought someone was being disingenuous.

"I think he's good already," I said with a smirk.

"Oh, but you don't know him like I do. My youngest needs to grow up a bit, and he's on his way with the bar he's opening with Aaron, but you'll be a help. I'm proud of him for how everything is lining up."

What was he talking about? *A bar? With Aaron?*

"What bar?" I asked. "What do you mean?"

His arm dropped from my shoulder, and he took a step back, pressing his lips together like he knew he said something he shouldn't have.

"Did I mention my son also needs to learn to handle his own shit without leaving it to others?" He laughed.

He was a handsome older gentleman. His sons took after that part of him. I hoped that was where the similarities ended. My annoyance was measured in uncomfortable silence with the occasional giggle from Delilah down the hall until Mrs. Matthews showed who I knew the boys took after in other aspects.

"For crying out loud, Daniel," she said. Her kind eyes turned to death stare in seconds, proving she had the wife-mom superpowers. "Mind your own business."

"It is my business," he mumbled.

"Yeah. Well, look where it got you last time you stuck your nose in where it didn't belong. Need I remind you, dear, that unsolicited advice is still unsolicited."

"But—" he said before Mrs. Matthews cut him off.

"And we are always proud of both of our sons."

"Leslie, all I wanted to say was—"

"And furthermore, darling, shut up."

Her death stare turned to ice, and it caused Mr. Matthews to close his mouth that had words on the tip of his tongue.

"Evelyn, you go on ahead. I know Abel is waiting for you," she said.

I tried not to be too obvious about how fast I wanted to escape, and when I hurried off, I was sure my pace came across as a sprint. An uneasiness swirled around my stomach about what Mr. Matthews had said. It wasn't that he was going into business with his brother, but the fact that he didn't tell me. As I followed the sound of Abel's voice, I concluded that there probably was, in fact, a reason why he didn't. My mind jumping to a conclusion fraught with deception wasn't fair to him.

I hesitated outside the first room on the right, pausing to take it all in. Abel was sitting on a flowered blanket on the floor, his legs tucked into his sides as he tried to fit into the square. Across from him was Delilah, Aaron's daughter, who had to be one of the most beautiful little girls I've ever seen with white-blond hair and a bob of tight ringlet curls. Every time I saw her I couldn't get over what a sweetheart she was, inside and out. While there had been times I might have had some negative thoughts about Aaron, he'd done such an amazing job raising her on his own when his wife took off.

He turned as I leaned against the doorway; he smiled, dimples deep. Mini teacups and saucers surrounded him, along with tiny cookies stacked atop a china plate. "I had to finish the tea party Delilah set up for us."

"No worries. I'm sorry for being so early. I hope I didn't ruin your party, Delilah," I said.

She shook her head before picking up a small, pink-frosted sugar cookie and holding it out to me. "Want one, Evelyn?"

"Of course," I answered, taking the cookie from her.

I joined them on the blanket and popped the entire cookie in my mouth. "So yummy, right, Delilah?"

She nodded. "Can I have another one?"

I picked up a yellow frosted cookie and handed it to her.

"Nothing wrong with a little bit of sugar, right?" I said to Abel with a wink.

He leaned over and whispered in my ear, "You can't talk to me like that in front of a child."

He stood and held his hand down to me to help me up. Once standing, he took my face in his hands and kissed me.

It was chaste, very unlike the passionate ones I was used to. It was expected considering our audience.

"Are you leaving now?" Delilah asked.

"Yeah we are, squirt," Abel said. "But thank you for the cookies and tea party."

Her face frowned and her head hung as she stared at the patterned blanket. I didn't know how this little girl had everyone she knew wrapped around her little finger, but she did. Me included.

"Hey," he said, squatting down in front of her. He lifted her chin up with his hand. "Who's my best girl?"

She thought for a moment before answering. "Me?"

He kissed the top of her head and stood up. "Always."

And just like that, anything I thought he was keeping from me slid to the back, and I knew I was falling even harder for him.

He took my hand as we left the room and continued down the hall toward the door. I glanced at the framed photos on the walls, various stages of life pictures of the Matthews family. One of Aaron holding baby Abel, I assumed, caught my eye and I paused in front of it.

"Look at you two," I said, running my finger around the dark wooden frame.

"Yeah. I think it was the day I came home. Little dude didn't know what he was in for by being my big brother."

I leaned into him, resting my head on his arm as I continued to take in the picture. Aaron, who was around eight years old, was sporting the biggest "cheese" smile as the tiny Abel screamed from his swaddled blanket. The sports-themed wallpaper behind them indicated they had to be in Aaron's room.

"When were you going to tell me about the bar you're opening with Aaron?" I asked, looking up at him.

His eyes closed as he drew in a deep breath, his chest expanding as he did. "My dad, I assume?"

"Yeah, but in his defense, he thought I knew. I think I should've known as well."

He pulled me around, positioning me so we could face each other. "I don't want you to think I wasn't going to tell you. I was, but I was waiting for the right time after I figured some shit out."

"What kind of stuff?"

"How much of this I want."

My hand pushed against his chest, as I needed some separation from whatever he was trying to say. Abel's parents' voices carried down the hallway as they discussed where to make a reservation for dinner later that night. It seemed like such a regular conversation to have as Abel danced around the topic of how much of this thing we had, of me, he wanted.

"You're mad," he said. "And I get why."

I crossed my arms in front of me. "I'm not mad. I'm...wondering why you told me to come here if you weren't sure how much of me you wanted."

His brows furrowed as he shook his head. "Wait. What?"

"You said you didn't know how much of this," I said, waving my finger between us, "you wanted. This isn't really the type of conversation to have at your parents' house."

"Are you fucking kidding me with this?" he said, his lips gradually raising to a grin before he started to chuckle.

"No. And quit laughing at me."

"I'm not laughing *at* you, beautiful," he said. He grabbed my waist and jerked me back to him. "I'm laughing because what you just said is ridiculous. I was talking about going into business with my brother, not us."

Heat from embarrassment washed across my face. "Oh."

He bent down, pressing a kiss to my forehead. "Crazy girl."

"Then what did you mean?" I asked.

"I was talking about the whole bar thing in California."

"California?"

"Yeah. Partners."

He should've been excited, but his expression was anything but. That was when I understood. It wasn't what he wanted to do, but something he thought he had to do. Teaching was where his heart was, and with no real prospects on the horizon, he was feeling the weight of his career decisions all over him.

"Look," he said, holding my face in his hands. "I didn't mean to keep it from you."

"I know, but—" I stopped myself, considering my words. "But I'm here for you to talk this stuff out with. It's why we have a thing, you know?"

He nodded. "It's an awesome opportunity, but I'm not sure it's the right one for me. For now, I'm going with it until I have to make a definite decision."

It was just like I'd thought.

"I'm not going to say you lied," I said. "But withholding is lying once removed. I don't like it and promise you won't do it again."

"Promise," he said, holding out his finger.

We intertwined our pinkies and shook on it. It was good enough for me at the moment and hopefully it was for him as well. He'd need to learn to trust me as much as I needed to do the same. It made me realize I had to say one last thing.

I stood up on my tiptoes and kissed him. "And I think it's amazing, you taking this on. If you decide not to because you want to make the teaching thing work, well, I think that's just as amazing."

"Come on," Abel said, tugging my arm. "Cheeseburgers and...other things await."

His parents were nowhere to be seen as we headed toward the front door. As Abel opened it, he shouted, "We're heading out. See you later."

"Bye, Evelyn!" Mr. and Mrs. Matthews said simultaneously.

"Bye!" I said as Abel shut the door.

As the door clicked shut, I found myself pushed up against it, Abel pressing his body into me. He swooped down, pressing his lips tightly to mine before opening his mouth and allowing his tongue to find mine. Deep kisses, his hands in my hair and mine gripping the back of his neck, led to a now-familiar sigh falling from his lips.

"That's more like it," he mumbled against my mouth. "I missed you."

The words, along with his beard, tickled me inside and

out. He missed me. It was like Callie had said—we were gooey. He smiled and rested his hands on my hips. His fingers fumbled around the middle of the jumpsuit I was wearing before he reached around my back, his hands smoothing across to my ass.

"What are you doing?" I asked.

"Trying to find your skin so I can touch you."

I stifled a moan because it was the exact thing that made me weak. His moves in bed were amazing, but he had perfected his art of words very well. I would've liked to have attributed it to his English major background, but I knew better. He had a lot of practice.

"You can keep trying," I said. "But it's a jumpsuit. It's all connected."

He grabbed my ass, giving it a squeeze. "That's too bad. What else is too bad is I'm pretty sure you're not wearing underwear."

"That's for me to know and you to figure out."

"It's not going to be all that I'm trying to figure out. Now. Back to cheeseburgers. Kuma's?" he asked.

It was a perfect May day, crystal blue skies and a hint of warmth coming off the mid-sixties temperature. The frigid Chicago winters turn everything gray and dirty. We see the city start to emerge as the snow all melts, and the temperatures begin to rise. It was why it wasn't uncommon to see locals wearing shorts and sandals this early on, which we did as we walked, hand in hand, to the "L."

The train was crowded for a midday Sunday and was standing room only. I wrapped my arm around a steel bar, leaning against it for balance. Abel, with no place else to go, lifted his arms above me for a grip, trapping me under him.

I looked up at him, and it took everything in me not to jump his bones on public transportation with children and clergy present. His turquoise T-shirt made his panty-dropper eyes appear bluer than normal while muscular arms held me so I didn't fall. He made me feel safe. It wasn't something I'd ever thought I needed or wanted, but a sense of safety was surrounding me. It wasn't just physical. I was beginning to trust him. Giving someone else your heart was the ultimate act of trust, asking them to keep it safe, and I was slowly allowing him to do that.

"You're locked in pretty hard there, beautiful," he said, looking down at me and smiling deep dimples.

Embarrassed I got caught staring, I shook my head. "Just thinking about cheeseburgers."

He laughed. "Mm-hmm."

He wasn't buying it and who could blame him?

* * *

Kuma's Corner, a heavy metal bar where every burger was named after a metal band, was always packed. The lines start forming an hour before they even opened so people knew they'd get a seat. It seemed ridiculous to wait so long for a burger when Chicago had tons of other amazing options, but there was an easy answer: the Lair of the Minotaur. A burger topped with Brie, caramelized onions, and a bourbon-soaked pear.

For Abel, I found out, it was the Black Sabbath, a chili-and-pepper-jack cheeseburger.

"This is the best thing I've had in my mouth in ages," I said. I held my massive burger in front of me and took the most ladylike approach to taking another bite. When I tore my eyes away from the meat in my mouth, I noticed my man meat was stifling a laugh.

I covered my mouth with a napkin. "What?"

He ran his hand down his beard before lifting his beer bottle to his mouth for a sip, his lips still turned upward in a smirk. The longer he didn't answer, the more paranoid I got. I wiped at my face, looked down at my shirt…anything to figure out what he was laughing at.

"What?" I snapped. "What are you laughing at?"

"The best thing in your mouth in ages?" he asked with raised eyebrows. "I'm offended."

"God. Do you guys ever not think like thirteen-year-old boys?"

"Not that I know of."

I stole a fried pickle from the basket next to him. "Okay," I said. "Second-best thing, okay?"

"Now I don't know if you are talking about the pickle or me." He gave me a fake pout, looking for reassurance.

Men were so stupidly predictable. Everything about their egos was wrapped up in their penis—whether they disguised it as a joke or not.

"Your pickle euphemism isn't lost on me, handsome," I said.

"I'd expect nothing to get past you. You still didn't answer my question."

I picked up my beer and chugged the last half, placing the empty bottle on the table.

"Nice," Abel said with approval.

I wiggled my finger, motioning for him to come closer. He leaned across the table, and I whispered in his ear, "Palate cleanser."

"Meaning?"

"I want the best thing ever, your cock, in my mouth so I can suck you so hard you come in my mouth and I can swallow every single bit of it."

His jaw dropped as he gradually eased himself back in his chair. "Fuck. Me."

"I plan on it," I said with a wink.

CHAPTER FOURTEEN

ABEL—

I almost took her in the bathroom and fucked her right there, but since our last go was in WET's bathroom, I decided to be a gentleman. Yes. I was the gentleman who waited until we were back at her place.

One of these days I was going to try the slow, seductive sex thing with her, but we couldn't control ourselves long enough to get that far. We tumbled into her apartment and down the hall to her bedroom, tearing at each other's clothes while our mouths never separated from our kisses. She lifted my shirt over my head and yanked me back to her with her fingers slipped into the top of my jeans. Her fingers began unbuttoning them as the palm of her hand started stroking my dick.

"How the fuck do you get this off," I tugged at the jumper-onesies-whatever-the-hell-she-was-wearing thing.

She giggled and reached behind her head, unbuttoning a tiny hook hidden behind her hair. It loosened the top enough for me to yank it over her shoulders and down her arms. Even though I was a master bra unhooker, I wasn't going to fuck around with her bra. I pushed the lace cup down and leaned down, taking her breast in my mouth.

She leaned against the wall behind her, digging her hands into my hair, and pulling me to her. I sucked and bit and did everything I already knew she liked. And the way she kept repeating my name, "God, Abel." Over and over, I knew she liked it a lot.

I pushed the rest of her outfit down before it fell to the floor and she stepped out of it. Just as I suspected, no panties. I tore myself away from her breast, running my tongue up through the center of her chest to her neck. Taking a handful of her hair, I pulled her head back.

"I fucking knew it," I breathed into her ear. "Now, get on your knees, Evelyn."

She yanked her head from me. "Take your pants off, Abel."

Toe. To. Fucking. Toe.

She sank to her knees as I unzipped my jeans and pushed them down along with my boxers. A tiny smirk emerged at seeing me so hard and ready for her. Her hand wrapped around my shaft, and she started pumping, twisting, up and down. It was good, but it wasn't what I wanted.

"Look at me, Evelyn," I said.

I waited until she obeyed, noticing her lips free of her lipstick, slightly (swollen) from all our making out.

"I want your mouth on me," I said. "Show me like you promised."

The words were barely out before she fucking took every inch of me in. She paused, looking back up at me, and brought her mouth back up to the tip. Her tongue ran round, round, before bringing me back in deep. My hips met the beat of her head, her mouth, her hands. Her hair fell into her face, so I brushed it away, holding it away from her face so I could watch her.

"That's my girl."

I moved, I moaned, and she got every cue. I tried to hold off, so I could finish by getting inside her, but the girl knew what she wanted.

I dragged my finger along her cheek, "It's time, beautiful," I said.

She increased her speed and grip just so, and I gave in.

And she did as she promised.

Every. Last. Bit.

She sat back against her calves and winked at me, clearly proud of a job well done. "That's my guy."

I was pleased with her performance as well, but my mind, my body, had already moved on to what I wanted to do to her.

"Stand up," I demanded.

She shook her head. "Remember last time? I told you I was going to be the boss this time. I let you get your kicks, now it's my turn."

Christ.

"On your knees, Abel," she said. Her eyes backed up her demand, meeting mine as I did what she told me.

There didn't need to be any further instruction. My mouth was on her, tonguing where she was so fucking wet from me that my dick was already in recuperation mode. I loved that I turned her on so hard. I loved that her giving me head made her so ready for me.

Her hand on the back of my head, her back arched into me. I slipped a finger inside, and with a few strokes as I tongued her clit, she cried out, coming against my mouth. I kept moving until she halted on her own. I was nothing if not a gentleman in the oral department. You don't stop moving until she does. Then when she pulls away, you stop. It was basic lady head protocol.

As I began to stand, I wrapped my arms around her legs and threw her over my shoulders, slapping at her perfect ass. She giggled as I dropped her onto her unmade bed. We crawled under the covers, and she tucked herself into my side. We lay quiet, both of us catching our breath after such a hard-core romp.

"Can I ask you something?" she said after a few minutes. "And if it's none of my business, you can tell me to buzz off."

"Evelyn, you're amazing, but even I need some down-time."

She lifted her head and playfully slapped my chest before returning to next to me. Her blond hair spread out, laid out across me. As I waited for her question, I raked my hands through it, dragging my fingers to the curled ends and repeating.

"Go ahead," I said.

"What did you mean earlier when you said that Aaron had no idea what he'd be getting himself into having you for a little brother?"

"Nothing." I shrugged. "I was joking, I guess."

Her head lifted, and she sat her chin on my chest. "You guess?"

"Well, I'm sure it's no secret that I'm a fuckup, and luckily for Aaron he's the one to bail me out a lot."

"Define fuckup. I mean, making some dumb choices doesn't mean you're a fuckup necessarily."

I sighed because I wasn't sure how much I wanted to tell her. It wasn't like I was an ex-con or anything, but it was humiliating.

"Let's just say, I've found myself in a sticky situation or two, and Aaron has always been there. Why are you asking?"

"Your dad said something odd to me, and I wasn't sure how to take it."

"Something more odd than spilling the beans about the California bar? He doesn't waste any time," I said, shaking my head.

"It was more what he didn't say. I'm sure it was innocent enough, but I can't stop thinking about it."

"It wasn't some dirty old man talk was it? Because he still thinks he's a player and can flirt, but it usually turns into him looking like a jackass."

"No, not dirty. He told me I'd be good for you, and he was proud, but you had some growing up to do."

A rush of anger came through me, knowing what he said, but as soon as it came, it was gone. When you've been witness to an older brother constantly being put on a pedestal, you've been viewed as nothing more than the prodigal son.

I sighed. "It's a not-so-subtle dig that I still haven't

found a teaching job, work at my brother's bar, but now while still riding Aaron's coattails, I'm going into business with him."

Her nails lightly grazed across my lower stomach, circles and zigzagging across the skin. "It's not like you're not trying, right? Sometimes the right job isn't as easy to find as people would expect."

"It's not that. They know I'm trying, but it was my choices that led me here."

"What does that mean?"

"If I had the business sense and was savvy enough like Aaron was, I wouldn't need to rely on them. Aaron has fronted most of the money for the California bar and is allowing me to pay my way in a little at a time. The whole thing makes me feel like I still can't measure up because it's not what I want for myself. I chose to be a teacher, and as anyone knows, it's not exactly a profitable career. Rewarding yes, but moneymaking no."

"So you're supposed to be feeling bad for picking a career you love? Something you feel passionate about? That's bull-shit."

"It is, but it also is what it is. And as much as I'd like to blame it all on a stupid career decision that's not all of it. They are right," I said.

"Well, I don't think they are. They should support you no matter what."

"They do. Kind of. I mean, it's not like I'm an outcast, but most of it was my doing."

"It sounds to me like you're taking the blame."

"Maybe I'm the one to blame. I was the one that stole my dad's Mercedes when I was seventeen, crashed and totaled it. I was the one who got caught cheating on my SATs, couldn't graduate with my class, and had to go to summer school. I was the one who almost flunked out of college after two semesters because I was partying too much. I was the one who drained my trust fund when I turned twenty-one by gambling and ended up owing a huge debt. Who do you think paid for that?" My voice had raised as I was talking, and I hadn't noticed until the last of it was out. "Sorry," I said.

"Don't be."

But I was. There would be time for her to understand family dynamics and for me to explain how different I was now. I was going to leave it all in the past—all the screwing around and shit.

"I'm the one that's sorry," she said.

"What the hell for?"

"You've been taking me out to such nice places, and it didn't occur to me that on a bartender's salary, it might've been tight. I'm sure—"

I laughed. "I'm not destitute. I can pay for dates."

Her head tilted to the side, her expression confused. "How are you affording the bar then, too?"

I shrugged. "I'm good at playing cards and shit for some extra money on the side. Plus, WET is more profitable than people realize. The clientele lends to that."

"You have your hands in all kinds of things don't you, handsome?"

Her eyebrows raised, and I knew she was questioning everything that was coming at her.

I hated holding back, keeping things from her. She didn't deserve it, but she couldn't know the truth. I couldn't stand the thought of her looking at me the way my father and Aaron do.

I held my hand against the side of her face, rubbing my thumb across her cheek. Tension was there. The doubt.

"Am I right to assume that this is everything you've been keeping from me?" she asked.

"Yes," I answered without hesitation. "Except for one thing."

"What's that?"

"I told Aaron I had doubts about moving there and managing the new bar. That was originally what I was supposed to do."

"Why?" she asked.

I lifted her chin with one finger and bent my head, kissing her. "You. That's why. Something's happening here, Evelyn. You're here."

"Are you insane?" she screeched. "That's the stupidest thing I've ever heard."

"Okay. Not the reaction I expected, but I'll go with it."

"We just started this thing. No one is making life choices or anything for anyone. I'm going to Charleston in a few months, and what happens then?"

"That's only for a few months," I said.

"But anything could come up at any time," she said, sitting up. She took the sheet along with her, wrapping it around her as if this conversation was now a place to find her modesty. "What if you got a teaching job out of state or what if Bridget wanted me to handle the Charleston office fulltime? I mean, I don't think either of us should be thinking about giving anything up for someone they just started dating. I mean, look at Aaron and Callie. They went into stuff all rushy-rushy, and it all blew up in their face. I don't think we should make that same mistake, not that I think we are, but it's something to consider. And that doesn't mean I'm not totally into our thing and not into you. I'm super into you. I'm probably more into you than I should be, but…"

She paused to take a breath, and I took advantage of the moment by letting out a laugh I was holding in. She was freaking out. She was dude freaking out, reacting as if she was a guy and the girl got too clingy.

"Relax," I said, pulling her back to me and tucking her back into my side. "We aren't Aaron and Callie. They didn't tell each other shit, and that was what blew up in their face. I'm being honest, and if that doesn't get me what I want, then it wasn't meant to be. So chill out, beautiful."

Her body began to relax again, her hands unclenched and rested back on my chest. "Sorry."

"Don't be. I don't want you to be sorry for anything you're thinking, but I also don't want you freaking out over nothing. No one is getting married or declaring the *l* word."

She giggled and pressed her lips to my chest before biting it.

"Ouch," I said. I rubbed my hand over the bitten area. "What was that for?"

"For being so on my level. From here on out, it shall be called the *l* word."

"Now that we have that covered, I'm done with all the serious talk," I said. I wrapped my arms around her and rolled her underneath me. "Now," I said, kissing her neck. "I'm ready."

* * *

I was a pathetic fuck and had no idea what was happening to me. All I knew was it was close to seven a.m. and I was staring at Evelyn, watching her sleep. In fact, I'd been up all night. After our round two, for which I win the award for holding out the longest and until she came three times, we both gave in to exhaustion. I don't know who drifted into sleep first, but I woke up an hour later. I could've blamed it on bartender hours and my internal clock always being messed up. But it was more than that and I knew it.

I didn't want to wake her, so I ended up picking up the book that was on her nightstand and started reading it. It was this filthy romance novel, which was a genre I never read, but was surprisingly good. I was getting to the part where they were finally going to start banging when Evelyn stirred next to me. She was curled up on her side, no doubt used to sleeping alone, before she rolled toward me.

Her eyes fluttered open and a sleepy smile spread across her face. "Hi," she said.

"Morning," I said. "Did you sleep well?"

"Mmm-hmm," she said, stretching. "You?"

I set the book down on my bare chest, laid open so I wouldn't lose my page. "Not bad."

She glanced at the book cover and raised her eyebrows at me. "I think you're a liar, and you're reading that? A romance novel?"

"Good literature isn't defined by such basic definitions, Evelyn," I said. "Plus, they're about to do it, so I'm committed."

She scooted close, the lingering scent of her perfume from the day before following her. She lifted my arm and wrapped it around her shoulder so she could snuggle in. "You know," she said, reaching under the blanket. "I've read that part already. I could show you how it went…" She paused, running her finger down my treasure trail, stopping at the top of my boxers. "…Down."

I groaned at her touch, the way the tips of her fingers ran just beneath the elastic of my boxers, the whole area oddly sensitive. Her hair was wild, and leftover makeup was smudged under her eyes.

"Oh," she said, sitting up. "I probably look a mess. Let me go take a quick shower."

She tried to slip out of bed, but I pulled her back, the book on my chest falling to my side. "Nope. You look perfect."

She glanced at me over her shoulder and shook her head. "Smooth as a motherfucker, as always, and also full of shit."

Okay. There was a little raccoon-eye shit going on, but seeing her so…herself really was beautiful.

"Stay there, handsome," she said. She rolled to the edge of

the bed and got out. Completely naked, and for only me to watch, her hips swayed as she headed into the bathroom.

Leaning back with my hands behind my head, I considered patting my own back. That girl.

All. Mine.

With that, an uneasiness brewed inside my gut, followed by a heated rage that moved throughout my body, when the realization of us being apart for three months hit me. The thought of her gone was one thing, but it was an entirely different thing to imagine who'd be sniffing around her when I wasn't around. My hand pulled at the back of my hair before I roughly ran it across my neck and beard. She captivated everyone around her—it wasn't only how gorgeous she was. She…fucking radiated something that made people take notice. I noticed and saw every other dude take notice whenever we were out.

I was freaking the hell out. First it was her last night and now it was me. It was how adult relationships were supposed to work, I guess. Only one person gets to melt down at a time.

And as quickly as it hit me, it was gone.

I heard the water running in the bathroom and knew I had a choice. Either wait in bed so I could give in to morning sex, which was always so good when you're waking up, but I'd been awake for hours. Hungry. Horny, too, but hungry a tad more. Or I could've gotten up and made breakfast. I shook my head and considered my deviant outlook.

Subsistence first. Dick second.

As I headed into the kitchen and checked out her fridge, I understood why she could eat like a linebacker but still have such a tight body. There was barely anything in it. I was lazy about grocery shopping, too, but my mom was always dropping leftovers or something off. She was like a magical fairy, dropping off meat loaf and lasagna—it being there when I got home.

Pickings were slim, and I was also no Iron Chef, so with something that resembled bread, eggs, and some coffee creamer, I decided to make French toast. If there ever was a doubt in my mind that she was the bachelor female equivalent to me, it became crystal clear after going through her kitchen. She had exactly one small frying pan that appeared to be from biblical times and a spatula that resembled a chewed cat toy.

I made do with what she had, and by the time she came into the kitchen, to my disappointment in a T-shirt and cotton shorts, the first slices of French toast were on the thing that used to resemble a frying pan.

She wrapped her arms around my waist from behind me, pressing a kiss to my back. "Well, look at you."

"Christ, Evelyn. We need to go to Williams-Sonoma or some shit. Where did you get this?" I asked, holding up a plastic fork. "Delilah's play kitchen?"

Her fingers poked at my side, tickling me. "Don't judge my utensils."

I flipped the French toast and turned around to face her. "Oh, that's not the only thing I'm judging. Why the hell do you have Steak-umms in your freezer?"

"Um. Because they're good and sometimes I crave a hundred percent real beef."

"The beef of what? Wait. Don't answer that. I won't even mention the Spam I found that expired somewhere around the year I was born."

"Spam expires?" she asked, confused. "Huh? Who knew?"

"If you weren't so hot, I'd be revolted."

"Speaking of the year you were born, when's your birthday?" she asked.

"August twenty-fourth."

"Shut up!" she said, slapping my arm. "It is not!"

"I will not, and yes, it is. Do you always have to hit? When's yours?"

"August twenty-fourth."

"No way," I said, turning back around to the stove. "There's no way."

"Do you want to see my driver's license?"

"Nineteen ninety-one?"

"Holy shit, Abel."

What were the chances? I was never good at math or statistics, but the probability of my girlfriend and me sharing the same birthday had to be really fucking slim.

I slid the French toast onto a paper plate. I tore the top open of a takeout syrup pack I found in the drawer of her refrigerator and drizzled it across the top of it.

"Come here, beautiful," I said, folding a piece in half because I was sure there wasn't another plastic fork.

I held it out for her, and she took a bite. She nodded her

head in approval. "Yum. Thank you," she said before taking in one more.

I popped the rest of it in my mouth, making a mess of the syrup running out the edge of it. "Shit," I said looking to wipe my hands on something. "Of course, you don't have paper towels or—"

I was cut off by her taking my fingers and bringing them to her mouth. She licked at the tops before sliding her mouth slowly down each of them.

I grabbed the plate. "Get your ass back in bed," I said.

"I can't. I have to get to work."

I glanced at the time on the microwave. She did have to get going, but I was going to bring out my best persuasive eyes to get a few extra minutes.

"You know," I said, raising my eyebrows. "I think your car has a flat tire. It's too bad you'll be an hour or so late until you can get it fixed."

"Or I can take the bus."

She smirked as she licked her own fingers, pretending she wasn't considering it. I could see the wheels turning, but her being her, she wasn't going to give in easily.

I pouted, turning my eyes down to the floor. "Please?" I begged before gradually raising my eyes back up to hers.

She shook her head, her grin turning to laughter. "Forty-five minutes, handsome."

I chased her back to the bedroom and plopped back on the bed. She climbed on top of me, straddling my lap.

"So, I got a question," I said.

"And I have an answer."

"This...thing," I said, waving my finger between us. "We aren't seeing other people. You're mine, right?"

She smiled. "Yeah. I'm yours."

"And vice versa?"

"For sure. You're my guy."

"So, with you away for three months, we won't be seeing anyone else then, either, right?"

She squirmed and pulled back slightly, her need for space becoming apparent again. I wanted to grab her, tell her, *Don't move. Don't try to put distance here because in a couple of months we'll have a thousand miles separating us.*

"What do you want to do?" she asked. "Three months is a long time. In fact, we'd be only dating the same amount of time when I leave for Charleston."

This entire dialogue made me further concerned. I knew what I wanted, but she wasn't putting out there what she did. If this was all or nothing, I'd need to hear that from her.

I brushed a hair off her forehead, placing it next to her face. "I asked you first, beautiful."

She looked into my eyes with strong intent. What she needed in physical space was being replaced with the desire to make herself verbally clear. "Can you be faithful?" she asked.

"Can you?"

Her stare turned hard and I wondered if she was angry. She shouldn't have been. This was covered territory. Maybe it wasn't politically correct to put us on equal playing fields, but at least it was honest.

When a smile lifted from her lips, and her glare softened,

I assumed she wasn't mad. We were going to be champion debaters. The more she grinned, the more my ability to hold my ground crumbled.

She had me.

She knew it.

"Yes, I can," I said, holding out my pinkie finger to her.

She crossed her pinkie with mine. "Me, too. Promise."

"Promise."

CHAPTER FIFTEEN

EVELYN—

The heat began creeping in, one day more than the next in the month of May, until all at once we were drowning in it. It was how Chicago summers went. This one was no different.

June.

July.

August.

Each brought their game, showing the world the blazing sun, and steamy nights were made for the most beautiful city in the world. Like a slow-motion run caught in between two worlds, my life stretched between sun and moon.

It was that heat, though. It brought the fire. The fire of earth and the one that circled Abel and me. It breathed into us, and with the breeze of every passing day, the flames fanned out more. The fear of getting burned didn't distract us. No. It only invited us closer.

The dread of me leaving clouded moments, but it wasn't something we discussed. It was like an approaching storm.

We knew it was there and knew it was coming. We just didn't know how bad it would be.

Wedding season was in full swing, and work was crazy busy. Weekdays were spent calming nervous brides, and weekends were spent running around, making sure that every detail was executed perfectly. My career was under the microscope while my personal life was in such a high gear that most days I ran on adrenaline. It wasn't a terrible place to be.

I also couldn't keep myself away from Abel for more than a day and vice versa. The night before our birthday, a Saturday evening wedding partied until well past one a.m. My mind was exhausted, but my heart and body needed my fix.

"Hey there, Evelyn," Tyler said, unhooking the velvet rope and opening the path inside to WET. "Nightcap?"

"Yes. Desperately. I had a flower girl puke on the bride's shoes during pre-ceremony pictures and had to run around the North Side looking for new but the exact same style of Jimmy Choos."

"Well, your guy is here, and I'm sure he'll hook you right up."

"Thanks, Tyler."

Entering the darkened space, the dwindling crowd finishing their last-call drinks, my eyes scanned the bar, looking for Abel. He was at the far end, leaned across the bar, talking with a couple. His smile, his animated voice, made every person he was near feel special. From far away, I could tell they were completely taken with him.

My aching feet walked me toward him at the same moment his head turned to see me. He straightened his body, winked, and smiled at me. Dimples so very deep. It didn't matter how many times I'd seen it. My heart still reacted the same—

"Hey, beautiful," he said as I approached the bar. "Come here."

He leaned over and kissed me across the bar. "I missed you," he mumbled against my lips.

"Same. It's why I'm here and also I need an Abel Manhattan."

"You got it."

"Can I steal you for just one second, though, first?"

His eyebrows lifted, mischief written all over his face. "Bathroom romp?" he asked.

"Nope," I said. I ran my finger down the length of the bar and wiggled my finger at him to follow me.

We met at the end of the bar where his hand slipped around my waist, bringing me close to him. He kissed the top of my head, lingering and sighing as he guided us into the dimly lit hallway.

"We can go in here for a minute," he said, pushing open a door. "Marshall's office, but he won't care."

He stepped aside as I entered, whistling as I passed him. "Hell, beautiful. That skirt. Your ass."

"Close the door," I said.

"You know I'm always down, and I have to admit there's something taboo about doing it in my boss's office, but—"

"Shut up, and close the door."

He showed his hands up to me, giving in to my demand.

After he shut it, he looked at me over his shoulder. "Should I lock it?"

"Yes."

The lock clicked, and before he could turn back around, I lifted the admired skirt. His eyes took a moment to narrow in on my panties, to what was written on them.

"A little something for my favorite bartender," I said.

His feet dragged against the worn carpet as he rubbed his hand over his beard. "Goddamn."

My panties were sporting a martini glass down the middle, with the words "I Could Use a Stiff One" printed above it. After I'd come across them in a catalog dedicated for bachelorettes, I knew they were perfect for my man. While not made for a day of running around or comfort, I snuck them in my purse and changed before I left.

He ran his fingers across the silver, embroidered letters, sliding them around just so they rubbed against my clit. His head lowered as his size surrounded me. It drove me wild when he commanded and encompassed my body. It was strong and man and mine all rolled into one.

"You bought these for me?" he asked.

I nodded, unable to form words the way his fingers, the palm of his hand, was working me over. His breath was sweet and warm as he rested his lips close to my ear. "I'm going to make you come so fucking hard for me in these."

A loud pounding broke the moment. "You two better not be fucking in my office! Payroll is all over the desk, and I don't want it covered in your spunk, Abel."

"Soon," he whispered. "I'll also give you the stiff one you

really want later. Right now, I'll make you a stiff cocktail."

After a quick kiss and a skirt readjustment, he grabbed my hand to leave. Once he unlocked the door, it flew open from the opposite side. Marshall's face was red with anger, his arms folded tightly against his chest.

"No offense with what I'm about to say, Evelyn," Marshall said. "But hell, Abel. If you don't go grab those bottles of gin I asked to you to get, I'll castrate you myself and you won't be able to fuck anyone ever again." He paused and seemed to regroup. "Sorry again, Evelyn."

"I'm sorry for stealing your office to show my boyfriend my underwear," I said.

"Be right back," Abel said, rushing out. "On it, boss."

Marshall jerked his head to the side. "Come on. I make any cocktail better than him," Marshall said.

I followed him back down the hallway, a few of the servers saying "hello" to me as they rushed back and forth. A well-dressed twentysomething, who looked like he was Brooks Brothers fresh, was waiting outside the bathroom. As I passed him, I recognized him from somewhere, but couldn't recall where.

"Evelyn, right?" he said, placing his hand lightly on my arm to stop me.

"Yeah?"

"I'll have it all ready for you," Marshall said, moving ahead.

"Thanks," I replied before turning my attentions to Mr. Brothers. "I apologize. It's been a long day, and I absolutely recognize you, but can't place you."

"I'd imagine you see a lot of faces at weddings," he said with a smirk.

He removed his hand from me and stepped back against the wall where he leaned up against it. Although it wasn't blatant, the back walk certainly gave him the opportunity to quickly look me over.

"I certainly do, so help a girl out?" I asked.

He extended his hand out to shake mine. "Michael. I was the best man at the Hobbs-Billings wedding last November."

"Right! Yes. You helped me get the drunk uncle out of the bathroom. Thanks again for that by the way," I said.

He gave a bow, complimenting himself and perhaps using his good looks to appear noble. "I think it was in the job description," he said.

His gaze became more aggressive, focusing on my chest while licking his lips, as he pushed himself forward. A slow swagger, a hand up above my head against the wall, and a head dip followed. He was all up in my space. "What brings you out tonight?"

"My—"

"Her fucking boyfriend, dickhead," Abel said from the darkness at the end of the hall. His feet pounded against the carpet as he approached us, a couple bottles of gin in each hand.

"No problem, dude," Michael said, lifting his palms to him. "Just recognized her from a wedding we were at together."

Abel stepped up close to him, towering above him by several inches. "I could see you sizing her up from forty feet away before inviting yourself into her space," he said.

Michael considered his words and obviously had a death wish. "I heard you. Now maybe you should go back to pouring the champagne for me and friends."

"All right," I said, grabbing Abel's arm. "Come on."

"Hold on a second, beautiful."

Abel shook his head and chuckled while glaring at Michael. "You ever look at my girl like that again or get too close to her, I'll be the one popping a bottle as I toast to how I beat the fuck out of you."

I was simultaneously scared of the rage that emerged from Abel and completely turned on with his alpha male dominance. "Thank you," I said. I tugged his arm again. "Come on. You owe me a drink. And Michael? You didn't stand a chance anyway."

I moved behind Abel and nudged him forward, but his stare never left Michael.

"It's about time," Marshall said as I slid into a bar chair across from him. "Did you guys have to go for round two already?"

Abel mumbled under his breath as he stomped back and forth along the length of the bar while banging the bottles down. He seemed sure he wasn't going to break those bottles, but I wasn't. I'd never seen him get so angry.

"Shit," Abel said. "We need ice, too. I'll be right back."

He stomped away in a huff as Marshall slid my Manhattan across to me. "Hey," he said. "Did he have trouble getting it up back there? Because the best thing to do in those situations, not that I would know but I've heard, is to ignore it.

He probably already feels like shit. I mean, our dicks are like our Holy Grail, all special powers and shit. Anything to do with that area and we're screwed. Plus, we don't want you girls to think it's you because face it you're really hot and—"

I patted his hand to shut him up. "No. There are no problems, like ever, in that area. And if you care anything about your penis or any other part of your body, don't let Abel hear you call me hot. He nearly tore a guy's head off back there and shoved it down his throat for talking too close to me."

"Pfft," he snorted. "I ain't afraid of him, but that does explain his reaction. He's crazy about you, and shit like that makes us guys crazy all over."

"What do you mean?" I asked, taking a sip from my drink. "Wait. Is this Russell's Reserve?"

"Wow," he said, nodding. "Impressive. A girl who knows her whiskey. I can see why Abel is so taken, and I mean that in a I'm-not-trying-to-pick-up-my-buddy's-girl kind of way."

"Don't tell him, but yours is better," I said, reaching for my purse. "How much do I owe you?"

Marshall curled his lip slightly as he shook his head. "Get out of here with that."

I never wanted to appear like I was taking advantage, so no matter if it was Marshall or anyone else, I'd hide some cash under my napkin, only to be found after I was gone. Abel appeared again, a bag of ice lifted onto his shoulder that he slammed down next to the well. "What are you two talking about all cozy-like?"

"Abel," I said warningly. "Lock it up, handsome. You're being cranky."

"I'm *not* cranky, but every time I turn around you're talking to another dude."

"Marshall isn't a dude," I said.

"Well, I am," Marshall said. "But. Yeah."

"And furthermore," I said. "Seriously. Lock it up."

Abel spun around and crossed his arms in front of him. "And by the way Marshall. Where the hell are the barbacks to do this shit?"

"I told you," Marshall said, raising his voice. "Two have the stomach flu, and one didn't show up. Deal with it."

Marshall raised his eyebrows to me before walking right past Abel. Me? I took a long sip from my cocktail, contemplating between leaving or waiting until he was done in an hour to yell at him properly. Putting him in his place and causing a scene wasn't my style—in fact, I hated couples that fought in public. However, he took a severe misstep and needed to be put in his place.

"Want a ride home?" I asked. "Or I'll just talk to you tomorrow?"

He wiped his hands on a towel before taking notice of a customer at the other end of the bar. "You drinking more?" he questioned.

"No. I'm not getting wasted and offering to drive you home."

"Do you mind?"

"I wouldn't have offered if I did, but if you're going to keep on not showing your dimples, I might reconsider."

He appeased me by flashing a quick smile before patting my hand and heading over to help the waiting customer. I sat back and watched him, how his hands moved to make a cocktail, how his smile flirted between warm and dazzling. He took everything that was on his mind and removed it to do his job. I loved watching him.

The bar slowly dwindled down, and when the doors were locked for the night, I hung back while they finished up their work. By the time Abel and I left, it was close to two a.m., but the heat from the summer's day still rose off the pavement. Once we were in the privacy of my car, I turned to face him.

"That," I said, pointing my finger toward WET, "was bullshit. What the hell is wrong with you?"

"What?" he asked, his voice going up an octave.

"Don't give me that. You all but decapitated that dude Michael and then went off on Marshall. Why?"

He ran his hands through his hair roughly before bringing them down across his beard. "I'm sorry, beautiful. I...don't even know what happened to me tonight."

"I do. You acted like a jealous asshole, and while I have no problem with you being all controlling in bed, I'm not cool with it anywhere outside of there."

"I know."

"Do you?"

"Yes. It was a dickhead move to call out Marshall like that."

"And?"

"And what?"

"The dude in the hallway. He was the best man in one of my client's weddings. It didn't look good, and it's bad for business. Bridget will flip her shit if she finds out."

"Wait. That's what you're mad about?"

"That's part of it and what started everything."

"Well, I'm not sorry about that part. That jerk was practically humping your leg, and girls don't see it like guys do."

"Do you think we're idiots? That I'm an idiot? Of course we know. We know exactly what you're doing. We also know how to handle it."

"But you weren't handling it. You were…letting…him."

"Letting him what? You're being ridiculous, and if you don't stop, you'll be spending our birthday alone."

He crossed his arms and started pouting all over again. It was infuriating and endearing all at the same time. While I knew he thought it was coming from a righteous place—the need to want to take care of me—he wasn't understanding that I didn't need to be taken care of.

"Abel," I said slowly in an attempt to calm my nerves. "I think maybe this was something we never covered. I don't need to be taken care of. I don't need to be saved. I don't need anyone getting jealous because I'm only talking to another guy."

"Okay," he whispered. "Sorry."

I removed his hand from his face, which he was rubbing at aggressively, and placed my hand there instead. "Look at me," I said. "Do you trust me?"

"Yes."

"You're my guy and I don't want anyone else."

He began to relax against my touch as his eyes shifted across mine.

Looking.

Searching.

I knew what he was doing. I'd done it so many times without him even knowing it. He was seeking the truth. He was trying to make sure he could trust me. I didn't even have to tell him that. I just knew he'd know.

"Trust me," I said. "I'm working on it, too."

He leaned across our seats and kissed me, lingering longer than normal. "I want to do everything better for you," he mumbled against my lips.

An ache shot through my chest, burning my heart so much so I lost my breath for a moment. There had been many men, a lot of sex and more intimate moments than I cared to recall, but no one had ever made me feel so whole. Completely Evelyn. He was seeing all of me, and I was letting him.

"Let's get you home, handsome," I said, starting my car and pulling it out of gear.

He rested his hand on my bare knee as I drove, dancing his fingers across the top. "Things go well earlier?"

"Yeah," I said with a sigh. "Same ol'. Same ol'."

"You look tired," he said.

I shrugged. "My brain is but I'm wired everywhere else. Wedding season, leaving for Charleston soon and all the work there has me so tense everywhere."

The streets were nearly empty except for cab drivers and others heading home from the bars. Abel's hand inched from my knee up between my thighs, his fingers lightly brushing over my panties.

"What are you doing there, mister?" I asked.

"Remembering you wore those for me," he said. "Plus, I want to try and take some of that tension away I feel a little bit responsible for."

The light turned red, and I stopped, but his fingers didn't. "Can you, um, wait until you get me home before…"

His dimples went deep as he scooted closer to me. "Don't worry, beautiful. I won't let you come yet. Promise."

It all happened so fast. The light turned green and I gunned it, my tires screeching against the pavement at the same moment as Abel ducked his head into my lap.

In one swift move he pulled my underwear to the side, and his mouth…his tongue…was on me. His head was banging into my steering wheel, and in an attempt to balance my boyfriend giving me road head and driving, I fumbled with the level until it was out of his way.

One hand on the steering wheel and the other in his hair as my body grooved against his mouth. I secretly hoped for a red light or somewhere I could pull over, but we were so close to his building.

"God, Abel," I moaned. "You're going to break your promise."

He lifted his head for moment. "Oh no, I'm fucking not."

He dipped back down and, with even more rapid aggression, worked me *all* over as my foot on the accelerator pressed harder. I turned into the underground parking garage and sped down the ramp. I was so close to coming as I pulled into a parking spot and threw the gear into park.

"Right there," I panted. "Yes."

His head popped up and he smirked at me as he wiped his mouth. "Not yet, beautiful."

I pouted. "That's mean. Why would you do that?"

"Because I'm going to take you to my bed and fucking feast on you. I want my lips, my tongue, and my dick all over you so you won't even be near another guy without him knowing you belong to me."

He exited the car, leaving me shocked and my jaw hanging open. It took me a few moments, but I came to and rearranged my undies back into place.

Abel popped his head back in from the opened passenger side door. "You all right there?" he asked with a wink.

He shut the door and leaned up against it, giving me the perfect view of his ass. His loud chuckling also didn't escape my attention.

Cocky motherfucker.

I exited my side, the smell of car oil and the fireworks that had been set off earlier at Navy Pier lingering in the air. There was no else around. With one wave of my finger, Abel followed me across the dark garage. As we waited for the elevator he leaned into me to kiss my neck, but I jerked back.

"Nope," I said. "It's your turn to wait now."

The elevator door opened, and as we stepped in, Abel pushed me forward up against the back of it. "Is that so?" he asked, stretching his arms up above my head.

The door closed and began ascending, but Abel slammed his hand on the control panel. We jerked to a stop as the tip of Abel's teeth gingerly sunk into my neck. "I'm planning on finishing what I started. Right here," he said.

He sunk to his knees, and there was no doubt he wanted to keep his word.

* * *

I was glad we kissed and made up all night long because I would've felt guilty for sleeping in past ten a.m. His side of the bed was empty, and when I ran my hand across the sheets, it was cool. He'd been up for a while. I stretched my arms above my head, yawning loudly.

"You awake finally, sleepyhead?" Abel shouted from the other room.

"Yes. And how are you such an earlier riser when you're used to sleeping until noon?"

"Because I had an agenda this morning," he said, entering the room holding a plate in front of him.

Two large cupcakes, swirled with frosting and sprinkles on top, sat on top of the plate. Two birthday candles flickered from the middle of each of them as he cautiously crossed the room before sitting on the edge of the bed next to me.

"Happy Birthday, beautiful," he said, holding the plate out to me.

It was a small thing, but it was one of the most thoughtful gestures any man had ever done for me. So many thought it was about flowers and expensive jewelry to get us excited, but it was always the subtle things. He smiled, his hair still messy and his glasses were on, making him look so unbelievably sexy.

"Happy Birthday, handsome. This is…amazing," I said,

looking at the cupcakes. "Should we blow them out together?"

"Count of three?"

"Wait. Which one is mine?" I asked.

"You can pick. This one," he said, pointing to the cupcake
with the yellow candle. "Is vanilla birthday cake flavored
with buttercream frosting. The other one is chocolate with
peanut butter swirls and a milk chocolate ganache."

"Oh," I groaned. "Chocolate peanut butter. You sure do
know the way to my heart."

"I do my best," he said with a wink. "Are you ready?"

I nodded, and he counted down as I thought of a wish.

One...

Two...

Three...

We blew our candles out at the same time, our wishes released into the air for the universe to place. I leaned over,
kissing him as a thank-you for his thoughtfulness.

"Can we eat them now?" I asked.

"Fuck yes. It's our birthday. Cupcakes for breakfast are a
given," he said, picking off the candles.

"Where did you get these so early?" I asked.

"Well, it isn't exactly early anymore, but since I didn't
know when you'd get up, I snuck out a few hours ago to go
to one of those cupcake ATM thingies."

"You did?" I asked, flipping my bottom lip into a pout.
"So sweet, Abel."

He leaned in and kissed my forehead. "That was the plan,
get you all full of the sweet."

He set them to the side before peeling away at the liners on each of the cupcakes. He picked up mine, and I frowned, assuming he was going to steal mine.

He held it in his large hand, bringing it close to my mouth. "You first," he said.

I bit into the side, taking in the most delicious mixture of chocolate and peanut butter my mouth had ever known so early in the day. It was his turn, so I picked up the vanilla cupcake and repeated the same motions.

We nodded to each other as we swallowed our bites before I remembered I had something for him.

"Hang tight right here," I said, swinging my legs out from under the covers. "I have to get something from my purse."

I got up from my bed, my naked body on display for him as I searched around for my undies and something to throw on.

"No need to put anything on," he said, taking another bite of his cupcake. "I'm only going to have you naked again so we can ride out our sugar high."

I flipped my hair out of my face to look at him as I was still bent over. He raised his brows, and I decided I'd let him have that one. He did surprise me with cupcakes. What was a little morning romp for the birthday boy going to hurt?

I stood and headed out of the room to grab my purse. As I walked about his apartment in the buff, I was reminded of how comfortable I'd become around him. While confident in my body, an open view was something I thought most women had issue with. It wasn't only with nakedness, though. Smeared makeup and dirty hair would've had me running for the shower, fearful of him seeing me less than perfect in the morning. If he wanted me then, called me beautiful with bedhead and bad breath, I knew he wanted me at all times.

I pulled the small gift bag from my purse and returned to the bedroom to find Abel staring at his cell phone, his face frowning.

"What's wrong?" I asked.

His head snapped to me, his face pale. I moved toward the bed, worried, because I'd never seen him with such an expression.

"Abel?"

His eyes searched around my face, and after a few moments, he shook his head. "Sorry, I was a—" He paused, blinking his eyes and clearing his throat. He tossed the phone back onto the nightstand. "Nothing. It was nothing."

"Are you sure? You looked like you saw a ghost."

"I'm sure. Now why aren't you back in bed with me yet?"

Whatever it was, it was gone now. I wanted to press a bit more, but it was our birthdays and I didn't want a petty debate over nothing to get in the way of that.

The shirt he was wearing was off, and he was under the top sheet in bed. It was folded down and over at the end of his treasure trail, his toned lower ab muscles creating a V that reached beneath the covers.

"What do you have there?" he asked as I slid back into bed next to him.

I set the bag on his chest. "It's your birthday, isn't it?"

"It is and it's yours as well. Look underneath your pillow."

I sat up and flipped the pillow over. Several strands of red ribbon were delicately wrapped and secured with a bow around a vintage-looking book. The worn edges, the color, which appeared to have once been dark green or blue, was now discolored to a muted tone. A gold leaf pattern, something resembling feathers, while also worn decorated the cover. The intertwining ribbons blocked the book title from me identifying what it was.

I picked it up and laid it on my lap, looking over at Abel. His eyes crinkled together in nervousness, and I had to laugh. "What's with the face? I don't even know what it is yet and I love it already."

He shrugged. "Go ahead and find out then."

I gently tugged at the ribbons and pulled them away, the title *Pride and Prejudice* in the same gold letters appeared.

"Oh my God," I said, covering my mouth. "Are you serious?"

I choked back tears as his hand palmed the side of my face. "Do you like it? It's not a real first edition, but it is from the late 1800s."

My fingers ran across the front as a few tears got out. "This is literally the best gift I've ever gotten," I said, turning to him. "Thank you isn't strong enough."

His hand still on my cheek brushed away the tears with his thumb. "Then you're welcome."

"Please open yours so I don't ruin the moment by freaking out about how expensive this probably was and how you shouldn't have and all that other bullshit."

I watched him lift the small glass bottle from the bag,

turning it back and forth in his hand, trying to figure out what exactly it was. "Okay, don't think I'm a dick, but it's one of two things. It's either a really expensive shot of tequila or unicorn piss. Either way, I'm stoked."

"Ha-ha. Take the top off and smell it."

He untwisted the cork top and, while looking at me, brought it to his nose. "Clue me in, beautiful."

"So, you know how I made my own perfume? No one else has this scent. Well, I made one for you."

He grinned and let out a strong laugh. His hand brushed up and down his beard as he inhaled it again.

"It's dumb, right?" I asked. "I didn't know what else to do, so I mixed this because it reminded me of you. It has cedar and sandalwood with this light coffee extract, but to balance it out, I added in some citrus with the tiniest hint of tobacco to make it super sexy. Oh, and—"

His mouth on mine cut off my babbling while his lips still tasted like sugar. "You made this for me?" he mumbled against my lips.

"Yes."

"And no one else has it?" he asked, moving from my lips and dragging kisses down my jaw to my neck.

"Nope."

He pulled away and stared into my eyes. "I didn't even make a wish when I blew out the candle because *you* are everything. You are everything I would've wished for."

* * *

We'd talked about what to do on our birthday for a while and had planned a beach day, dinner, and drinks with Aaron and Callie. However, our plans changed. We had sex and napped through most of the day, watching a movie in between. A swanky dinner was replaced by takeout from our favorite Thai place. There was no choice but to keep our plans to meet Aaron and Callie at a bar on top of the roof of one of Chicago's ritziest hotels.

They were waiting for us by the host stand when we arrived fashionably late.

"Late enough?" Callie asked with a joking glare.

Or what Callie would call just plain late.

"You're lucky it's your birthdays," she said, pulling me into a hug.

After a round of hugs and "Happy Birthdays" all around, we followed the hostess through the crowd across the breezy rooftop bar. We were brought to a cozy booth in the back corner, dark wood benches with matching railings surrounding us.

"I have to go to the ladies' room," I said before sitting.

"Actually," Aaron said. "So do I. You know, with all that waiting around, it will make anyone have to go."

"What? Go to the ladies' room?" Abel asked Aaron.

"Ha-ha. Grow up."

"You want me to get you something?" Callie asked Aaron.

"Yeah. The usual."

"Usual for you, too, beautiful?"

The subtlety of knowing my drink choice was probably overlooked by the others, but it spoke volumes to me. Callie and Aaron were in that comfortable, daily spot in their relationship and ordering a drink was the norm. To imagine Abel and I were nearing a point where we knew something so basic made our thing much more solid.

"Yeah. Thanks, handsome," I said, leaning down to kiss him.

"Oh God," Callie snorted. "You two make me sick."

"Like we both haven't had to sit through hours of you two and your gross love shit."

Aaron's hand rubbed Callie's back. "We're still into all that gross love shit."

He kissed her on the cheek before I shook my head and turned to head toward the bathroom following Aaron. Weaving our way through the crowded bar, Aaron would gently tap on a shoulder to move, and when one very large dude didn't want to, Aaron grabbed my hand while checking the dude out of the way.

"What the fuck?" Big Dude said. "You made me spill my drink."

He stepped up to Aaron, and I got nervous. The Matthews temper was nothing to mess around with as I've learned, but it was rare to see it out of Aaron.

Aaron leaned into him, shouting in his ear over the music. "I'll get you another drink and a round for your friends here, but you move out of the way when a lady is trying to get past."

I didn't know how he did it. His tone, his delivery was smooth as melted chocolate, and the guy ate it right up. A slap on Aaron's back as a thank-you, and we continued on with Aaron holding my hand until we made it through.

When we made it to the hallway connecting to the restrooms, I breathed a relieved sigh. "Risky, Aaron, but I'm impressed."

He shrugged. "You're like a sister to me now. I don't want anyone to mess with you."

"That's sweet. Thank you."

"And that goes for my brother, too," he said, his eyebrows furrowed tightly. "I've never seen either of you happier, and it seems to be going well. I'm happy about that. And it goes without saying that I'd lay my life down for Abel."

"I know that."

"Just...he missteps at times, and you need to be prepared for that."

"What does that even mean?"

"Be careful."

"I want to tell you I am being careful, but I'm not. I'm being so reckless with my feelings and everything with him that I can't see straight sometimes, but what is the alternative?"

"I don't want you, either of you, to get hurt."

"You know you can't control that."

"I know," he said, sighing. "You're right. I can't control it. I just care about you both. His track record—"

"I'm in love with him, Aaron."

He tilted his head to the side, and with a moment's delay, a small grin emerged. "You are?"

"Yes. And that's the first time I've said it out loud. He doesn't know. Hell, Callie doesn't even. I maybe didn't even know until this moment, but I am."

"I won't say anything. I promise."

"And I get where you're coming from. I hear it from you, Callie, your dad, and even Abel. He never feels like he could measure up."

"I know he internalizes a lot of shit. My dad and I joke, but there is an element of truth. He needs to get his feet firmly planted, and I know he's getting there, Ev. I see it. It's why I'm going into business with him. I'm proud he's taking it on because I think, at this point in his life, he's finally ready."

No one knew Abel better than Aaron. I had always assumed, but now I was certain. Abel was so confident on the exterior, but I saw more than that. There was a drive, a desire, behind his doubtful interior. It warmed me to know Aaron was starting to see that, too.

"I think so, too, and I know it means a lot to him. Okay," I said. "Now if you'll excuse me, I have my own business to take care of."

We both went in our respective bathrooms, and when I came out, he was waiting for me. As we approached the table, I could hear Callie dirt dishing to Abel.

"And that is why she can't or, rather, *shouldn't* drink tequila," Callie said.

"Are you kidding me, Cal?" I asked, sliding into the booth next to Abel. "I was gone forty-seven seconds and you had time for the tequila story? That was, like, over two years ago, and I stand by my story that *that* tequila was tainted or something."

"As a professional mixologist, the tainted tequila problem

in Chicago is out of control," Abel said, stifling a laugh.

"All right. All right," Aaron said, lifting his Scotch. "Can we drop the tequila so we can toast? Happy birthday to the double twenty-fives."

We joined our glasses together, a mix of "cheers" and splashing booze from overfilled glasses rained over us.

CHAPTER SIXTEEN

ABEL—

Seriously?" she asked as I pulled up to the restaurant.

It was our last night together, and I had a special evening planned. Judging by her confused look, she wasn't feeling it.

"What? I thought you enjoyed some beef from time to time?" I asked, putting the car in park.

"It's Carson's Ribs. *Ribs.*"

"Yeah? And?" I asked, smiling. The valet came to my side and impatiently tapped his fingers against his leather coat. "Ready?"

"Ribs are pork, Abel," she said.

"No they're not. They're beef."

"They can be but these," she said, pressing her finger against the passenger window and leaving a mark, "are pork."

"You afraid of getting a little messy?"

"I'm never afraid to get messy. You should know that by now."

"We can go somewhere else," I said. "You know, if you

aren't game for the whole maybe-pork-maybe-beef-but-not-afraid-of-getting-messy thing."

She rolled her eyes and swung the car door open, placing her high heel on the wet pavement. "I'm game for anything."

They were pork, and while I wasn't satisfied by this development until verified by two different waiters and one of the chefs, it didn't hamper the rest of dinner. We feasted on warm corn bread, loaded baked potatoes, and barbecue baby back ribs. Dessert was key lime pie, which we were sharing, when she tapped my hand with her fork.

"In light of our last night together for a while, tell me something that no one knows, like something you'd be embarrassed for people to find out."

"Hmm," I said, thinking while scraping some graham cracker crumbs onto my fork. "I don't know. I've left myself a pretty open book for you."

"Everyone has something. Like, what is the thing you do when no one else is around? Me? I like to listen to and sing ABBA and Dolly Parton songs. I'll blast it and dance around my apartment, pretending I'm on *Star Search*. Your turn?"

I scooped up a piece of pie. "Same."

She smacked my arm. "Don't be a dick. I just admitted to something mortifying."

"Okay," I said, pulling her hand into mine. "I've been fiddling with a book, writing one, for three years."

She set her fork down. "What? Are you serious?" she asked, her eyes wide.

"I know it's silly, but it's one of those things I've always liked to do, even when I was little. It started off as a final year project in college, and I don't know. It kind of stuck with me. I can't even explain the feeling I get when I'm doing it or what it feels like when I'm not. I think it's something I have to do with some regularity, in some form, or I'm not me. I know it probably doesn't make a lot of sense, and I wasn't specifically trying to hide it from you, but I don't know. It's my thing."

Her expression was hard to read, even after knowing her so well. She appeared to be stuck somewhere between confused and humored. I shifted in my seat and glanced around the room to avoid whatever it was she was thinking.

She squeezed my hand. "Handsome, you were supposed to tell me something embarrassing. You writing a book is spectacular."

"Well, you said something that no one else knew and that's it. It's a little embarrassing because I'm not very good at it, but—"

"Look at me, Abel," she said, interrupting me. "This is amazing. You have a passion. Do you know how special that is?"

I shrugged. "It is, but it's nothing worth bragging about."

"I don't think you get to be the one to say that, but I want you to promise me something when I'm gone."

"What's that?"

"Use the time that I'm away, the time you'd been spending with me, and put it into your writing."

"Why?"

"Because your expression changed and your words sounded different just by talking about it. There's obviously something there, and I want you to dig further in because I don't think anyone has ever told you how incredible you are."

"You've never read anything of mine. You didn't even know until this moment. How can you say that?"

"I don't have to read shit to know *you* are amazing and to know I believe in you."

I almost took my fork and stuck it right in my heart because I was done. There were so many times I didn't think what Evelyn and I had could get better, but then she'd say something like this, and my fucking soul would go up in flames. It was heat and devotion and it warmed my entire body. It was the shit song lyrics were about and sappy greeting card commercials. Hell. If I could buy the world a Coke in those moments I would because everyone on the planet should know this kind of rush.

I stood up only to lean back down and kiss her. "I promise," I said, my lips almost touching hers.

She gave me so much and I was unsure how much I was giving in return. Promises between us were sometimes the only thing I could do to make sure she knew what she meant to me. It seemed juvenile in theory, but keeping my word was all I was sure of.

I'd mentioned earlier I wanted to take her to see a play after dinner so leaving Carson's full and slightly buzzed was a nice transition to the next part of the night. The wind had picked up slightly, blowing her blond hair around her face and the scent of her perfume in the air. She looked like she always did tonight, but there was something different.

"What are you staring at?" she asked.

We were stopped in front of an old cement building, with a ticket booth, and a cracked window. I hadn't realized I was staring.

"I'm going to miss you," I blurted out.

A smile crept across her face as she pushed her hair out of her face. "Well, aren't you a sugar?"

She stepped close and stood on her tiptoes to kiss me on the lips. My thumb brushed against her cheek while my mind knew to commit to memory the touch of her smooth skin.

"I'll miss you, too," she said, grinning against my lips.

I buried my head in her neck, breathing and drinking her in. "And that fucking perfume, too. You're going to need to leave something of yours at my place when you leave."

"Aww," she said. "I definitely will, especially because I have a very strong sense of what it does to you."

"You do, do you?"

"Mm-hmm," she said, nuzzling my own neck. "A... reaction...to scent is a very normal...response."

With the subtlety only a woman could possess, she covertly ran her fingers down the seam of my jeans zipper.

"Shit, beautiful," I hissed in her ear. "I've got jeans on. You know it gets all tight in there if you get me hard."

"Sorry I'm not sorry."

Was there a polite way to say her perfume gave me an instant blood-to-my-dick type response that made me wonder what parts of her body that perfume was applied to? Back of the ears, neck, between breasts, navel…the possibilities were endless. My mind went to all those places on her body, her skin, nakedness, my fingers running across…

"You ready to move on?" she asked, interrupting my thoughts. "Or do you need another minute to get your boner under control?"

Was she fucking kidding me?

"Close your mouth," she laughed. She patted my chest. "Nothing to be embarrassed about."

"Who says boner anymore?"

"I do. This it?" she said, pointing to the building.

It didn't look like much of a theater, but then again it was Chicago. Shit was old here. Dilapidated on the outside usually meant it was full of amazing history and architecture on the inside.

"Yeah, it is. Let me go get the tickets," I said, walking to the booth, standing at the end of a line three people deep.

"This is the Nickerson Theater right?" I asked when I reached the front.

"Yeah, that's it," said the guy behind the glass. "You're here for Cannibal Cheerleaders on Crack?"

"Yeah. Two tickets, please." I mean, it was a weird name, but Marshall said, when I had asked him for ideas on something different to do after dinner, this was the perfect spot. A humorous satire based in an apocalyptic world where no taboo is off limits. Money was exchanged and he slid the tickets across to me. "Enjoy," my new friend said. "Sit near the front. Best place to be."

"Cool. Thanks."

As we stepped inside, Evelyn tumbled a bit, and I grabbed her arm to prevent her from falling.

"Shit," she whispered. She looked down at the floor. "The carpet is all torn up. No wonder."

"Well, that's a liability. You okay?"

"Yeah. I'm fine. I'm going to run to the ladies' room, okay?"

"No problem. I think it's over there," I said, pointing to the far corner with a dimly lighted, retro RESTROOM sign.

"I'll be right back."

I watched her walk away, hoping she wouldn't turn around to see me staring again, but I couldn't help it. The last few months had gone by so damn fast with one day running into the next. I didn't even have time to think before some papers were waved in front of my face.

"Here," said a burly guy with gray hair and a beard. He shoved a couple programs at me and walked away.

"Friendly bunch," I said under my breath.

While she was in the bathroom, I took the time to take in my surroundings. The carpet was, in fact, ripped in several places, and the walls didn't have much of the architectural flair that I thought I might see. In fact, the walls were covered with a stucco, popcorn-like surface, some of it crumbling in certain areas. The carpet underneath had a good dusting of it, which showed that either the building was falling apart as I stood there, or it hadn't been vacuumed in a long time.

I shrugged. Everything wasn't the Civic Opera House. I was sure the performance would be great.

I glanced at the front of the program: a production of *Cannibal Cheerleaders on Crack*.

Well. That was a hell of a name. It was obviously very satirical, but now I was questioning how much. The people waiting to get in all looked like a normal bunch.

Opening the program, I found it read like any other I'd seen, except for one spot at the bottom that read:

If you have any concerns with the clothes you are wearing getting stained, or if projectile liquids freak you out, we suggest moving farther from the first four rows.

What the fuck did that mean? Clearly it had to be a joke because—

"Want to go sit?" Evelyn said, stepping up next to me and sliding her hand into mine.

"Yeah, sure."

I looked down at the tickets and noticed there was no seat numbers or rows. Just a short note about general admission and no flash photography.

"What the fuck?" I whispered, noticing we'd be sitting on milk crates instead of chairs.

"Oh," Evelyn said. "Well, this seems…cozy. Where do you think we should sit?"

"I'm not making you sit on a milk crate for a show that has a projectile liquid warning in the program."

She laughed, squeezing my hand. "You're not making me do anything. Plus, I'm sure they're just being ironic. Come on."

With that smile, how could I refuse? I guided her to our seats, third-row front milk crates.

"Cozy," she said, leaning into me. Her hand rested on my knee, and I noticed her nails had a fresh coat of burgundy polish on them. She always had some sort of red on her nails, and I didn't think it questioned my masculinity at all to notice it. It was one of those things I noticed and thought was insanely sexy, especially when her hand, those painted fingers, were wrapped around my cock.

My body tensed when I realized she probably had them done earlier that day in anticipation of leaving. She'd gotten her hair done, or bleached, or whatever the hell it was she did to it, the day before. She'd been primping for weeks actually—new clothes and shoes getting delivered to her apartment. One pair of shoes had a label on it with a price that almost made me pass out. She had been getting ready for a while. I hadn't been.

I slid my arm around her, gently nudging her closer. "I think I can deal with this under these circumstances."

"Thanks for everything so far. I'm having a good time."

"So am I."

Those blue eyes of hers were staring straight into mine as she fit perfectly into me. As the lights dimmed, I curled my arm around her next, to bring her lips to mine, which were sticky and sweet from her gloss.

Then the stage lights came on full blast, and the moment was lost. Our kiss broke, and our attention was directed to the stage where an actress, dressed in a cheerleading costume, was on her knees, simulating a blow job on an actor in a three-piece suit.

Satire, Abel. Relax. It's only a metaphor for the rest of the play.

"Ohhhkay," she mouthed to me.

I shifted uncomfortably in my milk crate seat and hoped that this was the worst of it. I mean, how much worse could it get?

The actress that was on her knees stood up, lifting her short skirt, exposing a bright red thong. She reached around to her hip, lifting a knife from a holster.

She lunged toward suit guy and began stabbing him repeatedly, screaming as fake blood began to squirt out of him. *Squirt* wasn't quite the right word. It was, like they had warned, projectile.

And it came right at us.

And it went all over her.

All. Over. Her.

"Holy—" she said.

"Shit!" I shouted.

I guess she wasn't afraid to get a little messy. I just didn't think it would happen here. I was going to fucking kill Marshall for this.

* * *

I unlocked the door to my apartment, and once we were inside, I slammed it shut. I was so frustrated with the way things went down at that play. I had wanted the night to be perfect. What I got was my girlfriend standing in front of me with a ruined shirt and my dignity wounded.

"Get that shirt off, beautiful," I said.

"What?" she said with a wink. "No foreplay?"

"Ha-ha. Very funny. I want to get it in the wash. How the hell do I even get," I said, motioning up and down her shirt, "fake blood or Kool-Aid or whatever the fuck it is out of it?"

She stepped close, wrapping her arms around my waist and looking up at me. "I don't care about this shirt."

"And you obviously don't care about mine, either," I snapped. "You're getting whatever is still wet on me."

I untangled myself from her and began rapidly unbuttoning my shirt, but when it wasn't coming off fast enough, I ended up yanking it open. Buttons flew everywhere, echoing against the floor and wall.

"Fuck," I said, throwing the shirt on the floor with it.

I ran my hands through my hair before pressing my palms against my temples. Why the hell did it have to be tonight? Nothing I planned was right, and I wanted it to be.

Evelyn's eyes were wide, her eyebrows lifted as she watched my temper tantrum. She did not seem impressed. I couldn't say I blamed her. I was ruining our last night.

"Hey," I said, reaching for her again.

But she backed up, and without a word, she lifted her light blue shirt over her head. "I'm going to try some cold water and dish soap on this, and when I get back, you better have a new attitude; otherwise this will be as close as you get to me for a long time."

"Come on, Evelyn," I said.

But she walked right past me, her hand up to stop me from saying anymore. An unjustifiable anger rose through me, a different one than being angered at a night gone bad. She was being so calm, so…fine with everything. Wasn't she feeling sad or scared about leaving? I bent down to pick up my shirt and scattered buttons, but those clear kind were a bitch to find in my light-colored carpeting. I was crawling around on my hands and knees, searching, when Evelyn returned and stood in front of me.

She tapped her foot against the carpet before nudging me with her toe. "Better?" she asked.

I crawled closer to her legs and wrapped my arms around her at her knees. "Yes. I'm sorry," I said, looking up at her.

"For?"

I sat up on my knees, running my hands up from her knees to her ass. "For acting like a fucking baby."

"And?"

I pressed my lips to the bottom of her bare stomach, planting kisses all over the area and then following the same path with the tip of my tongue. "And for being a dick over nothing."

Her hands tangled into my hair, gripping it in bunches to pull me tighter. I ran my fingers along the top of her jeans before unhooking the button and pushing the zipper down. My mouth was back on her skin, her breathing increasing with each pass I took.

"And?" she whispered.

"And for not using the night to show you, in every single way I could, just how much I'm going to miss you."

"You're forgiven."

I took her by the hand to my bedroom, but once we entered, we separated and I went to sit on the bed. She stood in the center of my room, her hair falling over her shoulders and her tits spilling out of the top of her light pink bra. I knew her panties were the same color, even though I'd only seen the lacy top of them. I usually liked her in the dark bras and matching underwear, but something about the pink against her skin, how it almost looked like another layer of skin, made my cock respond. Heavily.

I pushed myself to the back of the bed, resting against the headboard. "Take off your clothes for me, Evelyn."

She obeyed and did it exactly how I would've wanted her to. Starting at her jeans, she finished unzipping them, and before she began to pull them down, she turned around. Her fingers hooked the sides of the jeans around her hips, and she bent from the waist as she eased them down her legs. It was the most perfect view of her ass made only more perfect by a thong in the same color as her bra. She turned around again and stood still, waiting for me.

"I want it *all* off, beautiful," I said.

Her arms extended across her back to unhook her bra. It loosened, and she let the straps slide down her shoulders…her arms and then off. I was still looking at amazing tits, and while it wasn't anything I hadn't seen before, I knew it was going to be a while before I'd see her like this. Before telling her what to do next, she continued by removing her panties, letting them fall to the floor at her feet.

I'd never get tired of how beautiful she was or how incredible her body was. While her body could turn me on in a second, her confidence and trust she had with us that allowed her to be completely vulnerable in front of me drove me wild in a different way.

"Your turn?" she asked.

"I don't know," I said, unbuttoning my jeans and lowering the zipper. "I need to be sure you're ready for me.

"Is that so?"

I slipped my hand down to the outside of my boxers, running my hand over my erection. "You see, beautiful. I'm so ready for you. I need to be sure you're just as ready."

"I am."

"Touch yourself. I want you to prove it to me."

A tiny smirk lifted one side of her mouth as she traced the tips of her fingers around and between her breasts before working her way down. My hand wrapped around my cock, and with tame strokes, I gave it the attention it needed without going overboard. The palm of her hand skimmed the top of her pelvis until it descended between her legs. I gazed at her, touching herself for me, and knew she was my weakness and strength all rolled up into one.

"I'm ready, handsome? Are you?" she asked.

I nodded as her naked body approached the bed, and she reached out for my hand as she climbed on. There was no part of me that didn't want to take her immediately, get inside of her and be as close to her as possible. Tonight was going to be different. I wanted to take her slow, languish over every inch of skin.

I slipped off my shirt and jeans, followed by my boxers,

and brought her in close to me. Our naked bodies inter-twined, but not fucking yet made my heart race. I tried to ease the panic settling into my bones by kissing her lips, run-ning my tongue over them to remember her taste. The air buzzed around us, an electricity was created.

It was all overwhelming me. The thought of her leaving and being gone for months. Before the words even left my mouth, I hated myself a little for asking it.

"Do you have to go?" I asked.

A soft sigh breezed across my bare chest as her hand reach across my stomach for mine, intertwining her fingers with mine. "Yes."

I nodded because I didn't know what I could fucking say that didn't make me come off as more of a pussy than I already was. Not like my silence could be misconstrued as being even more pathetic.

This was all happening so fast. It was too fast. My mind, my body, every single cell making me up was erupting in chaos. It was completely taking me over. The closer I got to her, the more scared I got she was going to slip away from me. Women were always replaceable for me, the next one waiting in the wings to satisfy whatever need I had. Evelyn was irreplaceable.

Panic crept into every part of me, enveloping me. What the hell was happening?

"What are you thinking about?" she asked, running her fingers up and down mine.

I sighed, unsure of how much or how little I should say. "I've never felt this way about anyone. Ever."

"Same here."

"And I don't know, like, how to compartmentalize it all. Me wanting you to stay, but wanting you to go out there and kick ass. Me knowing I'll feel this loneliness, this empty part of me with you gone, and not knowing how to deal with it."

I'd been afraid to look at her, wondering if what I was saying was wrong or if she'd think I was being a sappy asshole. But when I glanced at her eyes, her fingers that had been dancing across mine halted and she was all eyes. Eyes on me, on mine.

Her forehead creased so slightly, but enough for me to recognize she was worried, that there was something she was holding back, too.

I brushed my hand across her cheek before brushing a lock of her hair behind her ear. "Now it's my turn. What are you thinking?" I asked.

"I think," she said, pausing and pressing her eyelids together tightly. "No. I know. I know, I know."

"What?"

Her eyes flickered open, and with a strong stare, she said, "I'm…falling in love with you."

I sucked in a rush of air, the power of her words leaving me breathless. It was exactly what I wanted to say. I wanted to say more. So much more.

I leaned my forehead against hers. "I'm right there with you, beautiful. Completely. You're…everything to me."

CHAPTER SEVENTEEN

Evelyn—

I stood over him as he slept, the white cotton sheet wrapped around his lower hips and every curve of his smooth chest illuminated by the hint of the early morning sun filtering through the slits of his blinds.

I didn't want to leave him.

I had only just let him into my heart, trusting him with it, and now I had to leave.

"It's only three months," I kept telling myself, but the ache in my heart fought against logic.

It was every cliché I never believed. How the words he spoke to me the night before sunk into my skin, attaching itself to every part of my insides. How I swore our hearts were beating in unison when he moved above me, inside of me. How it wasn't just sex anymore for pleasure. It was getting as close as we could, our bodies intertwined, and our breaths came out as one so we didn't know where one of his started and the other ended. What I had with Abel, even in the short amount of time together, was nothing like I'd had with Patrick. Once that realization hit, I knew I was safe with him. He wouldn't hurt me, and that knowledge, the notion that weight carried was lifted off me, made me relish in only the amazing things Abel and I shared.

I glanced at the clock beside his bed: 7:23 a.m. I had to go now.

"Hey, handsome," I whispered in his ear, running my hand across his warm chest. "I have to go."

He stirred, stretching his arms above his head before his eyes fluttered open. That moment when you're leaving sleep, when you're still in dreamland was always the best. But the next moment was the worst, when the realization of what the real world was holding came crashing down around you. I saw it happen to him before my eyes. A sleepy smile and tug on my hand to bring me close to him before it all faded and his dimples disappeared.

He sat up against the headboard and wrapped his arms around my waist, tugging me to him. I crawled up and sat on his lap, resting my cheek against his strong, muscular shoulder.

"Be safe, beautiful," he said, his voice broken from sleep. "I'll miss you madly."

I placed a kiss on his shoulder, my red lipstick leaving a mark on his skin. "I'll see you next month when you visit for the weekend, right?"

"Absolutely."

We sat silent for a few minutes, and I knew I couldn't wait any longer. I pulled away, placing the palm of my hands against his cheeks. I'd wanted to tell him I loved him. I wanted to tell him before I left, but I chickened out the night before by only saying I was falling in love. It was a lie. I loved him.

His hand met mine on his face, and his eyes closed as we both tried to drag out the final moments. When his eyes reached mine again, I thought I saw the same thing there I'd been hiding myself. The conflict just below the surface, the confusion in the wrinkle between his forehead that let me know he was fighting something.

Tears prickled my eyes, but I wasn't going to let him see that, so I pushed them down. It was fine. It was all fine. We were going to be fine. I trusted him. I did. He'd given me no reason not to. No matter what anyone else said, I trusted him.

He took my face in his hands and brought me to his lips. Kisses so soft, so chaste, I breathed a sigh against his own. I wanted the taste of him, the feel of his hands dragging through my hair, even the noise of the traffic below us, to be committed to memory. I had to do it because I knew I'd need it.

"You stay here," I said, pulling away. "I want to walk out of this room, thinking of my sexy boyfriend lying all naked in this bed."

"Call me when you get there?"

"Sure."

"Okay."

"Okay."

Bridget asked me to stop by the office for a minute before I headed to the airport. It was a pain in the ass considering all my luggage, and after leaving Abel, I wanted to just be on my way. The longer I stayed in Chicago, the more I'd want to run right back to him.

Dragging my two suitcases, carry-on bag, and purse through the office door was annoying enough. The fact that Bridget was standing there watching me struggle, snorting into her coffee cup made me downright cranky.

"Keep laughing," I snapped. "And I'll have no choice but to tell you I quit."

She set her white cup down on my desk, no doubt leaving a ring on the glass top. "You'll never leave me."

I sighed as I dropped all my bags by the door. "What did you need that couldn't be done over email? Or phone? Or when I was here yesterday?"

"You're going to want to drop the attitude if you want what I have."

"That depends on what it is."

She reached below my desk and lifted out a white Birkin. It looked exactly like her precious. A rare, genuine smile spread across her face as she held it out in front of her by the two straps.

"What?" I asked. "You need me to drop it off somewhere? Does it need a repair?"

"No. I want you to take it to Charleston with you, Evelyn."

"Oh no," I said. "I'm not dragging another thing with

me there because you want it monogrammed or some shit
at a place there. I'm sorry, but overnight it there or something."

"Is your brain in one of your suitcases? This is yours."

No way. There was *no* way. I didn't know what to say, so
I stood there with my mouth hanging open because there
really was no way.

"What is your problem?" Bridget asked, swinging the bag
back and forth. "You don't want it?"

"Of course I do! I…I…I—"

"I figured you'd need your own power bag while you're
down south, working it on my behalf."

I inched toward her, holding my hands out to the Pretty.
My fingers gingerly brushed against the smooth leather and
the flawless design until Bridget released it into my grip.

"Do you want the dust bag or—"

"No," I shouted. "I mean, no thank you. I'm using it now,
and I promise I'll take such good care of it."

"Of course you will. I'm counting on you, Evelyn."

I knew she was and why her giving me the Birkin was so
much more than a gesture. This trip was going to make or
break my career. It was my time to rise above expectations. It
was why when I looked down over Chicago on the plane ride
to Charleston, the ache in my heart that was missing Abel already would be mitigated by what I'd be doing there. I had
worked for so many years for this. With the Birkin next to
me, sitting in its own empty seat to my left, I knew. I knew as
we lifted toward the clouds, the Chicago skyline below us, I
was ready.

* * *

Charleston was as beautiful and as quaint as I thought it would be. Old Southern charm surrounded by historic buildings and wisteria plants. The new By Invitation Only was on a lovely magnolia-lined street in an old building with large bay windows overlooking the bustling downtown action.

The office was simple but sophisticated, a little Southern, but definitely had Bridget's flair decorating it. The moment I walked in, I was taken by the bright sunlight reflecting off the white, polished furniture. We didn't have much of a view in Chicago, and during the winter months, all we'd see was gray and snow. A few months in Charleston would be enough sunshine and warmth to last me through the frigid temperatures I'd be returning to in December.

I'd been there two weeks, although in some ways it seemed like I'd only just arrived, but in others it seemed like months already. The work kept me busy, but my heart was back in Chicago with Abel. I was missing him so much more than I'd imagined I would. It was why when I had a free moment, I'd scroll through the pictures on my phone of us, to take the sting away. I was doing just that when Trinity popped her head inside my office.

"Biscuits?" she asked. "They're still warm."

"Come on in," I said, setting my phone down.

Trinity was everything Bridget claimed she would be. A spunky petite Southern belle with reddish-purple hair and a smile that could light up a room. She placed an open box of Callie's Hot Little Biscuits on my desk and sat down opposite me.

"Everything good?" she asked.

I pulled a big, flaky biscuit from the box and brought it to my mouth. "Mm-hmm," I said, taking a bite. "Except I'm going to gain ten pounds if you keep bringing me these."

She waved her hand around. "You are lovely no matter the size."

I pulled my planner close to me with my free hand and picked up a pen. In my list of things to do I wrote: "Send Callie Callie's."

"What do you have for me?" I asked.

She flipped open the turquoise-colored notebook she always had with her and retrieved a pen from behind her ear. "I called Lulu's about the floral arrangement samples and told them it was unacceptable. We asked for white roses and hydrangeas, not blush or some sort of hint of yellow. She got a little snippy with me, but I told her if that was her attitude, I knew there were other florists that would be happy to do what we asked."

I nodded. "Okay. What else?" I asked, taking another bite.

"We have a meeting at one after your standing Wednesday morning meeting," she said with a wink. "The Fitzgerald wedding wanted to finalize a few odds and ends and shouldn't be a big deal."

"In that case, why don't you take care of that and touch base with me after."

She sat up straighter. "You sure?"

"Absolutely. I'm here to make sure things are running smoothly and you see to that already. I have no worries."

"Perfect," she said, writing in her notebook. "One more thing. That twit from the Chamber of Commerce called again. I told her I'd drop off the basket for the silent auction this afternoon to give you privacy during your meeting, and she was as happy as a dead pig in the sunshine. Bless her heart."

I laughed because this was what I liked about her. She got shit done professionally, but her Southern charm hid the shade she threw in a heavily disguised way.

"All right. I'm taking one more bite of these, and then I have a call in with Bridget," I said.

"Okay," she said, rising from her chair. As she went to leave, she started to close the door but leaned back to wink. "Enjoy your date."

"I will. Thank you."

Wednesday at eleven a.m. were Abel's and my Skype date. While we'd sneak in other times to do it, it was our standing time between the hellish hours I was working and the nights he was at WET.

Our connection met and there he was, all sleepy eyed but sexy as hell looking.

"Hey there, handsome," I said.

"Hi, beautiful. Let me sit back a minute," he said, slouching down slightly and folding his hands behind his head. "And let me take in my hot-ass girlfriend. What's shakin'?"

"Not much. So busy I'm not sleeping much, and which is why I look like hell."

"Shut the hell up. You're the sexiest thing in Charleston. No doubt."

"Well, blame Trinity if I come home a little fluffier than I left you. The food here is amazing. I can't wait to take you around. Plus, we hit up the Belmont the other night. It made me think of you with the speakeasy vibe."

He tilted his head to the side and smirked. "You flirt with any cute bartenders?"

"Nope. I only have eyes for one bartender and he's in Chicago."

Our conversation, the familiar banter, continued for the next half hour. Our times like this didn't replace being together physically, but it helped a lot.

"Have you been writing?" I asked.

"I have. Diving back into it wasn't as hard as I thought it'd be, but it all feels right. I'd forgotten how much of a rush it was."

"That's great."

"It also solidifies my crippling self-doubt when it comes to anything I write because the whole thing sucks so bad right now."

"Who cares? You're getting something out of it. It seems part of what you should be doing. Keep doing it, handsome."

"I am. I promised, and a promise is a promise. For right now, though, I have to run. I promised Delilah a trip to Sprinkles."

I pouted. "I miss Sprinkles with you."

"We'll have a lot of other birthdays together, beautiful," he said, winking. "After I drop her off, I'm heading out to play a little poker."

"Again? Didn't you just do that a couple times last week?"

I didn't like to question him on many things because it wasn't my place. He had a mother doing almost everything for him and the rest of his family always keeping a watchful eye. However, I knew the gambling thing was a bit of an issue in the past so I wanted to touch base about it.

"Yeah. But I'm bored as fuck without you around. So, if I'm not working or messing around with the writing thing, I don't have a lot of desirable choices except if you count hanging around with Callie and Aaron, who talked for forty minutes the other night about tile for the new bathroom remodel. What the fuck do I care? There were over seven hundred swatches for the color white—no, not white. Beige. Or was it cream? I don't know, but seven hundred fucking colors."

"Ha-ha," I said. "Okay, no remodel talk for you tonight. They'd probably ask you about paint colors next."

"Cotton White was too white, but Choice Cream seemed to be a winner. Believe me, beautiful, it was hard enough for me not to make a joke about that color without Aaron asking if I thought Buffy Blue was too blue."

"God, I miss you," I said.

The line went quiet before he said, "I miss you crazy."

"How many days until you get here?"

"Fifteen days, twelve hours, and twenty-seven minutes. Not that I'm counting."

"Well, we can handle that, right?"

"I don't know. I miss you, but my dick, beautiful. It misses you even more."

"Is that so? Maybe I could help."

"Oh yeah?"

"Uh-huh. Ask me what I'm wearing under this skirt," I said, standing up and turning around. "In fact, hold that thought. Let me go lock the door and close the blinds."

"That's my girl."

That was the last time we spoke.

I wished I'd known it would be.

It would've given me something to hold on to, to remember, because all I could recall was what happened next.

He missed our next Skype date. No call, no text, no him.

Technical problems, I told myself. *Something with work. Buried in his writing.*

Afternoon turned to evening.

Something was wrong.

I waited until I was back at the house I was renting in Charleston before calling Callie and Aaron. They didn't know, either. Concern was hidden behind possible explanations, even after he didn't show up for work. I heard it in their words, their fake soothing tones, though. They knew something was wrong, too.

Night brought the day and back to night again. That was the way it always worked even when I wished so hard for it to because then I'd have to let the reality of how long he'd been gone settle into my bones.

Something was wrong.

I thought it would be the greatest relief of my life to hear his voice. But I was wrong.

Almost thirty-six hours from when our Skype date was

supposed to be, my phone buzzed, sitting next to my hand, on my desk. His name and photo popped up on the front, and I answered it before it was even done ringing.

"What the hell happened to you?" I shrieked. "I've been out of my mind worried."

"Sorry," he said in a flat tone. "Crazy night."

I paused before responding because he had to give something more than that. A blasé attitude wasn't going to cut it.

"Which night?" I asked. "Last night or tonight, the night that is almost over?"

"I said I was sorry."

His apology was flippant, at best, and it pissed me off. I never questioned him on his whereabouts, but when he was nowhere to be found for over a day, I was owed a little something more than a half-assed sorry.

"Abel," I said in a controlled tone. "You have to give me something here. I don't need to know where you are every second of the day. I think you know me well enough to know that, but this is bordering on disrespectful and I don't think that's very fair."

He sighed loudly. "I tied one down pretty hard the other night. I didn't get home until early morning. I slept most of the day and I fucked up. I know I did."

That wasn't like him. Nothing about the phone call and him being missing was like him.

"You're saying you went out and got so wasted you lost an entire day?" I asked.

"Something like that."

I didn't know what to say or even how to feel. I was trying

to get him to explain on his own, but he wasn't having it. He wasn't giving me a thing. I stood from my chair, and began pacing around my office, hearing the muffled sounds of Abel tapping something against a hard surface. Work had piled up on my desk after wasting so much time thinking he was hurt or something worse. It was why I was still at the office so late, something that hadn't even registered to him.

"I can't come to visit," he said. He paused, clearing his throat before continuing. "Some shit came up and I can't make it work."

Dread pressed against my chest, and I could barely find my voice.

"What kind of stuff?" I asked quietly.

"Work and some stuff I need to figure out."

There was another brief pause, and the anger I'd been holding back while giving him the benefit of the doubt came flooding out.

"Are you screwing around, Abel?" I shouted. "Because if you are, you need to tell me right now. Don't lie or whatever. Tell me and you can put yourself out of your misery."

"No," he said without hesitation.

"Do you want to think about that?"

"Fuck, Evelyn," he shouted back. "No. I'm not fucking around. I went a little hard the other night, and I didn't call you. I said I was sorry, so can we move on for now?"

"That's bullshit. You know it and I know it, so until you're ready to get your head out of your ass, we can take a breather. I have my own shit going on here, and you being MIA for over twenty-four hours didn't help."

"I don't *want* to take a breather," he whined. "Can we forget about it?"

"About what? That you're not coming here and aren't telling me why? That you're clearly lying about shit? No. Pull up your big boy pants and stop moaning."

"Let's talk about this when we both chill out a bit," he said. "I can't right now."

"That's fine, Abel. You chill out, and when you're ready to come clean, call me. And speaking of calling, you should probably let your family know you're alive because they didn't know where the hell you were, either."

"Okay. Talk to you later."

He ended the call without a response or even a good-bye. Something was more than wrong.

Something had happened.

CHAPTER EIGHTEEN

ABEL—

The booze made me numb.

The snow in November helped. It hadn't snowed in so long.

Balance burned the edges, but the cracks allowed the darkness in.

She'd be home soon.

There were always choices, and I'd live with mine because protecting her meant more.

I was standing in front of the firing squad and was ready to take as many bullets as came my way to protect to her. To protect my family.

My beautiful Evelyn. She'd never forgive me.

I don't think I'd ever forgive me.

She was everywhere and then nowhere. Everywhere in the button I found under the dishwasher from my shirt that was torn off the last night she was here. Nowhere when I had to keep pushing her away to keep her safe from me. It hurt me to do it, but hearing the sadness, the conflict, in her voice was excruciating.

I wished on every one of those fucking dandelions. I threw the jar across my apartment and watched the shards of glass anoint everything I owned, everything I touched.

I'd created my own hell.

CHAPTER NINETEEN

Evelyn—

Something was wrong.

It had been wrong for a while, but I kept pushing it further and further away.

Let me get home and everything will be fine.

It was what I kept telling myself, but Abel's attitude and the distance in his voice told me otherwise. A couple nights of him missing, followed by the cancellation of his trip was one thing. In the weeks that followed, he seemed to have drifted from me. His calls were sporadic. A broken computer ending our Skype dates.

"Callie. You would tell me, right? I mean, of course you would, but something is off," I said to her on the phone.

"Of course I would. What kind of a question is that? We've been super busy so we haven't seen Abel a ton, but when I have, he's been the same him."

"Are you sure? Things have been so weird."

"Weird, how? I know he couldn't come down to visit, but

Aaron mentioned something about WET losing two of the other bartenders."

"It wasn't only that. He's been short and distant."

"Maybe you being away was getting to him. Guys react in all kinds of messed-up ways when they're feeling stuff. It'll be back to normal by the time you get home."

It was the same thing I kept telling myself over and over, but it never sat right with me. Before I took off from Charleston I texted him:

Me: About to leave. See you tomorrow? I miss you.

Abel: Have a safe flight.

It was those kinds of responses that made my eyes burn and my stomach hurt. I knew something was wrong, and as my plane landed on a late, snowy night, dread hung over me. There was little time to sleep when I returned home, not that I wanted to. I just wanted to get into the office, play catch up, and then go find him.

I unlocked the door to By Invitation Only and flicked on the lights. Everything was still in place, exactly how I'd left it. It wasn't as pretty as the Charleston office, but it was home.

After tossing my coat on the back of the chair, I powered up my computer to see what Bridget had for me. The heel of my shoe tapped with worry and anticipation, but a deep breath helped take the edge off. I tapped through today's schedule and was grateful Bridget was going easy on my first day back. There was a nine a.m. appointment with a new client who would be arriving at any minute.

I wondered if there was time for a quick coffee run across the street, but a knock on the door let me know that wasn't going to happen. A tall, beautiful woman stood smiling, waving at me through the glass.

I waved back. "Come in," I said, standing up.

She pushed the door open and stepped in. "Hi. I have an appointment."

"Of course, Ms. Rossi," I said. "Come sit down. It's nice to meet you."

"Oh, there's my fiancé now, texting me," she said, looking at her phone while walking at the same time. "He works late nights, so he probably won't be able to make it."

"That's okay. We won't need him until we start making some decisions on things."

She typed away at her phone sending and receiving several messages in a row before sitting down opposite me.

She was stunning. Long dark hair with caramel-colored highlights framed her beautiful face along with deep chestnut-brown eyes that only accentuated her elegance. Her smile was warm, and she seemed to have a maturity about her—from the way she walked and sat down elegantly to the way she shook my hand and patted the top with her other.

"Can I get you anything to drink?" I asked, leaning over to our mini fridge next to my desk.

"No, thank you."

I opened it and retrieved a bottle of water for myself before I opened up a new file on my desktop. "Well, we like to start off by asking some questions about you, your fiancé, and initial wedding ideas, okay? You want an April wedding?"

"Yes," she said. "I know it'll be quick, but it's what we want. Is it too soon?"

It was an odd question, and I wasn't sure what she was exactly asking me. "April is really the start of the wedding season, so it will be tight planning, but it won't be a problem."

"That's good. I'm also grateful for your help. I don't have a mom or family here to help, so my mother told me to find the best planner in Chicago to help."

"Well, you definitely have found that. No one will take better care of you than Bridget. Let me get a bit more information from you. What's is your fiancé's name?"

"Abel. His name is Abel."

My fingers hovered over the keyboard, my eyes stuck to the blinking cursor. Hearing his name, which was unusual, was like taking a bullet to the gut. It was an instant, painful reaction.

I cleared my throat. "Okay," I said, typing his name into the groom slot. "What's his last name, Ms. Rossi?"

"Matthews."

Another bullet. This time it was my breath that caught it. A chill ran through my body, and I couldn't make my mind respond. There was a mistake. I made a mistake. It was her accent.

"Can you…repeat or spell the last name, please?" I asked.

Instead of typing her response, I picked up my water and unscrewed the top, listening to her recite every letter.

"M…A…T…"

I know I heard her right, but I'm still wrong.

"…T…H…"

He's playing a joke. It's something he'd do.

"…E…"

Except I heard it in his voice yesterday. And I heard it the day before that.

"…W…"

It can't be him.

"…S. Matthews."

I typed each letter she'd said, watching his name appear in front of me.

I couldn't swallow the water that was in my mouth as nausea threatened to bring it right back up. It was his name, but the cursor blinking taunted and teased me. I couldn't stop staring at it.

…blink…blink…blink.

"I'm sorry," she asked, concerned. "Do you feel all right?"

My eyes focused on the white blank space around the rest of the screen, but the cursor continued to mock my denial. "What does he do for a living?" I asked.

"He's a bartender."

"Matthews?"

"Yes. Well, not a bartender forever. He's waiting for teaching job. For now, he works at his brother's bar and—"

And then I couldn't hear anymore.

I needed to find him. I needed to get to him.

"Hey you!" I heard Bridget exclaim.

I didn't even see her come in or rush over. Her hands wrapped around me from behind, but I still could only see that cursor and hear his name. I could only keep seeing his name.

"Hi, I'm Bridget Harrison. You must be Dafne. We spoke yesterday."

Blink.

Blink.

Blink.

Dafne.

"Are you okay?"

"I...I need to, um, leave. I—" I struggled to say while trying to find my breath. "Not feeling well."

"You're pale, Evelyn. Are you going to faint?"

Blink.

"Evelyn?"

I had to answer her, so I tore my eyes away from the screen, but my eyes settled on Dafne instead of Bridget. My trembling fingers pulled at the fabric at the top of my sweater, trying to get air anyway I could.

She was beautiful. Her eyes were kind as she looked at me, concerned, wondering what was wrong with me. It was funny, so I laughed, but then...blink...blink...blink.

"Evelyn!"

My head snapped at the sound of her voice, and adrenaline came rushing in like a tidal wave taking over my body.

"I don't feel well. I think it's the flu and jet lag, and...I'm sorry."

I was unsure of what I said next or how it all appeared, but I grabbed my purse, bolting from the office. Digging my hand into my purse to locate my phone, I raced down the hallway toward the elevator. Once I found it, I called Abel's number, but it went right to voice mail.

"Son of a bitch," I said, ending the call.

The elevator was on our floor so there was no waiting as I stepped in and slapped my hand against the "1" button. Back at my phone, I started typing: "I need to talk to you. I don't know what is happening. I can't believe this is real until—"

The elevator door opened, and I ran out, hitting the revolving door so hard I almost lost my balance. My head was down, frantically trying to finish my text, when I pushed my way out of the revolving door to outside, slamming into someone.

"Sorry. I—"

I almost didn't recognize him. It was him, but it wasn't.

His beard was gone. Maybe that was why he looked like he'd lost so much weight. I wasn't sure. Maybe he was working a lot and that was why the skin under his eyes was darkened to purple. No smiles. No dimples.

My heart and brain were so conflicted. I knew the reason for all of it, but my heart only knew how much I missed him.

"Why?" I asked because it was all I could manage to say. I didn't even know what I was asking. It didn't appear like he did, either.

His lifted his head to look up at the building. "Are you working?"

"I was."

He still couldn't look at me, but I was going to make him.

"Look at me, Abel."

Nothing.

"Look at me!"

"What?" he shouted back as his eyes finally connected with mine.

"What did you do?"

He let out a sigh, shaking his head. "You know."

"Know. What?"

"I wanted to tell you first. You have to know I wasn't going to let you find out this way. It's just…I didn't know she was coming here today. I missed her text this morning and—"

"What. Did. You. Do? Just answer me. Stop saying her. Her. Her. Tell me what you did."

His body went uneasy, his hands shook while he shifted back and forth on his legs. This dance and his blatant avoidance didn't do much for the indignation building inside me. I wanted to hear the words from him before I could unleash it.

"Do you want to come back up with me?" I asked with abrasion. "You can help me fill in some of the blanks."

"Can we go somewhere and talk about this? I didn't want you to find out this way and—"

"Stop!" I said, pushing my hands into his chest. "I don't want to talk. I want you to tell me what the hell you did when I was gone. Tell me! Tell me how you couldn't wait until I was gone so you could get your dick into someone else. Tell me how you were seeing her the whole time we were together."

"No," he shouted. "No. It's none of that."

"Then say it!"

He ran his hands through his hair, pulling hard while pounding his foot into the pavement. "I'm getting married!"

And there it was. It was what I wanted and I still didn't believe it.

"What?" I asked, blinking my eyes at him. It was like I could clear the moment out of existence, that if I couldn't see it, it would all go away.

"God," he said with his voice cracking. "This is why I wanted to talk to you alone, private. I can't do this here."

"Well, your…fiancée…is waiting upstairs for you to plan your wedding."

I spit *fiancée* out like it was rotten, leaving a sick taste in my mouth. His shoulders sagged as he reached his hand out to touch me, but I jumped back before he did. I wasn't going to let him keep burning me.

"What kind of twisted fuck are you?" I asked.

His hand was still outstretched to me when he looked toward the ground. "I don't know."

I'd never encountered such a wave of emotions all at once. I was angry, hurt, confused, and devastated. One would rise to the top and as soon as I recognized it, another would replace it.

My body shivered, the frigid temperatures so much colder than what I'd left in Charleston. Even though I'd known Chicago winters, it didn't occur to me it was going to be so cold already. I thought it'd be warmer when I got home. I thought there would be time, so much more time.

I had to get away from the cold. I didn't know who he was. I never did, and whoever he was now, I didn't want to be near him.

I tried to step around him, but he blocked me. "It's not what you think," he said.

"There is no room for me to misunderstand, and if you think you can talk your way out of this, you're more of an asshole than I thought."

He bit down on his lower lip, hard, his teeth digging into the precious flesh. Those lips I'd kiss endlessly. The words that fell from them, and the smile that had lifted from the corners. It was all tainted now. All of it.

"You are disgusting," I spat, pushing past him. "I don't ever want to see your face near me again. Ever."

"Evelyn," he said, grabbing my arm. "Let me—"

I whipped my arm out of his grip. "And keep my name out of your fucking mouth."

* * *

My apartment building was like an apparition, appearing without me even knowing it was supposed to be there. I didn't know how I got there. I didn't know how I managed to walk so far, from the office to home, in heels that sunk into the slushy snow. I was cold from the inside out—my heart so much colder than my numb fingertips and wet feet.

Once inside I headed straight in the direction of my bedroom. I dropped my purse to the floor with such weariness the contents spilled to the floor with a crash, my cell phone making the most noise. I left it all behind as I crawled up on my bed and curled tight into myself, my muddy shoes dirtying the top of my ivory duvet cover. I didn't even care.

It started snowing as the sun tried to shine right through the flakes until the moon took its place. It was so beautiful, so, so exquisite. It wasn't enough, though, to take away all the black hanging over me.

He was the one. *Was.* Now he was someone else's one. He belonged to someone else. She seemed lovely, but the hate I had for her was deeper than any other malice I'd ever known. It was misplaced, though. The ugliness directed at her should've been directed at him instead, but I couldn't find the place in my heart or my head to do it because I loved him.

I love him. In love with him.

I'd known, of course I'd known, but the terror of saying it out loud, with no reservations was bigger than me. Now, it was probably the reason I lost him.

Married.

Fucking married.

We'd never even spoken the damn word to each other even though there were times I caught glimpses of that life with him, flashing in my mind like photographs. It was like a dream, but that was all it was. A dream.

Darkness covered me, and it was the only glimpse of hope I had that maybe it would bury me. There were no tears, no frantic phone calls, only the snow.

But then the darkness turned to light again, and I had to come to grips with the reality the same thing was going to keep happening.

I dragged myself off the bed, my body aching from laying in the same position, in my clothes, for hours. As I undressed, dropping my clothes into a heap on the floor at my feet, my eyes glanced over my down comforter. It was ruined.

It was all ruined.

I retrieved my cell phone and had missed several calls and texts. Callie, Bridget, but none from him. I didn't want to hear from him, but it burned my insides the same that he didn't.

The hot shower, as hot as I could make it, did little to help my shivering, pained body. I took the scalding water like a warrior, hoping it would wash away the pain, but as I exited the shower, it was still there. The pain. The fear. The snow.

I stood staring into my closet, glancing at my wardrobe consisting of almost all things I hadn't worn in months while I was gone. There wasn't a single piece that didn't remind me of him. Every piece of fabric he once touched, every article he slipped from my body made me recall each precious moment.

But I had to keep moving. It was the only way to not drown.

I picked out the least painful outfit, did my hair and makeup as I always did, and as I stepped back out into the real world, I appeared to look like I always did. Inside, though, I was shattered.

Bridget was already at the office when I got there, digging around my desk with one hand and holding a large Styrofoam cup of coffee in the other.

"Hey," she said, looking up. "Did you get a chance to send out this invitation yesterday before you—"

Before.

"Huh?" I asked. "What?"

She narrowed her eyes at me, and the invitation dropped to my desk. Her glare never faltered as she crept around the desk to face me. "Are you still sick?"

I took a deep breath and stepped around her, unbuttoning my coat. "No. I'm fine. What were you saying?"

"You're still really pale and it looks like…something."

"I said I was fine," I snapped. "Now what did you want? It's going to take me forever to get through this mess you made."

"Have you had your coffee yet? And when was the last time you ate?"

I threw my hands up. "Does it matter? Is informing you of my liquid and caloric intake part of my job description?"

"What is wrong with you?" she asked, raising her voice. "I'm okay with your usual sass, and maybe you being away for a few months has made me forget, but I'm not okay with this."

"Yeah, well maybe working for you is the problem. Maybe if I never left, then—"

"What?"

Maybe I needed to say it out loud. Maybe it would be easier.

"Abel and I aren't…he's…"

"I'm not following you. You guys broke up?"

No, we didn't break up. Breaking up would have required a conversation, a conflict, but I didn't get the luxury of either.

"Did you get a chance to look at the names for the new client yesterday?"

"Hold on. We'll get to that. Tell me about Abel."

I sat down in my chair and pulled up the most recent client file. When his name appeared, I turned the screen toward Bridget.

Her eyes scanned across it and widened immediately when she saw what I was trying to tell her. "No way," she said under her breath. "There's no way."

"My thoughts, but it's true."

"Are you fucking kidding me?"

"No. And I don't want to talk about it anymore than we already have. I obviously can't be involved with this wedding at all. If there is any lucky part of it, it's only in four months, so…"

"What kind of asshole do you think I am? We aren't doing this wedding. I had no idea when I talked to her last month who she was. I'll handle it, but—"

"Last month?" I asked.

"Yeah. I think so. I'll have to look it up, but it was definitely November."

While I was missing him, longing for him, he was asking her to be his wife. I'd never felt more foolish, or disgusted with myself in my life.

"Stupid, stupid dumbass," I mumbled. For the first time, tears began to back up in my eyes, but I shook my head to bring myself back to reality. I wasn't going to cry in front of Bridget. I wasn't going to cry and allow the wetness on my cheeks to remind me of what he did.

"You got that right. He is a stupid dumbass. He's worse than that. I can't believe he did this."

"No. Me. I'm the stupid dumbass."

* * *

There was no place I'd rather not be than at Aaron and Callie's, after the last two days I had, for a Christmas party. However, I wanted to face it all at once. I wanted to know why my best friend kept something like my boyfriend is engaged to someone else a secret. I didn't want to do it, but I had to do it.

The door opened, and Callie rushed into me, hugging me so tight it made my heart ache even worse than it already was. I'd already lost the boy, and now…I was probably going to lose my best friend, too.

"I'm so happy to see you, Ev. I haven't been apart from you for this long since…well, ever since we've met," she said into my hair.

Tears started to burn my eyes, but I'd done enough of that earlier. I didn't want any more.

I untangled myself from her and stepped back. "I can't stay. I'm only dropping off a gift for Delilah."

I held the pink-wrapped box out to her. She swatted it before grabbing my hand. "No, you're not only dropping off. Come on. We've all missed you."

"I can't," I said, yanking my hand away.

Her expression shifted, happiness turned to worry so fast I knew she could sense something was wrong already. "What's going on?" she asked.

My eyes looked at the ground, my feet planted on her weather-worn welcome mat. She needed a new one after the cold, snowy winter. It always would've been me to point these things out to her.

"Why didn't you tell me?" I whispered.

"Tell you what? You're freaking me out."

I pushed my eyes upward, level with hers. "About Abel."

Still nothing.

"What about him?" she asked. "Won't you come in and let's talk about this?"

Her refusal to admit anything only fueled my anger. I couldn't hold back.

"How could you not tell me about Abel getting engaged? I came home and was completely ambushed. A guy…and one you knew how I felt about, but whatever…is one thing. But you? You lying to me? I don't even know how you could do that?"

She stared at me, her jaw hanging open, speechless. It took me a moment, but because I knew her better than anyone else, even myself at times, I could see her expression was genuine. She had no idea what I was talking about.

"Get the hell in here," she shouted. "Now."

I followed her in and I was barely past the threshold when she slammed the door closed behind me. "You're talking nonsense, Evelyn, and acting completely out of control. What is wrong with you?"

"Are you telling me that you, who lives with Abel's brother, had no idea he was getting married?"

She snorted. "Abel? Where did you hear that?"

"From Abel!" I yelled.

"What? That's ridiculous. I'm sure he was kidding."

I was trying to separate everything coming at me again, sort out what I thought I knew, but what was really true. It was like I was dancing through land mines and didn't know what I'd step on next.

I drew in a deep breath. "I came home very early yesterday morning around two a.m. I took a quick nap and headed into the office. The first appointment for the day was a new client. This amazingly tall, very beautiful Italian girl, Dafne. Her fiancé? Abel Matthews."

"Oh, I'm sure that—"

"I know what you're going to say. Oh, there must be some mistake. I couldn't wrap my brain around it, but then it all started coming together. How he canceled his trip out and has been withdrawing more and more. The final piece? When I ran out of the office because I was going to go find him, and he was already there, going to meet his fiancée."

Her eyes were so large, and her face was a shade of deep red. It was a level of anger I'd never seen in her before. Callie's MO was to cry first and get ragey next. This…was all new to me.

"Aaron! Come here now!"

Delilah's head poked out from the end of hallway. "Why are you screaming, Callie?" she asked nervously.

Callie closed her eyes, mouthing "shit" under her breath. "I'm sorry, sweetie. I was happy to see Evelyn and wanted Daddy to come see her, too."

Delilah still seemed unsure, gripping the tulle of her ivory party dress in her little hands.

"Hi Delilah," I said. "I have a present for you. Do you want to come get it?"

She looked at Callie, and when she nodded in approval,

Delilah raced down the hallway, with us meeting her halfway. I handed her the pink box, which contained the newest Barbie and assorted outfits, and squatted down in front of her.

"I think it's okay for you to open this one now before Christmas," I said.

"Callie?" she asked.

"Yes, you can. Why don't you go up to your room and I'll be right there?"

She took off running and up the stairs, passing Aaron who was on his way down.

"What's wrong? I was just getting out of the shower," Aaron said. "Welcome back, Evelyn."

I wasn't prepared for seeing Abel's brother in the flesh, with the same blue eyes and strong jawline. They were so similar. My stomach turned, the same sour reaction I had since yesterday.

"Evelyn is really upset and I'm fully confused," Callie said. "I'm wondering if you know anything about it."

Aaron stood next to Callie, his eyebrows furrowed together in concern. Another Abel thing. "What's going on?"

I shook my head because I knew if I said the words again, the tears would start. The last thing I wanted was for them to see how destroyed I was and then to report to Abel. There was no way I'd let him know he ruined me.

Callie turned to face Aaron. "She said Abel told her he was getting married. I mean, that's ridiculous, right? Why would he say such a stupid thing?"

Aaron closed his eyes, his lips drawn into a tight line before whispering, "Shit. What the fuck?"

"What the hell is wrong with him?" Callie said, raising her voice.

His eyes opened, but he was confused with whom to turn his attention to. Callie or me. He picked both, shifting his eyes between us both.

"Look, I didn't know what exactly was up, but he started asking a lot questions about marriage, divorce—" he said before Callie cut him off.

"Wait," she said, lifting her hand up. "You *knew* about this?"

"Of course not, but there was something going on with him I couldn't put my finger on. Evelyn, I'm so sorry."

My brief moment of relief knowing Callie hadn't kept this from me was replaced by the betrayal that Aaron knew something was wrong and never said a word. I needed to get away. I needed to get out of that house and away from them. Away from Aaron's face, his voice, and his fucking devotion to his brother.

"I have to go," I said, turning and rushing toward the door.

"Wait!" Callie called after me. "Don't leave. Please."

She reached me, and her hand wrapped around my arm. I fought against her grip. "I have to. I'll—"

"Aaron," she cried. "How could you do this? How could you not tell her? Or me? Look at her!"

"Please, don't you two argue over this," I said. I looked at Callie, tears falling. "Promise me."

Her grip loosened and I pulled free. "Tell Delilah I'm sorry I can't stay for the party," I said, opening the door.

"I'm coming with you," Callie said. She pushed Aaron out of the way, flew down the hallway and up the stairs. "I'm getting my shoes!"

I stared at Aaron, hoping he'd offer something of an explanation, something to make it hurt less. That night of our birthdays when the four of us thought we were so damn lucky. Best friends and brothers. Was there anything more perfect?

"I promise we won't argue," Aaron said quietly.

Callie's footsteps, followed by her voice telling Delilah she had to run out for a bit, echoed above us. I didn't have time.

"You and your brother are so alike, Aaron," I said. "Both of your promises mean nothing to me anymore."

I shoved the door open and ran down the steps. I ran and ducked between houses until I couldn't hear Callie's voice anymore.

But because she knew me, loved me, she was already at my apartment when I got there. With no questions asked, she crawled into bed with me and held me until the tears, the screaming, forced me to lose my own voice.

CHAPTER TWENTY

ABEL—

I was going insane. People threw that term around, but now I knew what it legitimately meant. My mind wasn't my own anymore. It was too crowded with thoughts of Evelyn and the agonizing expressions she had on her face when she left me. The hateful tone in her voice repeated over and over again in my brain.

"What kind of twisted fuck are you?"

"You are disgusting."

"Keep my name out of your fucking mouth."

I deserved all of it and even more. There was no rationalization I could give her. Not now. I couldn't even wrap my brain around how I'd do it in the future, but I would. I had to. I only hoped she would listen.

A moment, just a small moment, would come and I'd imagine it was all a dream.

A nightmare.

Then a reminder would come.

It was no illusion. It was all real.

The debt I owed Benji was $400,000.

Two days, or two years, was never going to be enough time to settle with him.

"I'll forget all about it, Abel, if you do this one thing for me," he said.

And if I didn't?

An evil smirk spread across his face. "I'll have to go to your family. Your parents. Your brother."

I couldn't stop him if that was what he was going to do.

But then he continued.

"Accidents can always look just like that, you know?" he said. "Remember Cody Torres? It was a shame how he fell off the roof of the fraternity house in college."

He played poker with me. With us.

Was that Benji who did that to him? Cody was paralyzed. That was back in college, and nausea rolled over me, considering how much more he was probably capable of now.

"Abel," he said with a chuckle. "I hear you have a girlfriend. South Carolina is really far away. Maybe I should pay her a visit?"

There was no fucking way he was getting near Evelyn or my family.

So I agreed.

All would be forgiven in exchange for a "favor" that would last three years.

Yesterday, I got a text from Benji:

Debt will be forgiven as promised. Keep working your end of the deal. I heard you have a niece. That's nice.

I'd wait for another moment so I could slip away into delusion, but sometimes they wouldn't come for a while.

If only Dafne had waited to talk to me first before going over there. No. It was my fault. She didn't know. Maybe I should've had my phone louder so I could've heard the text message come through. Or maybe I should've been awake by midmorning instead of sleeping off my drunkenness. No. Maybe I shouldn't have fucked myself so hard that I was losing everything.

It was all on me and that was exactly where I wanted it to be.

My days were spent with clouded, confused judgment, but there was one thing that was crystal clear. I was doing the right thing. No one would understand the why or how except Dafne, Benji, and myself, but when left with the choice of saving myself or saving everyone who I loved around me, I knew there was no choice.

There was no joy, no laughter in my life at all. It was all emptiness.

There was only one thing I could do that would fill my mind with anything else but dread. Write. The book she told me to keep writing. The book she said I would find my passion in. It was the only way I could get close to her, as if I was writing every word for her. I buried myself in every word, every paragraph, until the words bled together. Then I'd take a break and go back to it. Two days after she returned home, it wasn't enough.

I saw the bottle of cologne she made for me sitting on my dresser. It made me miss her signature scent. There was one

T-shirt she had left behind, on purpose I'd assumed, but like the pussy I was, I slept with it every night. The scent had faded but I could smell it. There wasn't going to be much more time until it all disappeared. I flipped my bottle over and read the name of the store where she made it.

There was one way to keep a piece of her close to me.

I grabbed the shirt and went to Scentsory, the custom fragrance maker.

"Can I help you?" asked a cheerful, late-teen girl.

"Yes. I need to make a scent or perfume or whatever the hell you call it."

"Okay, well we have over a hundred oils for you to choose from so—"

"No," I said, interrupting her. "I don't need to choose. I already know what I want. I think."

"Great," she said, walking toward the various bottles of oils arranged in circle. "Where did you want to start?"

"It's a bunch of vanilla and some flower with a *p*. Wait," I said, pulling her crumpled T-shirt from my coat pocket. "It's on here."

I shoved the shirt at her, but she stepped back. "Ah. What?"

"Can you smell this and tell me exactly what it is?"

Her eyes shifted back and forth like she thought I was nuts. That was no longer debatable. I didn't have the energy to try to pretend, either. I just wanted to get what I came for.

"Look," I said. "It's my…girlfriend's…scent. I want to surprise her. I'm not being a creep. I took one of her shirts because I know her perfume is all over it."

"That's so sweet! No offense, but it did come off as a little creepy. Here," she said, taking the shirt from me and bringing it to her nose.

I watched as she moved around the white cotton, breathing in deeper and deeper, before finally handing it back to me. "Sorry," she said. "I don't smell anything?"

"What?" I snapped. "Are you serious?"

I inhaled against the fabric and it was all there. All of my Evelyn. How could this chick not smell it?

"Do you have a cold or something because it's all over this," I asked.

"Ah. No. I don't have a cold. We can try mixing some together to see if we can't get something close enough for you."

"I don't want close," I said, tightening my grip around the shirt before jabbing it back at her. "Can you try again? Please?"

She didn't take it from me, but with her hands tucked into the pockets of her yellow hoodie, she leaned down to take a whiff. It was like watching an animal sniff out something, her nose moving all around to detect what she was looking for. After a minute, she took another step back and she shrugged.

"Sorry," she said.

"Shit," I shouted. "Is there someone else here who can help me? I mean, how can you work in a perfume shop and not smell shit?"

An elderly woman rushed out from a side door, stepping next to the girl helping me. "What is all that yelling?"

"This guy," she said, pointing at me, "is being weird because I can't smell his girlfriend on the shirt he brought in."

"I wasn't being weird. I only wanted—"

"Get out," the elderly woman said, cutting me off. "I don't tolerate anyone talking to my employees that way."

My head turned all around, seeing the staring eyes of the other customers and the looks of judgment. I placed Evelyn's shirt back into my pocket and quickly exited the store.

I was fucking out of my mind. The insanity, the anger, drove into me until at certain times I crashed into a brick wall. An out-of-control wreck and I was barely a survivor. I picked up my sagging jeans, all of my clothes fitting looser and looser since I could barely eat and had quit working out. I shaved my beard because every time I looked at myself in the mirror, every time I touched it, it reminded me of how much Evelyn loved it. Her touch was all over it, and it got to the point when it was another memory that made me crazed. Food, people, my thoughts all left me sick, and I preferred to stay empty of all of it.

I stepped off the elevator at the floor of my apartment and could see Aaron standing next to my door. The hits were going to keep coming, but like the poison I chose to swallow, I had to keep taking the ramifications.

"So, I hear congratulations are in order," Aaron said, following me into the apartment. "I wish I could say Callie or Evelyn send the same kind of best wishes, but they're not quite there yet."

It was bound to happen, but I wanted it to be in my own time. I certainly didn't want it to be when Evelyn accidently found out and went to Aaron and Callie.

Who the hell was I kidding? There wasn't going to be a good time or any time that would make sense.

I was never much of an actor, but I was going to have to put on an Academy Award–winning performance in front of the person who knew me best. The backing behind was solid, though, and I knew that was what would carry me through. Protecting him, Callie, Delilah, and everyone close to me was worth it. I just hated myself for the way I was going to have to make sure that happened.

I unzipped my coat and tossed it on the couch before plopping myself down next to it. "I was going to tell you."

"That's good to know. I'd hate to be the last to know my brother is getting married to someone I never met or even heard of until recently."

"Her name is Dafne," I said.

He shrugged. "I didn't ask. I'm sure she's a bystander in whatever the hell you're doing, so I don't mean to disrespect your future bride, but the whole thing reeks of shit."

I rubbed at my temples. "Do we have to do this now?"

"Would you prefer we waited until the rehearsal dinner?"

I hated that he was mocking me, but I was going to take it. I was going to take whatever judgment and anger he was going to dish out. His stepped in front of me and folded his arms across his chest. He was waiting.

"No. I suppose you'll meet her before then," I said.

"You sound thrilled. Now, cut the bullshit, and tell me what the hell you're doing."

"I don't seem to remember me getting this pissy when you decided to marry Lexie and we all knew what a fuckup that was going to turn into."

His nostrils flared at the mention of Lexie, his ex-wife. "I dated Lexie for a while. We were having a baby, and while in retrospect marriage wasn't the right thing to do, it was hardly a surprise."

I was trying to be aloof, almost callous because it was the only way for me to remain detached and handle this. It was the only way without Aaron, the person who knew me best, seeing right through me. It would take so little for my resolve to break, to want to tell him everything, but doing so would only put him in danger. Benji made that clear.

"Whatever," I said, rolling my eyes. "You justify your marriage your way, and I'll justify mine my way."

"And what kind of justification would yours be, Abel? There's are a lot of us that would like to know."

"I'm getting married. Dafne is going to be my wife. Is that good enough for you?"

"No, but if it is for the both of you, then there isn't much else to say."

"Oh, hell. Say it, Aaron," I yelled. "Go ahead and fucking say it. You're probably coming all over your expensive boxers right now with how bad you want it."

"It's nothing I haven't had to say before," he said calmly. "I've come to accept the fact you and I are going to lead our lives in very different ways."

"What the hell does that mean?"

"It means you're going to live your life for you. I'll never understand the choices you make, but I don't have to. You'll have to."

"You're talking like a fucking psychologist. Talk to me like a brother! Tell me what you're thinking!"

I could see it building with every breath he took, all he was holding in, and he was right on the edge. He needed a push, and luckily for him, I had nothing else to lose.

"Remember when I found you drunk and stupid when you threw Callie out," I said, standing up and stepping up close to him. "When I told you what an asshole you were be-ing? I told you what you needed to hear. Fucking give me the same respect. Fucking. Say. It."

"You knocked her up, didn't you?" he asked, glaring at me.

"No."

"You don't have to marry her. If you haven't learned that from all I went through with Lexie, then you weren't paying very close attention."

"She's not pregnant."

He ran his hands through his hair and shook his head. "Then you've lost me, Abel. If she's the one, I'll treat her like a sister-in-law, but after seeing you with Evelyn, I have a hard time believing it."

"Please don't say her name," I warned. "I've lost her be-cause I fucked up, and the only way I know how to save even a little bit of the respect she might still have for me is to move on."

Aaron's mouth contorted in a disgusted expression. "That's so twisted. Respect? You're marrying someone else. She's heartbroken."

"And you don't think that kills me," I said. I pressed the palms of my hands into my eyes. "I hate that I hurt her. I fucking hate myself for doing it, but all I can hold on to is the hope she'll forgive me someday."

Forgive me. That was laughable. She *hated* me by now. She had to.

I released my hands from my eyes, and as my vision began to focus, I could make out Aaron shaking his head. "What the hell have you gotten yourself into, Abel? None of this makes sense. You don't love this other girl."

I didn't. He knew it, too.

I took in a deep breath, desperate to find the strength I needed to continue. "It all became bigger than us, Evelyn and I."

"What became bigger?" he asked, confused. "Make me understand. I'll be right there with you. You know that."

I did. He would. I knew he would, but it wasn't worth the risk. It was why I couldn't tell him. I couldn't tell him I'd fucked up. *Again.*

It was the same reason I couldn't tell Evelyn I was marrying Dafne. The ship was sinking, and I was saving her while I helplessly drowned. I hurt her, would continue to hurt her, in the most unimaginable way. Knowing that was bad enough, but my own sadness, the realization of all I was losing, compounded it. There was no room in the equation for me to be selfish, to think about how this decision was affecting *my* life, because there were too many other people who I loved more than myself to protect.

It was a lose-lose situation.

"What can I do, Abel?" he asked.

"Be my best man."

CHAPTER TWENTY-ONE

EVELYN—

Y ou've been working crazy hours so how about if I take you for a drink?" Bridget asked. "And before you say anything, we won't go to WET."

I wanted to decline, but I knew I needed to get out. A drink would probably do me good and seemed like a better option than binging on reality shows and eating my weight in Cinnamon Toast Crunch cereal, which was what I was doing every night. "Okay," I said. "And it's a Tuesday. He usually doesn't work on Tuesdays, so I don't care if we go there."

I wasn't sure what possessed me to say that, but all I could figure was I was trying to prove how strong I was. I didn't want Bridget, or anyone for that matter, to see how badly I'd fallen apart over Abel. Showing up there with my head held high would get back to him, and the added bonus was I was saving face in front of my boss.

"Are you sure?" she asked with raised eyebrows. "I can call and make sure he isn't."

I shrugged even though it was a good idea.

Her long red fingernails tapping against the buttons as she dialed and waited for an answer. "Marshall? Hey, honey, it's Bridget. Look, I have a quick question," she said, eyeballing me. "And I don't mean to put you on the spot. I want to stop in with Evelyn and—"

She paused as I detected Marshall's voice through the receiver. She nodded at me and gave me the thumbs-up. I breathed a sigh of relief because it was going to be a lot easier knowing for sure he wasn't working.

"Thanks, honey. I'll see you soon."

She dropped the phone in her purse and put her hands on her hips. "He's not there. Let's go get you tipsy."

I hadn't stepped onto that side of the building since I'd been home. There was always a fear I'd see him or some memory would hit me too hard. We rushed toward the star, the cold wind blowing through us, but when I didn't see it, I stopped.

"Where is it?" I asked.

"What?"

"The star. Did I miss it?"

"You're a few steps short, and it's not a star anymore," she said, smiling. "They added a little something new."

I followed behind her until she paused on a white dandelion painted on the ground. I stood above it, my eyes tracing the white floaties drawn next to it, looking like they were being taken off by the wind.

"I know a star wasn't anything big, but I have no idea why they'd put a weed here instead. What do you think it means?"

"Wishes," I mumbled. I lifted my head and faced her. "Someone wants you to follow the wishes."

I had no way of knowing if it had anything to do with us. It probably didn't, but it still stung seeing it there. Bridget knocked at the door, and it opened immediately, a grinning Tyler holding it open for us.

"Well, look at you two strangers looking as beautiful as ever," he said.

I smiled because the voices in my head telling me this was a bad idea left me speechless. He gave me a knowing nod, almost pathetic, like I was going to fall apart right in front of him.

"You don't need to walk us, sweetie," Bridget said. "We got it."

"If you say so. Enjoy, ladies," he said with a wink.

Bridget threaded her arm through mine. "Less talk. More drinking, right?"

"Yes, please."

I thought it would be okay, but it wasn't. Stepping back into the dimly lit room made it even clearer I had no business being there. It was all too soon. It was too soon for the back of the mirrored bar and the candles reflecting against the martini glasses. It was too soon for Marshall to put his arms around me and tell me Abel was a fuckup. Bridget did her best to shoo it all away, but the only savior was a Marshall Manhattan.

"Do you think I'm pathetic?" I asked Bridget. We were tucked in the very end of the bar, out of view of most people.

"No, and before you ask, yes. I would tell you if you were."

I drained what was left of Manhattan number three before my unsteady hand placed the glass back on the bar with a thud. Bridget eyed me above her own cocktail, a dirty martini with two olives.

"Pathetic, no," she said. "But I do think you're drunk."

I waved my hand around. "Nah. I can hold it fine."

"Is that so? Then why is your ass so close to the edge of the chair? You're going to fall off."

"I was starting to get up. I have to go tinkle," I said, sliding off the stool. "Be right back."

The mixture of drinking so quickly and the fact I hadn't been eating much did in fact make the drinks hit me harder than normal. I was unsteady as I made my way to the bathroom, balancing myself by holding on to the sides of the walls as I made my way down the hallway. Girls had it good when it came to the pissing thing, especially when drunk. We got to sit down, gather our thoughts for a minute, and do our business. I wondered how guys kept their aim on target when loaded. I giggled to myself as I washed my hands, considering what the inside of a men's room might look like, or worse, what it smelled like. I was going to ask Bridget her opinion on the matter, but I heard her shouting the moment I exited the bathroom. Making sure I wasn't going to face-plant, I hurried back down the hallway, my feet dragging against the carpet.

I peeked around the corner, and my heart stopped.

"You stupid asshole," Bridget said coolly. She picked up her drink and took a sip. "I hope for her sake she enjoys sleeping with garbage every night because that's what you are. Vile garbage."

Abel recoiled at her words, the sting written all over his

face. His shoulders slumped down, his once-fitted, white work shirt hung loose. He looked like a mess, and while I should've been pleased, it only made things harder.

He turned his head, and when his eyes met mine, there was nothing coming off him. No deep dimples. No excited eyes at seeing me. It was like he didn't even know me.

"He's covering for someone else tonight," Bridget said. "Marshall didn't know until now. Let's go."

"No. I want to finish our drinks," I said, glaring at him. "I won't let him ruin anything else for me."

"Marshall," she shouted. "Get this stupid fuck out of my face before there is blood all over your bar."

Abel raised his hands in surrender and backed away. I watched as he headed back to the bar, leaned over it to whisper something in Marshall's ear before disappearing down the hallway.

"Okay, well, that's over. If I can't make you leave, at least let's do a shot of tequila to take the edge of whatever you're feeling right now."

"I'm not feeling anything." I shrugged. "Nothing at all."

She snorted. "Yeah, right. You're a liar. You look like…a frazzled llama…or something equally terrible. Plus, you need to get your hair done. Seriously."

I needed to hang in there long enough for everyone to think that running into Abel didn't affect me. If that meant doing a shot of tequila or two, which is how Bridget wanted it, I was going to do it. It wasn't a smart idea, considering how drunk I already was, but I wanted to be able to keep up a good front.

"Okay," Bridget said. "Are we done here?"

"Thank God, yes."

"Let me run to the ladies' room, and we're out of here." She leaned over to whisper in my ear, "I'm proud of you, sweetie."

Mission accomplished.

I breathed in a sigh of relief knowing I'd made it. I made it and was still standing. Well, I was hopeful I'd be standing. There was no telling what was going to happen when I got up from the stool, but judging from the way I was rocking back and forth on it, walking might be a problem.

I dug through my wallet that I had sitting on the bar, wanting to leave a little something extra for Marshall in addition to what Bridget already gave. My eyes were trying to focus on the numbers on the cash, but my vision shifted when a hand I recognized slid something in front of me. By the time my eyes lifted, Abel's back was already to me, exiting the back of the bar.

I glanced down, and it was white cocktail napkin with WET embossed in gold lettering across the middle. It was like all the other napkins there. Confused, I leaned in closer and could see ink dots soaking through the front of the napkin. I flipped it over, and there, written in Abel's chicken scratch handwriting, it said, "I'm sorry."

I stared at the words, the ink running into the paper and making smudges. Tears came to the surface of my eyes, blurring all the words together into one big mess. Why did he have to do this to me? I was doing so well and now...I was not.

I needed to get away before I made a scene, crying and

making everyone uncomfortable. I stood up and steadied myself on my heels before I attempted to walk. Gripping the side of the bar, I inched down the length of it until I bumped into Bridget.

"Whoa," she said, grabbing me by the shoulders. "You need a pit stop, too?"

I looked behind her, and Abel was up against the hallway wall, one foot propped up behind him. His head hung low as he pinched the bridge of his nose.

It wasn't the tears I needed to hold in anymore. I pushed past Bridget, stumbling on my right heel before I ended up leaving the whole shoe behind so I could make it to the bathroom.

I did make it, but only as far as the sink before I vomited everything I'd been holding in. All the booze, heartache, and loss came out when my body couldn't take it anymore. Looking at myself in the mirror above the sink, my face blotchy and my eye makeup smudged, I didn't recognize myself at all. I was a wreck, standing with one shoe on, in a bar bathroom, puking over my ex-boyfriend. I was like a deranged Cinderella who lost one of her glass slippers, waiting for her prince to return it. Too bad my life was nothing like a fairy tale anymore.

* * *

Dreams were like listening to your favorite radio station. You turned it on, and more times than not, you were okay with whatever played. However, there were times when no matter how long you listened, the most dreadful tunes played one right after the other. My dream state after returning from WET and flopping down onto my bed was like the bad songs on my favorite radio station. A horrible dream about having to be a bridesmaid during Abel and Dafne's wedding. I was pleased when the banging of the drumline following them out of the church wasn't part of the dream, but someone knocking loudly at my front door.

Still somewhat tipsy, I dragged myself out of bed to see who would be here at close to three a.m., who I didn't have to buzz in. I looked through the peephole and wanted to sink down to the floor under it. If I was quiet, maybe he'd go away.

"I know you're in there, Evelyn," Abel said. "Your neighbor was outside with his dog and said he saw you come home a couple hours ago."

"Shit," I said, unlocking the door. I opened it a crack. "I've had enough of you for one night."

"Please let me in," he begged. "Just for a minute. I'm sorry I made you puke."

Bridget and her big mouth. That was mortifying. I didn't want to let him in, but I worried about the other neighbors being woken up. I opened the door the rest of the way and stepped aside to let him in.

His black leather coat was spotted with droplets from snow. I didn't know it had started snowing again. I looked him over, and he seemed cold. Good.

"What?" I asked.

"I can't stay away from you anymore," he said. "I need you to hear me out."

I crossed my arms. "Fine. Go ahead."

He took a deep breath in, running his hand across his face where his beard used to be. "I owe you so much more than an explanation, and I'll give it all to you, but I need you to trust me."

I laughed, a from-my-belly roar of a laugh. "Are you kidding me? I'd no more trust you than I would the rats that live behind the building."

"Okay," he said, shaking his head. "I deserve that. Can you remember when you trusted me? You did at one time, right?"

"At one time."

"Well, maybe if you can find that place again, you can remember everything we said, everything we promised."

"Are you kidding me?" I repeated. This had to be a joke. "Have you lost your mind?"

"Yes. I'm pretty certain I have."

"Look, it's done, Abel. You've moved on, and you coming over here is making it really hard for me to do the same. It makes you look like even more of an asshole."

"Please just listen to me," he pleaded, his hands cupped together in front of him. "I'm trying to explain why I did it, why I'm doing it."

I glared at him as I forced myself to ask a question I'd been too afraid to ask before. "Is this because I didn't say I loved you? Did you find someone else because I couldn't say it to you before I left?"

"What? No. Of course not."

"If that's true, which who knows at this point, then this

is what I need to tell *you*. When I said I was falling in love with you, that was a lie. I was already in love with you. I was so crazy, crazy in love with you, but I was also crazy scared. I wanted to tell you, but there was this nagging feeling in the pit of my stomach that something was going to happen when I was gone. I didn't expect this, but I knew something was going to go wrong. And the last thing I want to do is blame myself for that. That I should've told you I was in love with you and maybe you wouldn't be doing this. You wouldn't—"

I paused, taking a deep breath, but Abel snuck in when my guard was down for a moment.

"This is all on me," he said. "All of it is my fault. I was in love with you, too. I'm in love—"

"Shut up," I shouted, holding up my hand. "Just…shut up. I let you in," I shouted. "I trusted you. And you broke that."

"I know! I did the same, but—"

"But…nothing! You moved on and forgot about me the second I was out of view and now you're getting married. *Married*. Which, by the way, I find hilarious," I said, snickering again, but this time it was a cold, hard laughter.

He shrunk down, his shoulders slouching like he was being crushed from the inside. I paused, waiting for him to say something, to give me some sort of justification for what he did, but there was nothing. Just silence.

I knew it was my chance, maybe my only chance to let it all out. I wouldn't deny myself that or have any regrets about anything left unsaid. The torment in my heart superseded any rational thoughts I had. I wanted to hurt him as much as he'd hurt me.

"You have my blessings, Abel, because you'll need them. So will she. You couldn't even stay committed to me when I was gone for just a few months. Now you're going to promise to be faithful to her…forever. That's a tall *fucking order*."

His eyes wouldn't dare look at me. When he spoke, it was to the floor. "I can't…explain it to you the way I want. I wish I could, but I can't. I'm trying to protect you from so much and I don't know how to tell you so you'll understand. Just know, I have never, ever felt for anyone the way I feel about you."

"Felt," I spat. "Maybe how you felt. Past tense. And while we're on the topic of the past, retrospect is a painful but appreciated thing. You made me forget everything I ever promised myself about falling in love, that it was a word that held nothing but hurt in my life. I'm mad at myself for disregarding everything that anyone who gives a shit about me told me when I got involved with you. Bridget, Callie…shit, even your own brother! They all said not to, but I thought my own judgment trumped that. I'm glad for it, though. I know I'll never make the same mistake again."

"It wasn't a mistake! It was everything. I just…need to do this."

"You don't need to do anything except be honest, but I can see that isn't going to happen. None of this makes any sense, and the more you try to find some…explanation…the more I think you're trying to hurt me further."

"This is *killing* me. My fucking heart, Evelyn," he said,

pounding his hands into his chest. "Look at me. Don't you know that you fucking *own* me. Everything. Everything you see. Everything you feel. You own it."

His face, across where his dimples would appear when he was happy, was void of anything. There was nothing there. It was…empty.

"Not anymore," I whispered.

"You own it," he repeated. "From the second I saw you, you've fucking owned my heart."

There was one more question I needed to ask. It made me the most terrified of all, but I had to know. "Is she pregnant?"

I watched his chest heave, the weight of my words catching his breath. My head used to rest on that chest as I listened to his heartbeat. My fingers would run across his smooth skin until he'd roll me under him to kiss me so deeply I'd be dizzy. It was like a magic spell.

Spells, like promises, broke though.

"No," he said, staring right into me.

It was supposed to be a relief, but it only proved to make me even more confused. Confused and angry.

"You're locked in pretty hard there," I mocked, remembering when he'd say it to me. "Do you use that on your fiancée?"

"No."

It was all falling apart.

Fallen.

My insides, my spirit…broken. Now, I wanted to let myself indulge in the pain because it was all that was left. The tears, the screaming…all of it.

"I want you to leave now," I said, gathering what little was left of my strength. "And if I so much as see you on my street, I'll call the cops. Understand?"

"Evelyn," he pleaded. "Please. I need you to understand. I need you to just…give me time…to make you understand. Please don't do this. You…you're…my beloved, remember?"

I did remember, the flowers he sent me that got mixed up with a funeral arrangement that said BELOVED on it. I would remember it all because I'd never imagine in my life I'd believe in the fairy tale.

I touched his face, tears running down his cheeks. He leaned his head to mine, our foreheads touching. I knew it was the last I'd have of him, and selfishly my heart told me to take it. My brain would catch up. I knew it.

It was excruciating. Every cell inside of me screamed, telling me not to let him go, and that was wrong. He wasn't mine anymore. He never was.

"Please," he whispered through a cracked voice. "Please."

I slowly untangled myself from him and stepped back.

Back.

Back.

Until I backed up against the door. I reached around and blindly turned the knob. Stepping aside so I could open it, my eyes never leaving his. Without any room for him to misunderstand, I chose my next words carefully and said them with a razor-sharp tone.

"Fuck you, Abel."

CHAPTER TWENTY-TWO

ABEL—

It was a bad idea to go and try to pick out my wedding band the day after I saw Evelyn. I stood in front of the jeweler, eyeing the different selections in front of me, and all I felt was sick. The shiny gold bands were supposed to mean love and forever, but to me, it meant a lie. I left without getting shit.

I was walking home when a text from Dafne said she was waiting for me at my place. I gave her the key since it made sense to, but I hated myself for doing it. Then I hated myself more for hating it in the first place. There was no doubt she wanted to hear about how the ring purchase went, and I dreaded having to disappoint yet another person.

"Hey," I said, calling from the front door when I entered.

She was in the kitchen, steam rising from a pot above the stove. "Hi," she said, smiling. "I'm making dinner."

I shrugged myself out of my coat and sat down on the couch, exhaustion from doing nothing running across my body. "Okay," I said.

"How did the rings go? You find something you like?"

I listened to her drain the pasta or whatever she was making into the sink, waiting for my response. Everyone wanted answers from me all the time, and I was fresh out of them. I hadn't had any answers in a long time.

"No. I didn't," I said.

She stepped away from the kitchen and joined me on the couch. Her face frowned, the disappointment I'd anticipated written all across it.

"Is everything okay?" she asked.

"I don't know."

I did know, but I couldn't tell her that. She scooted closer, resting her head on my shoulder.

"It will be okay, sweet Abel," she said, placing her hand on my leg. "I know it isn't what you want at all, but three years isn't that long."

I looked at her out of the corner of my eye as she licked across her bottom lip, but keeping her burgundy lipstick in place. Her hand on my leg, her head on my shoulder. I hadn't been touched by anyone in so long, not since Evelyn left.

"Dafne," I said, placing my hand on top of hers. "I can't."

"You can't do what?" she asked. She rose from next to me and stood in front of me, before kneeling down in front of me.

I couldn't pick out a ring or plan a wedding.

I couldn't eat her food and pretend we were something we weren't.

I couldn't stop the nausea that came over me, knowing that three years *was* a really fucking long time.

I couldn't stop wishing with every breath I had that she would go away and I'd get my Evelyn back.

She leaned closer, placing her palms on the sides of my face. She stared into my eyes, searching for something, validation or some shit, but there was nothing for me to give her besides what I was already doing.

And it was all so wrong. Her deep chestnut eyes weren't the blue-colored ones I wanted looking back at me.

Her hands on my skin weren't the ones I wanted. It wasn't her.

And the way she smelled. It wasn't the sweet, flowery perfume that only Evelyn wore. It was a clean, fruity scent.

"I can't do any of this, Dafne," I mumbled.

She exhaled a hard breath, blowing her hair out of her face. I didn't know if it was for the sake of her hair that she did it or if it was her way of trying to figure things out, too. The almighty cleansing breath—breathing in answers, breathing out questions.

"I know," she said. "I've tried, Abel. I've tried to make the best out of this."

"How the hell could it be anything but awful? We don't love each other. I'm not even sure I like you at this point. You think the next three years will be anything but agony for me? You're getting what you want so I don't expect you to understand."

"You don't think I understand?" she asked, raising her voice before she stood. "You aren't the only one losing. I don't want to marry you. It's a means to an end. So, I'm sorry you've lost your girl, but the man I want will never be completely mine. This was an arrangement. It was to save us both, but I don't know if I can go through three years, let alone three months of this with you."

She was getting upset, and it was something I'd never seen from her before. She'd always been calm, together, but her tone, the way her accent deepened with each word made something inside me crack. In the center of my chest, something split open and the truth surfaced faster than I could comprehend.

I wasn't going to do this.

"What?" she asked.

I hadn't realized I said it out loud, but I did. It was out there. It hung in the air like smoke, the charred remains of everything I had burned.

"I'm not going to do this," I repeated. "I can't marry you."

Her head lowered, her hair shielding the expression on her face. "I...don't know what to say."

"Neither do I."

I didn't. How could I? One mistake was leading to another, creating a domino effect that was destroying everyone and everything around me. I thought I was saving everyone I loved, protecting them, but the hurt I was causing was doing that anyway. I had to end all the lies because the one thing I was trying to save was the very thing I was destroying.

"You are so unhappy," she said, staring at the ground. "You're filled with so much sadness and so much..." She paused, waving her hand around as she searched for the word she wanted. "Torment. So much torment."

I didn't know what the next move was, but I was going to

let her take it. Yes, she went along with it all, but I knew she was a victim, too, in some way.

And when her head lifted, I expected to see anger or hurt. Instead, I got something I completely didn't expect: relief.

She dragged her hands through her hair and held it tightly before twisting it around behind her. "I," she said, blowing out a sigh, "tried, Abel. Now that you've said it, I know what is true. It can't."

"I'm so sorry, Dafne."

"Are you?" she snapped, glaring at me.

"Yes. I shouldn't have done it. I shouldn't have gone into this knowing I wasn't going to be strong enough to marry you when my heart belongs to someone else. She's the one, *my* one," I said, running my hands through my hair. "I don't even know if that makes sense."

"It does make sense because you aren't the only one with love. I love Benji. Everything I have is because of him, but he belongs to someone else. If he could marry me, he would. I know he would. But he is promised to someone else already." She paused before shaking her head and continuing, "There is nothing left to say if you've made your decision."

I didn't know why, but in a way I was sorry for her. She was like me in a way. Stuck in a situation needing to find a way out. I felt the need to tell her that.

"Dafne, I'm sorry. I... I just... I don't even know how this all happened."

"Because you danced with the devil, Abel," she said as she stood and walked to the door.

I danced with the devil.

He brought me to hell and the only way to redemption was to either marry Dafne or pay up. I thought going to my parents would be the worst thing, having to admit to them I had gotten myself in trouble again. No. The worst thing was realizing I was getting exactly what I deserved by making deals with Benji again.

The final bridge had just gone up in flames. Now I was going to have to see how I could put out the fire.

"You know what?" she asked, leaning against the door. "Make something out of your life that is held with truth. Living a life running from who you are is hell. I will always run."

I wasn't sure what she meant, but I could guess. It wasn't like I ever asked why she needed to stay. Everything I did, every word spoken and step I took since the night of the poker tournament, when Dafne found me drunk outside an abandoned fast-food restaurant, was based on lies.

She snatched her purse and shoes from the floor by the door and flung it open. "*Vai a farti fottere*, Abel," she shouted before walking out, her shoes not even on her feet.

I wasn't sure what it meant, but I hoped it was something along the lines of, "Go fuck yourself, Abel."

And like that, another woman walked out of my life. There was something about thinking you'd hit rock bottom, but thinking and actually being there were two different things. I didn't need to think anymore if I was there. I was. I looked around my darkening apartment, and there was no hint of light. I was at the bottom.

The truth had me in a choke hold for months, and now, with no other place to turn, I had to release it.

I picked up my phone and scrolled through the names until I found the one I needed. I dialed and then I waited.

One ring.

Two ring.

Three…

"Hello?"

"Look, I know I'm not your favorite person right now and there's a lot of shit to cover, but I need you. I need your help, and I don't have anyone else to go to," I sniffled. My voice cracked as I continued, "You have no reason based off everything I've done, but I'm begging you to at least listen to me. Can you come over?"

There was a long pause, and I didn't know if the silence was the connection going bad or something else worse. But for the first time in months, I took in a breath that wasn't backed with fear when I heard Aaron say, "I'll be right there."

And he was.

The moment I opened the door his expression changed from annoyance to real concern, so quickly it even surprised me. In the half hour I waited for him to arrive, I'd prepared myself for everything he was going to throw at me— disappointment, judgment, anger, and all things in between. I was going to take it like the medicine I needed, the thing I deserved, and swallow every single bit of it.

He stepped inside, and as he unzipped his coat with one hand, he placed the other on my back. "All right. Let's do this," he said.

We went over to the kitchen table and sat opposite each other. I needed to look him in the eyes when I told him everything, so there was no room for him to think it was bullshit. I was coming clean, and in order to do that, I had to get all the dirty, disgusting truth out there for him to see.

I wasn't even afraid. I was ready. It was time. Because I knew this, could feel it in my bones, the words fell from my lips with candid ease.

His expression never changed, not even for a second when I told him that I lied about teaching online classes. Every cent I gave him toward the bar was made through gambling. There wasn't a shift of any kind in his posture when I told him that I awoke one morning after an all-night poker game with hardly any recollection of what had happened the night before. The night before I had racked up a debt in excess of $400,000. Aaron continued to hold steady as I explained I was given three choices: Pay the debt in the next two days; marry Dafne, who was Benji's girlfriend, so she could secure a green card; or do neither and put everyone I loved around me in danger.

Aaron barely took a breath when I said I would give up my life for three years to marry Dafne, to pay off the debt, but more importantly, to keep him and everyone else safe.

He leaned back against his chair and folded his hands in front of him. "Abel, you have really screwed up good, but it would've been a lot easier to work through if you would've come to me months ago. I'm not trying to be condescending, but how could you not trust me enough to know there isn't anything I wouldn't help you through? That there is anything I wouldn't do for you?"

I shook my head. "I wasn't going to put you in that position, Aaron. Benji doesn't fuck around, and I wasn't going to put you in danger. It was my problem to deal with, or at least, I thought it was."

He rubbed his hand across his jaw, letting the weight of my words sink in. There was a lot there, and I wasn't sure if he would or could believe me.

"You think we should just pay him?" Aaron asked.

The way he said "we" made tears sting my eyes. I didn't know why I ever doubted him or thought he wouldn't be exactly where he had always been: right by my side. I didn't want him to save me, and I didn't think he was necessarily doing that. He was just doing what he always did—be a brother.

"I see no way around getting out of it," I said.

He slapped his hand on the glass table, shaking the vase sitting in the middle. "Shit, that is a fuck ton of money. I can't just write a check for that amount and go on my way. I'm going to have to sell off some stock or figure something else out. Hell, Dad is probably going to have to kick in because I don't know right now if I can swing it all."

He was offering before I could even ask. Of course he was because that was what Aaron always did.

"I didn't want you to bail me out again," I said. "You and Dad were finally looking at me like I could do something for real with the bar and shit."

"Oh, for Christ's sake. Have you made some poor decisions over the years? Yes. But you know what? So have I. So has Dad. So has everyone in this world. Okay, so this is a biggie, and we'll figure it out, but I'll only do it if you promise me one thing."

"Of course, I'll pay you back. Every single cent. I wouldn't be able to live with myself if I didn't because—"

"It goes without saying. I'm serious as hell, Abel. You're going to pay in every sense of the word."

"And I'm going to get help," I said. Years ago in college, I chalked it up to me being a screwup. Now? It was something more than that. I didn't know how to name it, or even recognize it, but it was there. "I wanted to be your equal with the bar. The gambling was a fast way to make money, and it was working well for a time. I might have been fooled, but I never should have been there to begin with. Now, the money is the price I'm going to have to pay, along with probably having already lost Evelyn forever."

Aaron gave me a sad, confused look. "Why would you think you ever had to be my equal?"

"Because I never felt like I was."

He shook his head. "What? Because I ran a few successful businesses? That's bullshit, Abel. You are everything I'm not. You're fearless and insanely talented. You don't run away or hide your feelings. Your career path? Your desire to be a teacher? It's noble, and you choose it because you have the heart to want to give back to kids. Now, if you don't think that's amazing, if you don't think there were times that I hoped I could be more like *you*, then you have more issues than just a gambling problem."

The tears began to fall, and I wasn't even embarrassed about it. "There is so much shit to sort out I don't know where to begin, but I know I need help."

"There's no shame in that, Abel. When Callie and I had

our shit, I didn't know which way was up and which way was down. I had to see a therapist to figure my own issues out."

That surprised me. I always thought he had it figured out. Even if he made a mistake, I thought he knew how to fix it right away. He wasn't perfect after all, and realizing that eased my conscience slightly.

I pressed my hand onto the table, fingerprints marking the glass from my sweat as I wiped away tears with my other hand. "I'm sure I don't need to say this, but I can't pay anything more for the California bar. I should've said ages ago, and I realize the irony of this will be enough to make this whole conversation even more ridiculous, but I got a teaching offer. I got the call two days ago, but it's been a fucked-up two days. Anyway, it's for a woman going on maternity leave in March, so I'll still stay at WET a couple nights. If it goes well, they may offer me something else. I don't know."

"We'll figure it out, okay," he said. He rose from his chair and walked over to me. His hand rested on my shoulder. "*You're* going to figure it all out."

I leveled my eyes to his and spoke straight from my heart, clear and with honesty. "Yes, I will."

* * *

I paced the alley behind the building that housed By Invitation Only. I knew which way she would head when she left and I was a safe distance away. Far enough away to hide, but close enough to catch when I needed to. The temperature was in the teens, but with the windchill, it was almost below zero. The wind whipping around stung my skin, but was no match for the burning anxiety I had waiting for her.

I saw her immediately, with only one foot into the alley to cross it, before I called to her.

"Evelyn? Can I talk to you for a second?"

She leaned back on the heel of one of her black shiny shoes and placed her hands on her hips. "What is it, Abel?"

"Please. It'll only take a minute."

She tied the belt of her red coat tighter as she headed toward me, the sounds of car horns and my heart echoing in my ears. It had been weeks since I'd seen her, and she was the same as I last remembered. Stunning and cold. The cold part had nothing to do with the weather, either. She was so strong. She was stronger than me because every step she took closer I had to force down the lump in my throat that was forming. The lights above the buildings cast a halo around her, illuminating her hair and the gold strands blowing in the wind.

She stopped an arm's length away and cocked her head to the side. "What?"

I should've planned better what I was going to say, but all that came out was, "I'm not getting married."

"Yeah?" she asked.

Her cheeks were bright pink from the cold wind, and I so wanted to reach out to touch them, to know what they felt like. I'd never touched her face in the cold.

I shoved my hands into the pockets of my coat. "Yeah. I wanted to…tell…you."

She shrugged. "And why would I care?"

"I don't know. I...I—"

"What?" she snapped. "It's cold as shit out here, and you can't spit out whatever it is you want to say. You came here. You wanted to say something. Say it!"

"I love you!" I shouted. "I'm not getting married because it was all bullshit and I want the chance to explain it to you if you'll let me, but I'm in love with you. I love you."

Her eyes were wide and her head shook, first slowly, then faster and faster. "No," she said. "No. You don't get to say that now."

"Why not? I should've said it before, but I'm telling you now. I'm so fucking in love with you and that should've been enough for me to not fuck up, but I did. I want to tell you everything. I want to tell you that I'm working on my book, and I got a teaching offer and how Dafne—"

She pushed her hands into my chest. "Don't say her name! Just...don't do any of this!"

She spun around and tried to run off, but I caught her arm, forcing her back to me. She needed to believe me. She needed to look into my eyes and see the trust, the thing I'd been hiding from her for months.

She pulled against my grip until she didn't. Her body turned, her back to me, and I saw the smallest movement of the shoulders.

Raised. Lowered.

Faster.

Shaking.

"Evelyn?" I whispered. "Are you okay?"

"No," she mumbled. "I'm not okay. I can't do this, Abel. I can't see you or hear your voice or anything."

Her voice cracked at the end, and I watched as her entire body almost caved in on itself. Sobs, heartbreaking, gut-wrenching cries emerged as she bent at the waist, her arms wrapped around her stomach.

I knew she didn't want me to, but I had to. I had to touch her. I had to do something.

I don't know how it happened, but one moment I was cautiously approaching, touching her shoulder with the gentlest of touches and the next she was in my arms.

She hadn't been so close in so long. Her smell, *her* smell wasn't just the perfume. I was never, ever going to be able to re-create it. It was all her.

Sobs shook her whole body as she gripped the back of my coat in her fists. I let her. I wanted her to make me feel it—the pain I caused her—so I could remember it. I wanted to hear it in her broken cries, her labored breathing. I wanted to taste it in her tears.

I cradled her face in my hands, wiping away her tears with my thumbs. There were too many for me to keep up with it.

I did this. I did this to her and it was killing me.

I wanted to tell her to stop, but I didn't have that right.

Her eyes, rimmed red and hued purple underneath, looked at me, tore into me. Desperate. Pleading.

I brought my damp fingers to my mouth and tasted her tears. Taking what I did to her into my body so I could swallow it whole.

She yanked my fingers from my mouth and pressed her lips there instead.

It was all madness.

It was tongues and biting and groans until I had her up against the brick side of the building, her legs wrapped around my waist. It was cold, but not cold enough to stop.

It was everything I missed. Everything I wanted. But it was different now.

She ground into me harder and harder, as I grew harder and harder. Then I made a mistake. I spoke and then it broke.

"I missed you," I said between kisses.

She paused all of her movements and stilled her lips on mine before retreating so very slightly. Then those eyes were back on mine, and all the hurt and anger filled right back in before me, replacing where the tears had been flowing.

With our lips only inches apart I couldn't brace myself fast enough.

"What are you trying to do, Abel? Do you want to fuck me to try and forget about her?"

I was naive and so fucking stupid. I carefully lowered her to the ground, and the moment her foot met the pavement, she ran.

Away.

Again.

CHAPTER TWENTY-THREE

EVELYN—

Two things grew from betrayal—pain and confusion. Both were like currents that had me drifting calmly for days on end until a sharp shift would propel me off toward one. I'd tried to hold tight to one, but the waves would be too strong and my body would crash into another. Pain and confusion were often equal parts of the sea, but the elements of rational and irrational measured the same. I found validation in both because they rose through me together. However, I wasn't drowning anymore. The truth gave me peace, a sliver of hope, but it wasn't enough to keep me from going under at times.

It was much like the March weather. Rainy dark days that rolled in violent storms biting at the skin with icy edges left over from winter. I'd watch the waves crash up against the barricades when I ran along the lake. It seemed like the sky didn't reveal the sun for days on end, but the days when the gray parted, only for a moment, the sun was still there.

I hadn't seen him or talked to him since I left him in the alley almost two months ago. Up until that day, I thought the hardest thing I'd ever done was leave him to go to Charleston. No. The hardest was turning my back, knowing he was free and clear, and walking away from him again. It would've been so easy, so seamless, to erase all that had happened, and slip right back until us. But the brain and the heart didn't work like that.

And I wondered about him endlessly. How he was doing. What he was doing. Callie and Aaron never said, and I never asked. The wounds were still so raw, and I hadn't been ready to throw salt into them. Maybe it was time or maybe it was two mimosas in me at brunch one Saturday morning at Flo's with Callie that made me ask.

I sliced into another area of my Fruity Pebbles French Toast, taking a piece to dip into the zabaglione cream. "How is he?" I asked without looking up from my plate.

Callie stopped mid-bite into her Cocoa Pebbles French Toast. "Who?"

"Voldemort," I said, rolling my eyes. "Who do you think?"

"Well, we shouldn't be discussing either of them, but if you really want to know, I'm not going to keep anything from you." She took a sip of her Bellini, taking longer to respond than I'd expected her to. "He's good."

"And?"

"And what?"

"That's it? Come on, Cal. You said you weren't going to keep anything from me."

She tilted her head to the side and frowned. "Why do you want to know?"

I pressed my fork into the cereal crumbs and again looked to my plate, not her. "I don't know."

"I think we'll need to make a deal if I tell you anything, okay?"

"What kind of deal?" I asked, raising my eyebrows. "You always have crazy conditions."

"Nope. No conditions. Well, that's not exactly true. There's one. I don't want you to get upset."

And there it was. Something was going on that I didn't know about. My mind began running into a million different directions. Did he change his mind and go back to her? Did he regret saying he loved me?

"Wipe the pout off your face," she demanded. "I haven't said anything yet and you're already sad."

"When you say you don't want me to get upset what am I supposed to think?"

She sighed and tossed her napkin on top of her plate. "This is all so screwed up and again I feel like I'm in the middle."

"I didn't mean to do that, Cal. I know you and Aaron have been through a lot with this and—"

"Do you?" she asked. Her voice raised in the way I knew meant she was upset. "I don't think you know. Aaron and I argued so much over the whole thing. There were hurt feelings between us. We've worked really hard to not let untruths come between us. So, I don't think either you or Abel know what Aaron and I went through."

She was right. I didn't. And even though I'd witnessed how upset they both were the night of their Christmas party, I'd never apologized for probably ruining it.

I slid my hand across the table and put it on top of hers. "I'm sorry. I'm sorry I've been too wrapped up in my own shit to even ask. I mean, I'd be lying if I said it hadn't crossed my mind over the last few months that you and Aaron both warned me it was a bad idea to get involved with Abel. I should've listened."

"We both told Abel the same about you. It wasn't that we didn't think you were good enough or whatever, but we knew if things didn't go well it would create such a mess. Like, my best friend hasn't been over to my house since the night she stormed out in tears. And my boyfriend's brother never comes around, either. He won't even go to his parents' for family dinner with us. So, what I'm saying is, I didn't want you to apologize. I wanted you to know Aaron and I miss you. We miss Abel. You two don't have to be together, but you can't stay away from us forever."

"It wasn't going to be forever, but you've been there. I wasn't ready."

"I know and that's why I waited until you brought it up first. Like, we're planning this amazing springtime *Alice in Wonderland* party for Delilah's seventh birthday. She asks about you all the time, and I know she'll be heartbroken if you *both* weren't there."

"Wow. You're bringing out the big guns with that kind of guilt."

"It's not supposed to be, but I don't know."

We were both quiet, sipping at our drinks and looking out windows. My hand retreated. There were so many people out for an early Saturday afternoon walk. It always got that way when the weather began to shift. The cold kept us inside all winter and at the first break, even if it meant only a little, we ran with it. It wasn't even unusual to me to see a man pass by in shorts and flip-flops, walking a big black Labrador.

"How is he?" I asked, still gazing out the window.

"He's good, sweetie. He's getting all his shit straightened out. Of course Aaron and their dad, have him on a short leash because of all of the money, but Abel has been going above and beyond. The teaching job is going well, and he's still working at WET a few nights a week. Plus, since he moved out of the building, it—"

I snapped my head toward her. "Wait. What? He moved out of the apartment?"

"Ah. Yeah. It was his idea, too. He figured instead of his parents letting him live there rent-free, he'd move out so Daniel and Leslie could get renters. It's more than what Abel could repay what his dad fronted for the payoff."

I had absolutely no idea what she was talking about. Every word made less sense than the next.

"Why do you look like that?" Callie asked. "Didn't you know he moved out?"

"No. He never said, not that we had much of a chance to talk about our current living situations. And what are you talking about the money? Why does he owe Aaron and Daniel so much money?"

Her jaw dropped open, which she immediately covered

with her hand. "Are you serious? You don't know?" she mumbled.

I slapped her hand. "What?" I shouted loud enough for the people at the nearby tables to turn around.

"I...don't know if I should be the one to tell you this. You really should let Abel tell you because—"

I was going to scream again, but instead of causing a scene, I decided to cause a bit of a smaller one. I leaned over the table and clasped my hand over her mouth. "Listen to me," I hissed. "You are going to tell me everything. I mean everything. I mean every single damn detail down to the minute. You're going to do this because you're my best friend and you don't want to see me lose my mind. Do you understand?"

She nodded and I released my grip. Both of us picked up our champagne glasses at the same time and drained what was left in them.

"What's that lotion you're wearing?" she asked. "Is it that stuff from Bliss? The lemon one?"

I glared at her as she motioned our server over. He stepped over, and Callie circled the table with her index finger. "We're going to need one more round, Omar."

"Ladies going hard-core at brunch," he said, picking up our empty glasses. "I like it."

He winked at me as he walked away, and although a bit on the vertically challenged side, he wasn't bad. This was the time I knew Abel changed something in me. There was a time I'd be interested. Now? All I could concentrate on was what the hell was going on with him.

"Yes," I said. "Bliss. Now, please tell me."

She took in a deep breath. "Okay. So, you know how Abel was going to get married to that girl Dafne no one had even ever heard of?"

"Yes. I seem to recall, Callie," I answered, my voice dripping with sarcasm.

"I'm prefacing. You don't need to be a bitch about it. Anyway, well, I guess they met when he was playing poker at those underground games. She was there one night when you were gone, and Abel lost big. Like, a lot big."

"Are you kidding me? Like, how much money? And how come he never told me?"

Omar came back, and we paused as he set the drinks down in front of us. He lingered a bit, looking between us, but without saying anything.

"Thanks," I said. "We'll let you know if we need anything."

As he stepped away, Callie gave me a dirty look. "Don't treat servers like that!"

"Like what?"

"Rude! That was me for a lot of years."

"I wasn't being rude because he was a server. I was being rude because we're obviously in the middle of a conversation and he was gawking. Regardless," I said, picking up my Bellini and taking a large sip. "Continue."

"I'm not sure why he didn't tell you. I guess he was really embarrassed. He had gotten in trouble with gambling before and swore he wouldn't do it again, but I guess, in an effort to try and go in financially with Aaron with the new bar, he started doing it again to make money. He lost big, and he didn't want to go to Aaron and tell him, 'Hey, I owe over $400,000. Can you give me a hand with that?' He and his dad were going on and on about being proud of him for getting his shit together. I guess he felt he couldn't go to them and you and tell you what he did."

It could've been all the sugar from the French toast or all the booze, but hearing $400,000 made me light-headed. "Shit, Callie."

"I know. Take a sip because you'll need it for this next part."

This worried me even more, but I did as she said.

"Okay," she continued. "Long story short, and to be honest, I can't tell you all the details because I only know what Aaron told me, and boys always leave out the best parts, but the debt was going to be forgiven if Abel agreed to marry Dafne, who happens to be Benji's, the head of all the poker games, mistress."

"Why the hell would he agree to that?"

"I guess Benji was threatening to hurt people Abel loved. He couldn't marry Dafne because he is already married. She's his side chick. So, with her visa expiring, they needed to figure something out. He was desperate. Done deal."

"No. It wasn't a done deal. He didn't tell me! He didn't…anything!"

"I know. And believe me, when I got him in my claws, I went after him so hard he'll probably be scarred for life. But now that time has gone by, I can understand why he did it. I'm not saying it was right at all. Not even a little bit. But I understand."

"How can you even say that to me?"

"Because I've done things I knew were wrong, and it wasn't because I didn't love Aaron. It was because I was trying to protect him."

"You fibbing about something is a little different than you getting married to someone else behind his back. And while we're on the subject, why didn't he?"

She shrugged. "I don't know. Maybe his conscience caught up to him. He came clean to Aaron and that's how it went down."

"I can't believe any of this. I mean, he was going to marry someone else instead of trusting any of us to help? It's ridiculous."

"I'm not disagreeing with you. It is. Sitting here with you and saying it out loud, it seems impossible, but he didn't see a way out. Plus, take some time to see it from his perspective. If someone was threatening to hurt or harm any of us, wouldn't you do whatever you could to make sure that didn't happen?"

I hadn't cried in front of her since the night of the Christmas party when she laid in bed with me. I prided myself on keeping it together, but after what she said, tears began to fall. There was no way of even knowing what part of the story was making me so emotional.

"I should've been his out," I whispered. "It should have been me."

* * *

There was a certain comfort in knowing the truth, but comfort didn't replace anger. So much hurt could've been avoided if he'd only told the truth. Even now, it would've been nice to know the whole thing was a farce so I could've stopped blaming myself. I'd said everything I needed to say to him already, but that was before today. There was so much I wanted to get off my chest. It was why I stood outside of WET later that night, or next morning, considering it was close to two a.m.

I paced back and forth at the corner of the building, a fine mist of rain dampening my hair and coat. It was chilly, but not cold. Or maybe the march I had going at kept me warm enough. It was a safe distance, knowing I'd see him when he exited, but still far away enough. Patrons wandered out, shaky on their feet and voices loud from too much liquor. Anxiety swirled around me, settling into my brain and telling me this was a bad idea. Was I going to be opening a door that should be kept closed? Was I inviting in more confusion and making it even more difficult to completely move on?

I wasn't sure so, I knew better than to take a chance. My car was parked on the opposite side of the building, so I had to step across the fading dandelion to get to it. Coincidence was a bitch because the moment my foot passed the dandelion the hidden door popped open. Tyler saw me and I knew I was caught.

"Hey, stranger," he said. "What are you doing out here?"

"Oh, well. I was going to," I said, motioning at the door he was holding open, but then wondering what to say. I didn't know how much or how little the people he worked with knew.

"Get in here. It's cold and rainy," he said.

"Actually. I was going to head home instead because I was, and then, I...don't think...and whatever."

There was no judgment from him over my babble, but only a warm smile, which led me to believe he knew enough to not pass judgment. "Listen," he said, leaning against the door. "There's only a few stragglers left. If you don't want to go into the bar, I can go get him for you and you won't have to leave the front."

Him.

It was why I was there. If I walked away again, I'd still have to carry all the thoughts that had been running through my head all day, all these months, with me for a long time. I was tired of carrying.

"Okay," I said.

The florets that guided me to the door were almost gone. As I stepped inside, I wondered if they were going to replace them with something else. I wasn't prepared for all my senses to remember WET all at the same time. I hadn't been inside since the night I came with Bridget and most of that evening was a bit fuzzy.

"Hang tight, Evelyn. I'll go get him," Tyler said, unhooking the velvet rope. He disappeared around the corner, but he stepped back. "It's good to see you."

I tried to run my hands through my wet hair, but a messy knot of tangles and hair spray made it impossible. There was no doubt I looked a mess, and while I wasn't here to impress anyone, I didn't want anyone to get the impression I wasn't okay. Weakness wasn't something I admired in others, nor myself. My hand dug around my bag searching for my lipstick, but with the dim lights, I couldn't see. Maybe I should've come earlier because it was so quiet inside. It made me uneasy. No. I came when I did because I knew he'd be busy otherwise.

I heard his voice before I saw him. My heart recognized it before my brain. It was funny how that worked.

I only saw half of him before I saw him completely. He was so tentative with his steps, curving around the corner and into the hallway. His expression was confused, like he couldn't believe I was there. I couldn't believe it, either. The beard was coming back in, more like overgrown stubble now, and his face looked how I'd always remembered it. His white button-down was like all the others he usually wore, and while he didn't look as thin as the last time I saw him, it still was big on him. Unlike the last time few times I saw him when he seemed like a different person, he was Abel again.

"Hey," he said, stopping several feet away from me. "Is everything okay?"

"Yeah. I, well, no, everything isn't okay. I mean, nothing urgent, but—" I paused to gather my thoughts before continuing. "I need to talk to you. I had brunch with Callie this morning and she told me...everything."

His head tilted to the side and he ran his hands through his hair. "Okay, well, I'm about done here. We can step into Marshall's office."

"Won't he mind?"

"No. He's in California for the next few days checking up on the new place."

"Why is he there?"

His fingers were fumbling with the cuffs of his shirt. "He bought out my share," he said without looking at me.

The money. Maybe he would've given it up anyway, but he was paying his debt. Chipping away at what he could control, the apartment, the bar, in a way he could.

"I heard you moved, too."

"Seems that she did tell you everything, huh?"

"Don't be angry at her. I made her tell me."

He shrugged. "I'm not angry at her. I would've told you myself, but—"

"But what?"

"Come on. Let's go somewhere private," he said, stepping back to let me through.

His hand brushed across my back, and even through my coat, feeling that little bit of him made me shiver. I tried not to look around too much as we headed to Marshall's office. There were too many memories. The nights I sat and watched him work, dazzled by his ability to make every customer smile. The nights Marshall and I would bust his balls and get him going, only to take him home to my bed where I'd lick his wounds. The nights I came with Bridget. The first time when I knew there was more to him than the overtly sexed and slightly inappropriate man. And the last time I was here, vomiting in the bathroom and knowing I'd never been lower.

Walking into Marshall's office wasn't any easier. My mind

recalled the night I showed him my "I Need a Stiff One" undies, and Marshall busted us fooling around. We were happy then. Even when he went alpha on me after we left the room, and he went down on me as we drove to his apartment, we were happy. It was love then. I just didn't know it.

I took in a deep breath as Abel shut the door behind us, and I heard him do the same. He stepped over to Marshall's desk and flipped down the hutch on top, retrieving a bottle of bourbon and two glasses.

"Provisions," he said, pouring the liquor into the crystal whiskey glasses.

"That seems like a smart idea. I'm not sure the two-finger pour will be enough, so I wouldn't put the bottle away if I were you."

He handed me a glass. "Not a chance."

We stood with our glasses, wondering if we should do the courtesy clink, but it seemed almost too intimate. Instead, he lifted his to his mouth, tilting it slightly as a gesture, before bringing it to his lips. I followed, taking in a large sip, letting the warmth of the liquor hit my veins to take the edge off my nerves. He took longer, and I watched him swallow once, pause, and then take in another.

It was just enough of the liquid courage I needed.

"Why didn't you tell me?" I asked.

He took one more sip. "I wanted to. I should have." He shook his head. "No. That's bullshit. I didn't tell you then because I was scared out of my mind. I was scared of anyone, of you, getting hurt because of a stupid mistake I made. I was also so fucking embarrassed. I thought you'd hate who I was.

It ate away at me. I couldn't bear the thought of you hating me, and even though in the end what I did was worse. It was all about me, and then it was all about everyone else and me trying to save you. I didn't figure that in. It was fucked up. I know that now."

"You didn't try. You didn't do anything except let me find out from Callie."

"You're right. I could stand here and say that wasn't exactly what happened. Or that it isn't how I wanted it to happen, that I thought I'd have time to figure out what to tell you. It would all be semantics."

"How do you think this makes me feel?"

He blew out another large breath. "I can't imagine. From my perspective, I wasn't going to assume you wanted to know about anything. I wanted you to be able to handle things in your way, in your own time. If this conversation never occurred, I would've had to be okay with it. I was leaving it up to you because I didn't do that before. Maybe it was another mistake, but with it all being laid out in front of me, I'm really trying to do the right thing *now*."

I'd come expecting an argument or, in the very least, a firm denial about his role, but it wasn't happening. He was owning up, and it was completely unexpected. I decided to push harder. It was almost like it was easy for him, and I wasn't going to let him get away with it.

"So, you chose to get married to someone else over me?"

"Yes," he said, bringing his glass to his mouth again. After he swallowed, he continued. "I needed to figure it out on my own, and I couldn't. I couldn't go to Aaron or my parents and let them know I messed up again. I was drowning and I was not going to allow any of you to go down with me."

I looked down at my shoes, the patent leather still showing droplets of rain. He loved these shoes. "I would've helped you," I muttered. "I should've been the hand."

"The money, beautiful. It was so much money. Plus, I didn't want you to know how much of a failure I really was. My mind was so twisted. I thought you hating me because I was marrying someone else would be an easier redemption than knowing how much I failed as a man. That was worse for me at the time. It was wrong. It was so fucking wrong."

It was the first time he'd called me beautiful. I didn't think he even realized he did it. I'd never forgotten, but what I didn't recall was how it made my bones ache, made my insides vibrate against every syllable.

It made me furious.

I set my glass down on the bookcase next to me. "You know, I hear the words. I hear every single one you've said so far. They go around and around my head," I said, spinning my index finger around my head. "All the time. I turn it over and over, and I can't make sense of it. So, I'm going to need you to explain to me why I meant so little to you that you could fuck me over so hard you didn't even think that telling me you were getting married wasn't the first thing you did."

He squeezed his eyes shut and shook his head. "Evelyn, first off. You didn't mean little to me," he said before his eyes opened to mine. "You meant *everything*. You were, you are, absolutely everything to me. And I wanted to be everything for you. I wanted to be the man you desired in every sense.

I wanted to, I don't know, provide for you, and take care of myself, and take you on vacation, and be strong and ambitious. I love you enough to want to be better, to be who you deserved."

"But that's ridiculous. I didn't want any of that. You were already all I needed or wanted. Was money ever an issue? Did I ever demand a vacation or jewelry or make you believe I gave a shit about any of that?"

"No," he answered calmly. "But it wasn't about you. That's what I keep telling you. It was all me. It was twisted and fucked up, but it was how I rationalized it. Hell, even now, me trying to explain my state of mind then, it sounds like I'm trying to justify it. I did, but that was *then*. I had to take it, and swallow it, and let it sink into my body before I realized it."

"There's no easy way out. Marrying someone else was easy. Telling the truth was the hard way. You need to think about that because if there is ever a chance for me, or someone else in the future, you have to be willing to deal with the hard. I would've dealt with it. We could have done it together. That's what couples in, what I thought was, a committed relationship do. Trust each other. You should've trusted me enough. You should've trusted *us* enough."

"I didn't know how to do that then. I know that's not a good explanation, but I couldn't tell you I owed that kind of money. There was no way to come up with it. And if I didn't pay Benji, then I don't even want to think about what he was capable of doing. A buddy of mine got thrown off a building because he couldn't pay up in time. Again, it's so delusional

I can't even believe it myself, but at that moment, when trying to put shit back together, I saw a way out. It's like when you tell a lie, and then have to tell another to cover it up. You want to come clean, but you look at the tangled web you've created, and you feel trapped. That was me. When it came down to it, I couldn't let the lies keep me from what I knew to be true."

My skin tingled because it was all so much. "You need fucking therapy, Abel."

He tipped what was left in his glass into his mouth, swallowing hard. "I know. I'm getting it now. Also, Gamblers Anonymous."

"Did someone make you do that?"

He shook his head. "No, I needed help. I realized that. Every move I made, walking into that first meeting, finding a therapist and shit was all me."

I was glad and surprised. There were a lot of things about this conversation that hadn't gone how I thought it would have. Maybe he wasn't the same Abel inside, even though he was on the outside.

I returned to my own glass, lifting it from the bookcase, leaving a ring behind. "What changed your mind?" I asked, downing the rest of mine.

"Sorry?"

"Why didn't you marry her? It could've all been over and done with, but here you are. You're trying to clean up the mess."

"I didn't marry her because of one simple reason. She wasn't the one. You're the one."

It burned stronger than the whiskey swirling around my stomach. The heels of my shoes swayed beneath me, but I knew I couldn't fall apart. I couldn't let the words that used to mean something to me let me forget.

He took a step toward me, only one, and paused. "It's unforgivable. What I did. It's all on me. I understand if you can't. I really do. I'm not sure if I'd be able to if the roles were reversed, but it would be unforgivable to myself to not try my damnedest to make you remember why you once loved me."

"Forgiving and forgetting are two different things," I said. "Forgiving I can work on, but I'll never forget. I don't know how I can look at you without thinking about it."

"Beautiful," he said. "I miss you. I miss you so much."

I missed him, too. I missed all the good things about him, about us, but the bad things clouded over all of it. There was a large part of me that wanted to say, *Screw it. He messed up, but it's over now.* But I knew the doubt I had for him would still be there.

"I…don't know how to justify this, Abel," I said. "I don't. I can't wrap my mind around forgiving you for this and still being able to respect myself. It'll always be in the back of my mind. Always."

"I'm not asking you to forgive me right now, but please. If you need time, and need me to leave you alone, I'll do it, for however long you need me to. If you need me to, I don't know, hell, go to Antarctica, I will. All I know is you're the one. You're the one for me, and we were special together. Look at me," he begged. "*We* know this was special. We know because we lived it."

"I know, but you didn't trust me. I trusted you and you broke that."

"I did and whatever comes from that I'll have to take. But I can't forget about us, what we had, and know how special it was."

An anger shot right through me, fierce and unexpected, and I wasn't going to hold back. "You're right. What we did have was special, and I think that is the hardest part of all of this because now I don't know what to do with this...feeling...of stupidity I feel like is written all over my forehead. It did seem special, and it was a love I'd never known before. Never in my life did I think such devotion existed. But now, I feel so naive for believing. I feel so damn stupid for believing in the fairy tale, but like those fairy-tale weddings I help plan, it was all an illusion."

"And that breaks me apart inside, beautiful. It makes me want to run and hide it hurts so bad, but I'm going to stand here and take it. It's my penance for what I did. Any other time in my life, I'd try to pin it on someone else or allow others to think, *Oh, that's how Abel is.* Not this time."

"Why should I believe you?"

"I don't know why. Maybe because this has finally made me grow the hell up. Maybe because when I lost you I knew my actions had reactions and I never want to feel that way again. Maybe because I'm getting help to understand all of it. Or maybe because I'm telling you everything, that I'm leaving it all on the table this time. There's nothing I'm holding back, and I know you can't trust in that right now, and I need to prove it to you, but it's everything I have. Everything I have I'm giving to you."

His pleading eyes broke through all I was holding together. A lump formed in the back of my throat, and I couldn't find the words to continue. I came looking for answers, but as I stood there, I had hundreds more questions.

"I need to go," I whispered.

He opened his mouth to respond, but before he did, his jaw snapped shut. "Okay," he said, nodding. "I'll walk you out."

The silent pauses between us must have lasted longer than I'd thought because as we exited Marshall's office, the bar was empty. The candles had been extinguished and the bar had been wiped down to a shine. I paused, running my fingers over the smooth surface while I recalled how I fell in love with him here. He was still here, but it was all different.

"Did you forget something?" he asked.

My back was to him as I considered if I did forget something. I'd said I wanted to leave, so why couldn't I?

"Evelyn?" he asked.

"You moved?"

"Ah, yeah. I'm sure Callie filled you in, but it was the right thing to do. I should've done it a long time ago. This makes sense considering how much money and…"

He trailed off, and I wasn't sure why. I had to turn around to see he was doing his own daydreaming. Night dreaming. Dreaming.

His gaze was focused above my head when he said in faint voice, "I forgot a lot of things, but mostly I was thinking about you seeing my new place. It's such a dump, but it doesn't really bother me."

"As long as you're happy," I said.

His eyes shifted as if he remembered where he was, who he was with. "I'm not unhappy, but—"

"No buts," I said, stopping him. "That's enough. And you're teaching, yes?"

He smiled, and it was the first time I'd seen his dimples in *months*. It was also the first time I'd seen anything resembling happiness come from him.

"Freshman high school English."

"I was always afraid you'd end up in high school."

"Why?"

"Because you're going to have a whole lot of young girls falling in love with you."

"I doubt that. I'm pretty hard-core."

"A dreamy-looking teacher with wit to match? Come on."

The dimples disappeared and he frowned. "Dreamy and wit? You still think that?"

"I never stopped thinking that."

The stare down that followed rivaled any epic battles. Everything around us stood still—time, the earth—except our breathing. With every rise and fall of his chest, my heart beat faster, harder. I'd never know who moved first or why, but we met in the middle. Two large strides for him, and nearly a sprint for me, before our bodies crashed into each other, creating the most beautiful annihilation.

Our mouths, our hands, all at once. It was like the day out in the alley, but it was nothing like that. The alley was all in vain and shrouded in torment. Today was a release, a remembrance.

He lifted me up onto the bar, but our kisses never broke. We'd already had so much broken. I grabbed at his shirt to bring him closer, as close as I could get him, with such force I was sure there'd be scratch marks on his chest left behind by me.

His lips tasted of bourbon and him. One familiar and the other a recollection backed by a flood of memories.

He pushed it all into me. Every lie, every regret, and he placed it all on me.

He gave me it all and I took every single bit of it. I took from his lips and in the fistfuls of his hair I held in my hands. I took his muttered words against my lips, the way he repeated over and over "I'm so, so in love with you."

He was so brave, so unafraid. I wanted to push him away for reminding me why I fell in love with him.

I took it from his tongue moving with mine because he still knew how I liked it.

I took it all because there was nothing left of me.

And he fucking owed it to me.

We were winded and weak not only from the kisses, but from all the things they were backed by. He leaned his head against mine, brushing his fingers up and down the back of my neck. My own touch moved across his stubble, his jaw and down his neck.

"The dandelion outside?" I whispered.

"It was the last wish I had."

"I need time," I said.

"And I'm going to give it to you."

CHAPTER TWENTY-FOUR

ABEL—

I never knew I could be so exhausted and so exhilarated at the same time. Working two jobs, along with everything else I had going on, left little time for sleep. As I sat in my car after school, I leaned back against the headrest. The warmth from the late-day sun shining through the windshield would be enough to gently nudge me into sleep, but there were too many other things to do. Grading papers, print shop, meeting, and since it was Thursday, a shortened shift at WET. I'd never known such a hectic schedule, but it all seemed right. The high school I was at offered me a full-time job for the fall teaching Senior English and acting as advisor for the school newspaper. It was a damn dream come true.

Except it wasn't.

She was always the one thing missing.

I started the car and pulled out of the faculty parking lot, which in and of itself was a trip, considering I didn't feel old enough to be a teacher. Almost two months since she showed up at WET and not a word from her since. When I'd promised her time, I didn't know it was an indefinite term. Then again, I didn't know much about anything as far as we were concerned.

My phone vibrated, shaking against the loose change in the cup holder, with a call. I hit the answer button, receiving from the speaker.

"What's up, Aaron?" I asked.

"Callie wants to make sure you're coming for Delilah's party on Saturday?" he asked. He sounded exasperated, which was probably a result of Callie standing next to him, making sure he was calling me.

"Yes. I'll be there. Although I don't know about the whole *Alice in Wonderland* thing."

"Yeah, well, me neither, but it's what the girls want. I'm sure you'll understand some day that giving in to the women in your life is a lot easier than fighting about...Ouch! What the hell was that for?"

"Hi Callie," I shouted. "Leave him alone. I'll be there."

There was a brief exchange of muffled words before Aaron returned. "Everything else cool?"

"Yeah. Everything is cool."

A several second pause followed, which I knew meant he was fishing for something.

He wanted to ask how things were really, if I was keeping myself in check. He wanted to ask how my new place was and if I got the leaky shower fixed yet. He wanted to ask how the teaching was going and if I'd talked to Evelyn. He wanted to ask, but he wanted me to tell him. We were both stubborn pussies.

"It'll be good to see you," he said. "Miss you."

I'd been scarce mostly for the excuse of being too busy, but before then it was out of pure embarrassment. Somewhere in the middle and bleeding into the present was I didn't want to see Evelyn. Excuses got me nowhere before.

"See you Saturday. Miss you, too," I said.

Maybe we were both just plain ol' pussies.

We hung up, and I continued to navigate my way to the other side of the city during Chicago rush hour, which lasted from three p.m. to seven p.m. most days. It sucked I'd have to hike it back to get to WET, but I could hit the other places on my list within one metered spot. A coveted parking spot like the one I found outside Lightning Printing was nothing to fuck with.

"Excuse me," I said to the woman behind the counter. Her green polo shirt with the business logo on the side of the collar was clearly too big since the open buttons exposed the top of a lacy black bra.

"Yes?" she answered, tossing her long braided hair over her shoulder.

"I sent an order over this morning and I think it should be ready."

"What's the last name?"

"Matthews."

She typed something into the computer, her fake teal-painted nails tapping against the keys. "I hope your first name isn't Matthew," she said glancing at me out of the corner of her eye.

"Ah. No," I said. "Abel."

"Good. I like that *much* better," she said. She focused on the computer screen before continuing. "Okay. You paid for it already and it's all set. I'll go get it."

She sauntered off, looking back at me when she did. It wasn't that she wasn't attractive, but I was fairly sure that when Evelyn and I ended shit, she took a piece of my heart with her, along with my libido. I mean, everything was still in working order, but as far as wanting to get it on with anyone, it wasn't there anymore. A year ago, I'd fuck anything with a pair of tits and a knowing smile.

"Here you go," she said, returning with a thick manila envelope. She slid the contents out, running her fingers over the text.

It bothered me. Those words weren't for her touch.

"Do you want to take a look? This is a pretty big...package," she said, looking me up and down. "There's no one in the back room if you'd like some privacy."

God. Was I that bad? Not only that, but was I that obvious and it worked? Guys didn't take much work. You offered, we'd take. It was simple. What we never factored in was that falling in love with someone took it all away. It was so amazingly fucked up.

"No thank you," I said, turning the stack of papers toward me. I tapped the sides to get it all lined up before carefully edging it back into the envelope. "I'm all set."

"Are you?" she asked, raising her eyebrows.

I grabbed the envelope and tucked it under my arm. "Totally and completely."

I didn't wait for a response or reaction because I didn't care. It probably came across as a douche bag move and I'd have to work on it, but one thing at a time.

I jogged across the street to Starbucks to grab a triple-shot Venti something with extra-caffeine thing. Glancing at my phone, I was glad it was only 4:27 p.m. It would be tight, but I'd have time to grade the last of the papers I had to do before moving on. Of course as luck would have it, the line was at least ten people deep when I entered. There was one empty chair at the bar facing the street where I could set up, but there was no telling how long it would be there. I unbuttoned my gray cardigan and stepped over to the empty chair, hanging the sweater over the back to call dibs before returning to the line.

Two girls in front of me, both petite with matching blond hair extensions, were laughing, looking at something on a cell phone. They were also identical in matching black yoga pants with YOU WISH in hot-pink letters across the ass.

"I mean, his jizz was epic and, like, not in a good way," the one on the left said. "Like, there was so much of it."

"Like what does that even mean?" Right asked.

"Well, I was only being polite and he was so hot so I didn't back down when he gave me the head tap he was about to unload, but had I known he was capable of shooting a gun loaded with a pint of Twinkie filling into my mouth, I wouldn't have been so nice."

I snorted because Twinkie filling was one I hadn't heard

before. My laugh must've been louder than I'd intended because both girls turned around at the same time, with an oddly similar disgusted expression.

Shit. If they weren't twins, then they needed to stop practicing to be the twins from *The Shining*.

I cleared my throat and mumbled, "Sorry."

"*Holy. Shit*," Lefty shouted. "Abel Matthews."

"No *way*," the other said.

Crap.

This wasn't good.

"Ah, hey," I answered. I couldn't say their names because I couldn't remember them, but there were body shots, I think, but definitely a threesome with the both of them.

"Jen," Right said.

"Jess."

"Of course. Sisters, right?"

"You know, you were a dick for what happened, standing me up for the sorority formal," Jess or Jen said. I'd forgotten already. "But you are an even bigger asshole, and a disgusting one at that, for thinking we're sisters. Do you think sisters do…that?"

"Yeah?" the other said.

Could I not catch a break today? It was as if the universe was trying to present me with a sampling of bad behaviors of the past, and with the printer place girl, trying to tempt me with the fruit I didn't want anymore.

All I could think was: *What the fuck? Is this the* This Is Your Life *version of my sex life?*

The line moved forward, but the girls stayed put. I glanced

out the corner of my eye, and there was a coffee shop full of people watching me getting my balls busted.

"Are you going to say anything?" Jess/Jen asked.

What could I say? I was a dick. I knew I was. I'd been nothing short of a deranged nymphomaniac from my teen years until recently. The girls standing in front of me were examples of that. It was no wonder that when the karma bus hit me with the Evelyn thing it shook loose all of the regret, all of the humanity I should've had. You don't know how bad it was going to hurt someone else until you felt the same hurt.

"I'm sorry," I said. "I know it doesn't make a lick of difference now, and it took me a while to get to realize what an immature shit I was. So, I'm sorry for the formal and sister thing and probably several other things."

For the second time in less than an hour, I walked away. I didn't need to see the looks on their faces or stand there for another beatdown. There was enough of it inside of me to do damage and it almost totaled me. There was no way to make up for the past. I could only move forward.

And I did. I went right out the door without coffee and graded papers. I stayed hidden undercover in my car until I saw the girls leave with their Frappuccinos almost an hour later. No doubt they needed that amount of time to get their rage out over me and the excessive jizzer who had obviously fucked up as well. They were laughing again, but then I noticed one of them fling my cardigan over their shoulder.

"Damn it," I yelled, slamming my fists against the steering wheel. "It was my favorite."

Karma bus hit me right into my wardrobe.

With a few minutes to spare, I darted back across the street, got my coffee sans run-in with ex-lovers or being propositioned and walked the three blocks to my meeting.

I entered the church; a lingering smell of incense and confessed sins came at me from every direction. Panic began to buzz through me, but as I descended the steps to the basement, I reminded myself I always left feeling better than when I arrived.

The cracked tile floor paved the way down a long dimly lit hallway. Every time I made the walk, I considered all the times I spent in other basements. A lot of the people had to, too. Maybe there wasn't a safe place for any of us, but hell, a candy shop smelling of chocolate and licorice would've been nice. Or even a bread factory. Who couldn't chill and want to get healed surrounded by freshly baked goods?

Outside the door, I heard the low voices of conversation happening inside. I both hated it and needed it. Sometimes the things you need the most take time, and you have to go through a shitstorm of emotion to get to it. I had to believe it was all worth it in the end. As I pushed the door open, a sign reading GA MEETING hanging above it, I knew I'd be okay.

* * *

Standing in front of a cracked, smudged mirror was doing nothing for my self-confidence. Neither was the fourth shirt I'd tried on.

"Shit," I said, unbuttoning it before throwing it to the floor with the others.

Another thing that wasn't helping my self-confidence was the fact I was turning into a girl by going through everything in my closet, wondering what Evelyn would like me best in. There wasn't so much a concern over looking attractive, but I wanted her to notice me. I dug through a laundry basket of clean, wrinkled clothes before retrieving a geometric blue button-down. After a quick sniff, because sometimes clean and dirty got mixed together, I put it on.

Hell, I wasn't even sure if she was going to be there. I'd been laying so low, but this was for Delilah. Unless she was still hell-bent on not seeing me, I didn't think there was any way she'd miss it. I stepped back in front of the mirror and knew it was the best I was going to get. The drive over to their house rivaled first day of school nerves. I didn't know what to expect or how I'd be received. As walked to the front door, the big manila envelope in one hand, and a gift for Delilah in the other, I knew no matter what, I was going to be okay.

I poked my head in the front door, and being fashionably late had its privileges. Judging by the noise level, the party was already in full swing, and when I stepped in, closing the door behind me, there was no turning back. The walk down the hallway was different than any other time I'd walked it before, but when Callie stepped across the foyer stopping me, I realized I was wrong. Things were still very much the same.

"Hey you," she said, opening her arms. "I'm so glad you're here."

I wrapped my arms around her, feeling comforted by her warm welcome. "Thanks for inviting me."

"Oh, pfft. This is practically your home, too. You need no inviting," she said, stepping back and looking me over. "Can I take that?"

"Here," I said, handing over Delilah's gift. "This is for the birthday girl. I'll just hold on to this other thing."

"Okay. Well, I'm going to put these with the others and be right back. Aaron is up on the roof with your parents if you want to say hello."

I nodded as she hurried off. No mention of Evelyn. I glanced around at the guests in the living room, and there were a lot of familiar faces, but not the one I was looking for. Taking Callie's advice, I headed up the staircase and down the hallway to the door that led to the rooftop. While usually password protected to keep Delilah away, the door was propped open for the guests to come and go as they pleased.

The sun was warm for May. We were owed an early summer after the hellishly cold winter we'd been through. A soft breeze coming off the lake blew table covers up and down and made the scattering of balloons attached to the tables sway.

I looked around again, and then stopped because there she was. Her long blond hair danced in the wind, and the tight white dress she was wearing made her look beautiful.

Beautiful. My Beautiful.

I didn't know she was going to be here, but I knew in my bones she would be. Wasn't it fucked up how that worked? It still scared the shit out of me.

She was talking to my parents, engaged and pleasantly nodding. As her eye caught on me out of her peripheral vision, her head turned. It wasn't instant or certain at first, but a small smile lifted from her lips.

Those lips. The same red. The same thoughts. They on me, marking me and loving me. I shifted my weight with a subtle leg adjustment to account for the hardness happening in my pants.

Yup. All still in working order and obviously coming at full attention the moment I was within a thirty-foot radius.

I inhaled deeply because I was ready for this. It could've all been a disaster, but I was ready.

Dodging little girls in feathered boas and their wine-sipping parents, I crossed the roof to reach her.

"Hi Mom and Dad," I said, leaning over to kiss my mom on the cheek. I patted my dad on the shoulder at the same time with him returning the gesture.

"Son," he said. "We were just catching up with Evelyn."

"I can see that," I said, smiling. "How is that going?"

"Lovely as always," Mom said. "Daniel, I think Callie can use us to help with the food. Could you excuse us?"

"Sure," I said.

"Nice to see you," Evelyn called to them as they walked away.

"But seriously," I said when they were out of earshot. "How did that go?"

"The same as ever. Your mom being as sweet as sugar and your dad being your dad."

I laughed because some things never changed.

I took in a deep breath, unsure of how much I was going to get out of her. "How've you been?"

She took a sip from her cup and nodded. "Good. Busy. Wedding season and all. Bridget has me running my own now, so it's been crazy."

"Really? That's great."

It really was. She worked hard and fucking deserved everything she wanted.

"How about you?" she asked.

"Um, the same," I said. "Busy. School will be wrapping up soon, but I'm doing this summer school program. I may have to ditch WET soon because there's only so much time in the day."

She nodded again and took another sip. It was awkward, but then it wasn't. I knew her every expression. I knew she was afraid of spiders, but wasn't afraid of petting a snake. I knew when she laughed really hard, she snorted, and when she slept, she'd tuck her left hand under her head.

I knew all these things about her. I was sure she knew just as many about me. How could it be awkward when you loved someone?

"Well," I said slowly. "I'm glad you're here because I wanted to give this to you."

I handed her the envelope, and she took it in her free hand, her wrist bending against the weight of it. "Oh, wow. What is it?"

"It's my finished manuscript."

Her eyes grew wide as her mouth gaped open. "What?"

"I finished my book."

"Abel," she said, cradling the envelope next to her chest. "That's amazing."

I shrugged. "I'm not sure how good it is, but I wanted you to have it. No one else does."

Her head tilted to the side in confusion. "Why?"

"Because you made me want to write every single word."

CHAPTER TWENTY-FIVE

EVELYN—

I didn't know if I was ready. I told him I needed time, and he had given me that. It was the time I needed to readjust my thoughts and consider all that had happened. There wasn't a magic spell to make all the bad go away, and perhaps it was foolish, but every day that passed, anger subsided and understanding moved in.

He gave me my space, but I knew he was there. I knew he was thinking of me. I knew because every week there was a different reminder that was delivered to me.

The first was a large black coffee and bottle of Russell's Reserve Single Barrel Bourbon I found left on my desk after getting back from lunch. I thought it was from Bridget, but the card attached read:

Beautiful,

In case you get thirsty while I give you time.

Abel

The next was a burger from Kuma's and a Sprinkles cupcake left outside the door of my apartment.

Beautiful,

In case you get hungry while I give you time.

Abel

The box the burger was in was still warm. The cupcake, chocolate peanut butter, was my favorite.

Beautiful,

In case you need something to look at while I give you time.

Abel

A large funeral arrangement, one similar to the spray that was accidently sent me months ago from him, found its way to By Invitation Only once again. Bridget didn't even get angry about it or make me throw it away.

Other deliveries followed at regular intervals. A Dolly Parton movie for when I needed to watch something, and new running shoes for when I needed to go for a run.

He knew me. He was reminding me, and little by little, I was letting him.

I didn't know if he'd be at Delilah's party, but I'd sensed in my bones he would be. When he appeared on the rooftop, in a blue button-down shirt and dark jeans, it was like seeing him again for the first time. His body had filled in again, leading me to believe he was hitting the gym, and his beard was nearing original status. It was all him, but it didn't seem real until I saw him smile. The dimples. I had no idea when the last time was I saw them, but it was a relief when I did.

I still didn't know if I was ready, but as I sat at my kitchen table with the envelope containing his manuscript in front of me, I decided to *be* ready. I flipped the top open and slowly pulled out the large stack of pages. A Post-it was stuck to the first page. In his familiar writing, it read:

> *Something for you to read while you think.*
> *I love you.*
> *I promise.*
>
> *Abel*

The title page read *In This Life* by Abel Matthews. I turned the page over and placed it facedown on the table. My eyes scanned across the second page, but they immediately blurred when I read the words:

> *To my Beautiful:*
> *"In vain I have struggled. It will not do. My feelings will not be repressed. You must allow me to tell you how ardently I admire and love you."*

It was a Mr. Darcy quote, and it was for me. I patted my hand to my chest to calm the rapid beating before turning the next page.

And then the next.

And the next.

And the next.

I didn't leave the table for hours, poring over every one of his exquisite words and beautifully imagined story. The book centered around a nineteen-year-old man working as the groundskeeper at a cemetery adjacent to a convent. A young nun befriends him, but when a romantic relationship blossoms, they must choose what the morally right thing to do is versus what their hearts are telling them. The story spanned several years with glimpses into the small Vermont town they both lived in. It was heartbreaking and hopeful, a tragedy and a blessing. My tears stained the final pages not only from the moving story, but also because I knew Abel had written them.

His talent was intertwined with his passion, and he had found it. People lived their entire lives without finding one or the other, but he found both. Pride overtook me, but I still wasn't ready. As I piled the pages back into a neat stack and placed them in the envelope, I knew I was getting closer, but still not there yet.

I wanted to run to him, kiss his lips, and tell him he was brilliant. I wanted to tell him I loved him and that the light in him I fell in love with shined on every single page of his book. I wanted to tell him I wasn't sure I could ever forgive him or if we could ever be the same as we were before.

I wanted to tell him my desire to have him in my life greatly exceeded any desire for him not to be.

I wanted to tell him. I was certain I would, but I wasn't there yet.

* * *

"You want half of this?" Callie said, holding a chocolate-covered pretzel stick out to me.

"Sure."

I took the tissue-covered end, leaving her to deal with chocolate fingers. We nibbled on our pretzels as we strolled around the outdoor Maxwell Street Market. Antiques and old treasures lined rows and rows of shelves. Callie and I had been going to the market for years, mostly to browse and sometimes to buy. It was nice to be together, walking and talking, since the last time I saw her was weeks ago at Delilah's birthday party.

"Did I tell you we're taking Delilah to Disney World?" she said, rolling her eyes.

"No, you didn't, and what's with the look?"

"I think it's all kinds of ridiculous. It's so expensive and so crowded, and you have to plan for everything. Frankly, I don't know who's more excited, Delilah or Aaron."

I tossed my pretzel in the trash and looked at a table of vintage purses. "I think it sounds sweet. It's your first family vacation."

"Don't get me wrong. I'm not trying to be bratty about it, but I think a relaxing beach vacation is more my speed these days."

"You feeling old, Cal?"

"No, but I am surrounded by children all day so forgive me if I'm burnt out a little."

"Well, then why don't you start dropping some hints to the hunky man about a little getaway, just the two of you."

She raised her eyebrows. "Maybe."

"It'll be good for you two. It can even be a long weekend, and I'll watch Delilah."

"You would?"

"Yes. Is it so hard to believe I could take care of her?"

She stepped down a row of used books, leaning over to look at the titles. "No, it's not, but I'm just surprised." She stood back up, tossing her auburn hair over her shoulders. "And it's very much appreciated."

I winked at her and scooted in next to her to scan the books. Some of the titles on the spines were completely worn away, making it impossible to see the titles without going through each of them. I loved old books, though. The smell, the worn pages, and the mystery surrounding how many people had read it before you. I had almost gone through them all when a particular one caught my eye.

It was the gold lettering that gave it away.

I sunk to my knees on the ground, carefully removing the other books on top of it. It was blue. I had thought it was, but mine was so much more dated.

It was the exact copy of the same *Pride and Prejudice* Abel had given me for my birthday. What the hell were the chances?

"Did you find something?" Callie called from a few tables over.

"Uh-huh," I mumbled, carefully opening the cover.

On the title page, written in blue pen, in beautiful cursive was:

To my Handsome
  Love,
    Your Beautiful

Oh my God.

"What?" Callie said, coming up behind me.

My hand covered my mouth as I lifted the book to her.

"Is this like yours?" she asked.

I nodded. "Open it," I cried.

"Oh my God," she shouted. "Are you kidding me?"

"What the hell? How?"

She shook her head and looked down at it again. "I have no idea, but there was, or maybe even still is, another couple who call each other Beautiful and Handsome who had the same exact book as the one Abel gave you."

I knew what she was going to say before she said it. I almost beat her to it, but she was too fast.

"Do you know what this is?" Callie asked.

"Yes," I said, taking the book from her and heading to cashier. "It's serendipity."

* * *

Serendipity was all it took to be ready. I didn't believe it or think it even existed, but when it stares you right in the face, in black and white, there was no denying it.

It was why I was standing in front of a building that looked like it should be condemned. Callie confirmed with me several times this was the place. The cement stairs to the second floor were crumbling and clearly a housing violation. Plus, the smell of cooking oil wafting up from the Chinese restaurant next door made the entire building smell of takeout.

I balanced all the things in my hand when I knocked on his door marked Number 4. I hadn't considered if he'd be alone or what it would mean if he'd truly moved on. Maybe I was too late.

"Holy shit," he said from the opposite side of the door. "Hold on. I need to get some pants on."

It's nothing I haven't already seen, Abel.

I could hear him rushing around his apartment, things falling down, and cursing in the background. The door flew open and it was him.

Happy and dimples deep.

"Sorry for just dropping by, but—"

"Don't be sorry. Just come in," he said, holding the door open for me.

My eyes scanned around the studio apartment, the Murphy bed still open from being slept on and wrinkled covers on top. It was about the size of his bathroom in his old apartment, but this was all decorated by him.

"I know," he said, shrugging and shaking his head. "It's not as nice as the last one, but this one is all mine."

"I think it's great," I said. "I, um, brought you a house-warming gift."

I held out the large Mason jar to him, the insides stacked full of dandelions. It wasn't an easy feat collecting all of them on such short notice, but when I told Callie what I wanted to do, she brought in reinforcements: Aaron and Delilah.

"I figured we could all use more wishes, right?" I said.

He looked at the jar, turning it over in his hands. "It's a good thing," he said, lifting his blue eyes to meet mine. "I'd lost all of mine."

"I read your book," I said, patting the envelope. "I almost don't want to give it back to you."

"You don't have to. I don't know why you'd want to keep it because—"

"It was amazing. I loved it, and I want to keep it because I'm so proud you wrote it."

He didn't ask, and I didn't mind because I was finally ready. He set the jar down on the floor before he pulled me into him, wrapping his arms around me. My head found the familiar place on his chest I loved, and I leaned right against it.

"I have a question, handsome."

He kissed the top of my head. "What's that, beautiful?"

"What happens now?"

He pulled away, one arm still wrapped around me. "You'll have to turn the page to find out."

Turn the page to read an excerpt from the first book in Melissa Marino's Bad Behavior series.

So Twisted

Available Now!

CHAPTER ONE

CALLIE—

I s anyone else getting a wedgie from these damn things?" I shouted to the other females I was working with. I hurried to the other end of the bar as I adjusted my hot-pink bloomers that were under my extra short patent leather skirt. Our new uniforms were about as functional as wet toilet paper.

"Hey beautiful, how long does a guy have to wait to get a drink around here?" I turned and saw a barely legal guy at the other end of the bar, clearly not needing another cocktail.

Luckily, the DJ had decided that was the perfect time to crank the music, and like that, the cries of the drunken were silenced.

It was eleven o'clock and the night was young. The bar was packed, which was good for my bank account, but bad for my dignity. Every hour that went by at Venom, the downtown Chicago club I bartended at that catered to the newly twenty-one crowd, lowered the IQ of my customers.

"What can I get you?" I asked the dude heckling me.

He leaned in. "You can get me a double vodka, sexy."

"Is that it?" I said, making his drink.

"No," he slurred. He leaned in further, practically drooling over himself. "You can get me your phone number."

I rolled my eyes. "Sorry, sweetie. I don't date customers."

"Who said anything about dating? I just want to see that skirt on my bedroom floor in the morning."

"Ain't gonna happen. Anything else?" I said, handing him his drink.

"Yeah, I want those shiny, knee-high boots wrapped around..."

I cut him off before I could hear the rest. "Twelve dollars."

He reached in his pocket and pulled out a handful of crushed bills. He picked out a few and handed them to me. Something was crunchy in that wad of cash. Something damp, too. I wanted to vomit.

"There's more where this came from," he said with a wink. Fuck my life.

"Wait just a second," Frat Boy Slim babbled. "You look familiar."

"Probably because you're looking right at me. Crazy how the mind works, huh?"

I attempted to step away, knowing that continuing a conversation with this guy would be as enjoyable as a two-day-old pulled pork sandwich that had been soaking in curdled milk, but he wouldn't let up.

"Wait!" he said, jumping and spilling half his vodka on his pink Lacoste shirt. "Aren't you in that um...math class...the one for teachers with me?"

"Mathematics in elementary school?" I asked.

He snapped his fingers at me. "Yes! That's the one. I knew I recognized you from someplace."

There was seriously no hope for our future if this was the kind of moron teaching our children.

"That must be it," I said. "Okay, then. I have to get back to work."

"Hold up. Do you live off campus? No way you still live in the dorms."

"No. I don't live in the dorms because I'm too old for that shit, and I only go part-time. Anything else?"

"Pfft," he spit, waving his arm around. "You ain't old. You can't be older than twenty-four or so."

I touched my nose, letting him know he got it right. "Einstein."

He nodded and snorted simultaneously. "Yeah. I'm pretty smart. And I think you are, too, so why don't you just tell me what time you get off so I can get you off?"

I wasn't sure if it was my disgusted look or the distraction of having a drink thrown in his face by the girl standing behind him who was listening to our conversation, but like magic, he disappeared.

I rubbed my temples, feeling the pain of a headache coming on. "Fuck my life," I said aloud before placing a smile on my face as fake as the skirt I was wearing before I approached the next customer. "Hey there. What can I get you?"

By the end of the evening—actually three o'clock in the morning—I was totally spent. As I walked out the back door, I stopped and unzipped my knee-high boots with the four-inch heels. I crossed the parking lot barefoot, and even though it was March in Chicago, the feel of the icy ground numbed my aching feet. After getting into my car and waiting a few minutes for it to heat up, I drove home. The streets were empty except for a few drunken stragglers, their arms draped over a new friend who will soon be a lover or maybe even an old lover who was never a friend. It hardly mattered which one it was because I was jealous all the same. Logically I knew half of them would be alone by morning, but for the night, they had someone close. They had deep kisses and warm bodies. All I had was hot chocolate and Garrett's Popcorn waiting for me at home.

Exhaustion hit me the moment I began the climb up the stairs to my apartment. My head pounded with pain, and every muscle in my legs screamed for rest. I dropped everything, except my phone, at the front door and dragged myself to the couch, where I collapsed. My bed would've been much more comfortable, but my room might as well have been a mile away at that point. I had just enough sense to set the alarm on my phone for seven a.m. so I had time in the morning for a quick shower before class. Hot chocolate and popcorn was going to have to wait.

* * *

I heard voices but refused to open my eyes. It would be admitting morning had arrived, and that couldn't be possible when I had just closed my eyes. The faint sound of my alarm grew louder and louder as I continued to deny the time.

Strong steps against our hardwood floors approached me, but then stopped abruptly and reversed. With a sigh, I peeled my eyelids open—which were stuck together from the glue of my false eyelashes and leftover makeup I hadn't bothered to wash off. I slapped my alarm off and cursed the sun for being, well, the sun.

"What is your problem?" Evelyn said, her voice raising. "I thought you were leaving."

"Someone is on your couch. A woman, and she's in her underwear," an unfamiliar man's voice answered.

"Will you knock it off? I told you I had fun and that I'd text you later," Evelyn said.

"It was fun, wasn't it?"

"Yes." She sighed. "So, see you later."

"But what about the girl in her underwear?" he asked.

"I'm not in my underwear," I shouted, opening my eyes.

Evelyn's head popped out of her bedroom door. "Oh. Yeah. Definitely not underwear."

A tall blond guy wearing a wrinkled white button-down and blue pants turned. He gave a quick nod and side smile, clearly hiding his embarrassment over his mistake.

"Hey there," he said, swinging a suit jacket over his shoulder. "I was just—"

"Leaving," Evelyn said, nudging him.

Evelyn's one-hit wonder began his walk of shame, but stopped in front of me. His eyes drifted down my body, stopping at my skirt.

"Yes?" I asked, sitting up.

His head tilted and he smiled. "You work at Venom?"

"For shit's sake," I said, standing and stomping to my room.

The last thing I heard before getting into the shower was Evelyn telling him he was an inconsiderate jackass with a small dick.

I love that girl.

While I was normally not a morning person, I was even less so when I'd only had three hours of sleep. I practically cried through my five-minute shower, but when the smell of coffee hit me, my spirits lifted slightly. When I came out of the bathroom, in my ratty robe and hair up in a towel, there was a cup waiting for me on the counter in the kitchen. She even put the right amount of my favorite peppermint mocha creamer in it.

I sat at the kitchen table, going through my class notes, when Evelyn came out of her room and breezed into the kitchen like the breath of fresh air she always was. Her long blond hair was curled into perfect waves, while her cream-colored blouse was tucked neatly into her black pencil skirt. I was lucky if I managed to leave the house wearing matching shoes.

"Thanks for the coffee," I said, yawning.

"No problem," she said, slipping on her black heels. "Everything good?"

I nodded. "Mm-hmm."

"You sure?"

I set my notes down and looked at her. She was nervously biting down on her lower lip, messing up her red lipstick. Something was up. She never ruined her lipstick unless she was nervous (which she hardly ever was) or she was getting lucky with a dude (which happened on a fairly regular basis).

I stood and crossed the kitchen. "What's up?"

"Nothing," Evelyn said.

I rolled my eyes at her as I poured myself another cup of coffee. "You're a terrible liar."

She twirled a lock of her hair and pressed her lips together tightly. "I'm worried about you."

"Worried about what?"

"Cal, you can't keep working like this." She moved and stood in front of me. "You're so exhausted between working these late hours and with school."

I took a sip and shrugged. "I don't have a choice right now. At least I'm not working two jobs anymore."

We had this conversation so many times before, and while I knew it only came from a place of concern, my situation wasn't by choice. Sometimes I wondered if she realized that.

"Look, you're sweet to worry, but we've been through this already. My student loans are through the roof, and while I know I can defer, it'll be more of an issue in the end. If I thought I could still pay rent and everything else by any other means besides bartending, I would, but that isn't happening. I'm just taking a larger course load now so I can finish next year."

She took hold of my hands. "Look, I was thinking I could ask Bridget if you could do some help around the office. With the wedding season coming…"

I shook my head. "Me, working for wedding planners? Seriously? Plus, I'd still be making more a few nights a week at Venom. The money is too good."

"I'm not trying to piss you off," she said. "I think that…"

I pulled my wet hair back, looking up at the ceiling to blink away the tears. "Ev. Please," I pleaded.

"Oh," she said, putting her arms around me. "I'm sorry. Please don't be sad."

I sighed and put my coffee cup down so I could hug her back. "You worry too much."

She shrugged when we pulled away. "Sometimes, although worrying is usually your specialty. But I know how hard you work, both with school and the bar, and I love you so stupid."

"I know. I love you, too, Blondie."

"I have to run." She walked over to the table and picked up her purse. "See you later?"

"Probably not. Work tonight."

Work. Work. Work.

* * *

I sat at a café by campus, the late afternoon sun glaring off the table's surface, reviewing material from my earlier class. I was on my third coffee of the day, but while the caffeine from my triple-shot latte was giving me just enough energy to keep my head up, it wouldn't last. My eyelids burned, and there was a serious nap in my future if I got everything done before work.

I returned to my notes but was interrupted when my phone rang. I dug it out of my purse, checking the caller ID. EVELYN.

"What's up?" I said.

"Hey, are you busy? I've got some news I think you might be interested in."

"Studying. Something going on?"

"Okay. Before I tell you anything, you have to promise me you won't get mad first."

"Why would I be mad?"

"I can't tell you that. You might get mad."

I put my pen down and took a sip of my latte. "Fine. Go ahead."

"So, you're promising not to be mad?" she asked.

I didn't like where this was headed. Evelyn only asked me not to be mad at her when she did something I told her specifically not to do. The last time she pulled the "promise you won't be mad at me" bit, she came home with a ridiculously expensive handbag I'd admired when we were shopping together.

I knew I had to give in if I was ever going to find out what she was up to. "Okay, I promise I won't get mad. Tell me."

"I think I found you a job."

"Huh?"

"Hear me out. Okay, a few days ago I was at the office, and a client, Leslie Matthews, came in. She's hosting an event for the Junior League of Chicago. While we really don't do party planning, just weddings, Bridget does this yearly event for promotional purposes. I got to talking to Mrs. Matthews, and she was telling me she was having knee replacement surgery in a few months."

I yawned. "Uh-huh."

"She told me she was worried because her son, Aaron, who's a single dad, really depends on her for when he's working. I met him at last year's event and recognized him as an owner of some of the clubs and boutique hotels we do weddings at. Anyway, he's looking for full-time help since Mrs. Matthews is going to be out of commission."

She paused, waiting for a response, but I had none.

I sighed and looked at the clock on the wall. *Come on, Evelyn, spit it out, I have a nap waiting for me.*

"Okayyyyy," I said. "Are you getting to the point?"

"Yes! Aaron needs a nanny, a live-in nanny," she said.

I thought for a second before responding. "This is really fascinating, Evelyn. I hope you alerted the *Tribune* to this development."

"Am I talking too fast for you?" She paused and sighed. "You could be his nanny."

"What? Why would I want to do that?"

"Because you can live in his house, which is amazing, rent-free and make more than what you're making at Venom."

I tapped my fingers on the table as I processed what she said. It wasn't totally crazy, considering I'd worked for several families over the years as a nanny and was studying to be a teacher. Plus, when my father died, my mom had to work multiple jobs, leaving me to care for my two younger sisters.

"Okay, okay, I know what you're thinking." She interrupted my thoughts. "I know you too well not to know that you're considering all the what-ifs, but seriously I think this could really go your way. Today, on the way to work, it just popped in my head. So, I called Mrs. Matthews, and long story short, I told her all about you, that you were an education major, still in school, and had been a nanny in the past. She got in touch with Aaron and he was thrilled. Remember when you had asked me to help you with your résumé a while back? I still had it on my computer so I sent it to him."

"You did what?" My voice soared an octave.

"He emailed me and asked if you were available for an interview tonight at seven. I said yes."

"Evelyn!"

"Nope. No getting mad remember?"

I could almost hear her smiling on the other end, proud of herself for putting this plan all together. If I was being honest, it did sound appealing. I loved working with kids; it was the whole reason I wanted to be a teacher. Plus, the idea of making more money so I could quit the hellish hours of working nights lightened the weight on my back.

"I don't know, Ev. What about my hours during the day for school and the rent for our place? There's a lot of things to consider."

"He knows you're still in school. I was clear with him about your need for flexibility. And as far as our rent, we'll cross that bridge when we get to it."

Was this something I could do? Was it something I *wanted* to do? I ran through a bunch of variables, considering worst-case scenarios and all the reasons why this probably wouldn't be a good idea. Evelyn was quiet, knowing I was processing it all. The possibilities were too enticing. An interview with this guy wouldn't hurt.

"First," I said. "Thank you. Second, I'm definitely interested, but I have to be at work at six, so I don't think I can meet him tonight."

"Callie, this is a huge opportunity for you. I think Venom will survive if you're a couple hours late."

She was right. If this played out as desirable as it sounded, I could throw my patent leather skirt in the Dumpster of that dreaded bar. "What should I do now? Should I call him to confirm?"

"Nope. I assured him you would be there."

"What if I'd said no?"

"You've forgotten who knows you best."

Again. She was right.

By the time I left the café shortly after, something inside me felt lighter. The feeling wasn't fleeting or riddled with uncertainty. It was just...promise. As I climbed the steps to the "L," I sent out all the positive vibes I had that this went well.

At seven o'clock on the dot, I stood outside the exquisite brownstone where Aaron Matthews and his daughter lived. A black wrought iron fence surrounded the brick house, while circle-topped windows decorated the front. I looked at the roof, adorned with hanging vines bare from the winter, but no doubt gorgeous in the summer. The vines intertwined through tall, thin pillars that ran the length of the roof.

I rang the doorbell and waited while I continued to admire the outside of his home. To the right of the door, I noticed a small Disney princess figure. I bent down to pick it up as I heard the door open.

"Hello there. Calliope?" a deep voice said.

"Hi." I lifted my face to look at him.

Then I almost fell over.

Oh. Hell. No.

Nope. Can't work for this guy.

My eyes scanning over him created a multi-visual experience, every bit of his presence capturing me all at once.

He was tall, very tall, with an athletic build and dark hair that curled slightly at the edges. He smiled, a smile that accentuated his perfectly straight teeth and full lips. When my eyes reached his, the real trouble started. They were blue, the color of the light, aqua edges of forget-me-not flowers, and piercing against his dark hair and features.

Forget-me-not. It was unlikely to happen.

"Are you all right? You look a little pale," he said, concerned. He moved from the doorway, stepping closer to me. "Do you feel faint?"

I took a deep breath and stood up. "Mr. Matthews, yes, I'm Calliope. Or Callie. Whatever. I'm so sorry. I'm just getting over a little cold and not quite myself yet."

Nice save.

He extended his hand to shake mine, gripping it tightly. "Nice to meet you, Calliope. And please, call me Aaron. Thank you for coming on such short notice, especially now that I know you haven't been well. Are you sure you're up for the interview?" he asked.

"Oh yes, of course. Ah. Here," I said, shoving the Disney princess at him.

He smiled and nodded, taking it from me. "Everywhere. They're absolutely everywhere. Thank you. Well, why don't we go in so we can talk?"

I followed him inside, desperately trying not to stare at his ass along the way and failing miserably. I reminded myself there was nothing wrong with a basic human reaction. We were animals by nature, and admiring another animal you found attractive was normal. Although…from where I stood, there wasn't much normal about the way he looked.

I unbuttoned my coat and looked around the exquisite home. Marble flooring lined the hallway and extended throughout as far as I could see. I trailed behind him down the large foyer, which connected to a narrow hall leading to the rest of the home. To my right was a formal dining room with a long glass-topped table and several high-back chairs.

If offered the job, it would've been far and away the most beautiful home I'd ever lived in. My meager background didn't lend itself to such expensive surroundings. It almost made me uncomfortable.

"Please sit down," he said, motioning to the table and chairs. "Can I get you something to drink?"

"No, thank you," I said, hanging my coat on the back of the chair. I looked across the table and saw a copy of my résumé and references that Evelyn had emailed earlier. I noticed a few notes in the margin.

"So, Calliope, why don't you tell me a little about yourself?"

"Well," I said, taking in a deep breath. "I'm a third-year

elementary education major. I've been going part-time so I could balance work along with it, but I hope to graduate next spring, so I've taken on more classes this semester. I work nights at a downtown club, but that's been temporary. My goal has always been to work with children."

"Which one?"

"Which children?" I asked, confused.

"No," he said, laughing, his bright smile lifting the corner of his mouth into a handsome grin. "Which club?"

"Oh. Right. Duh. Um, Venom? It's near Rush—"

"And Division. Yes, I know it well."

"You do?"

"Don't act so surprised. I'm not that much of an old man at thirty-one."

"No," I said quickly. "Of course not. I didn't mean to insinuate."

He held up his hand, continuing to smile. "You were right to assume it isn't my type of crowd, but I used to be part owner of it. I sold off my piece some time ago, but it's good to know it still has some wonderful employees there."

He paused, his eyes running across my face, as his smile faded. There wasn't a sound surrounding us, but the energy in the room more than made up for the silence. The quiet sound of something brewing. Shivers rushed across my body.

"Have you always lived in Chicago?" he asked.

"No, but I never want to live anywhere else. I love it here."

"Agreed. Best city in the world."

He paused, glancing down at my résumé. "Your résumé is very thorough," he said, running his finger down the margin where his notes were. "I really asked for the interview to see if we'd be a good fit, or if rather, you'd be a good fit for us."

I nodded, waiting for him to continue.

Or maybe I was fixated on the fact that the way he said *fit*, a normal, everyday word, sounded so sexy.

Or maybe I realized my ogling was going to get me fired before I was hired.

"Why don't I tell you a little bit about us now?" He ran his hand through his hair and smiled. "I'm sure Evelyn has explained my situation. My mom's having surgery this summer, and I'll need someone full-time to help with my daughter."

As the word *daughter* left his mouth, his entire face lit up.

"What's her name?"

"Delilah and she's four. She's very smart and very high-energy. I love the idea of having someone with an education background. I'd love for her to go to the museums, take classes, and things like that."

"Absolutely."

"And I'm sure as is the case with many four-year-olds, she's very stubborn and isn't afraid to let her opinion be known."

"It's very common. Testing boundaries and all that."

"Well, she can definitely win top prize in the most dramatic tantrum competition. But she's sweet, and while I'm sure I'm biased, I think she's the most beautiful little girl, inside and out."

"Is she here? Can I meet her?"

"I thought it best that I meet with any candidate when she was not here. She's actually spending the night at my parents' tonight."

"Well, she sounds like a remarkable little girl."

"I think so," he said with a nod. "I understand you'll need some flexibility with your hours?"

"Yes. Three mornings a week I have class, but that's only for the next six weeks until summer. Obviously I'll be completely available then during the summer."

"It wouldn't be a problem. Even though my mom has been watching her while I worked from home, Delilah has been used to having me here. I wanted to ease her into someone new for the first few weeks. She's really only been looked after by family, so as you can imagine, she has one overprotective daddy."

The way he said "Daddy" was so endearing I melted a little.

"Totally understandable," I said.

"So, in the fall, you'll be in your final year?"

"Yes."

"That's wonderful." My eyes glanced over the white collared shirt he was wearing and to the small patch of chest hair that peeked through.

He slipped a piece of paper out from under my résumé and pushed it across to me. "Would this be acceptable to you?"

I looked at the paper and the number on it referring to the weekly salary he was offering. It was more than I'd made in a week at any job ever. My eyes looked it over again and again, as he tapped his pen on the table. This was in addition to the free room and board. My mind was blown.

"Very," I responded as calmly as possible. "Thank you."

"Of course that includes room and board, meals and such. I'd like to check out your references and verify the background check before we go any further. However, I do promise to call you by Monday with my decision regardless of what I decide."

"Great. Thank you."

We stood and I grabbed my coat from the back of the chair. He walked me to the front door, and as he opened it for me with one hand, his other hand brushed against my back. His touch, as light as it was, sent a shiver through my body. "Thank you again for coming on such a short notice."

"My pleasure."

I stepped outside and walked down the stairs as I buttoned my coat. I stopped at the bottom and turned. He still stood in the doorway, watching me. I smiled and waved.

He returned the smile, and even in the chilly temperature, my body grew warm all over. If offered this job, it might be the best employment opportunity ever or a mistake of epic proportions.

I went to work that night and the following, thinking of not much else besides Aaron. I worried that if I did move in, my infatuation would only increase and cause me to screw up one of the best jobs I might ever have. I mean, a child was involved with this. Plus, one bad reference from a prominent Chicago figure could jeopardize my future teaching career.

I spent Sunday mulling things over and decided to relax until I heard from him. He may not even offer me the position, and in that case, all of this was for nothing. From working and worrying all weekend, I was exhausted. After a long shower, I put on my most comfortable pajamas and climbed into bed.

Sleep came fast and hard, and I didn't wake until my phone buzzed on my nightstand the following morning with an incoming call. Groggy, I tried to identify the number on the caller ID, but it was no use.

"Hello," I said, my throat full of morning phlegm.

"Hi, Calliope? It's Aaron Matthews."

I shot up, clearing my throat. "Oh, hi. How are you?"

"Good. I'm sorry if I woke you, but I wanted to catch you before you went to class."

"Oh no," I lied. "I've been awake for ages."

"Well, the reason I am calling is that I would like to offer you the nanny position. Pending the rest of your references coming through as glowing as the others, of course. Plus, I'd like you to meet Delilah beforehand as well."

"Really?" I said, excited. "That's—"

Fantastic?

Yes. I wanted to say it was fantastic. It was, but it was something else, too. The emotions I had when we met, the way my body responded, was not only out of character, but frightening. With my focus being solely on school and work for so long, I didn't have time to date, let alone even be completely attracted to someone. What would happen when we were living together day in and day out? That was a recipe for a very volatile situation.

"What do you think, Calliope? Will you be our nanny?" he asked eagerly.

I had a choice. Either I could turn down the job, fearing

my initial emotions would filter into my daily life. Or I could stop worrying about what might happen, take hold of this amazing opportunity, and know I could handle anything that came my way.

I mean, was there really a choice?

"Yes, of course, Aaron. I'm thrilled to be your nanny."

ACKNOWLEDGMENTS

I can say wholeheartedly I don't know where I'd be without my superstar agent and friend, **Kimberly Brower**. You push me, encourage me, and reassure me, all while juggling all your other commitments without missing a beat (or stopping to sleep. Ever). Thank you times a million for all you do even when I'm shouting, "I'm freaking out!" at you.

My amazing editor, **Megha Parekh**, at Forever Romance is an editor that authors dream of having. Thank you for your guidance and for helping me make this book, these characters, more than I envisioned. Also, **Lexi Smail** and the entire team at Forever Romance for their continued support and enthusiasm.

Amy E. Reichert and **Sarah Cannon**. You two are a piece of my heart. You inspire me creatively and always know when I need you. You both are unicorns.

To **Benjamin** and **Zac** at the Violet Hour for being so gracious with their time and expertise and for letting me sip on the best Manhattans in Chicago while I eavesdropped at the bar.

The keeper of my secrets, **Karin**, and the person who had a front-row seat to watch (and aid) in my evolution. You helped bring me here, and I don't even think you realize it. This book, my entire life, changed because of you. Thank you.

Sometimes there is nothing in the world better than watching *Friends* and eating cereal in bed with your best friend. **Muffin**, I miss you every day. Thank you for living in a place that has inspired me and for you having the soul to comfort me.

My MR Girls: You are the strongest and most courageous group of women I've ever known. You, my dear friends, have seen me through over a decade of the highest highs and lowest lows. Thank you for never leaving me lonely and representing true friendship.

My mom and dad, three big brothers, and my entire extended big Italian family for being the most enthusiastic cheerleaders a girl could ever ask for. Not a day goes by that I'm not beyond grateful to be surrounded by such love and support.

And to the two boys in my life, L and J. You both mean more to me than you'll ever know. Our love surpasses labels and the word "family" doesn't even begin to touch the devotion that encircles us. Thank you, the both of you, for being you.

About the Author

Melissa Marino is a full-time writer and part-time Stormtrooper collector. When she's not writing, you can find her watching *Friends* reruns, mastering her cupcake frosting swirl, and hunting for the perfect red lipstick. Melissa lives in Chicago with her husband, son, and very opinionated dachshund.

Learn more at:

Melissa-Marino.com

Facebook.com/MelissaMarinoBooks

Twitter, @MelissaWrites2

www.ingramcontent.com/pod-product-compliance
Ingram Content Group UK Ltd.
Pitfield, Milton Keynes, MK11 3LW, UK
UKHW022301280225
455674UK00001B/126